"Exceptional!"—*Romantic Times*

"Enticing!"—*Seattle Post-Intelligencer*

"Spicy!"—*Library Journal*

"Heart-stopping!"—*Publishers Weekly*

Praise for *New York Times* and *USA Today* bestselling author **CHERRY ADAIR,** the "hot talent" (*Romantic Times*) behind these romantic suspense novels

HUSH

"Addictively readable . . . Testosterone-rich, adrenaline-driven suspense . . . Packed with plenty of unexpected plot twists and lots of sexy passion."

—*Chicago Tribune*

"Gripping . . . Fast-paced and loaded with action."

—genregoroundreviews.com

"Hot and steamy . . . The sexual tension is magnetic."

—paranormalhaven.com

"Adair is a master of pulling together exciting adventure and burning passion to make a spine-tingling read!"

—*Romantic Times*

BLACK MAGIC

"Plenty of sex, and a hero who always comes to the rescue."

—*Publishers Weekly*

"A hot new adventure."

—*Romantic Times*

Afterglow is also available as an eBook

NIGHT SHADOW

"Smoothly blends sensuality and espionage."

—*Publishers Weekly*

"Pulse-pounding . . . all the danger, treachery, and romance a reader could wish for. . . . Exceptional."

—*Romantic Times*

"Cherry Adair . . . will make your pulse race and your palms sweat."

—*Fresh Fiction*

NIGHT SECRETS

"Tremendous!"

—*Romantic Times*

"The night sizzles to new heights in these novels of romantic suspense."

—*Fresh Fiction*

WHITE HEAT

"A steamy fusion of romance and heart-stopping suspense."
—*Publishers Weekly*

"Heart-stopping adventure . . . spicy."

—*Library Journal*

HOT ICE

"A relentless page-turner with plenty of enticing plot twists and turns."

—*Seattle Post-Intelligencer*

"A very sexy adventure that offers nonstop, continent-hopping action from start to finish."

—*Library Journal*

HIDE AND SEEK

"Cherry Adair stokes up the heat and intrigue in her adventurous thriller."

—*Romantic Times*

"Outsize protagonists, super-nasty villains, and earthy sex scenes."

—*Publishers Weekly*

"Gripping, sexy as all get out."

—The Belles and Beaux of Romance

"A reason to stay up way too late."

—The Romance Journal

KISS AND TELL

"A sexy, snappy roller-coaster ride!"

—*New York Times* bestselling author Susan Andersen

"A true keeper."

—*Romantic Times*

Also by Cherry Adair

Hush
Black Magic

Available from Pocket Star Books

CHERRY ADAIR

AFTERGLOW

POCKET STAR BOOKS

New York   London   Toronto   Sydney   New Delhi

The sale of this book without its cover is unauthorized. If you purchased this book without a cover, you should be aware that it was reported to the publisher as "unsold and destroyed." Neither the author nor the publisher has received payment for the sale of this "stripped book."

Pocket Star Books
A Division of Simon & Schuster, Inc.
1230 Avenue of the Americas
New York, NY 10020

This book is a work of fiction. Names, characters, places, and incidents either are products of the author's imagination or are used fictitiously. Any resemblance to actual events or locales or persons, living or dead, is entirely coincidental.

Copyright © 2012 by Cherry Adair

All rights reserved, including the right to reproduce this book or portions thereof in any form whatsoever. For information address Pocket Books Subsidiary Rights Department, 1230 Avenue of the Americas, New York, NY 10020

First Pocket Star Books paperback edition April 2012

POCKET STAR BOOKS and colophon are registered trademarks of Simon & Schuster, Inc.

For information about special discounts for bulk purchases, please contact Simon & Schuster Special Sales at 1-866-506-1949 or business@simonandschuster.com.

The Simon & Schuster Speakers Bureau can bring authors to your live event. For more information or to book an event contact the Simon & Schuster Speakers Bureau at 1-866-248-3049 or visit our website at www.simonspeakers.com.

Manufactured in the United States of America

10 9 8 7 6 5 4 3 2 1

ISBN 978-1-4391-5383-3
ISBN 978-1-4391-6712-0 (ebook)

For my brother, who will never read any further than this.
You are my second favorite male in the whole PTO.
I love you.

AFTERGLOW

✦ ONE ✦

Monte Carlo

Rand Maguire could just see the headline now: *XXX WEDDING HOLLYWOOD STARS BARE ALL!*

One leak, one Tweet, one goddamned Facebook picture, and a hundred lives would be affected in ways no one could predict. The wedding had been, literally, a clusterfuck of gigantic proportions.

As security specialist to the stars, Rand's job was to protect the celebrity guests from danger while they attended the destination nuptials of Tinseltown's hottest young couple.

Possible hazards? Paparazzi, stalkers, ex-lovers, kidnappers. Hell, possibilities were varied and endless.

Not on the damned list of potential threats?

Aphrodisiac.

It was barely six the morning following the reception, and forty-plus of the major players—bride, groom, immediate family—gathered in the Presidential Suite of the Monte Carlo hotel, looking to Rand for answers. Why the hell *wouldn't* they? However one looked at it,

Maguire Security was responsible for the debacle. It was Rand's ass on the line.

The only thing he and his men had figured out in the hours since the reception was that the drug had been added to the toasting champagne. Which meant all the guests had drunk at least a few sips. Within minutes all hell broke loose as everyone lost their inhibitions in a spectacular display of unbridled lust.

Clothes were ripped open or completely off as couples screwed where they stood, lay, or sprawled on a table or chair. The sophisticated formal wedding became a sexual free-for-all. A porn-movie orgy come to life.

Rand hadn't had enough manpower to pull everyone, humping like dogs in heat, apart. Even when his crew tried, they were fought off as if the participants had to fuck or die. Whatever the hell the drug was, he'd never seen anything like it.

It had been a hellacious and exhausting couple of hours before he and his men managed to wrangle the hundred guests to their suites and lock them in for their own safety.

It was fortunate the wedding and reception took place on this floor for security reasons. Damned fortunate that it had been contained and not in the gardens as the bride had wanted.

Working with hotel management, he had the outside phone lines blocked, called in a team of doctors to minister to the guests, and started a full-scale investigation into the why and how of it. The local authorities were going to have to be called in, he knew. But for now, he had a couple of hours, tops, to figure this out.

He paused beside one of the ornate stone pillars, his back to the breathtaking, million-dollar view of the Mediterranean beyond the closed French doors. All the better to survey the bickering mass of celebrities and elite as they debated whether to lynch him now or save the ass kicking for later when the rest of the wedding guests showed up.

". . . absolutely couldn't control myself . . ."

"Favorite dress . . ."

The guests, gathered in small, feral knots, looked no further for a scapegoat than the man paid to protect them.

Glamorous actresses had skipped hair and makeup to put in their two cents before the other guests woke up and demanded his attention. Most, still feeling the sting of embarrassment, wouldn't meet his eyes, and those who did make eye contact didn't hold back the anger. Or fear.

The simmering tones in the suite threatened to boil over as Rand waited for everyone to find a seat. He'd better resolve this clusterfuck *fast*. If it became known that Maguire Security allowed something like this to take place on its watch, he'd lose every top-tier client he'd spent years cultivating.

He prowled the edges of the spacious suite, its Louis XIV furniture and 18-karat gilding gleaming in the sunlight streaming through the windows. He felt the weight and heat of a dozen pairs of eyes tracking his progress. Like a shark, he kept moving, eavesdropping on the conversations around him as he spoke quietly into his lip mic as his teams reported in.

"Anything?" he asked Walters, who was situated in the hotel security room. Like the rest of them, he and his splinter team had been at it all night, going through the hotel security videos from the previous evening. None of them had taken a break, let alone slept.

"Nothing solid yet," Walters admitted, sounding as frustrated as Rand felt.

"Stratham and Rebik are following a lead—one of the waiters who, some-fucking-how, managed to get out before we locked everyone in," Rand informed him as he prowled. "So far, that's our best bet. Let's hope to hell *that* pans out. Everyone else is accounted for."

He headed for the buffet. The private chef had loaded the table with fruit, pastries, juices, and large pots of coffee. Clean. A day late and a dollar short, but Rand checked anyway. Not that it mattered now. The damage was done.

The cold clench in his gut had been there all night. Disaster brewing, escalating tempers threatening to erupt, and still no goddamned answers. "The natives are getting restless," he said quietly into the mic as he scanned the restless group. "Find me something before it gets any uglier."

"Will do, boss."

Rand poured hot, fragrant coffee from a giant silver urn into a fragile-looking cup that barely held two swallows. He drank and filled it again, observing the milling guests behind him in the mirror over the buffet. Exhausted. Embarrassed. Pissed.

How in the hell had anyone gotten past his men to compromise security in such a spectacular way? Jesus.

Compromised was an understatement. In this case, that was just a fucking euphemism for *catastrophe*.

Rand had achieved a certain amount of fame for his stunt work in the film industry before branching out into the security business four years ago. More balls than brains, some said. But they were wrong. He was always three steps ahead of the stunt. Yeah, he'd taken some ballsy risks, par for the course, but they were calculated risks. Back then he placed his own life on the line daily with barely a qualm. Now he was responsible for the security and well-being of clients who paid him shitloads of money to make sure they remained safe.

He'd fucked up.

He'd landed this job because his security company was one of the best. He knew the business, and he knew the players. He understood the need for safety, combined with the desire for privacy, important to celebrities, and difficult to provide. He knew how they ticked. And the current situation was a public relations nightmare for any actor, other than a porn star.

He had a lid on outside contact, so the press hadn't got wind of what happened. Yet.

Early-morning sunlight spilled across the creamy marble floors and glinted off gilded picture frames, ancient tapestries, and plush, stylish furniture. The smell of stale perfume mixed with the heavy scent of hundreds of white hothouse roses in three-foot-high Carrara marble urns was stifling even with the air-conditioning on.

Rand was sorely tempted to fling open the doors and windows, just to get some decent air. Not that he would.

All this situation needed was someone with a zoom lens or a directional mic. He had to keep a lid on Pandora's box for as long as possible.

Walters's voice buzzed in his ear. "Still nothing. Tover wants to know if they should come back to the hotel and help herd cats."

"No." Rand kept his voice low, his gaze moving around the room so he could keep track of all the players. "Cole should be back from the airport anytime now. Keep looking. One of those damn devices must've caught something." He put the empty cup on one of the small tables, hoping his personal assistant was bringing more than reinforcements—what he needed was a fucking miracle.

Damn it to hell. His men were well trained and hyper-vigilant. How had they missed this? How had no one seen a damn thing until it was too late?

Walters rang off just as Ligg, another member of Rand's security team, beeped in on the other line. Every team, every fifteen minutes. For all the good it was doing. Ron Ligg, with his four, had taken point on the audiovisual in Rand's suite down the hall, a few doors away from the Presidential Suite where the reception had been held.

Armed with high-speed computers, they were going through all the data from every phone, camera, and video device confiscated from the guests the night before.

All of whom had meltdowns when told to give up their phones. His men had ultimately convinced them all that it was the only way to keep the all-too-damning evidence off the Web. Rand prayed he'd been in time. A picture was worth a thousand lawsuits. . . .

And just might offer a clue. "Anything useful?"

Ligg's team was looking at every bit of footage, every image, taken between six yesterday evening, when the wedding ceremony started, and about eight, which was when all hell started breaking loose at the reception. Anything captured after the toasts at about eight fifteen would be completely useless.

Unless, Rand thought grimly, it had been filmed with blackmail in mind. Then someone was sitting on a gold mine.

"No, sir."

"Keep looking. Record what we need and be sure you wipe the devices. Everyone gets their gear back clean." Gut tight, Rand disconnected. He wasn't taking any chances. He caught a brief glimpse of long red hair among the blondes and brunettes across the crowded room and felt a visceral, unwelcome clutch in his chest.

A moment later the illusion was gone, and he breathed more easily. It had been a trick of the light, a figment of his overtired imagination. He thought he'd gotten over reacting that way every time he saw a woman with that distinctive shade of red hair—but apparently not. He had more serious issues than revisiting a ghost from his past.

A dozen conversations were going on around him as he circled the room to gain a vantage point, preferably far from sharp objects and projectiles. As he moved, he felt the weight of collective gazes on his back, as if the guests were sighting collectively down a rifle scope.

". . . but God help me, I was *willing*. More than willing!"

The back of his neck prickled—a sure sign of danger—

as he passed the bride and groom sitting together on a sofa. The only danger left in this room was the fallout and repercussions from what transpired the night before. But he trusted that itch.

The danger was real and present, and while maintaining a calm façade, inside Rand was coiled and braced for the attack.

He saw his assistant, Cole Phelps, by the suite door. Ex-military, Phelps had ears that stuck out from his short sandy-blond hair, typical jarhead style. His square jaw and even brown eyes tended to project reliability—exactly what Maguire Security needed. At a fairly tame five eight, athletic rather than bulky, his physique wasn't what made him a good security specialist. The man had a head for details—facts, plans, organization. He was Rand's right-hand man.

Cole was caught in conversation with the redhead. Rand was certain there hadn't been a ginger at the wedding. He'd remember. He had a strong aversion to them. The woman's back was to him, yet every hair follicle on his body felt electrified, even though he knew she wasn't who his body thought she was.

"Mortified!" He identified that shrill voice as belonging to one of the blond, heroin-chic bridesmaids. The well-preserved middle-aged woman she was talking to was related to the groom. Aunt, Rand remembered. She agreed wholeheartedly, "Outraged!"

The room was large enough to hold a hundred wedding guests, but with everyone agitated, vocal, and moving about, it seemed overly crowded with less than half that number this morning. Cole and the redhead wove their way through the masses, making their way along the back wall out of the traffic flow. It took willpower for Rand to pull his gaze from the unidentified woman.

Hotel security? Another doctor coming to check on the wedding party? He had no idea who she was, other than a distraction he couldn't afford. It wouldn't be so distracting if he could get a glimpse of the woman's face to assure himself she wasn't who he thought she was.

"My mother . . ."

"Not my fault, baby, I swear. Your sister . . ."

". . . get tested, what if someone had . . ."

Rand lifted his head, his gaze skimming over the complainants and, like a filing to a magnet, back to the redhead just as she turned.

Ice-green eyes met his straight on.

Dr. Dakota North.

Impossible. Improbable. Incontrovertible.

It was that coppery hair that attracted him three years ago. But it was those pale eyes that had drawn an unsuspecting man like a moth to a flame. Windows to her soul, he'd thought back then. Cool, clear, and as refreshing as looking into a quiet pond. He remembered thinking her skin appeared luminous as if backlit. Glowing and silky smooth—

Seeing her here made something inside him go still— the quiet before the storm. Then he felt the impact of those familiar peridot-colored eyes like a physical blow to his solar plexus. A bomb of suppressed emotions exploded in his chest and splintered through him like shrapnel.

Bitch had *cojones*, showing up here. Now.

Rand kept his expression impassive, keeping a tight rein on his self-control so he didn't betray even a flicker of what he was feeling. Too bad that self-control didn't extend to his thoughts. He maintained eye contact for several more beats, giving her a cold look of inquiry.

Her chin lifted a fuck-you-right-back fraction of an inch.

Looking effortlessly hip in a simple white T-shirt tucked into dark jeans, completed with a black blazer fitted to her narrow waist, Dakota was thinner than the last time he'd seen her, her cheeks a little more refined.

Still so beautiful she made his mouth go dry.

He cleared his throat, tightening his resolve along with his jaw. He had no idea what the hell she was doing here or where she'd come from, but she could crawl right back.

She'd tied a mile of glossy red hair up in a just-got-out-of-bed untidy ponytail that hung over one shoulder and curled around her left breast before spilling like magma halfway to her waist. It was much longer than when he . . . they . . . than when he'd seen her last, but the color was seared into his memory. Fragrant living fire. Cool and impossibly silky to the touch.

In spite of, or hell, *because* of the situation, Rand instantly imagined all that wild red hair spread over her creamy naked body. Spread over *his* naked body. Even though he hadn't drunk the mickeyed champagne, watching nothing but sex for hours straight left an imprint on his brain.

11 Afterglow

His body *remembered* hers. The taste. The texture. The heat. It all came rushing back in an unwelcome surge of muscle memory. His skin felt too tight, and he was annoyed to find his heartbeat doing calisthenics.

What kind of sick joke had put Dr. Dakota North and an aphrodisiac in the same geographical location? Someone up there must be laughing his ass off.

Rand glanced away. What was she doing here, halfway across the world from Seattle, anyway? Because having Dakota just show up out of the fucking blue was not only annoying as hell, it was a stretch.

Cole had gone to the airport to pick up Zak Stark's handpicked Lodestone agent, and this was who he'd brought back? Even though Dakota was a chemist and could probably give him some insight as to what the drug might've been, she was a problem Rand didn't want. They were done. Had been for two years. He wanted nothing to do with her. Not then, not now, not fucking ever again. She'd destroyed his family.

And nearly destroyed what was left of him.

He met his assistant's gaze, telegraphing his feelings without a filter. Cole's ass was grass for bringing her here.

He must've bumped into her at the airport, or—hell, Rand had no idea why she was standing there as if she had a gold-plated fucking invitation to stay.

Where was the Lodestone agent? Zak had assured him he was sending his best man for the job. Rand needed the guy *now*. Judging by the raised voices around him, he couldn't wait any longer. They were edging toward hysteria, and it was time to take control.

Dakota's shoulders stiffened as she started picking up and comprehending snippets of conversation.

". . . make the Kardashian tapes look tame."

"Paparazzi?"

They each had an embarrassing story, each more horrific and humiliating than the last, and everyone in the room started talking louder, determined to be heard. It was definitely time.

"Quiet!" Yelling "cut" might be more effective. Still, the decibel level dropped as Rand snagged their attention. "Take a seat and calm down. You *all* had a bad experience, but trying to top one another is counterproductive." He paused. "Yes. You'll be getting your phones and cameras back. I'd like to remind you that you all signed nondisclosure agreements, and it's in everyone's best interest to keep this situation out of the press. Let's see what we know and go from there. One at a time."

Everyone talked at once.

"Enough!" His volume barely changed, but this time the group shut the hell up as everyone swiveled to face him. Their expressions ranged from fury to humiliation to fear. If looks could kill, he'd be stone dead.

And this was eleven hours *after* the incident.

"Arguing and pointing fingers isn't going to help us find the culprit." Rand kept his voice low and even. "My team has already spoken with each of you once, and we're going to go through it again now, one story at a time. You might not realize that you saw something that might help us with the investigation. Please be patient and wait for my assistant, Cole, over there."

Cole raised his hand.

"He'll come to you. Refreshments have been set up to make the wait easier. Thank you for your patience and assistance.

"And no, Creed," he added as the award-winning director and godfather to the bride opened his mouth to speak, "we *still* don't know if a wedding guest was responsible." Rand's people had grilled all of them like cheese sandwiches. And since no one had been allowed to leave the floor, the culprit was still there. They just had to figure out who that was, and/or wait for a blackmail demand.

"Then *obviously* it was one of the hires." Seth Creed's voice was tight and level. Rand started out as a stuntman, working his way up to stunt coordinator for the director. Creed was a lifelong friend of Rand's father. Rand was pretty sure they weren't gay, but they had an interesting relationship that was hard to define. One thing for sure, Rand liked Seth Creed a hell of a lot more than he did his father.

The director had guided his career from the start. Rand owed him a lot. Seth's stamp of approval on his security company had garnered clients before Rand earned them on his own. It pissed him off that this was the way he was repaying his friend for standing by him for years.

He'd always admired the director's even temperament. Creed didn't get flustered, never yelled or threw temper tantrums. His calm tones tended to keep people on his sets on an even keel, but that didn't mean he wasn't pissed as hell right now. His fair skin was flushed all the way to his receding hairline. His narrowed eyes warned that when he lost it, it was going to be extremely unpleasant for everyone.

"One of your security people—" Rand raised a brow, and the director subsided on the brocade settee, his expression grim, his eyes telegraphing his frustration. Unlike the others, he'd obviously taken the time to shower, and was dressed in jeans and a long-sleeved, crisply starched blue cotton shirt, buttoned to the throat. "Or one of the waitstaff," Creed finished. "You haven't found *anything* new?"

"I would have told you."

"It bears repeating," Brett Sing, royal pain in the ass and stepfather of the groom, stated flatly as he joined them, his voice rising as he cast an unfocused look around the room. He smelled strongly of sweat and booze. He was still wearing his tux pants and jacket, but somewhere along the way had lost his shirt. "Maguire's shecurity screwed up. Bottom line—*he'sh* responsible for this deviant getting in here in the first fucking plashe!" Again—or still—inebriated, he shot out a hand to brace himself as he listed to one side, sending a plate of croissants to the floor.

Rand bet the man would drink until he drowned out the memory of fucking his stepson's best man on the dais in full view of his family. "And I'm not saying any different," Rand said, keeping his fingers in the front pockets of his black dress pants in a deceptively calm posture. "Despite the fact that everyone here was run through a background check—twice—I take full responsibility for what happened." His gaze flickered to Dakota in the back of the room.

Her eyes narrowed as she too studied the room's occupants. He wondered what she was making of it all, then reminded himself he'd stopped giving a shit what she thought two years ago.

It wasn't nearly long enough.

With her expertise, she'd probably be of some assistance, he acknowledged. But given her track record, he didn't trust her. When the chips were down, self-preservation was the name of her game. He looked away and returned to the matter at hand. He and his people had done an exemplary job checking every aspect of the security for this gig. Including, Rand thought as he stared at Creed and the others, the entire guest list, the waitstaff, and his own security people. None of them had been exempt from intense scrutiny. The only person he trusted one hundred percent was himself. *Everyone* else was subject to suspicion.

Some, he thought darkly, not glancing at Dakota, more than others. "We have a strong lead," he briskly told the group. "We're going over every dotted *i* and crossed *t*. Again. I assure you, we *will* find the person or persons responsible and they'll be prosecuted to the full extent of the law." Before they were all blackmailed into bankruptcy, he hoped. And he lost his ass.

He walked over to what should have been the happy couple seated together on one of the ornate sofas strategically positioned to take in the view. Amanda Bennett, the petite, ethereal-looking bride, was one of Hollywood's new romantic-comedy superstars.

Judging by her wet hair, she'd showered before changing from her wedding dress into jeans and a baby-blue T-shirt; her feet were bare. She looked about thirteen. She blushed crimson as she burrowed under her new husband's beefy, protective arm. Her big blue eyes filled with tears. Not the tears that had won her three Oscars, a Tony, and several Golden Globes. These were the real deal. "My mother . . ."

"The doctor's seen her three times," Rand assured Amanda gently. Sara Tucker, a successful character actress, was too humiliated to leave her room. None of these people were at fault. Whatever the drug was, it was so powerful no one had been able to resist. It was doubtful if any of the wedding guests had even *noticed* when Tucker tried to rip the clothes off the nearest waiter and, when he fled, capped her bare breasts with the remnants of the wedding cake as she impaled herself on the groom's twenty-year-old brother.

Some people should never be seen naked.

One aspect of this job that he and his people handled extremely well, thank God, was that not a whiff of the wedding had leaked to the press. That in itself was a fucking minor miracle with two such high-profile stars. Coupled with the nondisclosure agreements that all of the guests signed before attending the wedding, it meant there was still a chance to keep a tight lid on the situation. *Everyone* was humiliated by what happened. They weren't going to say a damn word when they returned home. Even if someone *wanted* the publicity and was willing to go public about the incident, he or she would be ostracized by half of Hollywood for doing so, and it wasn't worth the risk. Salacious was one thing, but the events at the reception had guaranteed that nobody came out smelling like a rose.

Ligg and his team had better find something on the images. Walters would spot the bad guy on the hotel video. Or Stratham and Rebik would find the missing waiter. . . . They just needed a place to start.

"Your mother's fine now, sweetheart." Jason Dunham, groom and action superstar, rubbed his chin on the crown of Amanda's head as he met Rand's eyes. Like many of the people in the room, Rand considered Jason a friend. He'd doubled for him in a handful of successful movies in his time, and they'd remained friends even after Rand branched off into his security business.

"I have faith Rand. His guys *will* find the person responsible *and* bring them to justice. And yeah, it was all as embarrassing as shit, but nobody died. We'll all go home, go about our business, and never mention it again."

Amanda nodded from the safety of his embrace. He tightened his arm around his bride as he addressed the room at large. "Nobody can say we didn't create *the* most memorable wedding." He smiled his number-one box office, top-grossing actor smile, but Rand saw the strain around the new groom's eyes. "And thanks to Rand and his team, we've managed to pull it off without the paparazzi getting wind. Of *any* of it."

A soft chorus of voices rose in sour counterpoint to his little speech.

". . . appalling."

"I'll never be able to face my friends again."

"No way to keep this quiet once we all go home."

"Monica will talk first."

The bridesmaid who'd gotten up close and personal with the priest's genitals bristled at the accusation. "I will *not*, you skanky bitch!"

"*Nobody* talks." Seth Creed's voice carried clearly as he rose from the sofa and faced the crowd. "Not only will I sue anyone's ass who's stupid enough to want to get a little publicity for themselves, I'll see that you never work again. This was no one's fault—we're all victims, even Maguire Security, so shut the fuck up and listen to Rand."

Rand tuned them out as his Bluetooth headset beeped in his ear. *Give me a clue. Just one small fucking thing to go on so I can get this unraveled.* "Talk."

Oddly, with the one, curt word addressed to his caller, the room dropped once again into a thick silence. The tension was palpable, all eyes fixed on him. Unconsciously, Rand's attention snagged on Dakota. While he knew it was only skin-deep, her beauty made his teeth ache. Her vibrancy assaulted his senses. She'd always been Technicolor to everyone else's black-and-white. He scowled and turned away, pacing across the room to stare blindly out at the sparkling Mediterranean through the closed French doors.

"Found our missing waiter," his section leader, Mark Stratham, informed him, crisp and to the point. "Dead. Hotel room's been wiped. Ready for the address?"

"Go." Rand listened, committing the unfamiliar street address to memory. "Stay put. I'll be there ASAP." He disconnected as he turned to address the room at large. "We have a lead. Everyone chill. Don't leave this floor. And do not, I repeat, do *not* leave the hotel under any circumstances. And, yes, Mike, the no-outside-calls rule is still in effect." The teenage brother of the bride had been bugging to get his phone back for hours. Teenage angst was the least of Rand's problems.

He cut off the kid. "I don't care who anyone wants to talk to stateside. If the paparazzi get even a hint of this, *everyone* is screwed. We don't know if this was an act of terror, or if there was a specific target or agenda. This floor is secured tighter than Fort Knox. You're self-sufficient up here with your own chef and staff, and members of my security team are stationed outside everyone's doors. Nobody in or out until I get back with answers."

He scanned the room, seeing the challenge in Creed's eyes. "*All* the answers."

The director gave an imperceptible nod; his eyes said, *Don't fuck this up, your ass is on the line.*

Rand addressed Cole. "Make sure everyone has what they need. You." He pointed at Dakota, who'd pushed away from the wall when he took his call. "Come with me," he ordered in a flat, measured voice that brooked no argument.

✦ TWO ✦

Dakota considered tall, intense, and surly for a heartbeat before following him out of the room. Rand hadn't snapped his fingers, but his terse command was close enough.

Lovely. His loathing for her hadn't diminished in twenty-five months. If anything, it looked as if he hated her even more; she hadn't thought that possible.

The last time he'd talked to her, he'd called her some nasty names. She didn't care what they said about sticks and stones and about words never harming you. She'd rather he'd struck her than have him believe half of what he'd called her and accused her of doing. She probably would've recovered faster.

She straightened her shoulders and kept up with him. Clearly, he hadn't changed clothes since the wedding. His powerful legs were clad in custom-tailored tuxedo pants, paired with shiny black shoes, and a crisp white shirt with pin tucks down the front. The top two buttons were undone, the tie long gone. Rand never had liked formality, but God, he wore it well. He looked lean, and elegant and sexy enough to have all those little starlets looking at him with lust in their eyes.

This man, with his grim mouth, cold, intense eyes, and clipped speech was a stranger, and she'd treat him as such. Once, they'd been all heat and flash. Passion and need. Connection with little communication. When they'd been together she'd never seen him either cold or disinterested. Just the opposite.

Now . . .

Now she didn't know him anymore. Maybe she never had.

Despite her jacket, Dakota shivered. A primitive instinct for survival screamed for her to run like hell. As far and fast as her legs—or a private jet—could take her. But she wasn't going to run. Not from Rand Maguire, and not from what was happening here.

She'd fought hard to get her life on an even keel after he'd dumped her, but maybe if she'd seen *this* expression on his face when he'd done it, instead of just hearing his voice, she would've gotten over it faster. There was no room for interpretation, seeing the disdain in his eyes when he looked at her now. Rand wasn't even making a pretense at civility.

So be it.

She'd be as polite and nonconfrontational as humanly possible, even if it killed her. The past was the past. Water under the bridge. The bridge blown to hell, Dakota thought grimly as she practically jogged to keep up with his ground-eating strides.

He was wearing a shoulder holster with a very large black gun in it. James Bond had nothing on Rand Maguire, with his dark hair and flashing eyes, and a charm that was sorely lacking at the moment. Even the new scar here and there on his face and hands didn't detract from his sexiness. Probably added to his allure, Dakota thought as she matched his pace.

Just looking at him made her chest ache. She knew every dip and crag, every scar, intimately. She didn't want to remember, but being this close to him stole her breath and made her foolish heart pound. Her body's reaction to him hadn't changed in the years they'd been apart. Annoying but true.

The spacious hallway was lined with expensive-looking objets d'art and buff, black-garbed, well-armed guys standing guard outside various doors. Dakota was impressed. His company had grown and he was doing well, very well. The non-grudge-holding part of her psyche was glad.

Nobody in the room they'd just left appeared to have gotten much sleep. She'd bet he had even less. But other than needing a shave, he looked as fresh and sharp as a newly laundered shirt. Heavy on the starch.

The only plus was that he'd been taken unaware when he'd first seen her. Small satisfaction under the circumstances.

His dark hair was too long; he never could be bothered to go to the barber. His long-lashed dark eyes seemed to bore into her brain as he glanced at her when she caught up with him, halfway down the carpeted hallway. She felt a small hum of irritation in the back of her throat.

Don't let him get to you. This isn't personal. Remember that. She'd been lecturing herself since she'd left Seattle.

Not. Personal.

He paused to examine her face with a dissatisfied frown, his anger running icy, not hot like hers. "What the hell are you doing here, Dakota?"

Since she was here to *help* him, his irritation pissed her off, but she said evenly, "You know that the drug everyone in there was given was DL6-94, don't you?"

His frown deepened, the cold mask slipping for a fraction of a second as he grabbed her upper arm in the vise of his fingers. "What the hell are you talking about?"

The warm touch of his hand after so long was a shock. Dakota jerked her arm out of his grip and stepped back out of his unwanted magnetic force field. "The drug your father and I were working on at Rydell Pharmaceuticals." She strove for calm, but her insides were in revolt. "The drug formula that was supposedly destroyed in the explosion. The drug that one of my lab assistants referred to as Rapture. *That's* what your wedding party was dosed with."

His face hardened. "First of all." If his tone had been any icier, it would've caused permafrost on the crystal chandeliers overhead. "You were in that room for all of ten minutes, so you're basing your diagnosis on an erroneous assumption. Unless *you*—" He gave her a suspicious glare from hostile, narrowed eyes. "When *did* you hit town, Dakota? *Yesterday?*" He took an aggressive step forward, invading her personal space again. "Was this a sick experiment? Did you do it as some kind of perverted form of payback because I broke it off with you?"

"Don't be an ass." Her temper caught fire, and she curled her nails into her palms to keep from hitting him. She wanted to. Hard. And often. She wasn't surprised to discover that now Rand Maguire brought out the absolute worst in her. It hadn't always been that way, but it was that way now.

Heart thudding erratically, she lifted her chin and glared right back. Damn. She'd forgotten how big he was. He towered over her even though she wore heels. She stood a little taller and stared him down. He might be in an awkward situation with his clients, but she wasn't going to tolerate being intimidated when she was here—like it or not—to help him. "Cole picked me up at the airport and brought me directly here. Ask him yourself if you don't believe me." *Pathological liar* was the least offensive thing he'd called her in their last phone conversation. *Slut*, *bitch*, and *opportunist* had been some of the others. Based on *what*, she wasn't sure. But he'd acted on his convictions by telling her he never wanted to see or hear from her again. Ever.

Since he lived in LA and she in Seattle, that hadn't been hard to achieve. He'd refused to explain or to listen to reason. He'd rushed to judgment without a damned backward glance.

She'd learned a long time ago not to bother trying to explain herself to anyone. But it had hurt her deeply that Rand believed all those crappy things about her.

She'd thought he knew her better than that. Obviously not.

She started walking—heading, she presumed, to the private elevator at the other end of the mile-long hallway. "*You* were the one who called Zak Stark and asked for help, Rand. I'm the best kind of help you have. I know what you're up against."

"I don't need any more of your brand of 'help,' Dakota. Wasn't killing my mother enough for you? Did you want to up your body count and kill off half of Hollywood as well?"

"I'm not even going to dignify that crap with a response," she told him evenly. "You need me, and if you weren't so pigheaded, you'd be grateful that I put everything on hold to come. I'm one of the few people left who knows everything there is to know about this drug." She'd had nothing whatsoever to do with the drugs his mother had been given. Nothing. He hadn't listened then, and she wasn't going to try to convince him of her noninvolvement now. That wasn't the issue at hand.

"DL6-94 is a fast-acting, powerful aphrodisiac. Less than a microgram is all it would take to get the reaction your guests had yesterday. Enough to cause a loss of all inhibitions. For most people, that dose would be a powerful aphrodisiac, but for some it will bring out equally strong emotions they'd be unable to control."

He wasn't looking at her as she spoke, but his strides slowed down, indicating she had his attention.

"It's highly addictive and remains in the body. Eventually, if enough's ingested, leading to death. And since I worked at Rydell, Zak Stark thought you could use my expertise. Believe me, he had to do a lot of convincing to get me to drop everything and fly here to help you."

"How did he know what the fuck the drug was?"

"He didn't." She controlled her temper with some difficulty. "But since he knew I was a pharmaceutical chemist, he called and woke me in the middle of the night. We discussed the symptoms and what you'd described. I told him it might be Rapture. He asked me to come and help you. I *told* him in no uncertain terms that you wouldn't accept any help I could give you. He insisted. I'm here. If you don't need or want my help, I'll be happy to have a vacation before flying back to Seattle."

"How did Zak even know how to contact you?" his deep voice was soft and cold, his eyes hot. "Are you sleeping with him?"

Pigheaded ass. "I *work* for him."

His brow went up. "Doing what? Supplying drugs to unsuspecting citizens?"

He knew which buttons to push, but she wasn't going to react. "You don't really think I had anything to do with drugging those people?"

Faster than she could blink, Rand had her pinned against the wall, his thick forearms bracketing her shoulders, the massive wall of his chest hard and unyielding against her breasts. Sensations assaulted her, the heat and smell of him yanking her inside out.

"I was talking about the past. But now that you bring it up—*did* you have something to do with what happened at the wedding?"

The familiar heated sparks in his eyes forced Dakota to turn her head, leaving him breathing down her neck, literally. She shoved at him with both hands. "Keep making ridiculous statements like that, and you'll get your wish. I'll leave so fast your head will spin."

"It's quite a coincidence that you just *happen* to be here right in the middle of this mess." He allowed her to push him away. The wash of cool air was welcome and stunning after her close encounter with the man who was both her worst nightmare and her biggest fantasy. "Zak shouldn't have sent you. You've been misinformed—this isn't what you think it is. The doctors we brought in believe the guests were given a high dose of Ecstasy."

The scientist in her had to know for certain if this was her drug or just something similar. *Please God. Don't let it be DL6-94.* The wish, the plea, the prayer were all useless, she knew. She was just desperate to be proven wrong. "It wasn't E," she told him flatly, straightening her jacket and hitching her heavy tote back onto her shoulder. "I can tell you that even without knowing all the details. I need to see the blood work. I presume you had blood drawn for analysis?"

"Of course. We should have the results back in a couple of hours." He took the jacket one of his men handed him as he passed and shrugged it on. "You'll be picking up some rich guy on the beach by then."

"Oh, I certainly hope so," she murmured sweetly. A surge of raw emotion flooded her system. Anger. Grief. Fear. It was an unhealthy cocktail. "Have you contacted the local authorities?"

"Not yet. Eventually an alphabet soup of authorities will have to be called in. For now we're keeping a tight lid on it, with as few people as possible involved. Right now we have nothing."

"You have what the drug *is*. You know *where* it was first manufactured. That's something."

He didn't so much as glance her way. "Based on your word."

Which according to him was worthless. "Based on my *expertise.*"

"I'll take your opinion under advisement while waiting to hear from the experts here."

Dakota put her hand on his arm. A mistake. She felt hard muscle and tensile strength. She remembered . . . She let go, not wanting to feel the heat of his skin through the layers of his clothing. Not wanting to remember the strength of his arms. "News flash, Ace. *I'm* the expert. Be it in Europe or back in Seattle. Get me that blood work and I'll confirm that it's Rapture. We'll go from there." She forced herself to calm her erratic breathing.

It took several long steps before he noticed she hadn't kept up, but when he turned back to look at her, there wasn't anything sympathetic—or even open-minded— about his expression. "I hate to break this to you, Dakota, but this isn't about you. I'll have one of my men return you to the airport. Go back to Seattle. I don't have the time to wait out one of your moody sulks."

She was neither moody nor sulky, and she resented like hell being accused of both. "When did I *ever* behave like that?"

"When I repeatedly tried to contact you after my father was arrested."

She'd been in the hospital, in a medically induced coma, which he would know if he'd been less of an ass. The old hurt stung like new, but this wasn't the time or place to clear the air. If she had to explain *that*, she'd lose it.

"I can help you, Rand. If you'll let me. If not—" She lifted her shoulder and let it drop. "I know how to keep myself busy." *Give me something, anything, and I can track this guy down.* She could hunt down the guilty party, sure, but having Rand around would make what she had to do easier. And with *his* expertise—safer. Not that she'd ever let him know and give him that kind of leverage.

"I don't need—"

"You told Zak Stark you needed a tracker," she cut him off, remembering with bitter amusement when she'd found his stubborn side attractive. "Here I am. I knew as soon as Zak shared those few details you gave him that this was the drug we worked on at Rydell. I know it intimately, inside and out. I lived it, breathed it, dreamed about it for four years. This is the antidepressant we worked so hard to perfect. Our one massive failure. Trust me. It's Rapture."

Rand stared at her, his hands deceptively loose at his sides. She continued, hoping this once he'd hear what she had to say without being defensive and shutting her down. "Ecstasy and Rohypnol take ten minutes or so to act; both lower inhibitions, and often result in amnesia. From what I understand, all those people affected had *no* inhibitions, and they all remember in painful detail what happened.

"This can't be allowed to spread across Europe, Rand—we've got to stop it. This drug is more addictive than meth, and worse, is lethal in larger doses."

A muscle jerked in his jaw. "I told Stark the details in confidence."

"A confidence that would be shared with the Lodestone agent he sent to help you," she pressed, every bit as obstinate as he was. "Me. He knows I was a chemist, and we agree that I'm the best qualified to help you."

"Was?"

She didn't respond. Her life was no longer Rand Maguire's business. "If DL6-94 is already in production, there's a bigger problem than a handful of people getting their happy on. This has to be caught before it goes viral. This goes way beyond a few privileged wedding guests being embarrassed. It's a matter of public safety. We'd better hope to hell that Rapture *hasn't* gone into mass production, because if it has, we're looking at a drug that will outsell crack, E, and everything else put together. There'll be no stopping it. Right now I'm your best hope of finding whoever did this and finding out who's behind it. I have the ability to trace this back to the source."

"Alone?"

"Until I find who's behind it, yes. Then Interpol will need to be called in."

He cocked his hip, his gaze burning an acidic hole straight through her. "There can only be one person responsible for bringing that drug back into the mainstream, Dakota, and that's you."

"I'm not the only person who knew that formula."

His laugh sounded rough. "First you make sure my father is accused of killing my mother. Now, when he's securely behind bars, you're accusing him of formulating this drug? Out of an Italian prison? Seriously? You're crazy. And unwelcome. I don't want you anywhere near my father. The trial starts in two weeks. If the press gets wind that you're lurking about Europe, you and your crazy ideas are going to exacerbate the situation. Just leave."

Dakota planted her feet, ready for a fight—one she had to win to prevent more innocent people from injury. "Like it or not, you need me. I have the skills to locate whoever assaulted the wedding guests. I'll do what I need to do, with or without you."

He gave her a cold look. "Like what?"

"Like none of your damn business." She caught up with him as he started walking again, her footsteps muffled on the thick carpet. Her high heels put her eyes level with his mouth. His stern, well-shaped, *annoying* mouth. "Unless you're willing to work together and keep things amicable, I'm not wasting time explaining anything to you." She dragged her gaze back to his dark, unfriendly eyes.

"Would any of it be the truth?"

The truth would break you, you jerk. Her jaw hurt from clenching her teeth, and her fingers tightened around the handle of the heavy tote slung over her shoulder. Everything she'd brought on this trip was inside, as she'd purposely traveled light. "Go to hell."

"Been there, done that, got the scars to prove it."

He'd been a stuntman. The fool was covered with scars. "Who doesn't." After the lab explosion, she could match him scar for scar. "Do you really have a lead?" Not that she doubted his abilities; Rand always had a clear vision of what he wanted to do. When he decided on a course of action, nothing deterred him. He was the most decisive, focused man she'd ever met. He cared about those people back there, and he was going to deal with this disaster in the most efficient, expedient way possible. She'd been warmed by that caring once, until he froze her, cutting her out of his life without a backward glance.

Not that she cared anymore. She squared her shoulders. "It makes sense for you to fill me i—"

He held up one finger to silence her. "Ham called in a lead," he said into his lip mic. "Nobody on or off the floor until I give the okay." He barely changed tone of voice as he added to her, not slowing down, "I can't wait to get Stark on the phone. He better have one *hell* of a good explanation for this."

"Be my guest," Dakota snapped. She hitched her tote more securely onto her shoulder as she kept pace. Zak, smart man that he was, had put two and two together, come up with six, and had his plane readied for her. Zak had both sides of the story. Rand's and her own.

He'd believed that she was the *only* one he needed to send to Monte Carlo. Filled with hope that she could clear her name once and for all, she'd flown through the night to get to Monaco in time for breakfast. She hadn't been offered breakfast, but hope sprang eternal.

Rand slapped a hand on the call button and the ornate elevator doors glided open without a whisper. Dakota followed him inside and fought the urge to touch the plush gold-and-black wallpaper to make sure she had enough room to breathe. Claustrophobia was her Achilles' heel, and being in a small confined space with a large, angry male made breathing difficult. Being in the same space as Rand made breathing almost impossible.

She looked up as the door slid closed, feeling as if she were trapped inside a jeweled box with a Baccarat crystal chandelier. Only a few floors, she assured herself. She had enough issues to deal with without this anxiety kicking in.

Rand seemed to suck all the air out of the already airless space. His shoulder bumped hers, reminding her how large he was—not just in essence, but in physical presence. A good man to have on your side. A really, really bad man to have as an enemy.

She knew both from experience. Her heart picked up the pace, and she had the crazy urge to lean against him. She resisted burying her face against his strong, tanned throat and wrapping her arms around his waist by reminding herself that he hated her. Still really, truly loathed her, after all this time.

She backed away from his personal space until her ass hit the elevator wall, and she could catch her breath.

Her jaw set and her shoulders tightened. Claustrophobia be damned, she wouldn't show weakness now. "I'm not leaving." She met his eyes.

"Yes. You are."

"You can't force me onto a plane."

His grim look promised he'd give it his best shot.

She put her ace on the table. "You can't hunt down the bad guy if you don't have a clue. I'll find it."

He pinched the bridge of his nose, a gesture he made when he was especially tense, and she was immediately transported back three years ago to when they met. A cocktail party, hosted by the lab where she worked with his father. One look and Dakota was sunk. She'd kept her hands to herself by sheer willpower. Just because she was civilized enough not to act on her impulse didn't mean she hadn't enjoyed the rush of sexual awareness pulsing through every nerve ending in her body. Chemistry at its finest.

She'd never in her life experienced anything like the intensity of lust at first sight. It had been new and intriguing and wonderful. He'd been at the party at his father's persistent request, and she'd offered him an Advil after watching him wince with the pain of a tension headache. They'd gotten into a lively discussion over waiting out the pain versus the immediacy of man-made pain relievers. It rapidly progressed from pain to pleasure.

She'd thought it was real love, the kind that lasted forever. She'd been wrong. Unfortunately, she had some residual physical response to him after all this time. As long as Rand didn't know about it, the fact that she was having heart palpitations just standing next to him was none of his business.

God. When Zak told her what happened at the wedding reception, Dakota *prayed* the drug wasn't DL6-94.

After hearing the details, spare as they were, there was no doubt in her mind. None. She'd wait to confirm it until she saw the test results, but she knew what had been used.

"In case you aren't taking this, or me, seriously," she told him quietly, "let me explain in layman's terms just how bad the situation is. A person weighing one hundred and fifty pounds becomes addicted to DL6-94 after ingesting as little as five micrograms, be that one dose or five. It's downhill from there, because the eventual outcome of continued use is death."

He glared at her. "And if it's not Rydell Pharmaceuticals' formula?"

People will still die, but at least I can sleep easy knowing I had no part in killing them. "The drug needs to be taken off the street, Rand, no matter who's making it. Not only am I familiar with the ingredients and what it can do, I can track down the person behind the scenes. If it is the same formula, Rydell Pharmaceuticals will be responsible."

"We don't know that this is that far reaching," he told her without looking at her. "Blackmail is still on the table as a motive."

"Maybe. But doesn't it strike you as too coincidental that the drug your father was involved with was used at a wedding that you were working?"

His jaw clenched as he turned his head to look at her. "Paul is behind bars. Rydell's lab rats were all killed in the explosion. Do the math, Dakota. If this is Rapture, then the only person left is you. There is no one else." The caustic edge of his tone ate at her like acid.

In that moment she hated him all over again. "It's in Dr. Maguire's and my best interests for us to find the person responsible and put a stop to *whatever's* happening. At least you'll have to agree with me on that."

Rand speared her with an icy glare. "He's sixty-seven years old and has spent the last twenty-five months in a foreign prison, because of you. If you do one more damn thing to make his life a living hell, I'll come after you with everything I've got."

This had to be the longest elevator ride in the history of the hotel. Then she realized that he hadn't inserted the keycard to get the damn thing moving. "Much as I'm enjoying this delightful conversation," she said sweetly, "how about actually putting this thing in motion so we can get on with finding who we're looking for?"

With a shake of his head, he pulled his wallet out of his back pocket, removed the card, and rammed it into the slot. "What's your hurry?"

"Have you considered that whoever has the formula might be the one who framed your father?" Dakota didn't believe that for a moment. Paul Maguire had known *exactly* what he was giving his wife, and *exactly* what the ramifications were. Rand might buy into the accidental-death explanation, but like the prosecution, Dakota didn't buy it at all.

"The one-armed man? No. I know who did that."

She counted to ten, tired of proclaiming her innocence only to have it fall on deaf ears. "Let's call a truce for the duration."

"As long as it's a short duration." He gave her a bland look. "Stark assured me he was sending his best *man*."

Dakota leaned against the wall and forced a smile. There was that whole flies-with-honey thing that she'd better remember if she expected this inflexible man to cooperate with her.

No matter how much turbulent water raced under their shared bridges in the past. No matter how hurt, how angry, how damned well insulted she'd felt, looking at him now made her heart hitch on an annoying, primitive level. God, he was sexy. Not just in that haywire pheromone way. He looked damn good, always had. His eyes were a shade between chocolate brown and hazel, his face more craggy than conventionally handsome, and he had scars everywhere. Everywhere she could see. Many, she knew, in places she couldn't. She remembered them all. "In this case, his best man is a woman."

"We'll see." He didn't ask why a chemist was working for his friend, or in what capacity, and Dakota figured that was a truth that would have to come out sooner than later. Her special skill had never been relevant when they'd been together. Oh, she'd planned on telling him once all the excitement of their wedding was over, and their lives went back to normal. But normal had gone to hell in a handbasket, and that had never happened. She shrugged out of her jacket just as the doors opened, letting in the refined and subdued susurrus of multilingual conversations and the soft light cast by the antique crystal chandeliers. No one in the lobby gave them a second glance as they crossed the plush gold-and-blue carpet and emerged into the heat of the afternoon.

Across the street, the Mediterranean sparkled like diamonds on rippling aqua satin. Small white sailboats danced in the gentle swells, and larger oceangoing yachts, gleaming white and sinfully expensive, filled the nearby marina. Dakota lifted her face to the sun and breathed in fresh air scented with floral notes and brine.

Somewhere out there, someone was using what she and the team at the pharmaceutical lab had worked years to produce, to do . . . what? Drugging wedding guests seemed a strangely petty act, given the devastating potential of the drug.

Who? Who had escaped the lab explosion? No one but her. Yet here she was, halfway around the world—searching for a ghost. She rubbed the goose bumps on her upper arms the heat of the sun did nothing to warm. All those prayers as she flew here had been for nothing. What she'd dreaded and feared *was.* She'd thought the day Rand walked out on her had been the darkest day of her life, but if someone had the formula for Rapture, that episode would turn out to be a cakewalk by comparison.

She pulled her jacket back on.

"You can't be cold," Rand told her shortly. "It's eighty degrees."

"It's the temperature change from Seattle. I'll acclimatize."

"You won't be here long enough."

"We can't all have what we want, Rand. Like it or not, you need me, so you might as well stop flogging this dead horse. The sooner we find whoever's responsible, the sooner I'll be out of your hair." He didn't need anyone of course. He never had. He'd flicked her off his sleeve like a pesky fly the moment the going got tough.

"I'll reserve judgment."

A black midsize luxury car was waiting beneath the portico. Rand took the keys from the attendant, and within seconds, they were on their way. The rental smelled new. Rand smelled . . . hot, sexy, achingly familiar. The aura of danger vibrating about him was new, though. She stared out the window instead of at him.

"Where are we going?" she asked, realizing he was heading in the opposite direction of the airport.

"My men found the body of one the waiters at a hotel just outside of town. How did you get involved with Stark and Lodestone?"

She watched the naked people frolicking on the beach as they drove by. "He was my friend too. And we had something in common."

"Yeah? Like what?"

She suppressed a sigh of frustration and turned to face him as she fastened her seat belt. "I have the same sixth sense as he does."

"Yeah?" He couldn't have sounded more skeptical and unimpressed if he'd tried. "Do you see dead people?"

"Don't be an ass, Rand." There wasn't any heat in it; she couldn't summon the energy. She'd had *this* argument before, with everyone who'd ever learned about her ability. And subsequently dismissed it. "It's not that Hollywood."

"How convenient. How long have you had this?"

"As far back as I can remember."

"We dated for a year, and it never occurred to you to mention this incredible phenomenon?" If his tone got any drier, the Mediterranean outside her window would sink into a desert.

They'd been *engaged*, but it hadn't taken much to convince him that she was a liar and worse. She could only imagine how he would have responded to this news early in their relationship. Maybe they wouldn't even have made it to the engagement. Maybe that would have been for the best.

She kept her voice level. "It wasn't relevant."

His knuckles turned white on the leather-covered steering wheel. "Everything *about* you was relevant at the time. This is just one more thing you lied about and hid."

The injustice of the accusation didn't hurt less the more times he said it. "I didn't lie about it. I chose not to share it," she told him, her voice flat. "This isn't something I usually talk about, unless I want to spend lots of quality time with shrinks."

"Hard to understand how you didn't think it was something to share with your future husband."

"Maybe I had the sense you wouldn't ever *be* my future husband," she snapped, rewarded when a muscle ticked in his jaw. "It didn't have anything to do with who we were as a couple. And frankly, mentioning it has only ever caused me problems."

Her parents were vaguely loving, if they weren't distracted, but even *they* preferred she never talked about her gift. For two pragmatic academics, a daughter with an inexplicable sixth sense was awkward. It couldn't be explained or measured. They didn't understand it, and she was pretty damn sure Rand wouldn't have been any more accepting and open than they were.

The sun was hot on her arm as it shone into the car, but she felt none of its warmth.

"Suppose I suspend my disbelief," he began, tone cool, his white-knuckled grip no longer evident. He'd always had the ability to turn off his emotions like a calibrated drip line. "How does this 'sixth sense' work?"

"When I hold an item belonging to a missing person, I can track the person and/or the item." It might be an unusual sense but it wasn't that complicated. She saw numbers in a concise, endless stream. Data she'd learned how to process. She watched Rand's face to gauge his reaction.

He shot her an incredulous glance before looking back to the palm-lined road flanking the beach. "Have a crystal ball in that purse as backup?"

"Of course." She kicked off her high heels and wiggled her bare toes in the plush carpet as she got comfortable. He wasn't going to get to her. She couldn't *allow* him to get to her. "It's magical. All-seeing, all-knowing. How did you guess?" She'd had twenty-seven years of the same skepticism. Make that twenty-five, since no one had asked how she did what she did when she was a baby.

Rand tapped an impatient tattoo on the upper curve of the steering wheel with one finger as he maneuvered through the traffic. Eyes narrowed, he glanced her way again. "You're kidding. Right?"

"Unfortunately, yes. I don't have anything so mystical and cool as a crystal ball that tells the future." The beaches were crowded, the road bumper-to-bumper cars, and throngs of scantily clad pedestrians clogged the sidewalks in front of the hotels, high-end boutiques, and casinos. Normally she'd enjoy the smooth, powerful ride of the luxury car, but Rand's agitation, no matter how well masked, was boosting her own stress level.

She rested the back of her head against the passenger-door window, willing her clenched muscles to relax one by one. "Call it a . . . tracking sense, for want of a better description. Holding something the person I'm trying to locate has touched shows me where they are. I see their coordinates, latitude and longitude, like a continuous stream of numbers in my head."

He shot her an incredulous glance. "Seriously? A human GPS?"

"Pretty much."

"Does it work every time?"

She got her sunglasses out of her bag and perched them on her nose. "One hundred percent."

"And this has been proven?"

"Many times. You must know that Zak built Lodestone after he acquired *his* extra sense, following a near-death experience last year in Venezuela." It was oddly appropriate that the owner and developer of the incredibly successful online search engine ZAG Search would become a kind of search engine in the physical world.

"When we realized we had the same weird ability, it made perfect sense for us to work together." It had been such a relief to find someone who completely understood and accepted her.

"I was skeptical when *he* told me about it." Rand tapped an uneven beat as he waited to dart between two luxury vehicles with black-tinted windows. There was maybe an inch to spare as he took the gap. Dakota helped out by holding her breath until their vehicle was safely squeezed between them.

"Hell," he muttered, "I'd welcome voodoo if I thought it would solve this quickly and quietly."

"Sorry. No dolls with pins in them. But like Zak, I can track someone for you. His new company was built around this skill, and we're incredibly busy doing what we d—" Oh, God help her. "What we do," she finished gamely, as he whipped around a Porsche. So close she saw the whites of the driver's eyes as they passed. Rand was the most skillful driver she'd ever ridden with. And the most impatient.

Even when he took seemingly reckless chances, he was always completely in control and anticipated what was coming in the next few seconds almost before the other driver made the call. The other drivers, of course, didn't know this. Though she felt safe with him—in a vehicle—she still held her breath a few more times as he slalomed between cars.

His concentration on driving gave Dakota a few minutes to look at him, and she looked her fill. He had a new scar bisecting his left eyebrow, dangerously close to his eye. She used to run her tongue across the one on the bridge of his nose and the thin white mark just under his jaw. She contemplated the dark stubble, remembering how prickly it was when he stroked his face over her belly, or her breasts, or—oh, damn it to hell. She couldn't think like this. Not here. Not now. Not ever again.

"Trying to go fast in this traffic is impossible, and since Monaco is the size of Central Park, it can't possibly be necessary to kill someone to get wherever we're going a little quicker," she pointed out. Quite reasonably, she thought.

"Can you direct me if I give you an address?"

Dakota's smile felt strained. "Afraid not. It doesn't work that way. I'll plug that into the GPS for you." He rattled off the address, and she punched it into the system. They headed for a tunnel, and he passed half a dozen cars at an alarming speed. Although he handled the car like an expert race-car driver, she still dug her fingers into the center console.

He honked to let a white sports car filled with blondes know he wanted to pass. The car moved over, and the blondes waved and blew kisses. Irrationally, the gesture annoyed the hell out of her. "You always were a chick magnet, but it never crossed my mind to accuse *you* of cheating on *me*."

"Because I never looked at another woman when we were together."

"And I never looked at another man, so—"

His jaw tightened. "Shut up, Dakota."

"I shut up about this before only because you slammed

down the damned phone before I could challenge your accusation," she said, her simmering annoyance at his shitty attitude starting to boil over. "You accused me of sleeping around. Where's your proof? You had none!"

"If you're going to bring up old news, I'll drop you off at the airport." His voice was cold and hard as glass. "I'm taking you along against my better judgment."

"Let's agree not to drag the past into the present," she suggested tightly. "It's inflammatory and counterproductive."

"Fine with me."

Fine. Perfect. Back to the business at hand. "Rapture is administered on a pullulan wafer—an edible, tasteless polymer paper made from starch that's placed on the tongue or dissolved in liquid. So your theory that it was dissolved in the champagne makes sense. If everyone was out of control for only a couple of hours, it was a small dose, thank God."

Dakota knew exactly what behaviors presented. She'd observed test patients in clinical trials. The program had been shut down, on her recommendation, that same day. "It would be a simple matter to carry the wafers in. Hundreds of wafers and a small vial of the drug would fit into a matchbox. It's possible someone stole samples from the lab before the explosion and administered the drug here as a joke."

"Or a form of blackmail."

"Either would be a thousand times more acceptable than . . ."

"Than?"

"Than it's being manufactured as a street drug."

"Jesus."

"I need to hold something belonging to whoever administered the drug. What do you have? I can get started while we drive."

"I don't have a damned thing."

"Then you're shit out of luck. As good as I am at what I do, even I can't help you."

✦ THREE ✦

And so it begins, Monk thought with satisfaction. Years of preparation and sacrifice had culminated in this, a very public first demonstration of a new drug that would soon sweep the world. He almost smiled. Perhaps he should call it Tidalwave instead of Rapture.

"The buyer was pleased?" he asked the caller, who'd sent him several minutes of raw video footage from the wedding reception the night before. Of course the buyer was pleased. The demonstration proved the product superior in every way.

Fast-acting. Addictive. Cheap to manufacture, with the potential of multibillion-dollar profits. A win-win for sales, manufacturing, and the worldwide tentacles of street dealers who'd all be clamoring to get onboard to sell Rapture through their own vast networks. None of them cared about the end users, content to suck them dry financially and spit them out when they became too far gone with addiction or died.

They all died in the end. An unfortunate result of Rapture that he had yet to remedy. Still, there would be no end to users. The world was a big place. Millions upon millions of potential users. More money than he could dream of and, far more important, power beyond his wildest imagination.

Calm and always contained, Monk rarely felt anything as human as excitement, but the potential for more buyers of the product—in one form or another—actually made his heart beat a little faster as he sat in the stillness of his austere cell. He closed his eyes as his man spoke solemnly.

"Yes, Father. Extremely so. He placed a large order."

"Are we ready for the next demonstration?" This to the head of an Eastern European mob. The next level of use. Monk was able to offer buyers several options, including ingested and airborne, along with several price points. Like end users, there was no limit to potential buyers from the criminal element.

"Yes, Father. Everything is in place as you instructed. May I come to you now?"

Monk let his gaze rest on the muted colors of the ancient tapestry hanging on the far wall. Satisfied that the net he was casting would haul in more buyers as well as his ultimate prize, Monk disconnected without comment. After years of manipulation and sacrifice, Dr. North was being drawn into the elaborate web he was spinning just for her.

Monk leaned back, folded his hands across his belly, and sighed with satisfaction. Everything was going according to plan. He allowed himself a small smile.

SHE HAD HER BARE feet curled on the seat under her shapely ass, her back against the passenger door. The sunlight turned her hair to living flame. It seemed brighter, more vibrant, more alive than Rand remembered. His memories of Dakota's hair were pretty damned powerful.

He didn't have anything. For her to hold, or channel, or whatever the hell she claimed she did. And he sure as hell didn't want to remember the feel of those hot silken strands gliding down his body. "We'll be at the hotel where they found the body in a few minutes. Start channeling your inner GPS."

"Hopefully we'll find something useful there," she said without responding to his sarcasm. "A shoe, or some personal effect in his pockets—there's always something."

"Yeah. Maybe." His thoughts were anything but orderly, now that she'd shown up. Seeing her always short-circuited his brain, and today was no exception. He resented the power she had over his body. Fortunately, he'd managed to get her completely out of his system. Two years without seeing her effectively cured him. What hadn't killed him made him stronger. Yeah. He was cured. It was just the kick to his chest that churned up old memories.

Rand glanced at the route on the GPS, then back to the road. That she claimed to have this extraordinary sixth sense was ludicrous. True, his friend made the same claim, following his ordeal in South America, where he'd been kidnapped, shot, and left for dead. He had excuses that no one could blame him for—trauma, PTSD, grief. Dakota didn't.

Yet Zak had built a company based on his newfound sixth sense. Shit. Rand had no idea what or whom to believe. It pissed him off that he might need more than his own skills to crack this.

If she could help him find the person responsible for this, he'd bite his tongue and play nice. Which segued into the thought of him biting *her* tongue and playing naughty. He called himself six kinds of fool. She was everything he wanted in a woman, and pretty much everything he loathed in a human being. *Get a grip, Maguire.*

"I'm hoping like hell that when we get where we're going, there is *something.*" He was desperate enough to almost believe her. God. Her timing couldn't be worse.

If this *was* the drug that killed his mother, having Dakota—a key member of the Rydell team—suddenly show up in the same place as its reappearance was dangerously fortuitous. What were the chances?

Slim enough to make him suspicious as hell.

"So you're not a chemist anymore?"

Even her hair seemed to stiffen. "My lab was destroyed. People *died* . . . No. I'm not in that field anymore."

"You were *fired. Then* the lab was destroyed." More omissions. That had been almost two years ago. What had she been doing since? He didn't give a damn enough to ask—to brave her prickly field of *don't fucking bother*—and she didn't offer. Fine with him. He heard her take a controlled breath before she spoke again.

"Right." She turned those pale peridot eyes to him and waited out his sarcasm as she changed the subject. "Was anyone at the event *not* affected?"

"Other than my men and the majority of the wait-staff? No. *Everyone* drank the Kool-Aid, including the priest, the groom's eighty-two-year-old grandmother, all the band members, and two of my security people."

"How soon till we get the lab results back?" she asked.

"I asked them to put a rush on it. Later this afternoon, I hope." He turned down the tree-lined street indicated by the car's GPS. "What's your angle, Dakota? You're pushing hard to be involved. Why? You no longer represent Rydell, what possible interest could you have in the outcome of this investigation?"

"I was involved with every aspect of this drug. Why do you *think* I insist on seeing where this all leads?"

"We both know that's not it."

When her mouth tightened, deep lines furrowing between her eyebrows, he resisted every ingrained urge to reach over and smooth them away. Damn, she hadn't lost the ability to bring out his protective instinct. He squashed the urge to touch her.

"You have something to prove," he said mildly, when he felt anything but.

She shot him a fulminating glare, her chin tilted pugnaciously. "And what if I do?"

"Then your presence here is not only redundant," he told her, tone cooling, "it's a waste of everyone's time."

Her snort was eerily reminiscent of his. "Why don't you ask what you *really* want to ask?" She widened her eyes dramatically, hand on her chest. "Did you do it, Dakota?" she demanded gruffly. "Admit it. You just happened to know where this wedding was taking place, despite the fact that not even the paparazzi knew, and you dosed a room full of Hollywood stars with a drug destroyed years ago! Confess!"

Her mimicry nudged a reluctant smile to his lips that he suppressed. Nothing about this situation was amusing. Even if she could help, he damned well didn't want her here. "Apparently the formula wasn't destroyed in the explosion."

"Apparently not." She deflated slowly, her expression suddenly . . . what? Sad? Heavy with guilt? Yeah, that one he'd believe. "Only two people who worked on that drug are still alive, Rand. All of our notes and files were destroyed along with the lab. I was minding my own business in Seattle when Zak called me in. Cole met me at the gate after a twelve-hour flight. There's no way I could have done this. Even if I had the ability to be in two places at once, *why* would I have done it? To what purpose?"

He twisted the wheel and floored the gas pedal, overtaking two cars in the fast lane. He zipped in front of them, waiting a few seconds until the sounds of the car horns were lost behind them. "I have no idea how you think. I've *never* had any idea how you think."

"Clearly, I had no idea how you think either, so we're even."

It didn't matter what the hell the drug was—he wanted the person or persons responsible found and brought to justice. Dakota was right about that. "Blood work's been sent to a local lab. Let's see which of you is right." He ran his hand over his hair.

"They're wrong," Dakota told him flatly. "I told you before, Ecstasy could cause that kind of euphoria, but that spike in libido and total breakdown of inhibitions indicates DL6-94. It's not Krokodil, which is a completely different and dangerous drug, with completely different and dangerous side effects. The end result, however, is they both guarantee death. I can't confirm that this is Rydell's formula, but I'm taking an educated, well-informed guess. I won't know one hundred percent for sure until I talk to some of the victims and see the lab report. You must've questioned everyone affected. I'll start with any reports you've compiled—"

"Everyone's still at the hotel. Several under doctors' care. Two people had mild heart attacks, and Dunham's grandmother put her back out. Although," Rand's lips quirked, "she admitted to me that she'd never had such great sex in all her eighty-plus years, and she could now die with a smile." He shrugged. "She was the only humorous moment in the whole mess. What are the long-term consequences if this is what you think it is, Dakota? Am I going to have a hundred people die on me?"

She rubbed both hands over her face, then dropped them back into her lap. "It depends on the dose. One wafer won't do much more than make them horny and have zero inhibitions. You can tell the dosage by how much bloom they have on their eyes. Anyone—"

"Bloom?"

"Looks like a cataract. Did you notice anyone's eyes afterward?"

"Groom's stepfather got falling-down drunk. If anyone had a problem, he'd be the one."

"Have him checked again."

"Half of them are users of some sort of illicit drug," Rand pointed out. "I'm leaning toward somebody doing this to blackmail half of Hollywood's fucking elite." The embarrassment up in that hotel suite stuck with him, profound and palpable.

"I imagine it was terrifying for everyone when they finally recovered." Sympathy—guilt?—filled her voice. "Since the drug is lethal, you're fortunate nobody died. There's a dangerously fine line between pleasure and death. A microgram too much, and you'd be telling a different story this morning."

He glanced at the clean lines of her profile as she looked at the scenery whizzing by, then turned his own attention to the road as she glanced at him. "Will they keep this quiet, or is someone going to blab to the press?"

"Frankly, it's unlikely that everyone *will* keep their mouths shut. We're talking about *actors* here. This isn't like old Hollywood where scandal was kept hush-hush. These days, if Lohan gets a hangnail, it's front-page news. It won't remain a secret. Not for long."

"Then we'd better work fast and get them answers. Did someone happen to check the dead man's eyes?"

"No need. He was murdered. I don't have the details, but it wasn't Rapture. Let's hope there's something in the room for you to hold, because otherwise we're as screwed as the groom's stepfather, who did half the people in that room last night."

They were out of the center of town and the traffic moved at lightning speed. Dakota glanced at the GPS on the dash. "At this velocity, our ETA is two minutes. I'm taking a power nap. It was a long flight, and I didn't get any sleep. Wake me when you need me."

His eyebrows rose at that loaded statement. "White-knuckle flyer?" Another thing she'd never told him. One more he could add to the list.

She wedged her back more comfortably between the seat back and the door frame, and closed her eyes. "If God wanted us to fly, he would've given us wings."

"He gave us planes instead. There's no time for a nap, we're almost there."

"Hmm," she murmured, already drifting. Within seconds, her breathing indicated sleep.

Rand glanced over at her. "You're a complication I don't fucking need right now, Dakota North." His lips curved into a thin, humorless smile. "Thank God I'm immune."

THE HOTEL WAS TUCKED away in a cul-de-sac on the edge of town, too far away from the tourist destinations to offer much trouble for anyone but the locals. This was the kind of low-rent dive where casino losers came to lick their wounds as they counted their euros before going back to try their luck one last time. Night and day compared to where the wedding had taken place.

Rand parked the rental in a patch of shade under a stand of spindly palm trees in the weedy parking lot and glanced at his sleeping ace in the hole. He'd never met anyone who could fall asleep so fast, and so deeply. He knew a hundred ways to make Dakota wake up smiling.

He didn't plan on using any of them ever again.

Right now, there was no point waking her. She

needed, according to her, something tangible to hold, so until they found something the waiter might have left behind, he preferred she stay where she was. It was unlikely they'd even find anything. In which case, he'd have one of his men return her to the airport.

He was torn between the desire, no, the *need* to believe her tracking claim and the urge to be as far away from her as possible. The shadows of his once-frozen emotions were once again a tight, hot knot in his belly.

He peered through the window as he locked the car doors. Dakota flipped an arm over her eyes to block the sunshine but stayed asleep. He shook his head. How could she look so bonelessly comfortable curled in the seat like that? How could she look so *normal?* The liar that she was didn't show on her sleeping face. Instead, she looked beautiful and achingly innocent.

Looks, he knew, were deceptive.

Resolutely, he turned away and headed for the portico of the small hotel. The sun felt good on his shoulders, but back here in the alley there was no scent of ocean, just a sense of desperation and the stifling pressure of lost dreams. There was a reason the lavish casinos didn't allow Monaco residents inside to gamble.

He didn't gamble for money. Hell, Rand didn't gamble at all. He'd bet everything on love once and lost his ass. Lesson learned. Case closed. He didn't need her, he needed her skills. *If* she really had them.

He wasn't into woo-woo. He'd tried to keep an open mind when Stark talked about the strange new sixth sense he'd developed the year before. While traveling in

Venezuela, Zak and his brother, Gideon, had been kidnapped by terrorists. The details were grim. Rand could only imagine the burden Zak carried over his brother's death. When Zak sold ZAG Search on his return and started Lodestone, he'd tried to persuade Rand to join forces, thinking their two companies complemented each other. Security and tracking.

Probably would too. However, Rand had declined the partnership offer. He savored his independence. As a stuntman, then stunt coordinator he'd known to check every trick himself, seven ways from Sunday, no matter who told him it was safe. He was used to relying solely on himself, and he'd been slow to hire people for his company as it grew; it was difficult to find people he could have that kind of faith in. The kind of faith he'd had in Dakota.

Until yesterday, he'd been riding the wave. If he didn't find who was responsible and mitigate the damage before things spun even more out of control, he'd lose it all.

Still, Zak Stark was a good man and he trusted him. He'd kept meaning to wander by, knock back a few beers, and catch up, but Zak lived in the same city as Dakota, and Rand had let the friendship lapse because he hadn't wanted to be anywhere near her. Even his home in Los Angeles was too damned close to the Pacific Northwest.

With no leads and even fewer clues, he and his people needed all the help they could get. As much as he didn't want her around, he had to admit, he might need her to stick around after all.

Mark "Ham" Stratham and Derek Rebik waited for him just inside the front doors. Both wore black chinos and black T-shirts—no insignia. They didn't need uniforms or identifying badges to lend them a sense of authority.

"You made it in good time." Stress lines were carved deeply around Rebik's mouth.

"I'm motivated," Rand replied. "I left the Lodestone agent sleeping in the car. Go keep an eye on her, would you?"

Rebik raised a brow. "Sleeping?"

"Red-eye flight," was all Rand trusted himself to say.

The agent nodded and took off.

"This way." Ham led Rand across the empty lobby, past the unmanned front desk, and into the open cage elevator. He pulled shut the concertina-style door. "We're on the third floor." A chain-smoker, he smelled of cigarettes and the spearmint gum he used to disguise his smoking habit. It didn't fool anyone.

Rand pushed the button. Ham was a more than slightly overweight ex-cop with thirty-five years' experience on the Seattle homicide squad. Lines of strain tightened the skin around his eyes. His brown hair was buzz-cut, military style. Like Rand, he had no sleep in more than twenty-four hours. "How are our charges?"

"How do you think?" Rand stepped to the back of the elevator, crossing his arms over his chest. "Pissed, embarrassed, and a nanosecond away from a lawsuit against me, the hotel, and whoever else they can think of. What do we have?"

"Room was registered to a Daniel Perry. Fifty-three. Tempe, Arizona. US passport, been here a week," Ham said briskly. No fluff. "Hit the casinos hard, lost his shirt. Skipped early last night. Dead guy is Denis Brun. Twenty-five. Native Monegasque with a local address. Worked for the catering company for seven years and change. A couple of run-ins with the law over the years, minor drug busts. Clean for three years."

Rand frowned. "That was all on the guy's security clearance. Until his behavior changed . . . ?" Because he was using again and/or because he'd made new friends. Rand's educated guess was both.

Ham cocked a brow in acknowledgment. "A month ago."

The men's eyes met. "Bank account?" Rand asked, knowing there'd be a payment sitting there. The guy hadn't had time to spend it. Now he never would.

"Ten thousand euros deposited day before yesterday."

"Fingerprinted?"

"Yeah, and sent to our lab. We should have ID confirmation by the time we get upstairs."

"Where's Perry?"

"We're holding him at the airport, but it doesn't look like he had anything to do with this. Spent the night with some chick he met at a local bar. Went straight to the airport from her place."

Rand glanced at a man in nothing but his shorts who peered at them from his cracked-open door as they passed his floor. "Without his luggage?" Rand asked as his door snicked closed and the elevator rose.

Ham nodded. "Couldn't pay his tab and skipped. His shit is still in the room." He shrugged. "Happens all over the world."

"Didn't they hold his passport in the hotel safe?"

"Perry said he needed it to cash a check yesterday."

"So all they have him on is the Monegasque equivalent of defrauding an innkeeper?" Not that Rand cared. If Perry had nothing to do with what happened at the wedding, he was a nonissue.

But it was an *if*. Ham shrugged his beefy shoulders. "Pretty much. The locals are dealing with him. Our perp used his room to draw the waiter here. Did the deed and split. Nobody saw anything. No surveillance cameras, no fingerprints, no trace evidence. Nada."

"A professional?"

"Oh, yeah." The ex-cop was practically rubbing his hands with glee. The murder was right up his alley. Unfortunately, it just presented more questions. At least they had somewhere to start, and Rand knew this piece of the puzzle was in expert hands.

"Doesn't explain how the killer knew Perry wouldn't return." Rand leaned against the cheap paneling as the small box jerked upward in fits and starts. "That the hotel room was available while he gambled and lost, then went home with some woman to screw instead of returning to pick up his luggage."

"My thoughts exactly. I'll tell our guys to squeeze Perry some more." The door wheezed open on the third floor. The corridor had garish red-flocked wallpaper from the seventies and closed doors on either side of a black-and-red runner that looked worse for wear. The whole place reeked of strong French cigarettes, garlic, and death.

He acknowledged Becky Murry, another of his people, who waited directly outside the elevator as the door opened, weapon drawn. On seeing Rand, she relaxed and gave a curt nod, stepping aside.

Yesterday's incident affected everyone on the security detail. An unidentified drug had been administered to the clients under their protection. That the drug in question turned out to be an aphrodisiac was immaterial; it could just as easily have been a fast-acting poison. Then instead of embarrassment to deal with, Rand would have had more than a hundred deaths to explain to the authorities and the world at large.

His people all had a vested interest in apprehending the perpetrator, as quickly as possible. Their asses were on the line just as much as his. The two agents who'd partaken of the tainted champagne at the reception instead of doing their jobs had been fired. Not for fucking but for leaving their posts to drink on the job. Rand had zero tolerance. He had to be able to rely on the professionalism of every one of his employees at all times; no exceptions. Humiliated, they'd been sent home on a commercial flight at dawn.

"We haven't moved anything." Ham shoved the door to the room open. "But we went through it all with a fine-tooth comb."

Two more of Rand's men were inside; on seeing him, they relaxed and holstered their weapons as they stepped aside to give him room. They'd opened the window, and a muggy breeze moved the stink around and fluttered the cheap curtains. The body was on the bed.

Brun had been stabbed in the back, falling facedown across the tossed mattress, the knife still in him. Blood stained his shirt and saturated the covers and sheets. Not a pretty sight.

Pinkner took out his handheld computer. "ID confirmed. Denis Brun. We sent Shank and a couple of guys to his home address. See if we can find anything worthwhile there."

"Straight into the kidneys," Rand mused out loud. "Killer knew what he was about. Nice and quiet for the neighbors."

The hotel room was trashed. No defensive wounds, at least not at first glance, and most of the blood seemed fairly contained. No splatters, no spray over the scattered objects.

Deduction of the day: the poor bastard knew his killer.

"I suppose it's too much to ask for clues," he said without any real hope.

"Nothing, unless we can ID some viable prints we managed to lift from this." Using latex gloves, Ham offered Rand a second pair, waited while he pulled them on, then handed him a gunmetal-gray aluminum case the size of a paperback book. The outside still had traces of the fingerprint dust.

The hair on Rand's nape rose in warning. The box was light on the flat of his hand. Innocuous, really, but he felt a ponderous sense of oncoming doom. Christ. He opened the case.

Fucking, fucking, *fucking* hell.

He'd had his suspicions. The effects of the drug had been chillingly familiar, even before Dakota suggested it. But seeing the dense black polyethylene foam inside the case, with imprints for five vials and a shallow oblong depression, chilled his blood. Only one empty vial remained. The other spaces were conspicuously empty.

"What?" Ham gave him a piercing look. "Recognize it?"

Hell, yeah. "Any sign of the other vials?"

"No."

"We have the prints being analyzed?" Ham cocked a brow; of course he did. "Good man. Clear everyone out before the cops get here. I'll take this and see what the Lodestone agent can do with it."

"If anything." Ham didn't mask his skepticism. He'd met Zak Stark, liked him well enough, as far as Rand knew, but he made no secret of his conviction that the Lodestone premise was bogus. He believed maybe half of what he saw, and none of what he couldn't see.

Ham had told Rand flat-out that he was wasting their time asking for help from some freaky psychic or whatever Zak's agents were. Rand tended to agree with him, but at midnight last night, it seemed like a good idea.

"Yeah. If anything." Rand took the plastic bag Ham offered and zipped the case inside. "And to give you a heads-up, that agent happens to be Dr. Dakota North."

Ham's eyebrows shot up. "Dr. North? You're shitting me. What's that bitch doing here? Did she suddenly decide to do the right thing at the eleventh hour and agree to testify on Paul's behalf?"

"She claims this is the drug that she and Paul were working on at Rydell." Rand made a visual sweep of the room. Through the window, he could see the car in the parking lot, Rebik leaning against the hood.

Ham scowled, shoving his fingers into the front pockets of his pants. "Wasn't it destroyed?"

"That was the official report. Dakota swears this is the same crap. They called it Rapture at the lab."

"It was that and then some." Ham looked out the window, frowning as he looked back at Rand. "But Rydell was totaled two years ago. Saw it myself. Your father is in Capanne prison about to serve a life sentence unless there's a Hail Mary save anytime soon. He's more worried about bending over to pick up the soap than dispensing drugs at a wedding."

"It gets even more convoluted. This appears to be the same drug used to kill my mother." The thought was even more disturbing, because now Rand knew what must've happened preceding her death. He blocked out the very images.

"Are you fucking kidding me?" the eagle-eyed ex-cop asked, quietly coming to stand beside him. Ham gave him a speaking, narrow-eyed look and lowered his voice. "Funny how Dr. North is always somewhere in the vicinity of it, isn't it? You think *she* did the dosing yesterday?"

Rand shook his head. "No. Right now she's the only expert we have. But having her so close to the prison, Paul, and this close to the start of the trial could be problematic."

"She might change her mind and speak for him," Ham offered, clearly not believing *that* for a second.

"And admit she gave the drug to my father to administer to my mother? Unlikely. I'll use her expertise, but that doesn't mean I like it, and I sure as hell won't trust her farther than I can throw her. You can bet I'll be keeping a close eye on her. I don't want her fucking with Paul again. His position is tenuous as it is. It's imperative he keep his head." A thought occurred to him. "Maybe she's here to speak for the prosecution."

"No shit." Ham scrubbed his hand over the stubble on his head as he gave Rand a frowning look that spoke volumes. "Keep your dick in your pants and your head on straight, pal. Last time, she screwed with you and left you in the dust when you needed her most."

Rand crossed the worn carpet to get a closer look at the body. "I'm willing to try anything to get this situation contained." *Even if it means dealing with Dakota.* He didn't believe in coincidences. The Rydell Pharmaceuticals product showing up two weeks before his father's trial for murder, plus Dakota's mystical and hitherto unheard-of "sixth sense," smelled like a setup to him. He just didn't know by whom or why.

Ham had assisted Rand with an investigation to unearth any concrete proof of his father's innocence in both Seattle and Rome. They'd found nothing they could present to the Italian courts, but Rand still had people digging back in Seattle.

Eager to get out of the bureaucratic red tape of the public sector, Ham had switched to private and joined Rand's security company. Already an invaluable asset with his experience in homicide, Ham knew killers.

But subtle wasn't his gift.

"I'll go see my father and ask what he knows." It would be a waste of time, he was pretty damned sure.

Paul had been incarcerated for two years. From day one, he'd professed his innocence.

His friend clasped his shoulder. "Let me do it."

Rand hesitated. He believed his mother's death had been an unfortunate accident and was doing his best to forgive his father, but there was still a raw place that would never heal. Accident or not, Rand had lost his mother. Probably the only woman in his life who'd genuinely loved him back.

He wanted his father freed because it was the right thing to do, even though the thought of looking at the man turned his stomach. He could do it, but Ham would do it faster and didn't have personal history to blur the lines. "Yeah," he finally agreed. "Thanks. *You* won't be tempted to kill him. Last thing I need is a cell right next door to his."

"One thing we know for sure, he couldn't have done the wedding business." He jerked his chin to indicate the body on the bed. "Or *this* guy."

"Maybe someone who worked in the lab?" Rand looked down at the aluminum case. "One of the other lab rats, or . . . shit. *Someone* managed to get their hands on the old formula."

"Or it has nothing to do with that shit at all."

Rand stared at Ham. "You can say that after you witnessed the guests' behavior yesterday, coupled with Dakota's information? Obviously my father's not involved with the current mess, but he might remember something pertinent from his days at Rydell. Maybe give us a lead."

His father had always found a way under, over,

around any obstacle, but wouldn't have any resources in a maximum-security Italian prison. That said, Rand presumed his father had friends in Europe; he and Creed traveled together frequently to see the museums and galleries, which held no interest for their wives. So he wasn't completely cut off from the outside world.

"Seth and I went to see him last week. I want to know what other visitors he's had since he's been there," Rand ordered, turning toward the door. He needed out of the smell; the stench of the corpse hung in the thick air like a miasma. "Everything—when he saw his doctor, when he went to the clinic for a headache."

Rand received, and ignored, monthly reports. Merely seeing the man's name in print raised his blood pressure. Just because he was doing everything in his not inconsiderable power to give his father the best defense possible didn't mean he believed him completely innocent of the charges. No matter how it had come about, his father's hand had given his mother the drugs that killed her.

But after the trial, he never wanted to see his father again.

Ham assured him, "I'll take care of it myself."

"He's not going anywhere. Give it twenty-four hours. Take the lead on this as a priorit—"

Footsteps preceded a firm, feminine voice by milliseconds. "What can I—oh, my God!" Dakota stepped into the room, then took a hasty step back as she saw the body sprawled on the bed.

✦ FOUR ✦

The color drained from her face, leaving her freckles in stark relief. Rand knew how it worked: the stench, already a wisp of promise in the hallway, tripled in intensity as soon as the brain connected the sight with the smell. She immediately covered her nose and mouth with her palm.

Rebik, standing right behind her, grabbed her upper arms to steady her. Rand shot him a what-the-fuck-do-you-think-you're-doing look. The other man winced, released her, and said uneasily, "She's part of the team now, right? She wanted to—"

"See what the dead guy looks like?" Rand asked sarcastically. He wasn't annoyed at the sight of the man's hands on Dakota's bare arms. He was pissed that she was in the room at all.

Her eyes narrowed over the cupped hand covering her mouth, as if she was concentrating. Probably on not throwing up.

She was once again wearing her shoes, a good thing considering the condition of the carpet. Which put her almost a head taller than most of his men, and a few inches below his own six four.

"Your first dead body?" he asked.

Dakota didn't take her pale eyes off the bed. "It's more realistic-looking on TV." She paused. "I guess there's a reason Smell-O-Vision never took off." She wrinkled her nose.

Yeah.

Removing the small bag and its contents from his back pocket, Rand crossed the room. "See what you can do with this."

She didn't take it, but he could see that she recognized the shape, as he had. He smelled butterscotch as she tilted her head to look up at him. The fact that the scent of her favorite candy managed to underscore the sickening smell of spoiling meat said something about his state of mind. "Can we do it outside?"

"Sure." He gestured for her to precede him, then turned back to Stratham and the others. "Keep on this—"

"Yeah," Pinkner muttered. "Since it's the only sodding lead we have."

"Better than nothing. Call me when you get anything. I don't care how small." He stepped into the hall, bagged case held out to Dakota.

She waved him off. "I'll take that when we get to the car, okay? First contact always makes me a little dizzy."

Rand shrugged. He didn't care where she did it, just that she could somehow, any-fucking-how, give them a lead.

Dakota leaned against the wall of the small elevator as they rode it down. This close, he could see a scattering of pale caramel-colored freckles across her nose and cheeks. Rand found the smell of clean female perspiration, faded butterscotch, and light floral perfume as annoying as it was alluring. Nowhere for him to go. He was a captive audience for three floors.

She sighed. "That's a terrible way to die."

"It was quick."

She raised a russet brow. "I hope that's true, but you can't know that."

"A knife to the kidneys is always fast and silent." He didn't mention that it was the intense, excruciating pain that kept the victim quiet. "The killer was a professional."

She shivered, rubbing her arms. "Do you think there was a falling-out between thieves?"

The door opened, and they exited the small elevator and crossed the lobby. Rand waited until they were outside before answering. "The dead guy was paid ten thousand euros. We're working on the details." He disengaged the locks as they approached the car, then held the door open for her before he rounded the vehicle. As soon as he got in, he turned the air on full blast.

Dakota kicked off her shoes, pulled her feet up on the seat, and sat cross-legged. "Okay." She held out her hand, palm up. "Give it to me."

He had things he'd like to give her. Two years' worth of accumulated words that had never been said. Instead, silently, and with only a moment's hesitation, Rand slid the container from the plastic covering onto her extended hand. He was putting all his trust in a woman he didn't trust at all.

DAKOTA PLACED HER ELBOWS on her knees, trying to ignore the wash of vertigo that hit her the second her fingers brushed the case.

Beside her, Rand shifted in his seat. He watched her closely, like a skeptic trying to spot the trick. "You look like you're going to hurl."

"I don't usually."

"Do you need to close your eyes?" His voice held a huge dose of mockery. "Chant? Sprinkle it with juju dust?"

She shot him an unsmiling glance. "You're a man who likes to take risks." His expression did a slow spin before settling into an oh-so-serious look.

"You get that from just holding it?"

"I get that from sharing a bed with you for a year," she said dryly. "Are you trying to annoy me? Because it isn't working. I've heard worse, believe me. Now, shut up so I can see where your killer is."

After a few seconds, she leaned down and grabbed her large tote from the foot well.

"Nothing?" He sounded unsurprised.

She placed the bag in the cradle of her legs and rummaged around in it. "Oh, I know exactly where he, they, are. I want to show you on this." She held up a small GPS device. Dumping the heavy bag back on the floor, she turned on the handheld. "He's moving at a pretty fast clip. Hang on. . . ."

Dakota punched in the same GPS coordinates she was seeing in her mind's eye, then showed him the screen.

"Marseille?" He reached for the car keys. "I have a private plane at Nice airport. If you can make it a bit more specific, I'll—"

"He isn't in Marseille," she interrupted. "He's moving west. I'll show you." She punched in different coordinates.

Rand frowned at the screen. "Taking the scenic route? Where the hell's he going?"

She shrugged. "No crystal ball, remember? I presume that's rhetorical, since I can't see into the future." She tapped in the new coordinates as fast as they came to her. "Still heading west along the coast. What are we going to do?"

He started the car. "I'll drop you back at the hotel. We can keep in contact by phone—"

"Or," she cut in, "I can go with you and keep in contact by telling you as you drive." Dakota kept her voice level. "One is more efficient than the other, but I'm fine with hanging out at a luxury hotel. I can probably keep you updated from the spa."

Suspicious eyes met hers. "They have at least a two-hour head start," he warned. "I'm not going back for your luggage."

Or to drop her off, apparently. She was just fine with that. Dakota angled her back against the door to get comfortable. "No prob. I can buy anything I need when I need it." Which was exactly what she'd planned to do anyway.

"Location?"

The numbers in her mind's eye glowed softly, moving

as their quarry moved. "They aren't going fast enough to be on a plane or train. A vehicle for sure. Still heading west. How do you plan to catch them?"

Rand slipped dark sunglasses on, making him look even more remote and lethal. "I'll catch them," he said, his tone crisp and confident. He cranked the engine over and the rental car roared to life. There was no way this was just some regular car. It sounded too throaty and responded too well to his expert handling. Then again, this was Monaco. Maybe all of the rental cars here drove like Ferraris.

"If your driving gets too crazy, I'll close my eyes." Dakota felt something small untangle inside her, a tiny curl of hope. He wasn't going to take her back to the airport. He believed in her enough to take her with him. She let out the breath she'd been holding.

Reaching into his shirt pocket, he took out his phone as he drove. "Call Cole," he instructed the phone.

"Calling Cole," a mechanical female voice repeated.

A few moments later, his assistant answered. He brought the phone to his ear, excluding her from hearing both sides of the conversation. Rand filled Cole in on what happened at the other hotel, gave him instructions to pass on to the men, and told him to text him the lab results as soon as they came in.

Everyone was insisting they be allowed to return home. Once they were released into the wild, all bets were off as far as maintaining their silence went. It was a risk he was being forced to take. He couldn't keep the guests and waitstaff prisoners indefinitely, even if it was a gilded cage. "If the doctors give everyone a clean bill of health, then let them go. We can't hold them indefinitely. . . . Yeah. I hear you. Talk to Creed about getting some PR assistance before they leave." He paused to listen. "Send half our guys back with them." He listened for a few minutes, then said, "Okay. Keep me in the loop. Everyone is to go through you until I get back.

"Dr. North will give you our location and coordinates. Follow the bouncing ball, and keep the team in the loop."

Rand handed her the phone and Dakota read off the GPS coordinates of their quarry as she saw them in her head, then handed his phone back to him.

For the first time that day, his lips broke their harsh line and he almost smiled. "Let's see what this baby can do."

He kept to the fast lane, and a hair over the speed limit, weaving in and out of traffic like an Indy 500 driver. "You were a race-car driver in *Hearts Run*, this should be a piece of cake," she said lightly. He'd once told her that racing cars was his favorite gig as a stunt double, and he'd been in half a dozen movies where he put his phenomenal driving skills to the test. Those movies were her favorites. She had them all.

Now she was grateful that he'd worked so hard to perfect his craft and had never taken any of the stunts he performed lightly. His discipline and training served him well in his security business. She rolled her head on the seat back to look at him. He had a magnificent nose— one of the few things, he'd once told her, that had never been broken.

"You and Jason Dunham are friends from your stunt days, right?" The two men didn't look anything alike, but they were both tall with athletic builds. Rand doubled for the star in an action movie called *Tropical Storm* several years before he quit the business to become a stunt coordinator.

"Yeah. But Creed put in a word as well."

Seth Creed had given Rand his first stunt job, and she knew how much he admired and respected the director. He'd called Rand his lucky charm, and together they'd made a dozen blockbuster movies. Rand had the rugged good looks and charisma to have been a movie star himself, but he'd preferred being anonymous. He'd made a lot of money that way. And up until now, his upscale security business had been bringing in steady clientele. Dakota wondered how last night's incident would affect that business in the long term.

Nobody had died, and sex was big business. In a few weeks or months, it would be just a salacious story to whisper to their friends.

"Do you still think the motive is blackmail?" she asked, searching in her bag for a roll of candy, offering him one as well, which he refused, then she popped both in her mouth. It wasn't breakfast, but she had a feeling it was as close as she was going to get.

"Shit, I have no idea. If that's the case, I would've expected a demand first thing this morning. In a few hours everyone will be in flight, and by tomorrow most of the guests will be home. It's not out of the realm of possibility, but I don't see any reason for a blackmailer to wait."

She crunched on the candy. There were lush green fields on either side of the road, but she wasn't interested in scenery right now. "If not blackmail, then what? A way to discredit or ruin someone?"

"Yeah. That's what I'm thinking."

"Who?"

"Both the bride and groom are megastars, and Amanda is young and fresh enough that something like this could tank her career. Or it could be Creed. He's a straight arrow, no weird stuff in his life that I know of. Married, straight, no drinking, no drugs. Footage of his naked, hairy ass screwing a couple of bridesmaids would certainly impact his career. But he's big enough that I'm pretty sure something like this wouldn't matter beyond a mention or two on TMZ or Page Six."

"There's another option," she pointed out, pulling a bottle of water from her bag and twisting off the cap. It was warm, but quenched her thirst. "A hundred high-visibility people with money to burn. A hundred *customers*." She handed the bottle to Rand, who took an absent chug before handing it back. "Rapture is highly addictive, remember? It would take only a few more doses, and that would be it. Those people would do anything, pay anything to get their hands on more."

They drove through the dappled light of a tunnel of overhead branches, the plane trees lined like soldiers for miles, cows grazing in the fields beyond them. There were plenty of cars on the road. They could've been a couple out on a relaxing Sunday drive. They'd never taken a Sunday drive. Their times together had been so short—with her in Seattle and Rand living and working in Los Angeles—that they'd spent most of their time together in bed.

"Hell, that didn't even cross my mind, but yeah, that's certainly another option. It's that addictive?"

"The version we had in the lab was, and I don't doubt for a second that's changed."

"A hundred people, and word of mouth . . ."

He wasn't looking for a response, and she didn't offer one. For the next twenty miles they kept their own counsel. Dakota easily kept track of their quarry's GPS location. Whoever they were following was in no particular hurry and wasn't taking any detours.

Rand changed lanes and zoomed into a tunnel without slowing down. After several more minutes of silence, he slammed his palm on the wheel. "Damn it to hell. This pisses me off on so many levels."

She shifted to study him. "I'm sure it does." She pulled her sunglasses from her tote as they emerged from the tunnel, heading directly into the sun. "We'll find the guy." They were working *together*. God. She never thought this day would happen. "No one was permanently injured—they didn't receive a high enough dose. Embarrassment and maybe an STD will be the worst of it."

He shrugged one shoulder, a gesture she took to mean her words were small comfort. The only comfort they'd get would be when Rand caught up with the bad guy.

And she'd help him.

"You have a new scar on your eyebrow, I see. I thought your new career was supposed to be safer."

"Not as predictable, at least. Not dying's a plus either way."

"What happened?"

His eyes never left the road, flicking from cars to pedestrians to the mirrors in an easy, studied nonchalance that belied his skill. "My face got in the way of someone's fist."

Cute. "You didn't used to get hurt as often as I thought you would."

He shrugged. "Par for the course," he said after a moment.

Dakota smiled faintly. "You once told me you didn't miss it. Do you still feel that way?"

"Stunts are a young man's game. I wanted to do, not coordinate. The security business gives me plenty of action." He rotated his head, tilting it one way, then another. His neck cracked once. "How long have you worked for Zak?" He didn't like talking about himself. Never had.

"Almost a year. He saw a small piece in the paper about me finding a lost child, and contacted me." Dakota saw his jaw tighten. "People have all sorts of interesting abilities, but I'd never met anyone who could do what I do. To find a kindred spirit was incredible. He remembered me—" No, wait. She didn't want to go there. Swiftly, she amended it to, "—and before I knew it, he and Acadia took me to dinner, asked me a few questions, and offered me a job before we'd ordered dessert."

"And what were you doing the year in between?"

Between the explosion at Rydell and going to work for Zak?

Coming out of a drug-induced coma, screaming. "This and that. Temp work mostly." Dakota yawned and, borrowing a page from his book, changed the subject. "We're still on his tail, but we've closed the gap some. He's just over an hour and twenty minutes ahead. Looks like he's taking his time. Is there always this much traffic?" She smiled. "That was rhetorical. I'm guessing you don't drive the Côte d'Azur every day."

"The French hate tourists who drive like that." "That" was a couple of rental cars going slow enough that the locals were speeding past and blasting their horns. Rand was ahead of the pack, and in fact, picked up speed as soon as they passed one of the numerous speed cameras.

Dakota compared her numbers to the GPS again. "Looks like we're heading for Barcelona."

"What the hell is this guy's game? He gives a potent aphrodisiac to more than a hundred wedding guests, murders a waiter, and flees to Spain on the motorway in a low-speed chase?"

"It is odd," she admitted, pressing a hand to her growling stomach. She reached down and groped through her bag until she found a protein bar. "Want a bite?"

Driving with one hand held loosely on the wheel, he shook his head.

Dakota broke off a bite and popped it in her mouth. "Want to listen to the news? Maybe there's something about the wedding?"

"Unless one of the guests talked, there won't be. Between Amanda and Jason's people and my team, we did a masterful job keeping this quiet. Not even a whisper of this wedding was leaked to the press beforehand."

"That's an impossible task," she said, impressed.

"We managed to pull it off. Private planes, shell games, misdirection. As far as I'm aware, nobody knows any of them are in Europe. But all it would take is just one graphic photograph from the reception leaked. . . ."

"Seriously, though? In this day and age?" Dakota took another drink. "Would anyone care that the wedding guests had an orgy? How could you keep people from Tweeting that kind of thing in the middle of the show?"

"How would you feel if you saw your mother naked and having wild monkey sex with Justin Bieber?" Rand countered.

Dakota laughed. "Wild monkey sex?" She sobered. "Was he there?"

"No, and all the attendees were of age, thank God. But roll with the thought process."

She shook her head. "I'd freak out thinking about my mother having sex with *anyone*. But Hollywood people? They're always doing outrageous things. An orgy would certainly cause raised eyebrows in some circles, but since the general public probably thinks everyone in Los Angeles has plastic boobs and nose jobs and goes to orgies every night of the week, it would be a twenty-four-hour sensation, forty-eight at most." She rubbed the back of her neck and rotated her shoulders before settling back. "Then one of the housewives of whichever place would get a boob job or divorce her husband for the family dog, and the orgy would be yesterday's news. You'll stop the guy." She snapped her fingers. "Just like that."

"Yeah." He watched the road intently. "I'll stop the guy."

A PART OF RAND hoped to hell this *was* a blackmail attempt. It would all be so much simpler. He'd find the guy and make sure every scrap of evidence was erased. Unless whatever footage he'd shot was being electronically beamed to every fucking news service as they were driving hell-bent for leather across southern Europe. But he doubted it.

If anything went down back at the hotel, if there was anything on the news, Cole, who was coordinating operations in his absence, would call him ASAP. If Rand hadn't heard anything, it meant nothing new was happening back in Monte Carlo. As far as he was concerned, no news was good news.

Dakota suddenly opened her eyes and sat up straight. "He just stopped!"

Maybe he'd spoken too soon.

"What's the gap?" He was going on blind faith and a desperate need to believe she knew what the hell she was doing. They'd crossed the border awhile back, and just turned off into the business center of Barcelona.

Dakota glanced at the vehicle's GPS, then at the one in her hand. "Twenty-three minutes. We made kick-ass time. Can't you go any faster?"

As it turned out, he could.

The streets whipped by at an alarming rate, and Rand's lips twitched despite his intense concentration as she gripped the oh-shit handle above her window. They were in the center of downtown Barcelona in nothing flat, where the traffic became insane. There was no *faster* now.

"Plug your numbers in here, and see if we can pinpoint the address," he said. "Then set this GPS." Rand tapped the dashboard of the rental.

Dakota scowled at the car's GPS. "I don't understand this. What language is it?"

"The street names are in Catalan. Just read it off."

"C slash Picasso s slash n."

"That's c for *carrer*, which is street, and *sense numero*, which means no number," he explained.

"How can a downtown building not have a street number?"

"Punch it into the—"

"Ah-ha! It's Banco Bilbao de Inversiones."

"Why the hell would this guy drive six and a half hours from Monaco to Spain to go to the *bank*?" Rand demanded. "Doesn't make sense. No blackmail attempt, no high-speed chase. The guy doesn't appear to know or care if he's followed. He's kept to the speed limit all the way. He's making it too damned easy for us to catch up."

There was no logic to any of the guy's moves. If he wanted caught, he was doing a good job.

Dakota tilted her head, as if listening to a voice only she could hear. *What the hell*, he thought, *maybe she hears voices too*. Evidently she came to the same conclusion he had. "Either this jackass doesn't know we're hot on his heels, or he *wants* us to catch up." She slipped on her shoes and pulled a small compact out of her bag to check her makeup, which she didn't need. "We must've passed hundreds of banks today. Why come all the way to Barcelona? Or is his destination somewhere beyond the city?"

He'd never made the mistake of thinking Dakota was stupid. Quick-witted, intelligent, beautiful—and a liar, but not stupid. "Not the bank," Rand mused, taking a roundabout and weaving expertly across three lanes as he headed for a parking spot.

"Why not?"

"Banks typically close around one thirty or two thirty in Spain. It's after three. Maybe he stopped nearby."

"He hasn't moved by more than a hundred feet." Dakota shoved her wild ponytail over her shoulder.

Rand pulled over. "I'm going to see what I can find. Stay put." He unlatched his seat belt.

She looked out the window, then at him. "You can't go in there alone, Rand."

He raised a brow. "*I* sure as hell can. *You* stay here. I have no idea what I'm dealing with."

"That's the point!"

He opened the car door, adjusting the weight of the gun in the shoulder holster beneath his jacket. "Cole gave you his number back at the hotel, right? If I'm not back in ten minutes, call him. If our guy takes off, call me. Stay put. I'll be right back." He got out of the car. If it didn't involve a name, place, or time, he didn't really want to hear what came out of her tempting mouth. The long drive tempered his temper. The damned small space had been filled with the fragrance of her skin, the stuff she'd always used on her hair smelled like a tropical beach, and butterscotch candy.

One would think that none of those smells was a turn on. One would be wrong. He slammed the door with a little more force than necessary.

She shook her head and scowled at him through the window as he pressed the door-lock button on the remote control. A distinct *click* drove home his point.

The bank was an imposing gray stone building with enormous metal-studded doors. The street was lined on both sides with cars. Plenty of traffic, both vehicular and foot. The sun beat down on his head, and Rand felt a sense of anticipation as he paused before crossing, his eyes scanning the area even though he had no idea what he was looking for. His bad guy was unlikely to be wearing a trench coat and a fedora.

The women wore summery, sleeveless dresses, and everyone walked with purpose. He waited for a break in the traffic before sprinting across the four-lane street. He checked out the people around him as he moved. The metro station was right outside the building. People came and went. Organized chaos—the studied kind of flow every city cultivated.

In the distance, the unique Gothic spires of Santa Maria del Mar were sandwiched between modern glass-and-steel skyscrapers and quaint little shops in narrow alleys. Tucked on one side of the bank building was a dry cleaner, beside that a closed newsstand. Plenty of office buildings. In the crowded outdoor seating area of a nearby tapas bar, a group of young office workers were saying their good-byes near the black-painted doors. The street was alive with people; the savory fragrances of the many outdoor cafés permeated the afternoon air; and the smell of strong coffee made him consider a to-go cup.

Business as usual.

Except somewhere close by was a killer.

Rand looked up and down the car-lined street. Everyone seemed focused on whatever it was that brought them out—shopping, business, going back to work after lunch. It was a pretty summer day. Nothing looked unusual. Nothing appeared out of place, yet his gut told him everything teetered on the edge of horribly wrong.

He had to trust that Dakota was correct. That the person who'd last held the case containing the vials was somewhere close by. The bank? Why? And damn it to hell, *who*? Had he wanted to do some banking? Pick up a payoff? Make an after-hours deposit? But then, this whole fucking mess was odd.

He stood in the canyon of tall office buildings. Hundreds and hundreds of businesses. Thousands of places to disappear. He had no idea whom he was looking for in the metropolitan haystack.

Bank first, he decided. A highly polished brass plaque on the stone wall at the foot of the stairs gave the hours of business. The bank had closed an hour earlier. Either his guy was still inside—which was highly unlikely—or he was somewhere else. In which case, Dakota was wrong and they were screwed.

Would he have thought differently of her had he known about her ability to track people? He'd like to think that he'd have been fair. Shaking his head, he took out his phone to see if any of his team had called in updates. He frowned. They hadn't. What'd happened to reporting in? Oh, right—he'd told Cole to have everyone report to him. His assistant wouldn't call him unless he had news.

No news was good news right now.

Rand took the deep granite stairs three at a time. The towering, bas-relief–paneled bronze doors were closed. Of course they were. Fuck. Just for yucks, he tried the handle. His gut clenched in anticipation as the door swung open a few inches. With a quick glance over his shoulder, he slipped inside.

All the lights were on, he presumed for the cleaning crew. Not that there was any sign of life. No sound of floor polishers. No voices. No music; whatever piped Muzak the place used must have been shut off at closing time. Perhaps the guy was meeting someone in one of the private offices. Someone who'd orchestrated the ten-thousand-euro payoff to the waiter?

The floor in the vestibule was glossy cream-colored marble. Ahead was a set of elaborately carved wooden doors with heavy polished-brass handles. The doors had large panes at eye level, and as he approached, he could see into the vast interior of the bank. Even though there was no sign of anyone around, he withdrew the Glock from the shoulder holster and walked cautiously, listening for sound, aware of his surroundings as he moved.

As he cautiously opened the door, he was struck again by the unnatural, absolute quiet. Shouldn't there be someone around? Security? Janitors? Managerial types with paperwork to catch up on?

Then he saw the bodies.

Sprawled in groups on the floor throughout the silent marble and mahogany space, they were dead still. A faint cloying aroma of roses mingled with the stench of death. Holding his breath in case it was an airborne contagion, he did a quick visual scan of the large, open area. He'd gotten many gigs for his ability to hold his breath underwater—and thanked God for that training now. Because it appeared that the patrons of the bank had been gassed, and he could feel the insidious lethargy pouring through him as he stood there. *Crapshitdamnfuck.*

Bank customers and personnel were scattered about like dead houseflies, all in various stages of undress. Old, young. Didn't matter. They'd died while fucking like bunnies. Even after seeing something similar at the wedding, the sight was still shocking. A pornographic still life that was as disturbing as it was chilling.

Lungs burning, Rand crouched beside a conjoined young couple, felt for a pulse behind the guy's ear. Still warm, but dead. From beneath him, the woman looked up with eyes filmed a hazy white. A quick glance showed him that everyone had milky eyes.

Everyone had been interrupted mid-coitus.

Everyone was dead.

"Jesu—" The sweet rush of rose filled and expanded Rand's lungs. A surge of adrenaline flooded his body as euphoria engulfed his senses. His heart began to race, and his dick came to life with a vengeance.

He muttered "Fuck" under his breath, then held it on the exhale as he yanked the empty plastic bag from his back pocket and slapped it over his nose and mouth.

Was this the same shit administered to the wedding guests in their champagne? The positions of the bodies provided a graphic answer. Hell yes. It must've been introduced through the ventilation or air-conditioning system.

Just the couple of whiffs he'd taken already had a profound effect on his body. Rand was fully, painfully aroused, his senses heightened, his reflexes maddeningly slow. All he wanted to do was fuck. Anything. Anyone. It was a powerful, driving force, a directive he couldn't ignore. His skin felt too tight, his lungs constricted, and his dick so hard it was excruciatingly painful.

Get the fuck out. Pressing the plastic hard against his face, he craved a deep, liberating breath. *Now! No, damn it! Get a grip. . . . Get the hell . . .*

His breath tight in his lungs, sweat rolling down his temples, he forced his sluggish brain to take in as much data as possible. He tried to pin his focus inside the aura of light surrounding everything in a magical, truly beautiful way. It was the light he'd seen in religious paintings throughout Europe. The light of purity and love and holy fucking—

He slammed the Glock into his cheekbone. Barely felt it. He slammed his fist on a nearby marble counter. Pain, distant and disconnected, jolted up his arm. Behind the long teller counter, the vault door stood wide open. No one had stopped the robbers. Everyone had been caught in the throes of the powerful aphrodisiac, just as the wedding guests had been yesterday. A brief glance showed several security cameras smashed. No witnesses. No record.

His brain felt light. Fantastically light. Brilliant. Buoyant. Invincible—

Get . . . fuck . . . out . . .

His lungs burned with the need to breathe. He *needed* to breathe. And why the hell not? His body felt powerful, expansive, fucking incredible. He wanted Dakota in here. *Now*. He wanted to bare her breasts and taste the freckles on her skin; he wanted to plunge his hardness into her wet heat—

Drug talking! Get a fucking grip, Maguire!

The sunlight streaming through the high windows illuminated in exquisite detail the half-naked bodies, limbs entwined. Pants shoved around the men's ankles, the women's dresses askew, blouses ripped, breasts bared. Everyone had died in the throes of sex. And good sex, by the looks of rapture on their faces.

He *wanted*—

He *needed*—

Goddamn it—

"Rand?" The voice—sultry, feminine, fucking hot as sin—split the heavy silence of the corpse-strewn bank. "Rand, we have to go. The bad guy is on the move agai—oh, crap!"

He turned too fast, almost falling to his knees because his body was racked with overwhelming, clawing lust that felt like a raging, rabid animal inside him. Her red hair floated in slo-mo around her slender shoulders like living flames and licked the luscious swell of her breasts, outlined to perfection by the thin white T-shirt. He could practically taste the rose flavor of her nipples. Her hips looked womanly and lush, encased in tight jeans that accentuated her long legs.

Rand imagined the soft ginger curls at the juncture of her thighs, his heartbeat manic. He couldn't take his eyes off her face as he stalked toward her. He wanted her. Needed her. His heart threatened to explode in his chest. His dick throbbed, a painfully hard entity that demanded satisfaction.

Mouth dry, he forced out the words, "Get. Out. Now!"

"DAMN. DAMN. DAMN!" THE blood drained from her head as Dakota surveyed the bodies sprawled behind Rand, then fixed her eyes on his dopey smile. She sucked in a rose-scented breath, then mentally cursed a blue streak as she realized what she'd just done. Even though she'd never smelled Rapture in this form, she knew what it was right away. The effect was immediate and delicious. The silky pink smell curled through her, expanding her awareness of her body, urging her to tackle Rand and take him to the floor—oh, for crap's sake!

She grabbed his arm. "*Rapture.* Move it!"

The tanned skin was pulled taut over his features, giving him a feral look that made the hair on the back of her neck lift. He resisted her urging to race to the doors. His eyes glittered feverishly. His hair was mussed, and his mouth looked delicious.

What was it that she'd been saying? "Hey," she protested. Her mind shimmered into someplace warm and comfortable. Someplace without cold marble floors or dead people.

Just Rand.

"*Now*," she shouted, but the word edged on a groan as he placed his large hand on her breast, curling his fingers around the aching weight. Holding her breath, she grabbed his hand hard, trying to pull him with her. "Rapture. Don't breathe. Don't talk. *Move!*" But she'd already taken several breaths herself. The soft pink rose flavor of the drug seeped into every cell in her body, expanding her veins and blood vessels with pleasure and happiness.

But she knew they had to get out. Knew . . .

The tantalizing, sensual fragrance of roses perfumed the air. Her mind floated free, and she turned into Rand's chest, catching herself inhaling deeply. Eager for even a trace of the smell of his skin, that wonderfully hot, musky smell she remembered so well. He was so damn hot. Hot, sexy, and fiery to the touch. His skin burned as she ran her hand up his arm, feeling the tensile strength of muscles and tendons under her fingers. He had on too many clothes. A jacket. A shirt. She wanted to touch bare skin and feel the crisp rasp of the hair on his forearm. She rose on her toes to taste him.

His other hand shot out and his fingers curled around her upper arm. There was something metallic and cold in his palm, and he pressed it hard against her skin as he rasped, "Don't. Touch. Me."

She shoved hard at his chest but couldn't quite grasp why. She did it again, walking him backward as if they were dancing. Very romantic. Except for the gun aimed point-blank at her shoulder.

Did it matter? No, of course not. Damn it, why couldn't she think? Because she had trouble forming coherent sentences when she was around him, that's why. Their footsteps slowed as Dakota leaned into him, her tight breasts rubbing against his chest. God that felt amazing. She did it again, back arching just enough to change the pressure, the angle, to something decadently wicked. She moaned low in her throat, and tried to wrap her arms around his neck to pull him harder against her.

She ached and throbbed from the top of her head to the sensitized soles of her feet. It felt glorious. Magical.

Towering over her, he speared his fingers into her hair, drawing her face to his.

Rapture! "Rapture!" Dakota slammed her fist into his shoulder. "You idiot," she shouted, dancing him backward until she staggered. "We're *drugged*! Hold your breath and *move*!"

His reply sounded muffled, thickly indistinct. She blinked and glanced down to see what they'd stumbled over.

Two people lay tightly entwined on the floor. It was odd, really, but now that she thought about it, the marble looked cool and slick, and God, she was burning up. Her skin was on fire and felt too tight. Her nipples hurt, and moisture pooled between her thighs. The throbbing, pulsing heartbeat of an orgasm made her dizzy with lust as she reached for him again.

She had a wisp of a thought that she had to do something important. What had she been saying? It didn't matter. She knew what she wanted now. "Lie down with me," she urged, trying to tug her arms free of the shackles of his fingers. He was running his thumbs up under the short sleeves of her T-shirt in a sensual caress, making her breath catch and her mind fuzzy. "I think—I think that gun is supposed to be in your pocket." She laughed, filled with a wonderful euphoria that made everything around her glow and throb.

Her knees seemed to melt as she started to lower herself beside the couple at her feet.

Rand hauled her upright. "Up. Out. Now!"

"No, we don't have to. Everyone is having fun, Rand. Look!" There had to be two dozen or more . . . couples? She blinked them into focus as Rand spun her around, now shoving her back through the double doors of the lobby and hauling her unceremoniously outside into the sunshine.

The sun was extraordinarily bright and hot on her upturned face, and she had to squint to see him. "I think we should stay."

His fingers tightened around her arm as he forced her to move her feet or fall over. "Stop talking."

Dakota was vaguely aware of car horns blasting as he hauled her across the street. He unlocked her door and shoved her unceremoniously inside. "Stay!"

✦ FIVE ✦

The car was toasty warm. Womblike. Dakota's breasts ached—in fact, her entire body ached. Folding her arms over them, she pressed down. A little better. Best would be Rand's large hands squeezing her nipples. God . . . was she . . . ? Whatever that thought had been whisked away. She crossed her legs to ease the ache, and because it felt so good, squeezed. The orgasm hit her fast and hard. She was gasping and shuddering as Rand slammed his door shut.

Out of the corner of her eye she saw him grip the steering wheel with both hands, his knuckles white. He bowed his head over his hands and let out a shuddering breath.

Dakota reached out to touch his hair, but he jerked out of reach, eyes blazing. "Don't touch me! *Jesus.* Don't. Fucking. Touch. Me."

She heard and vaguely computed, but her hand slid across his leg to settle on the hard erection beneath his pants. She pressed her knees together, shuddering as another climax rolled through her. The blast of air from the air conditioner teased her sweaty skin, making her nipples painfully hard. She tried to pull down Rand's zipper. Impossible. Frustratingly impossible over the ridged length of his erect penis.

He grabbed her wrist, grinding her palm against his hardness. He was hot, even through his pants, hot and throbbing beneath her fingers. Leaning over the center console, she tried to get closer as she tightened her hand like a vise around him. She reveled in the hard length of him, *remembered* it. His penis jerked under her hand. She still wanted to undo his zipper, but she didn't want to let go of him long enough to do that.

So many decisions.

"Don't," he said thickly, but he lifted his hips to increase the pressure. Dakota tightened her fingers, and he groaned and flung back his head, the tendons in his arched neck throbbing. His body clenched as her thumb pressed against the head. She remembered the taste of his skin and came again, spasming in her seat, gasping for breath.

"Jesus . . ." His breathing was fast and labored, sweat rolling down his temple. His fingers clamped around her wrist. She pressed the heel of her hand down hard, causing him to jerk and cry out. His climax made her want him more. But this time, he was almost breaking her wrist in his attempt to pry her fingers off him.

Something prodded at the edge of her consciousness. Something bad. Something . . .

A man pounded on the side window, giving them an evil look, before walking away. Dakota frowned. What on earth . . . "Look around you," she gritted as a moment of lucidity shocked her into awareness. They were parked on a busy street; pedestrians strolled by, most unaware of what was happening inside the car.

Sensation flooded her body. Heat. Light. Need.

He shoved away her hand, then placed his own on the steering wheel in a death-defying grip so tight the bones shone through his skin. Color rode high on his cheeks, and a nerve jumped in his jaw. "We've been drugged."

"It'll pass," she insisted. She knew it would, but the feeling filled her to the brim, and she didn't want to be rational and sensible right then.

He gave her a cool look from hot eyes. "Whoever put the drug in the champagne at the wedding must've run it through the vents at the bank. Didn't you see everyone on the fucking floor?" He glared at her. "They were *dead*, Dakota. This time, the dose was lethal. We got a whiff. Thank God you had the presence of mind to get us out of there, but it was close, very close. Those poor bastards had no idea. They lost their inhibitions and were so busy screwing anyone who moved that they didn't notice or care what they were doing. The bank was robbed, and those people are all dead."

Think. She had to reel her brain back into functionality. Dakota wasn't sure if she'd sucked in enough Rapture for it to have such a profound effect, or if she just wanted *him*, any way she could get him—floor, car, on the freaking moon, if that was an option.

A small sliver of sanity parted the euphoria like a curtain. She forced herself hard against the seat back as his words resonated. "The drug's in our systems. It's going to be a bitch to fight it, but we can't stay here, Rand. We're right outside the bank! We have to leave. Can you drive?" She could barely form coherent words, let alone thoughts. She fought the insidious pleasure with all her might.

"I don't give a fuck what it is. I want you!"

"We're horny because of *Rapture*."

His hot gaze stripped her bare, leaving her breathless and wanting. How long had they breathed the drug? How long had it taken her to realize the smell of roses was Rapture? Rand had been inside the building a lot longer than she had.

Crazed and ragged, balanced on a razor's edge of succumbing to the effects of the raging want of the drug, she dug her nails into her forearm and searched his eyes for any sign of the bloom. His eyes were feverishly bright, glittering. Clear. The pain in her arm from her nails was dull, but it brought her a moment's clarity. "Everyone ripped off their clothes, grandmothers and housewives, bankers and office workers, falling to the floor and having sex with total strangers. In the middle of the bank. In broad daylight! Rand, listen to me! We have to get a grip. Straighten our clothes and go somewhere. *Anywhere*. Now!"

Her breasts ached, and she pressed her arms against them to ease the pain. The pressure didn't help. She wanted Rand's large hands on her. Cupping. Kneading. She wanted his mouth on her. She needed to be naked and spread wide. She wanted his body pounding into hers until she didn't know where she ended and he began.

Fighting for control with every fiber of her being, she snapped her fingers in front of his eyes as he reached for her breast. "Stay with me, Rand. Sta—" She blinked and brought his face into focus. It took a moment for reality to seep back into the euphoria. "Oh, shit! Let me see your eyes." Had she already checked? She didn't remember. "Damn it, Rand, let me—" She managed to grab his face and turn him.

She shouldn't have touched him. His face was rough and hot, his lips smooth. The smell of his skin made her dizzy with lust. The tiny logical part of her brain drowning in heat and need and lust screamed a warning, but too late. As she looked deeply into his eyes, she forgot they'd ever been at odds, forgot that she had so many secrets from him she couldn't keep track. She forgot everything as she drowned in hazel. Looking into Rand's eyes was like floating in a clear, cool mountain stream.

Burning from the inside, she wanted to let go of reason. Wanted to lose control. Wanted Rand to lose control. Here. Now. The heated blood racing thunderously through her arteries and veins demanded relief. She wanted to follow him over the brink into the heat and darkness of every carnal fantasy half imagined. She wanted to lick every scar on his body. She remembered where each was. There were new ones; she wanted to cry for his pain, then forgot that in the floating sensation of rising through liquid sunshine filled with effervescence.

He grabbed the back of her head, his fingers gripping her scalp. She reveled in the pleasure/pain. She blissed in the smell of his skin, the heady fragrance of her own arousal as she reached for him.

Dakota grabbed his arm, loving the flex and play of his sinewy muscles beneath the satin smoothness of his skin. She pressed her open mouth against his arm, wanted bare skin, and instead got fabric. She moaned her frustration and tried to reach his neck, where his damp skin gleamed in the sunlight and she could see the pulse of his blood pounding through his veins.

He wrenched out of her reach. Said something that was drowned out by the surging blood roaring through her veins. Her body yearned, ached, pulsed, craved. She whimpered, shifting across the center console to get to him. There was something—there in her mind for the flutter of a butterfly's wing—then gone.

Every molecule in her body vibrated with energy and light as she slid her hand across the flex of his rock-hard, masculine thigh back to the wet spot between his legs.

Her fingers closed around the pulsing, ridged length of him. "Mine." She didn't remember ever being this happy, this at peace, and yet so aroused that the brush of her own clothing against her breasts and between her legs made her breathing labored and as heavy as honey in her lungs.

Hard fingers closed in a punishing grip around her wrist, pulling her hand away. "—damn it, Dakota! Rapt—"

She writhed in his implacable hold, brought the other hand up to touch his hair, his cheek, his ear. So perfect. "Let's make it fast, so nobody sees us—oh, Jesus,

Rand! We aren't responsible for our actions. We have to resist. . . ."

His hair was impossibly silky soft, the rasp of his unshaven jaw rough and erotic against her palms as she gripped his cheeks in both hands. Her aching breast pressed against his biceps as she tried to climb into his lap. "Kiss me," she whispered thickly.

For one brief, tantalizing, agonizing second, his burning gaze dropped to her mouth. He ripped her hands from his face and started the car with a jerky twist of the key in the ignition. "Buckle up." His voice was raw as he checked his mirror before pulling into traffic. Tires screeched and horns blared. Dakota laughed.

IT WAS THE MOST uncomfortable, *painful* fucking ten minutes of Rand's life. Driving was a challenge. The only way to keep her from climbing all over him was to manacle her wrists in one hand while he attempted to steer with the other. It was impossible to block the alluring fragrance of Dakota's arousal as she fidgeted and shifted restlessly in the seat beside him. It was with overwhelming relief he was able to pull up outside a centrally located hotel without crashing, or jumping on Dakota while the damn car was in motion. He got out, tossed the keys to the bellman, rounded the car, and grabbed her hand.

"Rand." Just that, her voice thick with longing. He yanked her out of the car, making her stagger on her heels, flinging out a hand on his chest for balance. Her cheeks flushed a bright coral, her lips moistly parted;

her pale green eyes looked glassy and feverish as she stopped dead in her tracks. Her tight grip brought his fast-forward motion to an abrupt halt as she grabbed his shirtfront and practically climbed his body.

The blast of pleasure from her touch was so intense it bordered on pain and ratcheted his lust up another impossible notch. Every time he grabbed a sliver of rational thought—he knew what was causing this, knew and fought against it—the thought drifted out of his pleasure-saturated brain like pink smoke.

Her mouth opened greedily under his, her arms wound around his neck, and she wrapped one leg high on his hip.

Fuck finesse. Breathing was overrated. Rand kissed her back with everything in him. Her mouth was hot and sweet, her tongue agile as she responded with alacrity, pressing her soft breasts against his chest. Rand gave her all of his pent-up longing, pain, and loss wrapped in that everlasting exchange where nothing else mattered but the taste and feel of her. Jesus, he'd missed her. Missed *this*.

Vaguely he heard, *"¡Señor! ¡Señor! ¡Pare por favor!"*

The kiss was ravenous and carnal, juicy and supernova hot. Rand wasn't stopping for anyone. Teeth. Tongue. Hands. Her. Him. He gripped Dakota's jean-clad ass with both hands to bring her hard against the most painful cockstand he'd had in his life. The pressure didn't help.

He grabbed her thigh, pulled her leg over his hip, surged against the juncture of her thighs even as he was ripping at her clothes. He needed bare flesh, needed her wet and open and panting under him. He needed to be inside her *now*.

He heard people—the Spanish version of the cartoon gibberish *mwah-mwah-mwah*—in the background. Urgent hand on his arm. Shook it off.

Hard hands grabbed his upper arms, trying to pry him and Dakota apart. *"¡Señor! ¡Señor! Por favor, ven en el interior donde pueden ser privados!"*

It took several minutes for Rand to compute that he and Dakota were practically screwing outside the hotel right on the street. A small, horrified crowd gathered to observe the spectacle. He shook off the man who was trying to separate them, put a hand up in a stop gesture, and tried to get a grip.

Dakota gave him a wild look, reaching for him with both hands.

"Inside," he rasped, peeling her fingers off his damp crotch with difficulty and reluctance. Getting her to keep both feet on the ground was a challenge as well. He dug in his back pocket—another challenge—for his wallet, slid out a credit card, and shoved it at the man in a black suit who separated them.

The guy, as wide as he was tall, looked both horrified and fascinated by their PDA. Standing well back, he grabbed the card Rand offered. "A quick check-in, Señor—he glanced at the card—Maguire?"

"As fast as you can do it," Rand said in Spanish, wrapping a tight arm around Dakota's shoulders as she surged around to press herself against him like plastic wrap.

With Dakota corralled under his arm, and trying to bite his nipple as they walked, he crossed the lobby.

He had to carry his jacket in front of him because, despite coming several times, he was still painfully aroused. Thank God he was wearing black pants; the tell-tale wet spot on the front wasn't easily visible.

He checked them in—two connecting rooms—and hustled Dakota into the elevator to the sixteenth floor.

Maintaining a physical distance while she continually tried to twine herself around him like a vine was torture. They reached her room not a moment too soon. Everything, every-fucking-thing in him wanted to rip off her clothes and take her right there on the floor in the hall-way. As he'd wanted to in the elevator before. In the car before that.

In the fucking bank among the dead.

In the Monte Carlo hotel suite before that.

He untangled her arms from around his neck and shoved aside the leg she'd again wound around his thighs. She was like Velcro. Rand clamped his hands around her upper arms and held her still. "Take a cold shower. Stay in there until you're back to normal."

"It would be easier on both of us if you'd just do me," she murmured seductively, reaching for him with both greedy, grasping, urgent hands. Her skin glowed with sheen of perspiration, making it look impossibly smooth and soft. Her moist lips parted as she breathed his name. He could see the hard buds of her nipples poking through the thin cotton of her shirt.

Pulling up reserves he didn't know he had, Rand managed to corral all her moving body parts *and* unlock her door at the same time. A Herculean effort.

But as she fell into her room, as the bright sunshine beckoned from the open drapes and wide, scenic windows, Rand found his body crossing the threshold without his permission.

Found his hands reaching not for her arms again, but for *her.* All of her. Her eyes widened as he hauled her back against his body. Yanking her T-shirt out of her jeans, he slid his hand up her bare, damp midriff before kicking the door shut behind them.

He had her on the floor before the automatic locking tumblers engaged.

"Finally," she gasped as he roughly ripped the strap of her purse off her arm, tossing it away with a *thud.* It was the drug. That's all. Rapture.

A piss-poor name for what Rand was feeling now.

He couldn't wait. Didn't want to. Hell, he didn't even know if what Dakota was moaning was encouragement or protest—but the fingers in his hair as his mouth replaced his hand at her taut, silken skin didn't feel like protest to him. His lips traced the path his hands took, wet, open-mouthed kisses that did nothing for the raging hard-on wrenching the last of his self-control from him.

Her hair spread like a tangled skein of fire around her head and shoulders on the plush carpet as her legs moved restlessly. Sunlight slashed a bright wedge over them as Rand bracketed her hips with his knees and crawled up her body. His fingers were clumsy with lust as he tried to pull the rest of her shirt over her straining breasts. He cursed savagely when the material caught at her armpits, trapped there as she grappled with the zipper on his pants.

Curling his fingers around her rib cage, he bent his head to suck a hard nipple through her creamy lace bra into the wet cavern of his mouth. Her skin burned against his hand, the fever evident in her flushed skin and bright eyes as their fingers tangled, each with the same goal. Get naked.

"Yes," he growled as she trapped his hand between her legs. His dick was singing hosannas as he got closer to the prize.

The pressure of his hand against her mound was enough to arch her back, her head thrown back in a climax that sent deep rose onto her cheeks and contorted her face; then she screamed his name as she convulsed hard.

That easy.

His dick pulsed with need, desperate to be inside wet, warm, welcoming heat.

Any heat. Any wet.

Welcoming optional.

Rapture. A hell of a drug.

"Give me," Dakota gasped, pulling, twisting at his waistband. Every tug, every tightening of fabric against his dick sent him that much closer to another climax. Another euphoric explosion of sensation.

Roughly, he wrenched open his pants, rocked back on his knees, and yanked his own zipper down. His erection sprang into his hand, so tight, so hot he had to throw back his head, teeth clenched as his fingers wrapped around it.

So fucking good.

"No," she whispered. He sucked in a breath as another hand joined his—hers, softer. No less tight. No less dangerous. "Mine. God, all mine."

With no more warning than that, her lips closed around the head of his dick, and he couldn't stop himself. Didn't even know how to try. He twisted, pulled himself away, his climax rocking him to the bone as he cursed, hard and angry, savage and needy.

It wasn't enough. Damn it.

Dakota pulled her T-shirt over her head. Red hair and cream lace, freckles and smooth skin and jeans she was doing her damnedest to wriggle out of. "I want—"

He wrapped a hand around the back of her neck and yanked her toward him, banded an arm around her back, and didn't care that she hadn't managed to get her jeans past her thighs. That he hadn't even managed to get his pants more than open *enough*.

He lowered her to the floor, loomed over her, hemmed her in with his arms braced on either side of her shoulders. She tried to wriggle the damn jeans off; he didn't bother to try.

For a split second, her pale green eyes met his. Flared. Longing and need and visceral, sexual aggression. Fuck or be fucked.

They'd fuck.

And they'd *be* fucked.

And he didn't. Freaking. Care.

His dick slid against her damp, hot curls. She lifted her hips, tilted them at an angle that ensured his erection caught in the folds of her wet flesh. One twist, one exquisite tilt of her hips, and he was inside her.

So slick. So hot, so tight, made all the tighter because she couldn't open her thighs wide. Too much, too fast.

Her arms splayed, fingers grasping at the rug as she groaned in exultation and relief. Urgency.

The end.

God, he hoped the end. Rand pumped his hips hard, once, twice. Her breath hitched with each. Her eyes fluttered closed, her throat and chest stained pink with the onset of another climax.

So beautiful.

As her lips parted and her orgasm crescendoed on a scream, his own body—fueled by the drug despite all natural limitations—joined hers. Sweat plastered them together, made her skin slick and shiny, made his muscles tremble with exertion.

His orgasm, her orgasm, rolled over and over, twined together and shattered the world around them into a single, unified note of pain, pleasure, relief.

Maybe he'd passed out from pleasure; maybe the next minutes or hours passed in a drug-induced blur, but suddenly, the sun was at a far different angle.

He pushed up onto his knees, still rock-hard, far from satisfied as a sliver of rationality seeped into his consciousness. Rand staggered to his feet. Dakota lay on the floor, spread-eagled; she still had one leg in her jeans, her T-shirt by her head, her bra still clasped and angled across her magnificent breasts.

He shoved his other leg into his black dress pants, found his shirt on the floor, thrust his arms into the sleeves, and shoved the tails of his unbuttoned shirt into his pants.

Dakota raised on both elbows, her hair streaming down her back and clinging to the sweat on her gleaming skin. Her picture should be in the goddamned dictionary under *temptation*. "Come back down here. I'm not done with you!"

"Take that cold shower," he told her roughly, looking around for his shoes. "Do whatever you have to do in there. Keep the door locked. Move!" He hauled her to her feet. Dangerous, as she instantly clung to him, her arms hard around his waist, her lips and bare breasts on the open V of his shirt. He untangled her arms and backed toward the door. Wanting to stay, to keep doing what felt so insanely good . . .

When she came toward him, he blocked her with his forearm. "No more. No more, damn it! We're both going to regret this when the drug wears off."

"I won't—"

Rand wrenched open the door, slammed it closed behind him, and fell against the wall, breathing hard as he heard the automatic lock engage. Sweat rolled down his temples. He wondered if the erection would ever go down. He found his keycard and unlocked the door of his room. Closing and double-locking his door, he just stood there, eyes squeezed shut, heart hammering.

Then had to open them as he imagined Dakota right next door, stripping off the rest of her clothes. His dick pulsed. His heart pounded. Sweat ran into his eyes. He slammed the back of his head into the unyielding plaster wall.

The walls were thick enough he couldn't hear movement in the connecting room, but he could imagine . . .

He yanked open the door back into the hallway, and went in search of the gym.

PHASE ONE COMPLETE, MONK thought, swirling the intense, deep gold liquid in his glass. As the subordinate stood preternaturally still, he brought the Baccarat crystal glass to his nose and inhaled: apple tart with a sprinkle of demerara sugar, Sultana oranges, hint of nutmeg, clove, and aniseed underpinned with musky oak. With a deep sigh of satisfaction, he tilted the glass to his mouth and sipped, savoring the intense layers of delicious desserts in his twenty-eight-year-old Glenmorangie Pride whiskey.

No matter the visitor, a snifter of four-thousand-dollar-a-bottle whiskey was to be savored, enjoyed without haste. He took another sip, enjoying the expensive heat gliding down his throat as the other man waited.

His simple cell, with its stone walls and floor, could be frigid in the winter months, and even now, when outside the sun blazed, Monk had a small heater running to stave off the chill. A two-thousand-year-old Chinese rug covered the floor, and heavy burgundy velvet drapes disguised the fact that there was no window. Simple articles brought by his followers to ease his simple life.

He gave the man a small smile as he cradled the glass. Well satisfied, he had to force a mask of pleasantness to his features. He didn't like emotion, and in fact, rarely felt any. This satisfaction was more a comfortable warmth. But then he got that in the same measure from a good bottle of scotch. "The buyer was pleased with the demonstration of Rapture at yesterday's wedding, Szik. You did well."

The man puffed his chest and bowed his head. "Thank you, Father."

"Has Lucifer tempted you with too much pride, my son?"

"No, Father. I want nothing more than to please you."

Sycophantic asshole. Last night's display had netted Monk a sizable first order for the drug. Just the beginning. Production was already under way. There was just one player still missing, but that was soon remedied. Patience, as Monk well knew, was a virtue. He had nothing but time. The execution of the waiter early this morning had been a small bonus. One Monk hadn't witnessed firsthand, although the video had been well shot and gratifyingly realistic. Too short, of course, but effective nevertheless.

The buyer would prove to be a powerful ally. He already distributed an interesting selection of street drugs, and was ready to break into the European market. Rapture was going to net him billions, and for Monk, multibillions.

The man was eager to buy the uncut product after seeing the quick results at the wedding reception the day before. Buyers always responded better when they saw the results and potential of a new drug. This buyer was willing to put two billion dollars on the line for a quick turnaround.

Phase Two: a more powerful dose of Rapture had been leaked into the air-conditioning system inside a Spanish bank earlier today. That, too, had been a small but strategic display to whet the appetites of a different kind of potential buyer.

The only fly in the ointment was that Rapture was unstable at high altitudes, which would be problematic in Phase Three. By the time he was ready for the third unveiling, his new chemists better have worked out that wrinkle. No terrorist would want to drive a gas of mass destruction around in a fucking truck. Rapture Three could be manufactured anywhere, but Monk wasn't about to give away his closely guarded formula. If they wanted it, they would have to come crawling to his door, hats and money in hand. He was, and planned to remain, the sole manufacturer.

"As you instructed, our salesmen were allowed to keep the money they stole from the bank in Barcelona."

The money had been stolen just to show the buyers that, with a small application of airborne Rapture, anything could be done, right under the noses of anyone in attendance. The pleasant rose fragrance was an enticement to breathe deeply. Everyone enjoyed a fragrance that reminded them of something beautiful. Monk had spent a fortune perfecting that fragrance, using only the best flowers from the Grasse region.

"I'm afraid only one television station showed a small portion of footage of the customers five minutes after the gas was fed into the air-conditioner vents. The authorities shut them down. I hope the video our people took was sufficient inducement for our buyers?"

They weren't "our" buyers, Monk thought, mildly annoyed. They were *his* buyers. His invention. His blood, sweat, and faux tears. A lifetime of hard work and sacrifice was coming down to the next few weeks.

"The footage was adequate," he said dismissively. He had no interest in sex. Neither watching nor participating. He'd merely observed the activities as one would observe animals mating in the wild.

"There are a few prospects," Monk added. "We'll know more as word gets around." Word had spread like wildfire, and he already had more buyers for both applications. He'd have to see about hiring more chemists, more lab personnel. Bigger facilities . . . Monk sipped his whiskey. First, though, he had to keep Szik in his proper place.

"Did you masturbate as you watched the video?"

Szik hesitated, bowing his head, his tightly clasped hands a knot at his waist. "I did, Father. I couldn't help myself."

Monk leaned back in his chair, cradling the glass. "We must contact Branah and Raimi. I'm ready for Phase Three. You must be punished for your lust and pride," Monk said smoothly, with no transition between the thoughts, as he picked up from the table beside him a folded chamois, heavy with his favorite tools.

He looked up to see Szik still standing there, and said quietly, "Remove your clothing, my son."

AFTER A LONG, COLD shower that left him even more frustrated and no less horny, Rand jogged twenty miles on the hotel treadmill, which was damned hard to do with an unrelenting boner. He lifted weights until his arms quivered and sweat ran off him in rivers. Hit the sauna, and his fist, several times, ran again. Showered in the coldest water they had. He prayed like he'd never prayed before that nobody joined him in the gym. He'd used all his self-control leaving Dakota—what fucking little self-control he could claim.

During that first hour in the hotel gym, he would've fucked anyone or anything. For the first time in two days, luck seemed on his side. Nobody joined him. Nobody tempted him.

He went back to his room, took another icy shower, and called room service for hot coffee. Lots of it.

He'd been gone three hours. At least he could now do up his pants without causing himself irreparable damage. Dressed, and toweling his hair dry, he quietly opened the connecting door.

Dakota, wearing only a towel, was curled on the bed, her wet hair a wild coppery tangle across the white pillow and down her bare back. He noticed a faint red line on her upper thigh, a scar, near the edge of the towel, and frowned. That hadn't been there before. He looked more closely, his eyes traveling inexorably down her body.

It was no drug coursing through his system that made him want to run his hands up the smooth, creamy skin of her thigh. Gritting his teeth, he took a tactical step back.

"It's a good thing I've been taking care of myself for a long time, Maguire," Dakota said pointedly, opening her eyes. She rolled her head to give him the evil eye. "Where've you been?"

"Gym."

"Still?" She sat up, exposing even more of her long pale legs and a tantalizing glimpse of the upper swell of her breasts as she spread her hand across her chest to hold the white towel in place.

Rand's tongue stuck to the roof of his mouth. The harder he tried not to imagine her pleasuring herself, the harder it was to breathe. "You seem to be okay," he told her coolly, letting his eyes drift over her cinnamon-flecked skin. He wanted to lunge across the bed and take her. No preliminaries. Just nail her to the mattress. He gripped the doorjamb to anchor himself.

Her eyes narrowed, and she shoved a long hank of wet hair over her shoulder. "It would've been easier if you'd stuck around."

His nails scored the woodwork. "Nice to know."

Now her lips curved in a way that made him shake. Her wet hair was like a dark red cape around her shoulders, reaching halfway down her back. He wanted to fist it and bring the strands to his nose. Maybe bury his face in the damp curve of her neck and slide his hand to where he'd bet his last dime she was wet and aching still. Wanting what he wanted.

Her eyes were clear, light green, and dancing with amusement, as if she could read his mind. "I offered," she pointed out mildly. "Why didn't you accept? We would've had a better workout than you had in the gym."

"*If* we have sex again, it'll have nothing to do with sniffing any aphrodisiac, believe me."

She raised a copper eyebrow. "Maybe I won't want to have sex with you if I haven't been inhaling an aphrodisiac."

Always had to argue the other side, didn't she? He pushed away from the doorjamb, his equilibrium restored. "We'll have to wait and see, won't we?" There was a knock on the outer door of his room. Saved by room service. "That's coffee and food. Here or in my room?"

"I'll get dressed and meet you in there."

Too bad. "Good plan." He *really* could have gone for a round two. Rand pulled the connecting door almost all the way closed, and went to let in the waiter.

There was no reason that he should feel as though he'd just had a narrow escape.

DAKOTA DRESSED IN THE bathroom—pale-blue skinny jeans and a white tank top—then ran a comb through her still wet hair. Drying it was a pain. It was so long and thick it took forever. Her hair was her one vanity, but most of the time, having it hanging in her face and all over her shoulders and chest was just a nuisance.

Men liked her hair.

Rand liked her hair. Still. She could tell.

Not even glancing in the mirror, she pulled it up and off her face in a ponytail, tempted to take the band out and run her fingers through it before going into his room. Considering how inflammatory the situation was already, she decided against tormenting the man any more than she already had.

She didn't want to examine too closely her own behavior earlier. Even though there'd been no fragrance added to DL6-94 in the lab, she'd known almost instantly that she was inhaling Rapture at the bank. Known what would happen. And of course it had. In spades. Call her a fool, but she'd allowed herself to give in, allowed herself to give and receive the exquisite pleasure she'd found in Rand's arms.

Rapture had made their passion excusable and guilt-free.

She was damned if she'd second guess herself.

She was going with that.

Barefoot, she grabbed her tote and a plastic shopping bag, and walked into his room.

His bed was neatly made, so he hadn't taken a nap as she had; all those orgasms had worn her out. She speculated briefly on how he'd managed that wicked erection he'd had. He was sitting at the small table near the window, texting into his phone.

He glanced up and, with a small frown, waved his phone at her outfit. "You weren't wearing that this morning."

"I went shopping." She dropped the shopping bag

in his lap. "I got a few things for you as well, like dry pants and clean underwear." And a couple of T-shirts. And sneakers. "You can't walk around in a tux and dress trousers, stained ones at that, without attracting notice." Okay, that was mean. He wouldn't like being reminded that he'd lost control.

He ignored the bag as he ground his teeth. "Let me get this straight. We came here because it wasn't safe for either of us to be in public under the influence of a powerful narcotic. And you went *shopping*?"

She waved a dismissive hand. "That wore off after an hour; I didn't get as much as you did. Don't worry, I didn't rape and pillage anyone on the streets. I *did* have to make a few stops to . . ." She paused deliberately. ". . . relieve myself, but after a while, I managed to tough it out. Now we have fresh clothes. I saved us some time. You can thank me later." She dropped her tote on the floor and settled in the chair opposite him, pulling her feet up on the seat before taking the cup he extended with a stony face. She didn't give a damn that he wasn't pleased she'd gone shopping. She was a big girl. She didn't need his permission to do what she liked.

Including taking care of her needs if he wouldn't.

She breathed in the fragrant steam and hummed her appreciation, "Mmmm. Elixir of the gods." She sipped with pleasure.

"The guy's at least four hours ahead of us. If you were fully recovered, we could've gotten back on the road."

She waved her mug at him. "When I looked in on you in the gym, you still . . . had issues. I went out."

"I'm sure there's a boutique in the hotel," he pointed out, taking the toothpick out of a sandwich layered with what looked like every cold meat they had in the hotel kitchen, then biting into it.

Dakota's stomach rumbled. She removed the top piece of bread from her sandwich and picked off a couple of slices of roast beef with her fingers. "With sky-high prices and no selection? I think this portion of the conversation is closed, don't you?" She took a bite of the meat, spicy and delicious, then took another.

There went that muscle of annoyance twitching in his cheek again. "We're here to work, not go shopping."

"We're here to follow a lead." Dakota eased back more comfortably into the corner of her chair and scratched one bare foot with the other. "Not to get gassed with DL6-94, which was *never* its intended application, or to have to lock ourselves into our rooms waiting for it to wear off." She couldn't resist one more dig. "And we sure aren't here in this luxury hotel to screw each other, despite appearances to the contrary. But this is where we are. So what's next?"

They could've spent the last three hours having memorable sex, but for reasons she couldn't fathom, he'd declined her offer. Clearly, Rand's hate for her was stronger than the pull of a powerful aphrodisiac.

The realization was depressing. And irritating as hell.

Not that she was complaining—much, or not so much *anymore*, Dakota thought.

He rose from his chair and the shopping bag dropped unnoticed to the floor. Taking his coffee cup with him, he paced around the bed, then back again. He was the equivalent of a quickly tapping foot. An engine revving on idle. Coins jingling in a pocket. In other words, annoying and accomplishing nothing.

"You'll stay here," he finally said. "Use this as a command post. We'll keep in close contact via phone."

The coffee was hot and strong, just the way she liked it. Dakota held the cup between her palms and looked at him politely over the rim. "I don't think so."

He gave her a cold look. "You want to go back to Monaco?"

Cocking her head, she raised both eyebrows and opened her eyes wide. "Make me."

That muscle jerked in his jaw as it always did when he clenched his teeth. "Dozens of people died today because they breathed in *your* Machiavellian creation. I'm not dragging you all over hell and gone for no reason. Obviously, the shit that went down at the wedding wasn't about blackmail. Two acts can no longer be considered random. The next time—and there will probably be a next time—*we* might not be as lucky."

"You need me," she told him flatly. "It must be obvious to you now that my skill is one hundred percent accurate. I have to continue to use it if we have a hope in hell of preventing another attack."

She peeled a chunk of ham off the open face of her sandwich and held it between her fingers. "Don't think of me as a woman, Maguire." The way his eyes flared made it abundantly clear that's exactly how he saw her. She gave him a small, I-know-exactly-what-you're-thinking smile.

"Just consider me a professional GPS." Dropping the ham into her mouth, Dakota chewed with satisfaction. After swallowing, and allowing him time to digest that, she added, "I suggest you get over your snit, change your clothes, and let's get going."

She drained the last of her coffee, put down her empty cup, wiped her hands, and picked up her tote from the floor beside her chair. As she plopped the heavy bag in the cradle of her crossed legs, she glanced up to see Rand just standing there, gazing at her with that inscrutable poker face he was so good at.

"And just in case, I found these." She took out another purchase and showed him the package label. He barely spared her score a glance. "Emergency masks. They're really for use if your house is on fire, so you don't get asphyxiated by the smoke. They'll work on rose-scented happy gas in a pinch as well."

"*I* have to stop him," Rand said tightly. He didn't acknowledge what she thought was a halfway brilliant solution to the potential problem. He strolled over, and she braced for . . . what? A slap? A kiss?

When none came, she replied, "So do I."

"*Au contraire.*" He picked up the shopping bag and tossed it on the neatly made bed, then undid his pants and yanked down the zipper. "Your part of the program was unleashing this crap on the world in the first place. Mine, apparently, is to stop it from spreading."

"The *FDA* prevented it from being *unleashed*," Dakota informed him tightly, feeling the cold of his disdain all the way through her bones. He didn't care about her. Not even after that manic bout of sex.

They used to *love* each other. Love each other with a depth and breadth that had at times scared her with its intensity. She'd thought in the last two years that his apathy toward her was the worst event in her life. But his contempt was far, far worse.

Especially on the heels of all those endorphins.

Enjoy your last taste, Dakota. She knew she'd never have another.

✦ SIX ✦

R and kicked off the tailored black pants. He wore a knife in a black sheath on his left ankle. That was pretty much all he wore, and it wasn't the big knife Dakota was looking at. That was a minor detail. He was commando. His long legs curved into the tight curve of his ass and he was still almost fully erect.

"Boxers in the bag." Mouth dry and heart rate elevated, she couldn't tear her gaze away.

The sight of him in nothing but a once-white dress shirt and an ankle knife almost sent her over the edge. Okay, so maybe she hadn't completely recovered from the airborne Rapture after all. She looked at the sprinkler head in the ceiling until she got her brain back. "And I wasn't the sole person working on that formula, I'd like to remind you. There were six teams, your father being the head of one of them."

"Why did you swear in an affidavit to the prosecutor that you weren't the one who supplied him with the over-dosed wafers?" He removed the price tags from his new clothes with his teeth.

Dakota wasn't looking at his strong legs or mourning

that the shirt hung too low for her to get a glimpse of his ripped abs and lower. His words brought her out of the brief fantasy with a thud. She must still be breathing, although she couldn't feel the movement of her lungs as she stared at him, dry-eyed and bereft of speech for an entirely different reason.

"If you'd told the truth," he said, unbuttoning his shirt. "I would've stood by you. Got you the best attorney my money could buy. All you had to do was admit you made a fucking *mistake*, that you didn't intend the dose to be so high."

"I should have," she told him without expression or inflection. Because that lie would make at least *one* of them happy, and the end result was going to be the same anyway. There was already a bull's-eye on her back.

"The trial starts in two weeks." Watching her with a frown, he tossed the shirt on the bed and stood there gloriously, unself-consciously naked, and still semi-erect. His shoulders were broad, his chest delectably hairy, and his legs long. He had the body of a well-conditioned, honed athlete. She knew every hard inch of it, and every soft, tender spot as well.

Dakota felt absolutely nothing now. Not the clawing lust. Not anger that he hadn't changed in the intervening years. Not even sorry that he looked at her so emotionlessly. "Okay."

"You'll testify on his behalf?"

"If that's what you want." She heard her own dull voice from a distance. "Yeah, sure."

"Thank you."

She blinked him back into focus, puzzled to see him dressed in the new jeans and a black T-shirt. She must've checked out for a few minutes. Foolish. She needed to be on her toes. Especially now. Especially around him. She reached for her cup, tipped it to her mouth, and remembered it was empty. *Get a grip.*

"Are you well enough to travel? If not, I'll leave you here, and you can call in the coordinates."

"I'm peachy to travel," Dakota assured him. She would be. She just needed to give herself a pep talk about blood being thicker than water and people not being able to see the truth unless it bit them on the ass. She needed to pull up her big-girl panties and remember she had a task to perform before anything else happened.

Because as bad as the bank situation was, she knew the drug had the potential to produce much, much worse.

She put the empty cup on the table, then dug her GPS and the vial container out of her tote. She had to fake this till she made it. "Let's see where our person of interest has gotten to in the last four hours." The moment she touched the hard case, she swore under her breath.

"Damn it to hell. The trail's cold," Rand said flatly. He had sat down to put on the sneakers, and he looked over at her, ready for the bad news.

"No. The trail's still hot. The problem is, we now have *two* people to follow." She picked one set of numbers at random, as two separate strings of digits ran through her mind like a double ticker tape. She tapped the numbers into the GPS. "One's moving east across France. The other's headed north."

"Can you tell if they're traveling by land or air?"

"Neither is fast enough to be on a plane. I suspect they know the drug is unstable and loses potency if they fly."

"Can you track both at the same time?"

"I just did." Not that she'd ever had to follow two trails at once, but apparently it could be done, even when her insides had been scooped out by a dull knife. *Oh, shut up, Dakota! Don't be so dramatic.* She was a scientist. Pragmatic when she needed to be. As a realist, she'd known for years how Rand felt; this was no surprise.

One blissed-out session on a hotel floor wouldn't change that. If the man had been in his right mind, it never would have happened.

"Christ." Finished with the shoes, he ran a hand around the back of his neck. "We're spread too thin. I don't have enough manpower for this."

"Fortunate that you have me as backup womanpower, then, isn't it?"

"I'll have some of my people follow one trail, you and I the oth—" His phone rang. "This could be a real lead. Speak," he added into the phone.

They'd arrived in Barcelona following a *real* damn lead, Dakota thought darkly.

Damn it, damn it, damn it. This wasn't nearly as easy as she'd hoped, even though she'd known it wasn't going to be.

"SING JUST DIED," LIGG told Rand flatly.

"Brett Sing *died*?" The stepfather of the groom was an ass and, Rand suspected, an alcoholic. Perhaps a heart attack, or kidney failure? "Tell me it wasn't related to the drug."

"Sorry, boss, but the doc said yeah, it was. He was knocking back that champagne pretty good during and after the event. One of his symptoms—shit. How do I describe it? His eyes looked kinda like my grandma Ella's. Cataracts?"

"The bloom?" He looked over to see Dakota watching him intently. At those words, the flush drained from her face, leaving her skin pasty, the freckles standing out in stark relief. Her teeth dug into her lower lip as she listened to his end of the conversation. He turned the phone to speaker.

"Yeah. His eyes turned this spooky, milky white. Docs are pretty sure it's not E. They're speculating it's that new Russian drug, Krokodil. I have toxicology back, want me to text the summary report to you?"

"Right away," Rand ordered as Dakota nodded. It was no Russian drug, they both knew. Dakota could confirm it from the blood work. But they already knew the answer.

"Barcelona. Before I fill you in—any other news?"

"Yeah. The heist is all over the news. They're claiming they have a 'person of interest.' Don't know if they made you or are blowing smoke. But I'd watch my six."

Rand motioned for Dakota to clear the room. Grabbing her tote, she slid off the chair to scoop up the clothes he'd stripped off, stuffing everything into the shopping bag.

A video camera might have survived the heist and been

functional. God only knew he hadn't examined them at the time. Without positive ID, he could be anyone. There were a million tall, dark-haired men.

Dakota, however, with her mile-long screaming-red hair, was impossible to miss, and easy to identify if captured on the video. Right now, she was more of a liability than an asset.

Rand strode to the connecting door, glancing around her room. Other than the slept-on bed, it was pretty much an empty hotel room. There was a small, rolling overnight case that she hadn't had with her when they arrived, and several more shopping bags on the chair. He shook his head. In the midst of a drugged high, she'd fucking-well gone shopping. *Women.*

"Any footage?"

"Just a vague description and a grainy image off the surveillance video. Could be anyone. They won't be able to ID you off the surveillance footage. However, they do have a pretty decent physical description from people on the street."

There'd been pedestrians—plenty of them—between the bank and the car. "Hell!"

"They claim an arrest is imminent."

"Unlikely. But I'll be on the road ASAP."

Dakota stood in the doorway between the rooms, as still as a doe in headlights. He glanced around to see if he'd left anything lying around his own. He hadn't. He backed her into her room and quietly shut the connecting door. There was no point in trying to wipe away their fingerprints, between the bedrooms, the bathrooms, and the equipment in the gym. Hell, he'd used the corporate card when he checked them in earlier.

If the cops somehow traced them to the hotel, they'd be screwed. Besides fingerprints and his name on the hotel bill, there was their very public display when they'd arrived to tie them to what happened at the bank.

"Anything else?" he asked Ligg evenly.

"They showed a seven-second video of the scene before it was apparently pulled from the air by top brass. Pretty salacious stuff. Reports are that thieves got away with five hundred thousand euros. Seventeen dead. Cause unknown. Since I'm presuming you aren't now five hundred K richer, I'll take a stab that the perp got there before you did."

"Same shit as the wedding guests were dosed with, but clearly stronger."

"Not distributed in two-grand-a-bottle champagne," the man said wryly, "unless that's what they do now instead of hand over a toaster for opening a new account. What's your take?"

"Administered through the air-conditioning system. It has a faint scent of roses. Probably killed everyone within ten minutes?" He glanced to Dakota for confirmation.

She held up her hand, fingers splayed.

"Make that five," Rand corrected grimly.

"Son of a bitch."

"Keep me posted on any further developments." Rand disconnected and looked at Dakota, his mind still on what he'd seen at the bank. "Get your shit together. We've got to go."

Without asking any questions, she stuffed several small shopping bags in her tote and grabbed the handle of the suitcase. "Who died?"

"Stepfather of the groom." He held his hand out to indicate she wait while he opened the door and checked the corridor beyond. "Okay. Here, give me that." He took the small case from her and waved her ahead of him down the wide, well-lit hallway.

"Why are we sneaking?" They passed the bank of elevators and headed for the stairs. "Nobody could possibly know we're staying at this hotel," she pointed out as he opened the door into the stairwell.

"Want to stake your life on that?"

She shook her head. "You do remember that we're on the sixteenth floor, right?"

"Better pace yourself." The back of Rand's neck itched, and he glanced back and up. There wasn't anyone there, but he felt the need to get the hell away from the hotel and out of town as fast as possible. He couldn't afford to be taken into custody and have to go through some lengthy process to prove he and Dakota hadn't robbed the bank. Better safe than sorry now.

He took the Glock from his shoulder holster, and almost crashed into her when she stopped dead in her tracks. "Keep going. Don't stop, for Christ's sake!"

"My shoes." She slipped off her heels and stuck them in her bag. Then she ran lightly down the stairs barefoot.

Rand caught up and stayed close, almost on her heels. He could smell the heat of her skin, and the faint, intoxicatingly familiar lemon scent of her hair. Even in the relatively dim lighting of the stairwell, the color was a dead giveaway. "Got a cap or something to cover your head?"

"Or something." Still moving, she rummaged in her purse and pulled out a handful of light brown hair. "Hold this a sec." She shoved the bag in the general direction of his chest and started twisting her hair on top of her head. She held it in place with one hand and tugged on the wig with the other.

"How's this?" Dakota asked, turning to face him for a moment. Sleek brown hair brushed her shoulders, the straight-cut bangs skimming her long-lashed green eyes. "Better?"

No. He missed her red hair. "It works. Can you go any faster?"

She shot him a speaking glance, then turned around a little too hastily, and he had to grab her arms to prevent her tumbling over her own feet. Unperturbed, she asked, "Do you want a disguise too?"

He released her arm with a gentle shove to keep her moving. "You carry multiple disguises with you?"

She shrugged, not quite making eye contact, concentrating on not tripping again. "I like to change my look now and then, and like I said, I went shopping. I have this—" She pulled another hank of hair out of her bag, this time short and black.

"No thanks."

She stuffed it back into the tote, then rummaged in one of the shopping bags and handed him a black baseball cap. "Then here. Wear the cap. Oh, wait—what about these?"

He put on the baseball cap, took the reading glasses and put them on. Clear glass. "You're a regular Houdini." They passed a door leading to the third floor.

By the time they reached the sign indicating the sky bridge to the public parking garage adjacent to the hotel, she was sweaty and out of breath. Exactly, Rand knew, how she looked after a passionate round of sex.

"Now what?"

"We're going to boost some wheels." Dusk had fallen, and the garage was dim and half-empty. Commuters had left their offices for the day and the dinner crowd hadn't yet arrived, but there were plenty of cars to choose from.

Rand picked a nondescript station wagon. "Here." He handed her the small tool kit he always carried in his back pocket. "Go take the license plates off that van over there while I hot-wire this puppy."

By the time she got back with the license plates, the station wagon was purring. He switched plates, putting the van's tags on the station wagon, and vice versa. Satisfied, he jogged back. "It's not brain surgery, but it'll buy us time."

From the street below he heard sirens, then saw the flashing lights reflected off the mirror of a nearby car. The police could be at the hotel for any number of reasons, but Rand knew they were looking for them. How they'd tracked them so fast, he had no idea. He opened the driver's-side door and gestured. "Get in."

Dakota shot him a surprised look. "You want me to drive?"

"Do you have a Bluetooth headset?" When she nodded, he told her, "Get it out. You take this car, I'll get another."

"Really?" She just stood looking at him with her eerily pale eyes. "And how will you find the bad guys without me?"

"We're going to stay in contact by phone. You hold on to the case, direct me where I have to go."

She made no move to get into the car. "And I'm supposed to be . . . where exactly?"

"Keep that wig on, go back to my people in Monaco." He tried to make out what people were saying on the street several stories below where they stood in the shadows. But the voices were indistinct.

"I don't think so."

He turned to look at her. "You don't think s—"

Dakota stood, feet apart, a .38 gripped in both hands. "Wherever you go, I go."

"Oh, for—while I appreciate your skill in being able to track like a bloodhound, we may both be wanted by the local authorities." He tried for patience. It gritted. "I used my credit card to check in. If they haven't already, they're sure to figure out who I am, and by association, who you are. Those cops down there are hot on our trail. We need to split up if we have a hope in hell of not being caught. Do you really want to stand here and debate the merits of traveling together right now?"

"I'm not debating a damned thing. Make no mistake, Maguire, I *will* shoot you." Expression grim, she motioned with the gun. "Get in the damned car."

FOR SEVERAL UNCOMFORTABLE HEARTBEATS, Dakota thought Rand would refuse. But after a few seconds of deliberation, he climbed in and placed his hands on the wheel. He gave her a bland look from inside the car as she rounded the hood, keeping the muzzle pointed at the center of his forehead, then climbed in the passenger side. "Drive."

"Since when do you have a gun?"

Since she'd been jumping at shadows for the last month. "None of your damn business."

He jerked his chin at the gun clutched tightly in her hand. "Know how to use that?"

It was so small, only about six inches, and looked like a toy, but Zak had assured her it could do the job. "At this close range, you'd be hard to miss."

They wound down the spirals of the parking garage. Dakota fumbled in her overly full tote for the case and her GPS while maintaining her grip on the gun.

When they reached street level and the bottom of the ramp, she saw two police cars parked right in front of the hotel. Her heart stuttered, then started pounding loud enough that she couldn't hear anything else.

"Where are we going?" Rand asked, not sounding or acting freaked out in any way that he was being held at gunpoint or that the police were in their line of sight.

He probably didn't take her as a serious threat. So long as he did what she wanted, it didn't matter if he thought he was humoring her.

He eased onto the street and into traffic. It was getting dark, and the city lights twinkled around them. She pulled down the visor and flipped open the mirror to check behind them. As far as she could tell, nobody appeared to be following as the nondescript station wagon blended in with the early-evening traffic leaving the city.

"Head northeast. I'll tell you when to change direction." The coordinates of the two people carrying the vials were keeping a steady pace. Different directions, but similar speeds. She didn't know how to isolate one from the other, so the two long strings of numbers remained layered so close together that at times it was hard to differentiate them.

There was quite a bit of traffic. Rand rested his elbow on the edge of the window as he drove. "So we're still following the vials?"

"One of them, presumably—or at least the person who is carrying it. Trust no one. I'm adopting the Maguire creed."

He kept his eyes on the red taillights ahead. "Does that include you?"

"I can follow one trail on my own, which will eventually lead me to the source. I don't need you. But you need me." This was crazy. *She* was crazy. Dakota wedged her hands between her up-drawn knees, keeping the gun below the level of the car's windows and prying eyes. Her hands shook with adrenaline.

"Want to tell me what the hell's going on?" His voice was smooth, but a muscle below his eye ticked. "I've never known you to champion guns, or to have a tote full of disguises available."

How much to tell him? How little could she get away

with before he demanded answers she couldn't or *wouldn't* supply?

"Whoever these people are, I think they're testing the boundaries and applications for the drug. Presenting each application to potential buyers before it goes on the market."

"How do you know this?"

Because nothing else made sense. "It's an educated guess."

"Who's *they*?"

She ignored his crisp tone. "I believe it's the same people who had a vested interest in Rydell Pharmaceuticals going out of business two years ago."

He snorted with disbelief. "Are you getting this spotty intel from your crystal ball?" When he stopped at a light, he turned and plucked the gun from her hand as easily as taking a toy from a baby. She didn't even see it coming—blink and gone. Her fingers and her pride stung. "This damn thing still has the safety on," he informed her, his tone layered with disgust. "Next time you point a gun at someone, do it with the intention of firing it." He stuck it under his seat. "How deeply *are* you involved in this clusterfuck, Dakota?"

Her head itched beneath the wig, but she was afraid that the second she took it off, the police would drive by, recognize the hair she was so damned vain about, and arrest her on the spot. She settled for trying to scratch her scalp through the netting cap. "I don't even know where to start."

"Try the beginning."

"You have to promise to listen, without judging or jumping on the defensive. Can you do that?" She waited several hard, thumping heartbeats for him to nod, then drew in a steadying breath. It felt as though she'd been scared forever. "Odd things were happening in the lab several years ago—"

"When we were together?" His features hardened almost immediately. "And you didn't happen to mention it at the time?"

He'd been working his ass off to get Maguire Security off the ground, traveling a lot. She hadn't wanted to whine to her new lover about a situation at work that was an irritation more than anything else. "My work was classified, and what was happening wasn't alarming," she explained evenly, "just odd. I wasn't the only one who noticed. Notes went missing, then the file would suddenly show up in an unsecured location. It was as if we had poltergeists—"

He shook his head. "Come on."

"I'm not saying there *were* ghosts, Rand. It's a figure of speech." She swallowed. "We'd finished all the trials and blind studies for DL6-94—keep going northeast. We'd all worked so hard on this drug. It was going to revolutionize antidepressants, which haven't changed much in ten years. The greatest SSRI and SNRI combination on the market."

Rand took the next turn. Traffic in this part of town was lighter. Dakota kept checking the rearview mirror. It was impossible to tell if anyone was following them or not. It was nerve-wracking.

Rand reached out and flipped her visor back into position. "We can both do that, or you can relax. I've got it," he said. Strange comfort, but . . . Dakota took a deep breath, oddly comforted nonetheless. "Keep talking," he added.

"The side effects were too severe." That came out on a rush. Folding her arms over her chest, she sank back into the seat, trying to organize her spiraling thoughts. "We worked on ninety-four different formulas, and had six different trials. The very chemicals we were so excited about were the same chemicals that produced the most profound side effects—euphoria, total lack of inhibition. Not just the aphrodisiac properties, but off-the-charts highs and lows of emotion. Intense, homicidal anger, fear, or grief."

"One fucking hardworking antidepressant."

He was being facetious, but at least he was still listening. Dakota wiped one hand down the leg of her jeans. She felt as though she were precariously balanced on one foot on a high wire. This was the first time he'd *heard* her side of the story, and there was a relief in telling him the truth. Or as much as she could right now.

"It worked incredibly well as a serotonin-norepinephrine reuptake inhibitor. The downside, obviously, was that it was extremely habit-forming, accumulated in the body, and therefore was lethal after only a few doses. We worked hard to refine it, to lessen its aggressive edge—"

"You didn't think, '*Hey*, people could die'?"

She winced. "The amount of effort that goes into any new drug isn't a new thing, Rand. These difficulties happen more than you think, and there are so many useful drugs that begin life as more dangerous versions of themselves. All they need is time to fix them."

He said nothing. Disgusted, maybe. But then, he refused to even take an aspirin for a headache.

She couldn't completely blame him. Dakota had let herself get carried away. Lulled by the promise of a new dawn for the depressed and the hopeless.

She sighed. "The FDA, of course, didn't approve even the version that we thought *might* pass. It was a devastating blow to all of us who'd worked on various aspects of it for years."

Dakota curled her legs under her. It was easier to talk to Rand when he wasn't looking at her, but with the lights from the dash she could look her fill. The car was a quiet cocoon with just the sound of the tires on the pavement.

She saw Rand's gaze flick to the rearview mirror, then the side mirror, and then relax a little more. "No pharmaceutical company is going to produce a drug that's both highly addictive *and* a guaranteed death warrant. Particularly Rydell, which was already having financial problems because of a lawsuit dragging through the courts for ten years. Not to mention that the drug was unstable in high temperatures and *extremely* unstable at altitudes over one thousand feet. Impossible to transport by air. No distribution, even if it weren't all of the above as well, equals no funding."

"All that work for an unusable product?"

"Yes. Unusable for our application anyway." She rubbed her forehead under the faux bangs and settled into the angle between the seat back and the door. "The aphrodisiac qualities were perfect for a street drug, though. It had everything a user could want, and they'd keep coming back for more. One of many reasons we couldn't go any further with our trials. Rydell wasn't in the business of making street drugs, no matter how lucrative they are."

"The company invested a lot in it, and you're saying that Rydell had money problems?"

Dakota hadn't talked about any of the details with Rand, although at the time they'd been seeing each other. Rydell had all its chemists sign a nondisclosure agreement. What they worked on in the lab was strictly on a need-to-know basis, with small groups working on different aspects or different formulas for the same potential new drug. "They spent billions on all sorts of drugs, not just—"

Running out of patience, he snapped, "Cut to the chase."

"The formula and everyone's notes were gathered and destroyed. It was a major production. Everything that they wiped, shredded, or otherwise deleted was recorded and verified. *Nothing* was left of the original formula—it was too dangerous."

He gave the station wagon more gas as the streets became less congested. "Yet here we are, two years later, with someone producing, according to your expert opinion, the exact same shit."

"Yeah. Also in my expert opinion, I've been spied on for at least five weeks now. Maybe more. They've been in my house, several times. My garbage has been gone through a dozen times. My computer at home hacked, and my iPad stolen. . . ."

He swore under his breath. "What did the Seattle PD have to say?"

"They looked into the break-ins. They took my statements. They told me it was probably kids. I hadn't worked at Rydell for years and it didn't even cross my mind that my break-ins were related." She rubbed her face wearily. "Until Zak Stark told me what happened at your client's wedding."

He ran his hand over his jaw, and shot her a quick glance. "What am I missing? I don't see the correlation."

This was the tricky part. Zak's call hadn't come as a complete surprise. Weird stuff had been happening for weeks beforehand. "The police found my iPad a week after it was stolen. I didn't tell them this, but *all* of the team's notes from Rydell were on it."

✦ SEVEN ✦

Rand took out his phone, holding it against the steering wheel. He shrugged at Dakota's bold statement. "So you forgot to delete them." He checked the fuel gauge as they hit Autopista 7 traveling north. It was possible their destination was Paris. He keyed in a quick text to Ham, telling him to rendezvous in Paris ASAP. If their final destination wasn't the city itself, Ham would at least be able to backtrack and meet him somewhere in the middle.

"No," she told him flatly and with utmost conviction, yanking off the wig and running her fingers through her hair to release the tantalizing fragrance of lemon and warm woman. "*None* of the data was ever on my personal computer or on my iPad. I had the latest model, Rand, that model came out only last year—how could I put any data on it?"

At the look he shot her, she lifted her chin, stiffening. "And I didn't steal the data myself only to leave it, like an idiot, on my iPad two years later. The penalties for stealing intellectual property are steep. Stealing Rydell's formula falls under the Economic Espionage Act. Not only a hefty financial fine but years in prison. Someone *put* it there. Someone is setting me up."

Clearly. His radar had been on alert since she started talking about the past.

A couple of weeks before the lab explosion, his father, on his second honeymoon in Italy, was arrested for the murder of Rand's mother. Rand had flown to Rome as soon as he got word. He and his father always had a complicated relationship, and God only knew, given his father's propensity for struggling against the—what he called—tyranny of his wife's tight-fisted hold on the purse strings, Rand had arrived in Italy believing the worst. But after talking to his father at length and hearing from his attorneys, Rand knew his mother's death, while tragic, had not been his father's fault.

Her death devastated both his father and Rand. He'd had a close relationship with his mother. Paul Maguire was a lot of things, but he had loved his wife in his own co-dependent way. He'd stayed with her through her severe bouts of chronic depression, which hadn't been easy. Rand gave the man props for sticking by the woman he loved through some very bad times.

They'd both put a lot of their hope into Rydell Pharmaceuticals' new drug, and his father had worked night and day with the team, trying to perfect it through each necessary, painstakingly slow phase.

Dakota had been the one to give a month's supply of the drug to his father for the duration of the trip. She'd told him it was the batch number that had the fewest side effects. The one, she assured him, that was moments away from FDA approval.

After the tragedy, when Rydell had been thrown to

the wolves in the press, Dakota had vehemently denied sending the drug to Paul in Italy, and refused to testify on his father's behalf. At first, Rand had been stunned by her refusal to own up to her mistake. Then he'd been furious. He'd called her from Italy and broken it off with her. He hadn't given a flying fuck about a purchased wedding dress, or deposits to anybody. His mother was dead, his father in prison. He'd been in no mood to be fucking reasonable.

The explosion in the lab a few weeks later had been a mere footnote to his life at the time. He knew people had been killed, and he'd known Dakota wasn't one of them. She'd been fired by the lab, which was throwing its support behind Paul Maguire, and wasn't permitted back on the premises. Other than that, he didn't give a damn what she'd done afterward, or since.

What would anyone gain by putting those lab notes on her iPad? Especially since no one but Dakota even knew they were on her device? "Do you suspect anyone?"

She shook her head. "I've racked my brain. Obviously it has to do with Rapture suddenly coming on the market." Her pale eyes gleamed in the light from an oncoming car. "We have a timeline and we're on the clock. When we find whoever is responsible for the wedding and the bank, he'll lead us straight to whoever is manufacturing the product."

"And you plan on doing what, Dakota? Confronting the people who anticipate making billions of dollars from the sale of this drug? You're out of your mind. Entire countries can't put a dent in the drug trade, and you want to tackle this on your own? With that little toy gun you brought?"

"I'm the only one who can get all the way to the top of this particular food chain," she said stubbornly. "All I have to do is tell them I can stabilize the drug."

His heart skipped even though he had no reason to care. "You're insane."

She shrugged. "Maybe. But they might know, or certainly will soon, that they have a problem if they want to sell it to anyone wanting to move it in bulk from here back to the States, or if they want to sell it to terrorists."

"How so?"

"The formula is unstable at high altitudes. Unless they want to truck it, ship it, or use a low-flying hot air balloon, they aren't going to be able to transport it great distances. Additionally, terrorists won't be capable of using it from the air."

"Bullshit. If it has a stability problem, they can manufacture it wherever they need it." Something about Dakota's explanation, something about her demeanor and tone of voice, made every receptor in Rand's brain flash a warning.

"True. And maybe they will. But that's all I have to offer them at the moment."

"*Can* you stabilize it?"

"No. It can't be done. But *they* wouldn't know that, because I was one of the few people working on that wrinkle," Dakota said flatly. "Someone from that team must be here in Europe, maybe putting out feelers to buyers. What if the people we're tracking are two sales reps? We're . . ." She checked the GPS in her hand. "We're making good time. We're only three hours behind this one. If you have someone you trust to follow the other lead, call him. If not, I'll follow the leads one at a time."

"I thought we weren't trusting anyone?"

"We?"

He gritted his teeth, feeling as if he were making a deal with the devil, and gave a single nod.

"You know your men," Dakota said, her voice tired. "Pick whomever you'd trust with your life."

Rand pulled out his phone and speed-dialed a number with his thumb, keeping both hands on the wheel. He called Ligg, because Ham would already be on his way to Paris. Dakota gave him her secret GPS coordinates and the speed at which the target was moving. Ligg and a small team would fly to a likely destination, and Dakota would provide updated coordinates while en route. If they got lucky, the guy would stop and she'd be able to give Ligg the exact location. If not, Ligg would continue to tail him, with Dakota's aid.

Rand disconnected. "We might as well use this time to text the drug information to the doctors in Monte Carlo so they can complete testing," he mused. "The guests are scheduled to go home tomorrow, and the family insisted on sending the newlyweds on to their honeymoon a few hours ago."

"What about Brett Sing?" Her tone was carefully neutral. Was it a trick of the light, or was her gaze eerily haunted?

"They'll need to keep his body for testing," Rand said grimly. "The least the newlyweds can do is take a few days away. Come to terms."

She nodded. "Give me the phone. I'll write the text."

Rand waited the ten minutes it took Dakota to input the necessary information, then had her send the info to his team at the hotel to pass on to the doctors.

"You're delusional, you know," he told her flatly, his gaze going from the fuel gauge to the next exit. "These people murdered seventeen people in the bank today. The drug rep would take away your little popgun as easily as I did." He cocked his finger and held it to her temple. "Bang. Lady, you're dead."

"I won't be distracted."

"You won't have to be distracted. They'll kill you anyway."

"Believe me, once our guy contacts the head honcho and tells him I can fix the transportation issue, they won't kill me." She seemed very sure.

Then again, so was he.

"They will when you can't deliver. This is an insanely risky idea, Dakota."

She shrugged, as if losing her life meant nothing in the scheme of things. Maybe it didn't. Maybe she was so far gone this time she had nothing left to lose. And a hell of a lot to gain if she fell in with the manufacturers of this drug, he reminded himself unnecessarily.

"But it'll work. We keep working our way up the food chain until we reach the top."

"I'll make you a deal," he said abruptly. "We'll find him and keep a safe distance until I see exactly who and what we're dealing with. But when we do"——he sent her a serious glare——"you let me do the talking, and let me take him to the authorities. If he's willing to kill seventeen people to see how the drug works, and one more just to cover his tracks, he's willing to kill *anyone* who gets in his way. Deal?"

She bit the corner of her lip. "Maybe it's a she."

Yeah, he thought darkly. *Maybe it is a she.*

PARIS.

They'd switched cars a hundred miles south of Paris, then again near dawn as they neared the outskirts of the city. They traveled all night at breakneck speeds, only stopping when absolutely necessary.

"I don't know about you," Dakota told him, barely glancing around as they passed under the illuminated Arc de Triomphe and drove along the Champs-Élysées, the black sky lightening to navy over the rooftops, "but I'm seven steps beyond exhausted. I don't know how you can function on no sleep."

"I took a power nap at the last rest stop." And let her sleep for a full hour when he saw how pale and sleepy-eyed she was. He'd driven almost a hundred miles blind to give her that necessary rest.

He couldn't give her much longer, since she was the only one who knew where the hell they were going. At first she'd tried talking to stay awake, but he'd told her several hundred miles back that he preferred not to chat while driving. Having to listen to her soft breathing was distraction enough.

"I need at least a couple more hours of sleep before I go on. If you even suggest another energy drink, I might throw up." She grimaced. "In fact, I can guarantee it."

"Look, we made good time," he told her. "Closed the gap. But if we take more than a pit stop now, we risk being a step behind again." Rand was reluctantly impressed with Dakota's tracking ability. He didn't understand how it worked, but it did. She might be full of crap about a lot of things, but he was beginning to trust her on the one thing that was important right now.

He didn't want to stop, although exhaustion weighed down his eyelids, and his muscles felt shaky. He'd been awake for almost seventy-two hours. Not just awake but on high alert. The two long road trips, back to back, didn't help. He was an active guy, and sitting in a car for hours on end was exhausting in itself.

"I think we'll be okay." She yawned. "But we'll be better after a nap."

"I'm wiped too," he admitted, flexing his fingers on the wheel to get back some circulation. "I need some shut-eye to be on my A game when we catch up with this guy—or woman, for all we know. If we shut down for a few hours, our quarry could be in the wind while we're napping. We can't take the chance."

"I think *he's* sleeping; he hasn't moved by more than a few feet in the last half hour."

"Let's get to his location, see what we're dealing with, and then formulate a plan of action." It was difficult making his exhausted brain think beyond that.

"Sounds good. Turn left, three hundred feet." She cocked her head and looked puzzled. "Hmm. This is a new one for me. He's below street level."

"The catacombs?" Shit. A warren of tunnels and old

mine shafts crisscrossed beneath the city. Finding anyone down there would be next to impossible. Unless the
seeker had Dakota's Spidey senses, of course. Rand had
no intention of taking Dakota with him from this point
forward. What was left now relied on good old-fashioned
white-hat stuff. No need to put Dakota in danger unnecessarily.

Stark called his people "agents," but Rand doubted if
his friend hired people for their tracking skills expecting
to send them into mortal danger. Dakota seemed almost
relieved when he plucked the gun from her hand. He
had no idea what her real agenda was, but he'd bet dying
wasn't on it. There was still a place inside him that cared
for her . . . cared for her *safety*.

He'd protect *any* woman in exactly the same way. Just
because he'd loved her once, just because he'd believed
with everything in him that she was the one he'd been
waiting for, didn't mean he was motivated by any feelings
other than his general need to protect.

Drugged sex notwithstanding.

Rand found a small, overpriced hotel nearby, circled
the block, drove a mile, removed the plates, and abandoned the stolen car. They walked back to the hotel
through the balmy Parisian streets in the blue light before
dawn, while the city slept and the quiet seeped into his
tired bones.

It would warm up later, but for now, the air was cool
and smelled of baking bread and strong French coffee.
He could use several gallons of the stuff. A few people made their way to work; the streets would fill in a

few hours with tourists and commuters alike. With the brown wig covering her hair and his baseball cap pulled down an extra inch, he and Dakota passed everyone in silent anonymity.

They strode by an elderly man, tightly wrapped in a gray sweater that matched his uncombed hair, as he opened his newspaper kiosk for the day. The headlines on one newspaper read, in French: *INTERPOL CLOSES IN ON BARCELONA KILLER.*

AN ENORMOUS VASE OF pale pink roses in the elegantly understated—and expensive as hell—lobby of Hotel Édith filled the air with their perfume. She had always liked roses, but Dakota would never smell a rose again without thinking about what happened in Barcelona.

They checked in, using cash, and headed to the elevator. It wasn't the boutique hotel where she'd booked them for the start of their honeymoon, but small and intimate and similar enough to remind her of all she'd lost. Weird, odd, and painful to be here with Rand now.

She shoved the memories aside. She'd never completed her French language classes, which in light of recent events was unfortunate. Especially if she wanted jam with her croissant, assuming she ever got a real breakfast.

The bag slipped off her shoulder and she hitched it higher.

It was heavy, stuffed with their original clothes and everything else she was hauling all over God's creation like a turtle with its house on its back. There wasn't anything unnecessary in it, just bare essentials. The new clothes she'd bought were in the rolling carry-on bag, along with a few nonessential items, such as two new pairs of shoes.

As soon as the elevator door closed, Rand gave her an inquiring glance. He made no mention of their aborted honeymoon plans, and neither did she. It wasn't important now, and knowing him, he'd probably thrown off all those memories. No need for words; they were focused on the same endgame. "He's still underground. Maybe he's tired as well, and is taking a nap."

"Maybe he's dead," he suggested, propping the small, wheeled case beside him.

"Not if I'm seeing his numbers." It really wasn't fair that Rand didn't look as exhausted as she felt. They'd traveled together around the clock, making do with a few catnaps. She felt wrung out, limp, and grubby. He looked just as he always looked: tall and tanned, his eyes more hazel than brown in this light. And ridiculously sexy. He'd needed a shave twelve hours ago. As tired as she was, Dakota's nipples peaked beneath her tank top as her body remembered the countless times she'd felt the rasp of that rough stubble stroking her skin. She remembered the smoothness of his lips in comparison, and the urgency of his hands.

She remembered the weight of his body, the feel of his skin against hers, and his breath against her neck as he'd plunged into her like nothing had changed.

Damn. She wished she *didn't* remember all the textures and tastes of Rand Maguire in such a visceral way. Maybe she'd look into a frontal lobotomy when she got home. *If* she got home.

"I hate that damn wig," he told her, apropos of absolutely nothing, as they got out of the elevator on their floor.

Her feet sank into the plush green-and-navy carpet as she stepped out. "You try wearing it a while. It itches worse than a too-tight hat."

"Did you buy the wigs on your illicit shopping spree yesterday?"

No. She'd brought a selection of disguises with her on the Lodestone jet: the wigs, a reversible windbreaker, two pairs of light cotton pants, and the wrong color makeup. She had no idea *who'd* follow her, or what she'd need. She'd been a Girl Scout.

"My hair's too recognizable," was all she said as he unlocked the door to their room and ushered her in ahead of him. Her back brushed his chest as she passed him.

He hitched his stride, guaranteeing space between them before he followed.

She noticed. She tried not to care. Instead, she walked all the way into the room and looked around, taking her bag off her shoulder, where it left a red dent in her skin.

The slope-ceilinged room was small and overly ornate, and smelled strongly of French cigarettes. The bed was a queen, and there was little else in the room. Dakota stood, looking at nothing as she tried to gather her few remaining resources to do . . . something. Or, rather, to do nothing.

Was it wrong to want a man as much as she wanted Rand? God only knew he had no interest in her anymore;

she got that. But her body, starved of his for twenty-five months, urged her to turn into his arms.

He had to remember. This time, there was no drug to lower their inhibitions, no excuse.

Just good old-fashioned human contact. And comfort.

As she walked over to the bed and flipped on the lights, she imagined doing just that. Imagined the feel of his strong arms wrapping around her, the brush of his lips on hers. Her heart ached, as if she'd only just lost him for the first time.

Distance—time and space—hadn't helped. The lack of either wasn't helping now.

"Want to shower first?" She gestured toward the bathroom.

"Sure." He loosened the shoulder holster, but didn't remove it. Unlike her gun, his didn't look anything like a toy. It was black and lethal looking, and he handled it like he knew how to use it. "Order some room service and a big pot of coffee." He hesitated. "Or maybe not. You should sleep, at least for a few hours."

"Don't tempt me. I don't want to risk him moving again and sleeping through it, like you said earlier," she said wearily. Rubbing at her eyes didn't help wake her up, even a little. "Why don't *you* get some sleep, and I'll keep track. You need your wits about you more than I do at this point." She dropped the bag on the chair by the window and flexed her fingers. "I can focus okay. I'll have food. Coffee."

"First, it's the crack of dawn and barely light. The whole of Paris is sleeping, which, as you noted earlier, is probably why the bad guy isn't moving," Rand pointed out dryly, glancing anywhere but at her. Dakota's chest ached even harder, and her eyes stung. It hurt like hell that he couldn't even stand to look at her.

He went to the narrow window and held back the drapes to look out at the street below. "And what would you suggest we do with him if we got him right now?" He turned back. For all the emotional warmth he exuded, he could've been looking at a stranger. "Hold him hostage here in the room?"

"Well, no," she admitted.

His expression softened. "It's okay. I've contacted Ham. He's on his way. He and I will go in together later this morning, and you'll talk us to his location." He paused. "After a nap."

They used to take "naps" on rainy days in Seattle, curled together after making love in front of the fire in her Queen Anne Hill condo.

It didn't surprise her that he'd contacted his friend without telling her. She was too tired to be angry, too emotionally spent to fight. It took all she had not to burst into exhausted tears. She'd do well to remember the hardest lesson she'd ever learned: trust no one.

Especially not Rand.

RAND LOOKED FOR EXITS. One door, window onto fire escape.

"Never mind," he said abruptly. "You grab a shower first." He took his phone out of his pocket to let Ham know their location. He knew her; Dakota wouldn't get into bed without a shower first. He didn't want to hold up her—

His tongue stuck to the roof of his mouth as she yanked off the brown wig. His throat dried as she ran her fingers through her flattened hair. It sprang up in a wild mane as if happy to be liberated.

Over the year they'd been together, he'd spent many sleepless nights with her tucked against his chest, his nose buried in the fragrant fiery strands. Seeing her hair now, even in the dim lighting, was like a mule kick straight to his heart. "Check the guy's location again before you go in." He sounded annoyed, even to himself.

He couldn't help it. His entire body remembered every detail; even though intellectually he knew she was poison, he was sucked in like a moth to her flame.

"He's staying put," she told him decisively, picking up her bag and placing the case in her hand on the small bedside table on what they'd long ago considered her side of the bed. He wasn't the only one with muscle memory, it seemed. "I'll be quick." She walked to the bathroom and shut herself inside. The door didn't close fully, leaving a sliver of brighter light to spear into the bedroom, as well as a tantalizing view of Dakota.

Undressing.

The water turned on. Rand sat on the foot of the bed and called Ham. The phone kept ringing. He frowned. Ham had several hours' head start. He should be somewhere in Paris right now, waiting for his call.

Since his assistant was coordinating the various teams, Rand called Cole for updates. Mildly annoyed, he listened to the phone ring. None of his people had called in several hours. He wasn't too concerned, that would just indicate that they hadn't anything new to report.

What was of concern was Cole not answering his phone on the first ring as he usually did. Rand frowned as he got up and went to the window, held aside the drape, and looked out. Cole's phone clicked, but it didn't roll to voicemail. Just abruptly disconnected.

What the hell?

He squeezed the bridge of his nose. There were logical reasons for his assistant not to answer his phone. Before he went to DEFCON 5, Rand needed to eliminate the obvious. Bad connection. Damaged equipment. Out of range.

And Cole knew how to contact him despite those limitations.

Unless he was dead?

Shitdamnfuck.

Rand's gut had been signaling a warning for hours, but he'd put it down to the obvious. Now he wasn't sure. He punched in the numbers for each of his team leaders in turn. Each phone rang, then rolled over to dead air.

Would Ham show up? Or was he too out of the picture?

As far as Rand knew, he was on his own.

Double fuck.

He heard splashing from the bathroom. No, he wasn't alone. She was an added concern he had to decide quickly how to deal with.

The head- and taillights of traffic on the road below showed through the deep blue of early morning, in which colors were soft and muted, and the day was filled with possibilities. None of them good right now.

He'd known the moment they walked into the lobby that Dakota remembered their mutual past acutely. The pain and loss in her peridot eyes were impossible to miss, and the sadness radiating from her had been palpable. Or maybe, Rand thought derisively, he was projecting his own feelings onto her.

He rubbed his bristly jaw.

There was something he was missing, but damned if he could put his finger on it. Half his men were missing, and he couldn't figure out Dakota's real motivations for clinging to this like white on rice.

His men would show up. Or they wouldn't. Out of his control right now. If he took things at face value, he was starting to doubt things that he would've sworn to be gospel a week ago. Now he wasn't so sure that everything he'd been led to believe about Dakota was true.

He'd never given her the opportunity to defend herself, never given her a chance to tell her side of the story. Now wasn't the time. But later . . . ? He'd reserve judgment.

Now he wanted to know why she cared if someone else was selling the drug she'd helped create. Personal pride? *Professional* pride?

A cut in a billion-dollar drug deal?

For now, he had to be satisfied that she wanted what he wanted, to find the person or people responsible. Different agendas, same goal. The reality, as much as he hated to admit it, was that he needed Dakota's special skills. Without them, he had fuck-all.

The Spanish police were looking for him—possibly for *them*. Interpol was likely also involved, if they knew he'd left Spain. Did they know he was in France? How soon would they track him down? Hours?

It seemed to Rand that every time they figured one thing out, they were faced with more questions. One thing he wasn't ambivalent about was Dakota not going any farther. He'd use his power of persuasion to convince her they'd both be safer with her giving directions from the hotel. Since calling hadn't worked worth a damn, he decided to text everyone. He sent a 911 to call in reinforcements. Now to see who responded.

There was a *thump* as something hit the bathroom door; then it creaked open. Rand smelled soap and shampoo, and steam-warmed, damp woman, as she came out. He shoved the phone in the pocket of the jacket Dakota had bought him on her little shopping trip.

"It's all yours," she said, rubbing her shoulder as if it hurt. "I left a new toothbrush on the counter for you."

He glanced over his shoulder because he felt paralyzed by the familiar smell of her fresh from the shower. She wore the short white hotel robe, and her long legs still gleamed with moisture. She started toweling her hair, every move familiar, bringing back memories he'd managed to suppress for years.

Only that was shit. He hadn't suppressed anything. Not really.

"Ham isn't answering," he said, striving for business-like. Her face was scrubbed clean and rosy, her ice-green eyes level. God. She had weapons she hadn't even used, and he was flailing for balance. "I didn't order room service yet," he told her, knowing he sounded irritable but not giving a damn. "I figured you'd be in there an hour."

"I don't take long showers when I'm alone." A verbal slap. She didn't used to take short showers with him. "Let's order, I'm starving." She stopped blotting her long hair, then frowned. "Where's your guy?"

He shrugged. "Detained, I guess. He'll call back."

"How long are we hanging out here before we go and find the bad guy?"

"You say he's in the tunnels. I'm not taking you down there. There's no need. This is the endgame. You'll stay here, maintain contact on the phone."

He could see the argument already building. "What if there's no phone service—"

"I'm grabbing a shower," he said over her. "Order room service, then take a nap. I'll wake you when I leave." He walked around her and went into the steamy, floral-scented bathroom, then forced the door shut.

Before he put his hands on her. *Again.*

✦ EIGHT ✦

As soon as the shower turned on, Dakota tossed the small suitcase on the bed, rifled through it, and took out fresh clothes for both of them. Boxers for Rand. A fresh black T-shirt and dark-washed jeans. Black socks. An almost identical change for herself.

Easy and uncomplicated.

Dressing quickly, she wrapped the thin towel around her hair. Like her, Rand never lingered in the shower.

Not when he was alone.

If she were in there with him, it would be another matter entirely. They'd been known to deplete a large hot-water tank on more than one occasion. Cold water hadn't shortened the time they spent in the shower either. Many was the time they'd emerged from the bathroom, teeth chattering and goose bumps on their skin, only to fall into bed and make each other warm all over again.

She picked up the case that had contained the vials and curled her fingers around the hard surface. Their quarry was still where he'd been for the last hour. That was good.

The other guy was still headed in the direction she'd last given to Ligg; no need to call and update him yet.

Once he had the man, would Rand return to get her? Would he let her follow through with her plan? Or would he find it easier to leave her behind entirely?

Dakota stood at the foot of the bed, debating just how to handle the situation.

Despite her half-assed insistence, they both knew she didn't want to go into the catacombs. She was claustrophobic, for one thing, and for another, it was doubtful the bad guy would be alone. He certainly wouldn't be happy that someone followed him. A rat cornered was dangerous. Rand and Ham were professionals. They were armed. They were equipped to handle violence. She wasn't. The only thing Dakota had going for her was determination.

All very logical.

The jobs she'd been on involved finding people or things. The search usually lasted a day, maybe a week; then she was on to finding the next wandering Alzheimer's patient or the next missing artifact. She had to tell her boss his agents needed espionage training when they went into the field from now on. Tactical training? She smiled for a moment, picturing some of the other Lodestone "agents" throwing karate kicks and shimmying down black ropes in the dead of night. Nope. Not gonna happen.

Although, there was that one Lodestone guy—too bad he and *his* skill weren't here right now.

Discovering that she lacked the abilities necessary for survival or, say, optimal health at this stage of the game was scary as hell. Her brain was only going to get her so far. After that, she might need brute strength.

Hell's bells. After the running, chasing, wild monkey sex on a hotel-room floor, *and* more hours clocked in a car than she ever wanted to spend again, she'd hardly been capable of opening a stuck bathroom door.

As if just thinking it summoned him, the door opened, and Rand came back into the room wearing just his jeans, his chest bare.

He was created to go shirtless. His broad shoulders gleamed bronze in the lamplight. Water droplets sparkled in the mat of crisp dark hair on his chest, which tapered down to an arrow that disappeared into his open waistband. She knew every curve and ridge of those rock-hard abs. Everywhere his nerves and tendons ran beneath his hot, satin-smooth skin . . .

She dragged her eyes up to his face, and just like that, she changed her mind. "I'm coming with you."

One eyebrow rose as he saw the clothes she'd put out for him, but all he said was, "Fine."

His capitulation shocked the hell out of her. Rand was a man who took his job as a protector seriously. True, he didn't love her anymore. He had no obligation to watch her back, but that was just the kind of man he was. "Seriously?"

"You're a big girl, Dakota. I can't tell you what you can and can't do. If you want to go down there with us, I certainly can't stop you." He sat on the side of the bed and reached for the socks. She knew he was commando because she could see his underwear on the bathroom floor.

"There are at least sixty or seventy miles of subterranean tunnels, seven stories under Paris's streets. A maze of tunnels and unused mine shafts that rarely, if *ever*, see a visitor." He put on one shoe and paused, she felt, for maximum effect. "If you think you can handle the possibility of getting trapped down there, if you think that your claustrophobia won't kick in, be my guest."

She rubbed her bare arms, where goose bumps of the claustrophobic kind pebbled her skin. "Will you tell him I have the formula he needs so we can go up the chain of command?"

He didn't bat an eyelash. "Sure."

"Don't say sure. *Be* sure," she insisted. "Because I *will* go with you if you don't swear on your father's life that you'll tell him that, and come back to get me."

Rand glanced up, his glare icy hot, the muscles in his neck and back rigid.

She'd stepped on a line. Too far.

"Don't you mention my father, Dakota, unless you have a serious death wish," he said, much, *much* softer than the menace in his tone should have allowed. "You did what you set out to do. Have you thought about the consequences of what you're proposing? This is going to be dangerous. Seriously, crap-your-pants dangerous. This guy has nothing to lose—"

"And everything to gain if he believes I have something to offer that he can't get anywhere else," she told him. "Instead of attempting to hold a desperate man hostage, why not offer him something he wants? It's a win-win."

"God, you haven't changed at all, have you?" Rand put on his other shoe and got to his feet. His wet hair dripped unnoticed onto his bare, gleaming shoulders. A droplet of water slid slowly and enticingly over his collarbone. "You jump in without knowing how fucking deep the water is. Or who you'll land on when you take your swan dive." The bitterness in his voice stung, and she could see the anger in his eyes, despite the distraction of his spiky black lashes.

Dakota struggled to slow her racing heartbeat and held tightly to the towel, wet hair forgotten. She narrowed her eyes and lifted her chin. "That's not only untrue, it's not fair."

Rand was across the room and in her face faster than she could blink, the intensity and pent-up anger vibrating around him like a warning siren. "Explain that to my father if he's convicted and spends the rest of his fucking life in prison, thanks to you. Explain that to the investors, and the millions of patients with severe depression who were deprived of a viable drug. Explain that to a man who loved you beyond reason. Explain your lies and betrayal to all of *those* people, and then try to rationalize your behavior to yourself."

Her jaw hurt from gritting her teeth at the unjust accusation. "My God. You're giving me credit for having a hell of a lot more power than I actually had! Destroying the formula wasn't up to me. Rydell knew what we had wasn't viable. It was a corporate decision to stop production and move on."

Rand turned away from her, stalking back to the T-shirt she'd put out for him. "What did you think you'd do on your own? Apprehend a determined drug dealer by yourself?" It was as if she hadn't spoken as he pulled the fabric over his head. "No, of course not. Someone would have to ride in and rescue your ass. That someone would be *me*. Don't fucking think I don't know that you haven't told me everything. I've gotten used to that little game of yours by now. You're the tip of a giant iceberg, sweetheart, and I don't have the time or inclination to find out what the hell you're really up to." He didn't even stop to take a breath. "So, here's the plan. You stay put, you walk Ham and me through the catacombs—from here. Or from wherever the fuck you want to be. I don't give a shit. I don't want you with me."

Tears burned behind her eyes. She held them back with a force of will she didn't think she had the energy for. "Wow," she said softly. "You can't be any plainer than that. Thank you for your honesty." She felt as though a slow-acting, extremely painful parasite invaded her body. She'd thought she'd experienced all the unendurable pain a body could bear, but she'd been dead wrong.

Afraid she might splinter and disintegrate right before his eyes, she pulled back the covers and crawled into bed, tugging the covers over her bare shoulders, her back to him. With the ragged remains of self-control, she kept her breathing even and swallowed the howls of pain tearing through her. "Wake me when you need m—when you need my services."

THERE WAS A HARD rap on the door. Rand got to his feet. They were both dressed, finishing the breakfast he'd ordered from room service. Early-morning sunlight shone through the window beside her, but Dakota didn't feel the warmth. She finally slept, badly, for about three hours. She knew Rand had slept for a while, because the covers on his side of the bed were rumpled. He hadn't touched her, even by accident, and she'd woken to find herself clinging to the very edge of the mattress as she listened to him in the shower again.

Even in their sleep, they did everything they could to stay away from each other. Like she needed that reminder.

The numbers in her head were stationary, so their target was still where he'd been for the last several hours. At least someone was getting a full night's sleep.

The second string of numbers halted in Switzerland. Rand had texted his people with the information she'd given him over breakfast. All was right in Rand's world.

Everything was wrong in hers.

"I won't promise to do what you want because I have no idea what we'll find when we get there," he told her. He crossed the room and opened the door. "You'll have to be satisfied with whatever the outcome—hey, Ham."

Dakota didn't like Mark Stratham. She wasn't sure what it was about him, but she trusted her instincts, and her instincts told her he was still a jerk. Rand had sicced him on her after his father was arrested. He'd been in Italy organizing Paul's legal defense.

Detective Stratham was a thorough bulldog. He'd interrogated her as if she were on the witness stand, and was a hostile witness to boot. He'd been rude and verbally abusive, and had made up his mind about her guilt before she'd so much as opened her mouth.

The entire thing had been . . . unpleasant.

No, she didn't like good old Ham. He brought the stink of a three-pack-a-day cigarette habit into the room with him.

"Hey, Red." He barely glanced her way as he shook Rand's hand.

"Detective." The irony that the overweight ex-cop's nickname was Ham wasn't lost on her. She wasn't particularly fond of nicknames. Especially "Red." But his suited him to a T.

"Ready to rock?" he asked Rand. Pleasantries exchanged, duty discharged.

She was just fine with that.

"Yeah, good to go. We have a map of the catacombs, spare batteries for the Maglite, and extra ammo."

Spare batteries, Maglite, map, fresh clothes. And, oh yeah, destination. Thanks to *her*. Sit. Stay. "You're welcome," she said mildly.

Ham looked at her, the briefest glance that dismissed her just as quickly, then turned back to Rand. "What's the plan?"

"Since our target is approximately two miles from an official entrance, we won't waste time searching for a manhole or hidden entrance," he explained. "That will just eat up time, and have us risk him moving. We'll join a tour and split off. The actual mines aren't open to the public. Dakota's staying here to talk us through."

"No place for a woman," Ham said, with too much satisfaction for her taste. As if she'd insisted on accompanying them.

Dakota smiled sweetly. "Small, extremely tight places are no place for anyone with claustrophobia." She only stressed *tight* a little. He got her point, paling slightly.

He was a chauvinist and a womanizer, and she didn't know how he did his job because she'd bet dollars to doughnuts the man couldn't run, considering he was overweight and smoked like a factory stack. But he and Rand had been friends since Paul's arrest, and Rand clearly liked him, since he was now part of Maguire Security.

Maybe she and Rand had the same reason for the way they felt about the man. Ham had been assigned to Rand's father's case just after his arrest, and sided with Rand and Paul after the hearing.

He'd opposed everything Dakota had told them.

Okay, so it was personal. She didn't like being called a liar. Especially flat-out to her face.

By either man.

PEOPLE, MONK THOUGHT, OBSERVING Szik's valiant effort not to cry out, were a necessary evil. One needed them to fulfill tasks that one couldn't do oneself. But they were weak. Disobedient. *Always* a disappointment.

It was a rare occurrence that Szik screwed up. But he wasn't immune to Monk's lessons, and even a perfect record required careful handling. "Tell me again how you lost the woman." He took a puff of his cigar to get the tip red-hot, then brought the glowing ember down on the man's forearm. He enjoyed the sweet smell of burning flesh and the tiny flares of smoldering hair, mildly intrigued with the way the various muscles in the arm contracted as the pain registered.

"He—he took her from the hotel—"

"In *Barcelona*," Monk coached.

"He took her from the hotel in *Barcelona*, Fath—"

The cigar flared, then bit again. A little longer this time. There was no excuse for omitting details.

Szik couldn't contain his whimper, and his face contorted comically as he tried to breathe through the pain. His lip was bloodied from gnawing on it like a rat to maintain his silence for the past fifteen minutes.

Truly, some men needed harder lessons. Monk wasn't holding Szik's arm. He wasn't restrained in any way. It was the man's allegiance and devotion holding him immobile. His arms were braced on the table in front of him, palms up. Livid red marks marched in neat, symmetrical lines up his inner arms. Some old, some new.

Tears of gratitude trickled down Szik's smooth cheeks. He was appreciative that Monk took the time to school him. He knew he needed discipline, knew that losing the woman warranted his death. He was grateful that Monk was merciful, and welcomed the pain so that he could learn and grow.

Monk knew this because he willed it so, and Szik was a fine student.

Monk took a puff of the fine Cuban. "Continue."

A drop of sweat mingled with the leaking tears to roll off Szik's chin and plop on the polished wood surface of the table. Szik would spend the next few hours scrubbing the table with disinfectant for the infraction.

Monk eyed the man with distaste before glancing at the red tip. "There is no point," he told Szik without inflection, "in doing a job if one does not do it well, don't you agree?"

The man was rendered speechless as Monk gently touched the burning tip to the inside bend of his left elbow. "You were saying?"

"They switched vehicles just—just o-over the border into France."

"Excellent. Then you took her, and she's waiting for me—where?"

"No! I mean, no, Father. She somehow got away and we haven't been able to find her," he said in a pained rush. "*Yet!* Yet."

"*Belphegor.*"

"No, Father. Not sloth! I did my best to—"

"Be quiet, my son." Such children. Annoying that he had to guide and chastise, and always he had to think for them. "Dr. North is in Paris."

Szik almost passed out with relief. "Thank you, Father. I will go immediately—"

"Go *where?*"

"Ah—"

Monk saw the wheels turning in Szik's small, reptilian brain. "How do you propose to find one small woman in a city with eleven million people?" he asked gently. Dear God, must he do everything himself? "Because I want to help you achieve your full potential, Szik, I'll tell you. Dr. North is at the Hotel Édith on Avenue du Maine." Cornered like a lab rat, exactly as planned.

Monk leaned back in his chair to sip his fine Glenmo-rangie Pride whiskey, rolling the hint of nutmeg around on his tongue with the sweet taste of success. Simple pleasures. The endgame was within his grasp. Aside from the small glitch in Barcelona, everything was back on track and going according to plan. No thanks to his sub-ordinate's bumbling.

"I w-will take care of this delicate s-situation person-ally, Father." Szik gritted his teeth, loudly enough for Monk to hear and be annoyed by the intrusive noise.

Monk leaned forward and placed the round coal again, carefully to compensate for his irritation. The man, of course, was a moron. An idiot. Given that Szik could barely hold his head up right now without puking or doubling over with pain, he wasn't going anywhere. In any event, Monk wouldn't tolerate the delay of having Szik travel to Paris. A lot could change in the time it would take.

"Have Raimi and Branah deal with the situation immediately. There will be no more delays. Kill Rand Maguire—he's completed his usefulness. Have Dr. North brought to me." Monk placed tender fingers beneath Szik's sweaty, tear-dampened chin and looked deeply into his terrified eyes. "Do not disappoint me, my son. I would hate to punish you."

WIRED AND EDGY AFTER the men left, Dakota pulled the drapes open, letting in the bright sunlight. She took the tray of stacked dishes and put it outside the door, then went back to the table and spread her map out so she could see where Rand was and how far he had to go. Beside it she placed her GPS and phone, plugging both in to keep them charged.

Her internal GPS knew where Rand was, but having modern technology made it easier to visualize. After calling room service for more coffee, she settled in to people-watch, making herself comfortable with her feet propped on the chair Rand used when they'd eaten their monosyllabic breakfast. No surprise, since they'd shared a confined space in various vehicles for almost nine hours with hardly a word spoken.

It was, Dakota realized with a sudden pang, not that different from the time they'd been together. With Rand living and working in Los Angeles and her in Seattle, when they did get together the last thing they wanted to do was talk. Back then, their silences had been filled with murmuring and sighs of satisfaction. The silence in the car had been filled with unspoken accusations and regret.

"Where are you?" she asked when she hadn't heard any conversation in her Bluetooth for about ten minutes. She just wanted to hear his voice; she knew exactly where he was. She'd stuffed one of the socks he'd dropped on the bathroom floor in her pocket.

In her head, she saw his coordinates below the coordinates of the Paris bad guy, and the second bad guy, and made two marks on the map in front of her. Two miles didn't seem like a long way, but the tunnels of the old mines twisted and turned and went up and down. Way down. The thought of being seven stories under the city gave her hives on her hives.

"Approaching the avenue du Colonel Henri Rol-Tanguy entrance. Let us get in, then direct us." His voice was quiet and deceptively intimate. There'd never be any more soft murmuring in her ear, she knew. Dakota rubbed the ache between her breasts as she located the tourist center and the entrance to the guided tour on her map.

Paris Guy's numbers were still stationary. "He hasn't budged." God. What if she was wrong? What if she could still see his location, but he was dead?

RAND HEARD DAKOTA'S SOFT breathing in his ear as he followed Ham down the extremely confining spiral stone stairs. "You awake, North?"

"Following your progress. Slow going, huh?"

The lighting was dim, twenty-watt bulbs, but didn't necessitate using the small, powerful flashlights they had. "A lot of very narrow stairs."

"One hundred and thirty," Dakota told him. She was good that way, he remembered. Good with details, and she had a knack for remembering trivia. She'd been, his father had told him, excellent at her job at Rydell. Precise and methodical, with an attention to detail that had sometimes driven the other members of the team nuts. She'd loved her job. Didn't make sense that she was no longer doing a job she was good at and highly qualified for.

There must be plenty of pharmaceutical labs across the country who'd hire someone with Dakota's skill and training, yet she hadn't gone back into the field after . . .

"Man, this fucking place creeps me out," Ham muttered, his shoulders practically brushing the damp walls as they corkscrewed down to the first level. Ahead of them by five minutes was a family with three teenage boys; even though Rand couldn't see them, their voices were loud and echoing in the confined space.

"Our guy hasn't gone anywhere," he assured his friend as he came to the bottom of the stairs. The narrow corridor filled with the sound of Ham's labored breathing. "You okay, buddy?"

"Yeah. Give me a minute."

Before Rand opened communications with Dakota, he and Ham tossed around various scenarios about the lack of communication from the team. They'd have to wait and see who—if anyone—responded to Rand's texts.

While his friend wheezed behind him, trying to catch his breath, Rand tried to figure out what the hell a drug dealer was doing in the labyrinth of tunnels beneath Paris's streets. It seemed an unlikely place to have a meeting. It wasn't exactly well lit or signposted. There were a million more convenient places to do business. "You sure this is where he is?"

Ham glanced up. "This was your idea, pal—oh, talking to Red?"

He nodded at Ham as Dakota assured him, "One hundred percent. The numbers show he's two point eight miles south of your location."

Rand vaguely remembered reading an ancient magazine last year while waiting to see his father at the prison. The Paris underground was not only a labyrinth of old quarries and the ossuary; it included hundreds of miles of tunnels comprising the oldest and densest subway and sewer networks in the world. Beneath the streets of Paris were canals, reservoirs, crypts, and bank vaults.

Old wine cellars that had been transformed into nightclubs and expensive art galleries did a thriving business down here. It was a city beneath the city.

No one was allowed in most of the old tunnels, mine shafts, and catacombs anymore. Just this one-hour walk from point A to point B to see the millions of bones, then out the other side halfway across town, unless they had special clearance for research or repairs.

Without Dakota's navigational skill, they wouldn't have a fucking hope in hell of ever finding anyone down here. He'd noticed that some of the tunnels had street names, presumably correlating to the streets aboveground, but he suspected that was only on this level, not farther down where the public wasn't allowed to roam freely.

Rand stayed close behind Ham, who filled the tunnel with his bulk. Poor guy was already huffing and puffing. Garbage, newspapers, cans, and cigarette butts littered the stone floor, soaking up small spills of murky water that dripped from the ceiling and walls. Well-done graffiti covered the rough walls. Some people with a lot of time on their hands apparently spent considerable time down here. Druggies? The homeless? Counterculture artists? Away from the glare of the city's laws . . . why not? The subterranean lair of their quarry began to make a little more sense. Still . . .

Dakota would be hyperventilating in this confined space, and they hadn't even gone two hundred yards.

"There's a branch off to your right." Her voice in his ear sounded calm and even. "Turn off after you go through the crypt."

"Got it." He wiped a trickle of water off his ear, grateful when Ham picked up the pace. Water droplets gleamed inches over Rand's head. When they got into the tunnels where visitors were prohibited, he'd assume the lead. For now, they were well behind the family ahead and a good distance from the people bringing up the rear.

Sound rippled around him; indistinct voices, the crunching of shoes on centuries-old dirt, the uneven drip-drip-drip, and Dakota's even breathing in his right ear.

In the early hours of this morning, he'd listened to her breath hitch as he'd lain two feet from her slender, tense back, and a hundred miles from any connection they'd once shared. The smell of her skin and hair had made his dick hard and his fingers itch to reach out and touch her. God, he missed her.

No. No, he didn't miss *her*. He missed, with an intensity that rocked him, the *memory* of her. The memory of *them*. Not just the sex, which had been phenomenal, but the laughter. The connection. The communication without verbalizing. The quiet and the noisy. The soft and the hard.

"They used to grow mushrooms in the tunnels, did you know?"

"You don't have to entertain me," Rand told her shortly.

"I know. Sorry. I'm—"

"Ham. Get the lead out. Close the gap." He didn't want to hear what she was. Scared. Worried. Lonely. Her feelings weren't his business anymore. And he was glad of it.

The fact that their quarry had been wherever he was—not moving much—since very early this morning indicated he'd reached his destination, either a meeting of some kind, or his *final* destination. He was in the right place for a very private burial. He'd join the six million bodies exhumed and reinterred in the tunnels of the old mines, which had become an ossuary in the eighteenth century.

The air got cooler, smelling moldy and dank as he followed Ham, and tried to tune out Dakota's soft breathing directly in his ear. Her silence pulsed with unspoken words. He was totally fucking fine with that. Other than this business that brought them together again, there was nothing that needed said. Part of him regretted what he'd said last night, but he was glad he'd clarified his stance.

He knew in his gut she wouldn't keep her promise to help his father. He could even understand. To vindicate Paul, she'd have to incriminate herself. She wouldn't do that. He wouldn't ask again.

They came to the crypt with its walls of bones, disarticulated and anonymous. Some of their owners died more than twelve hundred years before.

"Holy shit," Ham said, looking around. "I thought they just, I don't know, *tossed* the bones in here. This took some serious work."

There was a macabre beauty to the way the bones had been arranged in elaborate and intricate patterns, but the two men didn't linger. Rand wanted to disappear down the side tunnel before the people he could hear behind them closed the gap.

Ham muttered a vile curse, yanked his hand off the wall, and reached for his weapon as something large, wet, and feral raced between his legs. "Hate this fucking place! Where next?"

"Stop. This is it." The black ornamental wrought-iron gate was right where Dakota said it would be, barring the tunnel they should take. It was quick work for him to pick its padlock with the tools he always carried. They slipped into the darkness, and Ham closed the gate behind them.

Rand set the padlock back in place and tucked in the post enough to make it look closed. Unlike the corridors used by the tourists, there was no light here. Turning on their Maglites, they continued. The ceiling was dark with soot from the oil lamps and torches of the past, and the path ahead was nothing but a stygian void.

It was a good thing Rand wasn't given to flights of fancy. The place seemed to pulse eerily; it was like being in the belly of a beast. Whole damn place was the stuff of horror movies. His mind moved along the line he'd seen on the map as it curved and jogged for another half mile or so. The chances of finding his man down here, alive, were slim to fucking none, and he knew it. But Dakota had been so convincing. . . . More fool him. Veracity wasn't her strong suit. She believed truth was something she could bend to suit her own agenda.

She had her own reason for finding this guy, and he'd bet it wasn't to stop him selling Rapture as a street drug. Someone reinvented the formula. Did she want in? God only knew the sale of any illegal drug was ridiculously lucrative, and the effects of Rapture guaranteed the dealer, manufacturer, and everyone else up and down the food chain untold billions of dollars.

The question of what she was hiding—of what she was *really* doing here, and why she was so intent on his heels—spun circles in his mind. Had Stark sent her, not knowing she had another agenda? Or had she lied to her boss to get him to send her? More immediately, had she sent Rand down here to get him out of the way while she did . . . what?

An enormous, mangy rat scrabbled by his foot, the beam of the flashlight picking up its red eyes. Behind him, Ham swore, a muffled sound of surprise. "Holy shit! Did you see that? Size of a fucking dog! What do those things eat? Steroids?" His breath rasped and he braced a hand on the wall for a moment, his head bowed. "You got a map, right?"

"We're good, buddy. Dakota has our backs." *Or not.*

"Wouldn't put it past the bitch to leave us down here with our dicks swinging in the wind."

Rand was surprised at his knee-jerk reaction to hearing Dakota referred to as a bitch. "Ease off, Ham." Not that he had to defend her honor, but the mic was open. "One thing at a time."

Ham cleared his throat. Fool should give up smoking before he killed himself.

"How're you two getting along?"

"Fine," Rand said shortly. He had no intention of discussing Dakota with his friend, who already had his own prejudices against her.

"How do you get a redhead to argue with you?" Ham asked, a smile in his voice. "Say something!" He whooped with laughter at his own unfunny joke.

"Keep it down, we don't know who's around." Rand's tone brooked no argument.

Ham, crude as he was, was not an idiot. "Point."

Whose, Rand wasn't sure. His shoulders brushed the narrow walls of the corridor, and he was aware of the ceiling a mere couple of inches above his head. Ham's heavy breathing seemed to fill the space around them. He felt for the guy; he was having a hell of a time squeezing between the damp stone walls.

Rand's light showed an uneven circle of limestone six feet ahead, just in time. Without the Maglite, he would've missed the small opening in the floor. "Stairs," he warned, his low whisper too loud in the dark confines of the passage. He'd almost dropped straight down the narrow stairwell. Another set of carved stone stairs spiraled into deeper blackness. If either of them fell here, they could remain unfound for a hundred years. Was that Dakota's plan?

"You okay?" she murmured in his ear.

"Going down to the next level now." Hands braced on the unevenly chiseled curved walls, he stepped cautiously down the worn, cracked steps cut out of the bedrock. The walls oozed moisture, and the lower he went, the stronger the stink of sewage became.

"Jesus, what died in here?" Ham's voice was right over his head as he took one cautious step at a time on the dangerously slick, triangular stone treads.

"That's raw sewage."

"Keep your hands away from your face, and walk *fast*," Dakota advised prosaically in his ear. "You're less than two thousand feet from him now."

"Can't see much farther than ten feet in front of me." The world was reduced to blackness, dank, smelly air, and Ham's labored breathing above him as they literally walked in circles to get to the bottom of the vertical stairs. At this point, it was unlikely that the guy they sought was even alive. "Are yo—"

Rand heard a familiar *pop* directly overhead, followed instantly by a muzzle flash. He braced, half-turned, but he was too late. Ham's full body weight crashed into him, knocking the breath out of his lungs and sending him down the remaining dozen stairs on his back.

Everything went black.

✦ NINE ✦

R and?" The faint crackle of the Bluetooth's feedback was all Dakota's straining ears picked up. No conversation. No breathing. She'd heard a *pop*, then static. She got to her feet, finger pressed to the small device on her ear. "What was that?"

Silence.

Silence.

Holding her breath was counterproductive, and she let it out slowly. *Think.* Law-abiding citizen that she was, her first thought was to go to the local authorities. Terrific idea, if she weren't on the run herself. They'd arrest her, *maybe* remembering to ask questions later. Not going to help Rand.

Her heart double-tapped. "Damn it, Rand, say something."

He wasn't alone. Ham was with him. . . . "But what if something's happened to *both* of them? Shit, shit, shit." She walked to the door of the room, then paced back to the window. "Okay. Not *alone* alone."

He had a team of highly trained security guys back in Monte Carlo, she reminded herself with relief. They were hundreds of miles away, but at least he had backup.

She curled her fingers around the sock in her pocket. His numbers glowed bright in her mind's eye. He was alive. "Thank God. Because one way or the other, Rand Maguire, we're going to have a come-to-Jesus moment one of these days, and *soon*. If I have to handcuff you to the bed—no, bad idea. No beds when we talk. Tie you to *something*, and sit on you—we're going to have the conversation you weren't ready to hear two years ago. Whether you want to hear what I have to say or not."

Through her fear and pent-up anger, Dakota was left with a stark and unequivocal truth. "I still love you, you jerk. You *better* be all right." Now all she had to do was find him.

Using the hotel phone so she could maintain her connection with Rand, Dakota called his assistant's cell phone. The phone rang, then abruptly went dead. Impatiently, she tried it again. Same deal. With a growl of impatience, she got the number for the hotel in Monte Carlo and asked for him, only to be informed he'd checked out. She frowned. Had he gone back to the States? Wasn't an assistant's job to stay close to his boss so he could assist?

Since she didn't know the names of any of Rand's other men, and the only guests she remembered were the movie-star couple—probably on their honeymoon somewhere—and the big-time director, she asked for Seth Creed. They'd been in his suite when Dakota arrived from the airport. It made sense that he was at the top of the food chain. Unless he, too, had checked out?

By the time the call went through, she was already regretting involving him. She wasn't paranoid, but as

Rand and Ham's sudden silence proved, they couldn't trust anyone.

"No comment!" Seth Creed said the moment he answered the phone.

"Mr. Creed, this is Dr. North. I'm working with Rand Maguire—"

"You found the son of a bitch who drugged us?"

"We're working on it. I wonder if I could talk to whomever he left in charge?"

"Don't you know who he left in charge?" he demanded, suspicion lacing his impatient tone.

"It wasn't relevant."

"And it is now?"

Not a fan of his cool tone, Dakota answered his question with her own. "Is Rand's second-in-command there, Mr. Creed?"

"Everyone split this morning. In fact, I'm on my way to go see his father before I head back home myself." He expelled an impatient breath. "Is there anything I can do . . . ?"

"No, thanks. It's no biggie. I'll ask Rand later. Thanks." Weren't they investigating on their end? Maybe not. Had he thought as she had—trust no one—and sent them all home? Maybe his men had accompanied Ham, and they were here in Paris already. Available to come to his aid if he needed them?

Dakota put the hotel phone back in the cradle and started pacing the small room. To the door. To the window. To the door. To the window. "Damn it! Okay. What to do? Breathe. Think. Form a plan of action."

She could tell the line was still open, but try as she might, she couldn't hear either Rand or Ham. The good news was that she knew Rand was alive. If he weren't, his GPS numbers would blink out. She had no way of knowing the condition of Mark Stratham. Rand wasn't moving, the guy he was looking for wasn't moving either, and she was stuck in a hotel room blocks away.

Or not.

The cavalry wasn't coming. Or rather, the cavalry *was* coming. Like it or not, *she* was the cavalry.

RAND CAME TO WITH a vengeance, pain spearing through his head in a white-hot sunburst. There wasn't a vestige of light, and the weight of Ham's considerable girth pinned him to the cold stone floor. He shuddered with the chill that seeped around his body. His clothing was wet—moisture from the seeping rocks, and possibly Ham's blood. He smelled it above the notes of mold and decay, the sharp, metallic stink of death.

He knew his friend was dead, but he fumbled to find a pulse at his throat anyway. Nothing. Goddamn it. He hadn't heard anyone approaching. But the noise Ham had made struggling for breath, Rand's own responses to Dakota's questions, and their feet scraping the gritty stone floor probably masked the approach of the killer.

He managed to roll Ham off him and pressed the lighted dial on his watch so he could look for his weapon and headset. He discovered both nearby. Automatically, he checked his weapon, something he could do with his eyes closed. The clip was still in it. That was the good news. The bad was that the flashlights—both his and Ham's—shattered on impact.

No phone reception, and no light source other than the faint and ineffectual blue light on his watch. He was effectively out of communication with Dakota and had no idea where the hell he was, or how to go on.

Staggering to his feet, he found Ham's weapon close to his body, and shoved it into the back of his jeans under his jacket. Someone had known they were there. Someone who'd been stupid enough not to check to see if *he* was alive or dead. The only thing Rand had going for him right now was that the killer wasn't aware he was alive and at large in the tunnels.

Dakota had said his objective was less than a quarter of a mile ahead. He could go back, up the stairs, back to the ossuary, and follow the tourists out. Or he could continue on the path that he was on.

Either he'd find his man and a way out, or . . . he wouldn't.

DAKOTA TWISTED UP HER damp hair, dug the short black wig out of her bag, and pulled it on, shoving the long strands of red hair under it as she would beneath a shower cap. She found her Smith & Wesson on the counter in the bathroom. Nice of him to leave it for her. "I'm out of my damned mind!" she muttered, tucking the gun in the back waistband of her jeans. The thing was *tiny* when she wanted a—a bazooka!

What had Zak Stark been thinking when he gave her the .38 at Sea-Tac? "Point and shoot. Yeah. Right," she muttered, looking around to see what else she might need. "A doctor? A gurney? Rand's missing damn security team? An army of armed soldiers. A Navy SEAL? All of the above?"

What she had was a GPS location and a six-inch gun with five rounds. *I hope there aren't six bad guys,* she thought with gallows humor. She'd never fired a gun in her life.

The chances of her hitting anyone farther than a few inches from the barrel were slim to freaking none. "Out of options. Woman up, Dakota Christina." Not sure if the S&W, small as it was, could be seen under her thin T-shirt, she slipped on her black windbreaker, stuffed the GPS in one pocket and her phone in the other, and left the hotel, heading toward the entrance to the catacombs.

The sun was shining and there were people everywhere, enjoying the beautiful day. She walked briskly, even though she wanted to break into a run or turn around and go back to the hotel. The streets smelled of urine, cigarette smoke, and the dog poop left where it had been deposited on the sidewalk. Parisians *loved* their dogs almost as much as they loved smoking.

In the dark wig and sunglasses, she was hardly memorable or even noticeable. Just another tourist in a city filled with them. Still, she felt as though she had a large red bull's-eye painted on her back, and her skin prickled with nerves. The stationary latitude and longitude numbers in her head showed her that Rand hadn't moved. Still alive. Same for the bad guy, who hadn't budged either.

They were down there, maybe a quarter of a mile apart. Neither moving. Dakota wasn't sure if the fact that they weren't together right now was a good thing or a bad thing. Do *not* think, she warned herself as her heart pounded and her hands, stuffed in the pockets of the jacket, grew increasingly sweaty.

Do not think about going—*willingly*—into *catacombs*.

Don't think millions of dead people residing there.

Don't think tight, confined spaces.

Don't think seven levels of hell.

Don't. Think. Claustrophobia.

The gun in her waistband was heavy for such a little thing. Her armpits itched with anticipated fear. She took a roll of hard candy out of her pocket and popped a butterscotch in her mouth to alleviate the dryness.

Think, she reasoned with herself as her footsteps got slower and slower with dread, of *not* going inside.

Imagine walking away. Imagine leaving Rand in there, injured or somehow incapacitated. Imagine no one ever finding him. Ev-er! "Damn, I hate it when I'm this logical."

"Allez-vous bien, coup manqué?"

She shook her head. She didn't speak French, but by the frown of concern on the older woman's face, Dakota guessed she'd asked if she'd lost her mind. No, *that* she'd lost years ago. When she'd believed Rand when he'd told her she was the love of his life. That they'd be together forever. That they were two halves of a whole.

Forever was apparently eleven months, seventeen days, and a handful of meaningless hours. He should have lis-

tened to her when she'd told him love didn't—couldn't—
last.

Obstinate bastard.

She'd been wrong, but she was still going to save
his ass.

The line to get into the catacombs was around the
block and all the way up the street. It was a tourist
attraction. What had she expected? That she'd just stroll
inside, one, two, three?

It was noon and too hot to be wearing even the thin
jacket, but she ignored the discomfort as she walked all
the way up the line until she was three groups from the
entrance. Nobody said anything. They just presumed she
was where she was supposed to be.

Taking out the map of the underground streets and
tunnels, she memorized each path and branch that
she'd advised Rand to take as the first group in line was
allowed in. Five minutes between groups, she'd read. She
shuffled to close the gap, closed her eyes, and walked
the tunnels in her mind. Looked at the map again, then
refolded it and shoved it in her pocket.

The couple before the family in front of her went inside.
Her stomach turned agitated, impatient somersaults, not
helped by the greasy smell of the burgers the kids near her
were eating while they waited. *Come on, come on, come on!*

Her heart fluttered in anticipation. She glanced at her
watch. It had been just over fifteen minutes since she'd
lost contact with Rand.

Was she overreacting? She was imagining him unconscious and hurt. Maybe they'd just lost cell reception? She

shuffled forward a few more steps. If that was the case, Rand would be furious if she followed him. God only knew, she'd be relieved if she didn't have to go inside. . . .

The problem was, there was no way of knowing what the hell the situation was.

When the laughing, joking, noisy British family of seven went in, Dakota sucked in a stabilizing breath and went in with them.

It wasn't as dark and confining as she'd dreaded. Just long stone walls with dim sconces every now and then, but her hands were still sweating, and her breathing became a little erratic in the narrow tunnel. There wasn't much to see, as the two older kids just ahead of her pointed out to their parents, who were marching ahead of the pack at a nice fast pace. Dakota appreciated that. The air smelled more of greasy hamburger than anything else. Her stomach rumbled.

"Where *are* the dead people, Mum?"

Rand's numbers glowed bright in Dakota's mind's eye.

A BEEP IN HER ear indicated a second call. *Ham!* Relieved, she put Rand's call on hold, and accepted the second caller.

"Rand's down."

"Mark?" Thank God Rand hadn't gone in alone. "What ha—"

"Ma'am, this is Chris Raimi."

Her heart was pounding so hard Dakota almost passed out. Not Mark Stratham. If this man had Rand's phone, he had Rand. "What do you want?"

"I'm with Maguire Security, ma'am."

Her breath came out in a *whoosh* of relief. "Thank God. You're with him. Is he all right?" It was a stupid question. Of course he wasn't. If he were, he'd be talking to her himself.

"We did not accompany Rand and Ham into the catacombs. We lost contact twenty-three minutes ago. We're on our way to you at the hotel. Please stay where you are." There was a faint click, but she was still getting feedback from Rand's Bluetooth, which meant his line was open, he just wasn't responding.

"Wait, I'm—" *Here!*

So Rand had lied when he'd agreed they'd follow the guy on their own. He had ordered his entire security team to rendezvous with him in Paris. No wonder no one had been in Monaco when she called. Instead of being angry, she was relieved that he had the right kind of help on the way. "Thank God."

Only the reinforcements were on their way to the hotel.

And Rand's GPS numbers were moving. Slowly and away from her. But moving.

She debated breaking her connection to Rand, to call him back, but decided against it. She was here, and had no idea how far away he was. When Raimi got to the hotel he'd call again, and she'd lead him to Rand and Ham then.

After making her way through the ossuary, she saw the wrought-iron gate Rand and Ham must have passed through. It was padlocked. Beyond it was nothing but black. Not only did she have no idea how to pick a lock, she didn't have anything to even try it with. Dakota was almost relieved that she didn't have to go beyond it, until she tried the padlock anyway and found it hadn't been completely closed.

Foiled, she thought, trying to find a glimmer of humor in the situation. There wasn't any.

A bead of sweat rolled down her temple as she struggled to compress the rising terror at being in an even darker, even more confined space. She assured herself that there was plenty of air to breathe, that the walls had stood for centuries. That thousands of people had walked right where she was, and they'd all gotten out the other side.

The pep talk helped only a little. Okay, not much at all. Made no damned difference. She was here, and she was going to find Rand. That was the *only* option right now. Finding Rand.

Now the passage smelled of old dead things and decay. Goose bumps pebbled her skin, both from nerves and the suddenly colder air seeping from the cross tunnel where she stood.

The good news was that Rand's numbers were once again on the move. She let out a ragged breath.

"*Move,*" she ordered her paralyzed feet. Unhooking the heavy padlock, she pushed through the ancient gate, then pulled it closed behind her. She replaced the lock as Rand had done, so his men could follow her, just as she heard the next group passing into the chamber she'd just exited.

Turning on the narrow beam of her flashlight, she followed the uneven stone floor, stepping over piles of trash and trying to ignore the scratching of what she was positive were giant rats scurrying close by. A full body shudder slowed her steps for several moments.

Breathe in. Breathe out. Breathe in.

Forcing each foot in front of the other, willing herself to keep going, she came to the spiral stairs that Rand had taken down to the next level.

The air became progressively colder and more stagnant, and she picked up her pace. She was scared going slowly, and she was scared going fast. Fast would get her out of there sooner. But it was dangerous. The floor was rough, uneven, and slick. Garbage of the stinky kind made the passage hazardous, and puddles of stagnant water were everywhere. The walls oozed water that caught the light of the flashlight, making her feel as if she were inside the bronchial tubes of some giant beast. Was the air getting heavier? It was certainly more of an effort to breathe.

She reminded herself again that there was plenty of oxygen, and she could indeed breathe. God, she wanted out of there. Now. Keeping the light on her feet as she took each step, she finally managed the dizzying descent and arrived at the bottom. Just about to step off the last step, Dakota swept the beam of her flashlight across the floor. Inches from where she'd just been about to step was a human hand.

Too frightened, too shocked, to cry out, she froze. Dear God . . . Rand? It took every ounce of fortitude she could muster to move. Raising her leg, she stepped beyond the extended arm at the base of the stairs. Another sweep of the light showed Mark Stratham, eyes open and unseeing, with a large, gory hole in the side of his neck. His shirt was saturated with blood.

"I'm so sorry." *Sorry you're dead. Sorry I didn't like you.* Would someone find him soon, or would he lie here undetected for years? She rubbed her arms, grateful for even the thin protection of her jacket.

In her head, Rand's numbers continued to move slowly ahead of her. Sidestepping Ham's body wasn't easy. The corridor was not only narrow but dark and spooky, and Ham was—had been—a large man. Once over—literally—the hurdle of Mark Stratham's body, Dakota started jogging to close the gap between herself and Rand.

She stepped into a puddle of water and staggered off balance, throwing out a hand to catch herself. The wall oozed slimy wetness. With a grimace, she wiped her hand down the leg of her jeans and kept going. Faster when she heard voices and cries indicating there were people nearby.

At first she thought her heartbeat changed rhythm, pounding in her ears as she moved down the corridor. But after several minutes she realized that what she was hearing wasn't her own erratic heartbeat but the faint sound of music. Not a melody, but the deep, resonating *thump-thump-thump* of the bass accompanied by shouting and laughter.

Her steps slowed, then stopped altogether as she listened. Definitely music and voices. Someone was having a party? Down here, several levels beneath the streets of Paris? Apparently.

A faint shimmer of lighter black indicated a light source down a side branch. Knowing Rand was some-where close; Dakota took a left and headed toward the tiny pinpoints of light.

Disappointed, she came to a dead end where an intricate black metal grille set into the wall like a large window prevented her going any farther. The sound of voices drew her closer. The illumination beyond the grille cast dots of golden light against the adjoining wall. Intrigued and curious, Dakota peered through one of the tiny openings.

There was a large room on the other side. No, not a room. It looked like a bar—a club of some sort, with dim lighting and wide, white-leather backless sofas scat-tered about a shiny black floor.

Her breath snagged in her throat when she saw what was happening on those low couches, on the floor, against the walls. A dozen or more couples were having animated, very *loud* sex. *Oh, hell. Here we go again.*

Distracted by what she was seeing, Dakota took a few moments to realize that not only were Rand's GPS coordinates stationary and very close, so were those of the guy he'd come down here to find. Was one of those writhing bodies Rand?

She pressed her face closer to the grille.

Even while her scientist's brain knew these people had been dosed with Rapture, it was hard not to be affected by seeing them in the throes of uninhibited sexual pleasure. She didn't smell roses, so they must have ingested the drug. It didn't matter. She couldn't tear her eyes away.

Suddenly, a steely arm wrapped around her midriff and a hard hand slapped across her mouth.

EVEN IF DAKOTA WEREN'T seeing Rand's exact GPS location inches from her own, she'd have known it was him by the scent of his skin and the contour of his body as he pressed against her back. Tempting as it was to lean backward into his heat, Dakota wrapped her fingers around his wrist and tugged his hand from her mouth. She turned her head to look at him, and raised an eyebrow. Probably hard to see under her faux bangs.

She trembled as he tucked an errant strand of hair behind her ear, feeling the caress in every receptor cell in her body. Looking down, she allowed him access to her exposed nape. A lover's pose.

He leaned close, whispering, "What are you doing down here? It's dangerous."

"Our bad guy's in there." The erotic sound of multiple people having noisy and energetic sex just a few feet away was extremely distracting. "We lost contact, and you weren't moving for a while." Dakota was pleasantly surprised to hear how calm and rational her voice sounded, considering the circumstances. "I thought you might need help."

"Ham was shot. He's dead."

And the possibility that it was you terrified me enough to make me overcome my claustrophobia and come find you. "I saw. I'm sorry, Rand."

His body radiated heat. She shifted so her bottom snugged against his groin. His braced legs bracketed hers, and she was surrounded by the heat of his body and the salty soapy fragrance of his skin. The bristles on his jaw rubbed against her temple. It was too dark to see more than the speckles of light from the grate shining on his black T-shirt and the lower part of his face.

"What about you?" she asked quietly. "Were you hurt?"

"I'm good." He put a finger across her mouth as several men in the room started talking, disconcerting because they were all in various stages of undress, and having sex at the same time.

Dakota didn't speak French, but Rand did a simultaneous translation quietly in her ear, and she closed her eyes because she really didn't need the sight of all these strangers having sex to remain imprinted on her brain for all time.

"Our guy is offering more samples. The buyer just pointed out that the Bad Guy happens to be boinking *his* favorite girlfriend." Rand's voice indicated amusement as he continued. "Buyer guy says he doesn't *need* more samples. He's ready to place a large order." Rand's breath moved strands of her hair across her face. "How soon? In production now. Three weeks. Buyer wants his shipment sooner, and wants to be the exclusive European distributor."

Dakota didn't need a translation. She opened her eyes again. Bad Guy laughed as he shoved the woman off him, then rattled off another stream of dialogue. It might've served as a distraction from feeling like the roof was about to close in on her head, if she'd understood what everyone was saying. Since she didn't, and having Rand safe and sound beside her, her claustrophobia was closing in on her. She tried to regulate her breathing, but she was prickly hot, then icy cold as wings of panic beat against her.

"Our guy just told him he can have France. Big concession, he says. *Everyone* wants Rapture, buyers are easy to find."

The buyer threw his legs over the side of the couch, shoving away the hands of the two naked women, who carried on what they'd been doing without him. He rose, gestured for Bad Guy to give the women more of the drug, and snapped his fingers to a man waiting in the shadows.

"He's telling our guy to call in his order. Arranging a down payment. Scheduling delivery . . ."

Dakota tilted her head as Rand kissed her ear, while the two men made the arrangements and the dozen other naked participants were handed what she knew to be paper-thin wafers with dots of Rapture imbedded in them. They each eagerly placed the dose on their tongues. It would dissolve in seconds. . . .

"God, I hate this thing." He pulled her wig off, letting her damp hair tumble around her shoulders in wild abandon. "You're beautiful, no matter what color hair you're wearing, but this"—he tugged on a long strand—"is my favorite. I used to have fantasies about your hair." His voice cracked, then roughened. "Damn it, woman, you should have stayed in the hotel room."

A hint of what he used to feel for her? Then *wham*,

shut it down again. Way to keep a girl on her toes, Dakota thought. "Don't yell. They'll hear us."

"Doubt it," he whispered dryly, his lips against her cheek. "Are you turned on by them?"

She gave a dramatic shudder. "Ick. No."

"Then slow your breathing before you hyperventilate. I'm right here, and this place has been standing for thousands of years."

"I *know* that. Logically. But I still have claustrophobia."

"Think about something else."

"Like what?" She was pretty much surrounded by sex. She let a small sigh of frustration escape, her body hyperaware of him, of the people in the other room, of *him*. . . . The naked men in the other chamber were now arguing loudly.

"It was supposed to alleviate depression," Dakota said, trying to work up anger and indignation to shove away her irrational fear of the confined space. Her body prickled, and sweat stuck her shirt to her skin. She wanted out of there. Now! "Not to create sex addicts."

Rand cupped her face, his thumb stroking her cheek. A shiver of a different kind skittered across her nerve endings, and her nipples tightened. She made a move to turn, but his large hand on her hip kept her in place.

"It was very brave of you to come down here."

"I wasn't brave at all," she assured him, tilting her face to rest briefly in his palm. God. She'd missed this. Missed *him*. Unfortunately, this was neither the time nor the place to have this conversation. "It took everything I had not to pee my pants and whimper all the way."

"Doubly brave, then." His thumb brushed back and forth in a maddening caress across her lower lip, and his other hand slid from her hip to flatten on her belly, drawing her closer. The ridged length of his penis pressed against her butt, hot and throbbing even through several layers of fabric.

"I forgot your tendency to race in where angels fear to tread. An extremely unscientific trait, I always thought, but one I admired."

Someone in the club let out a piercing cry as they climaxed. Dakota tried to swallow, but her mouth was dry, and she could feel the increasingly rapid beat of her heart in every pulse-point up and down her body. "I have to get out of here," she said desperately as the walls seemed to close in on her. A film of perspiration prickled her skin. Averting her gaze from people in the throes of Rapture wasn't compelling or distracting enough to stave off her claustrophobia.

It felt as though the entire city of Paris were pressing down relentlessly on her head. The very air felt suffocatingly heavy.

"Seriously, can we get the hell out of here now? We heard what we need to hear, and we can't nab the guy from here."

"Lean against me and close your eyes," he whispered against her cheek.

"Damn it, Rand. I don't want to play games right now. This isn't funny."

"I know. We can't leave until we know what the next

play will be. I can't let you stroll out of here on your own. Close your eyes and breathe with me. There you go."

Eyes squeezed shut, she felt the brush of his hand against her tummy; then his nimble fingers slipped the button of her jeans free.

"Remember when we had that picnic at Gas Works Park?" he murmured against her ear. After a few moments of struggling in the oppressive darkness, Dakota saw that day behind her closed lids. "It was cold and gray and drizzling, and we bundled in the blanket and ate our sandwiches there on the wet grass. We stuck it out because my flight was leaving in a couple of hours, and we couldn't bear to let each other go. So we sat there shivering, looking over choppy Lake Union. Remember the feel of the spray stinging your face and the wind cutting through our clothes? Hell, we didn't care. Just drank that great wine out of paper cups and talked about a quick trip to Tahiti. Remember?"

Dakota nodded. God, yes. She remembered every single moment of their time together. Made more precious because they lived a thousand miles apart and didn't see each other nearly often enough.

That day at the park was even more memorable because it had been the day Rand proposed to her. Their love had kept them warm, and the discomfort of the cold gray day had been swept aside by the prospect of their rosy future.

She'd missed him with an intensity that at times had been unbearable. Her throat closed on a whimper. She ached for more intimate contact. Surrounded by him wasn't enough, and she felt bereft when he stopped touching her face. But it was only temporary.

Skimming a hand beneath her tank top, he murmured, "Mmm," curling a finger inside the cup of her bra, his hard palm shockingly warm. With his fingertip, he raked the hard areola of her erect nipple, making Dakota moan low in her throat and press her bottom against his erection, rocking against him. She wanted to turn around. She wanted him to kiss her. She burned for him to kiss her, but instead, he eased her zipper down. "Rand . . ."

Need clawed at her. She made a muffled sound of mingled pleasure and despair. Nothing between them had changed, but she didn't *want* to say no. She didn't give a damn where they were. She squeezed her eyes shut, feeling the skim and glide as he slid his hand into the open V of her pants. Behind the darkness of her lids, all she could do was feel and hear the erratic breathing and sounds of sex a few feet away. That was quickly tuned out as her own breathing became ragged, competing with the sound of her own rapid heartbeat. He nuzzled her damp hair as he slid his fingertips under the elastic of her lacy thong to cup her mound. "Rand . . ."

"Shh." His fingers opened her, and Dakota shifted restlessly to give him better access. "You're wet." His rough voice had an incredibly sexy rasp, and her nipples tightened even more, to hard, needy points.

"And getting wetter." A haze of lust blurred the glow of the room in front of her. Stars and glitter. "Are you . . . going to . . ."

"Oh, yeah." He teased his way inside the damp seam, sliding two fingers inside her. She arched into his hand as her muscles contracted. He pressed the heel of his hand against her clit and brought her to climax so fast it caught her between one breath and the next. "More?" He bit gently at the distended tendons of her neck as he inserted another finger inside her, stretching her. He kissed the side of her throat, stroking his tongue around the shell of her ear. He remembered her body so well.

"God, yes." The fact that she couldn't spread her legs because of her tight jeans, and because he was leaning against the wall, his body bracketed around hers, made the sensation of his fingers inside her even more erotic. His arms surrounded her, his breath blew hot against her throat. His heartbeat syncopated with hers. Hard, rapid, loud.

This was familiar. The heat. The intensity. The want. This, she thought, choking back a sob, was the Rand she knew. And still loved.

"I remember what you taste like. Here." She gulped air as his fingers thrust impossibly deeper. "And here." His hand curved around her breast inside the cup of her bra; he rubbed the hard nipple with his thumb so it hardened even more, and ached for the wet heat of his mouth. "Salty and sweet."

The next muscle-clenching crest pulsed throughout her body, drawing tighter and tighter. . . . She flung her head back, gasping for air as her muscles spasmed around the hard spear of his fingers. His strong arms kept her upright when her knees threatened to dissolve with the pleasure as the second climax washed through her in a hard, bone-shuddering wave that made her dig her nails into his wrist, and she bit her tongue to keep from crying out with the pulse-pounding, driving orgasms rolling through her one after another.

Dakota wilted limply against his broad chest, her heartbeat manic, her brain fogged with lassitude and pleasure.

Sounds seeped back into her consciousness. Rand's slightly erratic breathing as he rested his chin on the top of her head. The nonstop action in the club, and the rasp of her own breathing. "What about y—"

His entire body stiffened. He jerked away from the wall, his hand still between her legs. *"Shit!"*

He'd done such a great job distracting her from her claustrophobia that she'd almost forgotten why they were there. "What?"

"Quiet." He withdrew his hand from her pants, set her aside a few feet from him, then brushed by her to get close to the grille.

Dakota mouthed, *What the hell?* Which he couldn't possibly see in the dark. He wasn't even *looking* at her. His entire focus was on the room beyond as he stepped closer. He leaned in to peer through the finely wrought iron.

Bang. Bang. Bang.

Their Paris bad guy's GPS location winked out of Dakota's head, and Rand said, "Our bad guy just fucking well got himself *shot.*"

✦ TEN ✦

As soon as they bolted the hotel room door, Dakota yanked off the black wig that she had put back on before leaving the catacombs. When this clusterfuck was over, he was going to burn the damn thing. She tossed the wig onto the bed, her pale green eyes a little dazed.

He'd gotten them out of the catacombs as the people in the club became marginally aware that someone had been shot. Nobody seemed to care particularly. Rapture did that. The situation had just gone from shit to fucked in a heartbeat.

He raked his fingers through his hair, dropping his hand when he smelled Dakota on his fingers. Christ. He couldn't go there.

She sat on the foot of the bed. "I don't understand what happened."

He went into the bathroom and washed his hands, drying them as he walked back into the room. She sat cross-legged on the bed, her bare shoulders gleaming in the sunlight shining through the window, and her hair looked like the finest cognac streaked with ginger. He walked to the window to stare out at the Parisian rooftops without seeing any of it.

Dakota's beauty stole his breath, making him do and think crazy things. Always had. "Apparently our guy went to the club last night. Waited for the owner-slash-prospective buyer to show. He supplied the buyer and his friends with Rapture. As you saw, it was a big hit. Big order. Then playtime for the rest of the night."

"Everyone looked . . ." Dakota's lips twitched. "Very happy. Why kill the man who was about to give them a lifetime supply of happy?"

"That——" He cut himself off when there was a coded knock at the door, and he went to yank it open. "——is the million-dollar question. A day late and several million dollars short," he told Ligg and Rebik as they entered. "What are you doing here? You're supposed to be following the other guy. And why weren't you answering your phones?"

The two men exchanged a look.

Ligg shrugged. "Crappy reception."

"I left explicit instructions for you to follow the GPS location Dakota sent you. Did you get any of *those* texts?"

"Nope." Ligg gave him a quizzical look. "Only one from Ham telling us to rendezvous with you here."

"Where's everyone else? Cole? Walters?" He'd brought twenty-four men with him for the wedding. He'd ordered half his men to return to the United States on the private plane with the wedding guests, which meant there should be eleven of them hanging around waiting for orders.

Rebik shook his head. "No idea."

"What about Chris Raimi?" Dakota asked, picking up on the tension. "He called and said he was on his way here."

"Who?" Rand asked, distracted by the men's inability to tell him where the others were. He shot a brief glance at her, then looked at Ligg for answers. "Chris Raimi? Never heard of him."

"You're joking, right? I *spoke* to him. He had my cell number."

Yet another fucking mystery. "He's not one of mine."

Dakota looked from Ligg to Rebik. "Do you know who he is?"

"No, ma'am," they said in unison.

She pulled out her phone and hit "last call." Rand watched as she listened, a scowl marring her pretty features. He already knew no one was going to answer.

"Ham's dead." He was pissed at the world, and he didn't bother hiding his anger and frustration. "And our quarry with him. What the hell took you so long, and where are the others?"

Ligg gave him a strange look. "You counterordered. Most of the team went home this morning."

Rand's gaze met Dakota's. She bit her lip. *Trust no one.* He turned back to his men. "Who passed along the order?"

Rebik frowned. "I thought Cole—"

"No," Ligg corrected. "It was Jakes."

Jakes was too far down the food chain to work independently, and it was unlike Cole to take orders from anyone but Rand. His assistant had been with him for seven years, hell, back when Rand had been Creed's stunt coordinator. He was as loyal and devoted as a golden retriever, and as protective and tenacious as a rottweiler. He wouldn't take anyone's word for it that Rand had told everyone to go home.

"Point is—it wasn't *me*," Rand informed them grimly. "If you were ordered to return home, supposedly by me, what are you two doing here?"

"I spoke directly with you after Jakes relayed the first order," Ligg told him. "We figured you wanted to keep this tight. Especially if the Spanish police and Interpol are on your ass."

Damn. "They ID'd me?"

Derek Rebik shoved his hands in his pockets, looking like he wanted to pace. Rand watched his men, trying to assess whether they really believed he'd counterordered, or whether they had their own agenda. Paranoia was insidious.

"Not that we've been able to find out," Rebik reported, running a hand over his shaved head. "They have one grainy video. So far, they haven't been able to ID the person in it."

Rand remained standing, but gestured to the small table and two chairs by the window. "Grab a seat, and I'll update you. When I was in the catacombs, I overheard the guy we were tracking as he was talking to a customer. He said that two men were sent to a meet with a prospective buyer at the Bennett-Dunham wedding."

"Wait. The buyer was at the *wedding*? As in one of the guests?" Ligg, who was about to sit, straightened. "It wasn't a blackmail attempt, or someone playing a gag that went balls-up? Jesus. We're gonna get our asses handed to us by a bunch of high-profile Hollywood lawyers!"

Rebik looked from Ligg to Rand and back again. "Or find our asses thrown in jail somewhere."

"All possibilities," Rand admitted. "Dakota and I think all of this has been a demo. That dead waiter was paid to drop wafers with the drug into the champagne glasses. The liquid caused it to dissolve. It was a small dose—" He looked to Dakota.

"Less than a microgram," Dakota explained, scooting back to lean against the padded headboard, "but more than enough to cause the uncontrollable reactions. That presents as sexual excess for the majority of people taking Rapture, but for others it will manifest as wild mood swings. Rage, fear, paranoia."

"Shit. Yeah." Ligg dropped into the chair. "That tall brunette bridesmaid couldn't stop bawling, and the old guy with the white hair was on a rampage, tossing tables and throwing shit he shouldn't have been able to even lift. It took three of us to restrain him long enough to tie him up."

Rand leaned his shoulder on the bathroom door-jamb as they talked. Who'd countered his orders, and why? Someone who wanted him swinging in the wind alone with no backup? On the run from the authorities? It sounded a little crazy to him, but he figured it wasn't paranoia if someone was really after him.

"According to the guy in the catacombs, manufacturing has barely begun." Rand shrugged. "While they work out the production details, they're giving firsthand displays of exactly what Rapture can do. These guys we were following are basically *salespeople*. The box you found in the waiter's room was a traveling salesman's sample case. We need the kingpin."

Rebik half-smiled. "The stuff will practically sell itself. What else does it need to do besides make you horny?"

"The effects are dose-dependent," Dakota told him shortly, clearly not amused. "In the realm of toxicology, we have several commonly used measures to describe toxic doses—"

"Cut to the chase," Rand inserted before she went all chemist on them and no one understood more than a word in three. When Dakota was on a roll, it was sometimes hard to stop her. "They get the gist."

She wrapped her arms around her up-drawn knees, but Rand knew her well enough to know she wasn't relaxed. She wanted to find the manufacturer worse than he did. And he wanted the guy *bad*.

"A dose," she told the two men, keeping it simple, "is the quantity of the chemical that impacts an organism biologically. When Rapture is made to be ingested, a very small amount—less than a microgram—is delivered on a soluble wafer. That would be your street drug. A *much* stronger airborne dose was inhaled at the bank. Strong enough to kill everyone who came into extended contact with it."

"Holy fuck."

Holy fuck indeed.

"The gas has a slight scent of roses, which wouldn't be detectable until the toxins hit the air, and by then it would be too late." Dakota's ice-green eyes met Rand's across the room. "As a weapon of mass destruction, Rapture would be unstoppable in the hands of a terrorist."

IT WAS LATE AFTERNOON, almost dusk, when Rand commandeered a pickup truck parked down a narrow, out-of-the-way side street a few blocks from their hotel. Once again, they switched license plates before heading south out of town. Dakota was getting good at popping them off and using her thumbnail to screw them back on.

He called Rebik and left a message when he didn't answer. "Damn it to hell, now where are they?"

"On the way to the airport," she reminded him mildly. The second bad guy had too much of a lead to catch up with him by car. Dakota had directed them to Innsbruck. From there, they'd rent a car to tail him. "Relax. They know you're already pissed. I'm sure they'll call you as soon as they land. Here, give me your phone, I'll text them, and they can read it when they get there." She texted the new coordinates, then shot Rand a sassy smile. "Want to add a love note?"

"I want to add a kick-your-ass-for-not-picking-up-your-phone note," Rand said dryly. "Just tell them to call me ASAP."

Dakota added the rest of the message and handed him back the phone.

"Where are *we* going?" she asked as he checked the

rearview mirror. The guy in the catacombs was dead, and Rand's men were following the other GPS coordinates.

"Rome. I have to talk to Paul."

He always referred to his father by name. The two Maguire men weren't what Dakota considered warm and fuzzy to each other. "Your father's been incarcerated for two years." She kicked off her shoes and curled her legs under her butt.

"Thanks for stating the obvious," he wryly observed.

"I meant that he's hardly in a position to be in the know, Rand. I think we should find a place to stop and rest for a few hours, and then catch up with your guys."

"No. We've all wasted too much time. I'll let them follow that lead. They'll call when they have him. We can decide how to handle it from there. My father won't know about the present application of Rapture, but like you, he knows this drug inside and out. He could have a puzzle piece you don't know or don't remember, and maybe he can give us a better, more direct lead. I'm sick of fucking zigzagging all over Europe like a pull toy. We need to get proactive and find a way in the back door."

She opened her eyes and straightened. "I'm all for proactive and kicking some butt. What's the plan?"

"I have a friend who'll charter us a private plane on the QT. I don't want to hit the large airports in case they're being watched. With face recognition software, it's not out of the realm of possibility that Interpol could be on our asses."

She rubbed her hands up and down her arms as a shiver of foreboding chilled her. "No argument there.

How many cars do we have to steal between there and here?"

"This one should do it. It's only an hour's drive to Fontainebleau. I haven't spotted a tail. I don't *think* the police are following us. If they were, they'd've hauled our asses in for questioning by now. But going to an airport and trying to take a commercial flight would up the ante."

The roads were clogged until they broke away from the city and left the lights behind them. Eyes gritty, she curled on the bench seat, fixing her gaze on the hypnotic beams of the headlights as they traveled very fast through the gathering darkness.

Rand was a terrific driver, and she'd always felt safe with him. In a car, that was. Her emotions hadn't been safe with him at all.

He surprised her with his next question. "How are your parents?"

"Golfing, comitteeing, and being normal," she said with a smile, angling her body and stretching out her legs. "They're going to Bora-Bora next month." Charming people, her parents. Both college professors, they loved but didn't understand her.

"What's their take on this sixth sense of yours, or did you somehow manage to keep it a secret from them too?"

"Here's an idea," Dakota murmured, eyes still closed. "Let's do our best not to make inflammatory statements until we've both had twelve consecutive hours of sleep."

"Fair enough. How *do* Dr. North and Dr. North deal with their only child's superpower?"

"They went through denial and isolation from my

birth to age seven. Anger from eight to about twelve. Bargaining in my teens, claims of clinical depression— theirs, not mine—in my early twenties. They skipped right over the acceptance part of the program. No A's for their daughter's superpower, that's for sure."

"That sucks, Dakota."

"They love me. They just don't understand how I see the numbers. They just don't get it. Or believe it. Or understand it. It's not scientific or rational. I accept their issues, and we don't ever talk about it." She turned her head on the seat back. "In light of the connection between Zak Stark's near-death experience and the advent of his skill, I think I had something similar when I was about two. I got encephalitis, and they told my parents that I'd died in the ER."

She shrugged. "There's no way of knowing if I'd had the GPS sense before that. I don't ever remember *not* having numbers streaming through my head. I had no idea what they were."

"What's it look like?" The curiosity in his voice was a far cry from the disdain she'd been hearing in his tone since Monte Carlo.

"The numbers? They appear as a string, no indications of latitude or longitude, no north or south. Just a long string of numbers on a never-ending loop. I've learned to switch it on and off, because when I was younger I'd see dozens of numbers if I was on the playground, or if I touched anything and everything. Eventually I was able to sort the wheat from the chaff and focus on just one . . . stream. The numbers are bright, for want of a better word, and when I see them they're superimposed over whatever is in my field of vision. Layered over everything."

"Annoying?"

She shrugged. "Just my reality. I've never had it any other way."

"How did you figure out what the numbers were?"

"My parents tried to pretend to themselves that I was a child prodigy instead of a freak, and that I was seeing some sort of mathematical equation that they never could figure out. But when I was five or six, our dog was stolen. I was devastated and cried for hours. Then I found his collar in the backyard near the fence, and the numbers changed almost immediately. That time when I told my father, he got out a map. One of my school friends had taken Snoopy, claiming the dog had followed her home. I never liked that girl."

"They were still in denial, even though you started that early?" Rand shot her a quizzical look, then turned his attention back to the road. The trees lining the road were becoming more dense. Beech, oak, and pine, black silhouettes against the night sky.

"It took a couple more years and a bunch more 'coincidental' finds to bring them around to the fact that, like it or not, understand it or not, it was a part of me. They showed me how to use a map, and eventually my dad bought me a handheld GPS for a birthday."

An oncoming car's lights illuminated Rand's face as she turned to look at him. He didn't look annoyed, just curious. It was a start. "Did you go to Zak and ask for a job?"

"No. I hadn't seen him since——" Since Rand had told her to go to hell. "For about a year. After I got out of the hospital." She cleared her throat. "The lab fired me, and I was unemployed for a while. Then there was a string of abductions of high school girls about a year ago. Five girls were taken as they walked home from school in the space of a couple of weeks. As soon as I heard about the case, I went to the local PD and offered my services."

"Let me guess——they didn't believe you could do it, and/or they thought you were the one doing the kidnappings."

"Both. But eventually I persuaded them to give me a shot, and they let me hold the last girl's cell phone. I found her in Olympia within an hour."

"Dead?"

Every now and then another oncoming vehicle's lights would illuminate Rand's face, making him look a little demonic, and grim. "No. Alive. My talent only works if the person I'm trying to track is still alive. The men had been holding her in a hunting shack in the mountains. The cops arrested both of the assholes and found the bodies of the other four girls buried on the property. The girl's parents went to the press, Zak's wife saw the newscast, and they contacted me. He and Acadia took me out to dinner and offered me the job."

"A waste of your education, don't you think?"

"I didn't lose what I learned just because I do this instead of being a chemist. Actually, the two jobs can work well toge——why do you keep looking back?"

They were in the boonies between towns, nothing

but fields and trees on either side of a two-lane road. A handful of vehicles traveled in either direction, lights on. The interior of the truck lit up as someone tailgated them.

She straightened, half-turning in her seat. "Is someone following u—" Oh, dear God. Rand had his gun in his hand. It looked huge and menacing. A quick glance at his face showed that so did he.

"For the last fifty kilometers." His voice was calm, but she could read the tension in the lines of his body. Her pulse sped up as he slid down his window. Warm wind blew her hair around her shoulders, it smelled of grass and pine trees.

"Put your shoes on and tighten that seat belt."

"I don't want to sound like Pollyanna, but they'll question us, we'll explain the situation, you'll show your credentials, and they'll let us go—right?" She slipped on her shoes, and turned, arm braced on the seat back to look out the rear window. There were several cars' lights behind them. She looked back at Rand, his features illuminated by the dash lights. She wasn't sure he was even listening to her. Eyes narrowed against the glare in the rearview mirror, he looked intense and focused.

"Okay, yeah, we were at the bank, but surely all it'll take is a few questions. They'll know we aren't *bank robbers*. Except—damn it. All those people died. So they're not just going to *question* us, are they? They're going to haul us off somewhere for serious interrogation."

The thought scared her to death. The laws in Europe were vastly different from back home. Rand would know this better than she did, thanks to his father's experience with the Italian police.

She started mentally tallying everything she owned, in the event it needed sold for her legal defense. There wasn't much. She'd sold her condo and was in hock up to her eyeballs, thanks to a gazillion dollars' worth of medical bills. She rubbed her arms through the thin windbreaker. "Are you going to stop?"

He had his gun hand braced on the lower curve of the wheel as he drove. "No sirens or lights. I don't think that's Interpol or the local cops on our ass." His tone was grim, and he cast another glance in the rearview mirror. His thigh flexed as he applied more pressure to the accelerator. The car shot forward as if jet-propelled. Someone honked loud and long as they passed. The trees alongside the road whizzed by at blistering speed in their headlights.

She frowned. "If it's not the police, then w—"

"Tighten your seat belt and hunker down." In case she didn't understand the "hunker down" part, he put his gun hand on her crown and shoved.

"Holy shit, Rand! Both hands on the wheel!" Dakota slid lower in the seat, her head sliding below the headrest.

He'd just wrapped his fingers back around the wheel when the truck was sideswiped with a loud crunching of metal and a bone-jarring shudder. A blare of horns from other cars trying to avoid being sideswiped by either the attack car or the truck reverberated in the night wind.

A metallic *bang-bang-bang* and the accompanying muzzle flashes indicated bullets hitting the body of the truck.

The blast of answering shots fired from Rand's gun made Dakota's ears ring in the close confines.

The bad guys volleyed back, a burst of gunfire peppering the steel body of the truck in a cacophony of bangs and metallic whines set her teeth and nerves on edge.

With a grinding, almost animal-in-pain sound, the car scraped down the driver's side. Their wheels squealed as Rand fought to stay on the road. "Fuck."

He could say that again.

He fired several more shots through his window, which were answered with several from the other car. Dakota saw the muzzle flashes in the darkness, and waited for a bullet to hit one of them.

No bullet through the brain, just the jolting impact of the other car slamming into them again, immediately accompanied by the shatter of breaking glass. The force jarred all the way down her spine as the truck slewed across the road with a high-pitched screech of the tires. "Son of a bi—"

"What?" She raised her eyes to try to see what was happening.

"Stay down!"

She buried her face in her lap. Something exploded through the window beside her, showering her with chunks of shattered glass that glimmered like diamonds on her clothing and hair in the lights of oncoming traffic. She squeezed her eyes shut and wrapped her arms over her head, bracing her feet on the floorboard as the car swerved and bumped over something, then swerved again. Blaring horns and squealing tires made her picture the drivers slamming on brakes and wrenching their cars out of the way of the careening truck.

Rand cursed again as the heavier vehicle slammed once more into the rear on the driver's side, pushing them partway into the ditch running alongside the road, a two-foot drop. The truck tilted dangerously, and Dakota grabbed the door handle and braced her feet.

"Don't worry," he yelled. "I'm still a member of the PDA."

"Public displays of affection?" Dakota yelled back, voice muffled by her lap.

"Professional Driving Association."

"Oh, yeah. That's the bunch that doesn't give disability insurance, right?"

"I've done dozens of high-speed chases. Just keep your head down. I'll lose them."

This wasn't a movie stunt where he had two or three rehearsals and several takes from different angles to make it look realistic. Rand wasn't going to lose them if they were attached like Velcro to the side of the truck. "Tell the director to yell 'cut' anytime soon."

The shrubs and tree branches in the ditch slapped the truck's body as he accelerated. The other vehicle body-slammed them from the rear, then again, shoving them forward toward a stand of trees visible in the cone of their headlights.

Another bullet whizzed through the truck, leaving the rear passenger window shattered, and the windshield with a vast spiderweb crack that made visibility difficult. Dakota dug her nails into the fake leather armrest on the door to prevent herself from shrieking every time the other car slammed into them, every time they got off another shot. Not for herself, hell, she'd be happy to scream her head off like a girl, but she didn't want to distract Rand, who was doing a masterful job.

He knew how to handle a car, thank God. However, when he'd done his job, he was working with other stuntmen. Not some homicidal maniac determined to kill him.

The truck lurched and bumped back onto the tarred road just shy of the trees, only to be hit again from behind. Her head snapped back. She didn't know what she could do to help. Shut up and not distract him was the best she could come up with.

She didn't know when she'd lifted her head from her knees, but if she was going to die, she'd prefer looking death in the eyes. She pulled the belt tighter across her body, keeping her head low but her eyes firmly fixed on the road illuminated in the headlights.

Rand's fingers were white as he clenched the steering wheel, then gave it a vicious tug that had her grabbing the dash with both hands as he swung the truck in an arc that left it pointing at their attackers—head-on.

No. No. No!

Aghast, she realized that far from slowing down, Rand was aiming straight for the other vehicle, a large black sedan with tinted windows, the front fender crumpled, one headlight shattered. A lethal Cyclops that Rand was going to play chicken with.

"Brace!" With a flip of his wrists, he sideswiped the

attack car, sending it skating across the road into an oncoming vehicle. Horns blared, lights tilted and dipped as the two cars spun out of control.

He floored the truck, did a wheelie, and kept going. Dakota smelled burning rubber. She pulled herself upright and turned to look behind them.

"I think you shook them." She swallowed. "You shook m—oh, damn it to hell! Here they come."

"See 'em." He had his foot hard on the accelerator. The truck shook and rattled with the speed. But this wasn't an Indy 500 race car. It was an old truck. The car behind them looked new, shiny, and heavy. And very, very determined.

He waited until they were inches from the bumper, then wrenched the wheel again, spinning the truck into a screeching, bone-rattling one-eighty. Dakota saw the other driver's face, his eyes wide as the two vehicles passed within inches of each other. Rand fired a shot, but they were traveling so fast Dakota had no idea if it found its mark.

"Got a hairbrush in that bag?"

Dakota slung the bag on her lap and rummaged through it. She leaned over, giving him the boar's-bristle brush without question.

"Here, stick this in there." He handed her his gun. "And this." His wallet and phone.

Dakota tossed everything into her tote and zipped it.

"Give it here." He took the bag, shoving it between his seat and the truck door. Not a particularly safe place to stash it.

"Slide over here, and hold the wheel." He manipulated the seat control and the seat slid back, giving him more legroom.

She had to undo her seat belt to accomplish that. Probably not a smart move under the circumstances. She slid across the cracked vinyl seat until she felt the heat of his body through her clothes.

"Eleven and three." He unbuckled his belt, then curled his warm hands over her freezing fingers to make sure her hands were where he wanted them. "Hold tight, they'll ram us again. Keep going straight."

Wind coming in the broken windows whipped her hair into stinging strands across her face. She had a death grip on the plastic steering wheel, her knuckles ghost-white in the near dark. She kept her eyes on the road, ignoring the trees and shrubs whizzing by in her peripheral vision. Rand contorted his body across her lap, thrusting his arm between her knees and down to the pedals to wedge the brush . . . somewhere. The truck's speed dropped so dramatically that the bad guy's car skimmed their bumper, then kept going right past them. Dakota had a glimpse of two men in the front seat, and then they were once again plunged into darkness.

"Get on my lap." Rand pushed against the door with his shoulder, then contorted to get his leg bent enough to give it a solid kick.

Horrified, she turned to look at him. "No wa—" He gave her a steely look in return. "You're *insane!*"

He finally managed to pop the driver's-side door open, and Dakota saw the black ground rushing below in the wedge of the open door as her bag flew out and disappeared from sight.

"Damn it to hell, that had all our stuff—" *Oh no, oh no, oh no.* Before she could retreat to her side of the seat, he grabbed her under the arms and lifted her onto his lap, facing forward, squeezed between his unyielding chest and the hard steering wheel. The truck swerved and danced across the road, and she had to grab his leg with one hand to keep her balance.

"You can't do this," she shouted over the crunch of gravel beneath the tires. The wind whipped her hair around them in a twisted tangle. "Rand, for God's sake. This isn't a movie set."

The steering wheel dug into her stomach. His chest was hard behind her, his thighs flexing as he rearranged his legs to accommodate her on his lap.

"It's going to be all right, sweetheart. Let me do the work. Keep your head down and tuck and roll. Let go of the wheel." He slid closer to the wide-open door. He half-stood, crushing her ribs against the steering wheel. Dakota wrapped her arms around the arm he had clamped around her midriff, cutting her circulation; his other arm protected her head. "Crazy damn man, who's going to protect *your* hard head?"

"That's my girl. Head down. Hold tight." His arms tightened like a vise around her, his body protecting hers. "Cowboy up. Ready?"

"No!"

Rand jettisoned them out of the car into the blackness of the night.

ELEVEN

R and landed hard, his left shoulder taking the brunt of the fall as he kept his body wrapped protectively around Dakota. No crash pad to land on in this stunt. Just skin meeting pavement. Not textbook-perfect in the stuntman's fall guide, but as far as he could tell, nothing was broken.

They slid, rolled, and bounced across the dirt verge for a hundred feet before slowing down on the softer grass. The slide felt like an eternity, but experience told him it was probably a minute or less before they came to a jarring stop.

Had anyone seen them bail?

If he had been capable of drawing a breath, he would have used it to curse. Having the wind knocked out of him still sucked after all these years, but he knew to take small sips of the warm evening air until his lungs inflated. His hand was over Dakota's breast, and he could feel her instinctively doing the same.

While it would've been excellent to stay right where he was in the cool grass, Dakota clasped in his arms, they needed to *move*. "How're you doing?" he whispered against her cheek as her breathing stabilized.

Her long hair was all over him. It smelled like lemons and crushed grass.

"Every bone in my body is broken," she informed him breathlessly, not moving as she labored to drag air into her lungs. "If you're not going to fling us into space again, could you loosen your arms a bit so I . . . can . . . breathe?"

Her bottom was pressed against his groin. Very much as it had been hours ago in the catacombs. Damned fool that he was, he didn't want to let her go. He loosened his grip, feeling the loss of her as she straightened her legs and rolled onto her back, panting.

He looked down the road, no curves, so he could see the taillights of their stolen truck as it kept going. A few seconds later, the sedan's headlights barreled toward them from the opposite direction. Thank God there were no other vehicles; the road was dark and deserted save for the truck and the attack car.

They were in the ditch, the darkness and long grass hiding them from view. But if the car stopped and the men got out, they'd be sitting ducks. Rand flattened his body, and watched the headlights spin as the car made a U-turn to come up on the rear of the truck. The truck was going about thirty-five miles per hour. Easy enough to catch. Two sets of red lights moved into the distance.

With a loud, grinding crash, the car slammed into the back of the truck, the sound horrifically close in the still night air. "Bad guys think we're still in there," Rand said softly, his attention on the road. No one would be looking back here, but he wasn't taking any chances with Dakota's life.

Another hard slam. Fainter this time as the vehicles moved away.

"Shouldn't we get going?" Dakota demanded, rising on her elbows to watch with him.

"Give it a few more minutes. If they see we aren't hunkered down in there, they're going to put two and two together and come loo—Jesus!" An earsplitting screech, ending abruptly in a loud crash and the sound of glass shattering, was followed by a ball of fire as the gas tank exploded. A spectacular display. Could've come from one of Creed's movies. Except this was real life, and someone wanted them seriously dead.

"God, what just happened?"

"They must have run the truck into a tree or wall or something immovable." Other than the distant glow of flames, the road was dark. No returning headlights. Not yet.

Dakota flopped her head back in the grass. There was enough starlight for him to see the gleam of her eyes and the sweat on her skin. She was disheveled beauty painted in black and white. "This is insane. Who *are* those guys?"

"I suspect the same people who killed Ham."

She frowned up at him. "How did they know where to find us?"

More important, *why* did they want to kill them? "An excellent question." He touched her cheek. Her skin was a little clammy from shock. And then, because he couldn't help himself, Rand curved his palm around her jaw. "Are you hurt anywhere other than bruises, lacerations, and all your bones being broken?"

"Isn't that enough? Why did you tell me to cowboy up? Was that some sort of code I should know?"

"In the business, it means doing a stunt you know is going to hurt."

"You could've filled me in on that little detail sooner."

"Still would've hurt." His chest hurt as he looked at her. A free fall would do that to a man, Rand knew. He'd experienced plenty of them. However, nothing in his life had given him the same sensation as when he looked at Dakota North. No matter what had happened between them, no matter how many questions remained unasked and unanswered, the sight of her stole his breath harder than a fall from a ten-story building. Or a moving vehicle.

He hadn't been able to stay with her, but he'd done a shitty job of living without her. Caught between a Scylla and a Charybdis. "Why are you here, Dakota?" *Here in France. Here in my arms. Here when I'd almost managed to forget you.*

She reached up and grazed his mouth with her fingertips, her lips curved in a Mona Lisa smile. "Some crazy guy threw me out of a moving car."

"Rude and extremely ungallant of him." He closed the few inches separating their mouths and bent his head to crush his lips over hers. Little flares of lust and greed exploded around his heart. Yeah, his dick was involved too, but he wasn't thinking that low.

Her mouth was hot as he speared his tongue inside. The familiar taste of her, butterscotch, went directly from his tongue to his groin. He ravaged her mouth, forgetting killers and unanswered questions. Forgetting past resentments and the grinding pain of losing her.

He fisted her glorious spill of hair. The scent of lemons, dust, and crushed green things filled his senses like a drug. Rand kissed her with everything he had. She responded by bracketing his face with her hands, murmuring low in her throat as her body arched to get closer.

He made love to her with his tongue and his lips, loving the heated sweetness of her butterscotch-flavored mouth, both hands tangled in the silky strands of fire spread across the grass.

He was out of his mind, Rand thought desperately, easing his lips from the cling of hers. He bent his head to press a kiss into the fragrant hollow of her throat, then reluctantly withdrew his fingers from her hair.

He lifted his head. "I think we managed to ditch them. Come on." He got to his feet—Jesus, everything hurt—and held out his hand. "We have a plane to catch." He pulled her to her feet. Her wildly tangled hair tumbled down her back, and she made a grimace of pain. "Seriously, how badly are you hurt?"

"Scrapes, bumps, and potential bruises. I'll live." Bunching her hair in both hands, she did some intricate knot thing at the back of her head that held it off her face. She glanced around. They were at the edge of an open field. Other than faint starlight, there wasn't another light to be seen. "Should I call a cab?" she asked lightly.

He brushed dirt and bits of grass from her arms, pretending he didn't see her wince, then looked back down the road. "Our turnoff was about a mile back. Can you walk?"

"Yes, but sadly, I can't dance. No rhythm. Lead on, Macduff. Oh! Wait. There's my bag! Woo and hoo!"

Rand walked a couple of hundred feet and picked it up from the middle of the road. Hooking it over his shoulder, he returned to where Dakota stood waiting.

"Thank God. Everything I own is in here. I can take it—"

"No. I've got it." Not trusting himself if he touched her again, Rand kept a couple of feet between them as they walked. She was a little stiff, but she didn't appear seriously hurt. Every muscle in her body had been jarred and would be hurting like hell, if not now, then come morning. Treating their injuries would have to wait until they were somewhere safe.

They kept to the verge where there were stands of tall trees and clumps of thick vegetation. Only one car approached. Rand pulled Dakota behind some low branches and waited until its taillights were red specks. A few minutes later, another car passed without fanfare; they ducked and covered, then continued walking. The trees thinned and the shrubs became more widely spaced for several hundred yards, leaving them exposed.

Rand debated skipping the small airfield, turning around, and walking the rest of the way into Fontaine-bleau, where he could find a hotel and check every inch of Dakota, making sure she was as fine as she claimed.

Honesty wasn't her strong suit. She'd walk with a broken leg if it proved a point. The airport sign, coming sooner than he'd anticipated, made the decision a no-brainer. "The private airfield is this way. It's a flight school as well, so they probably have someplace we can clean up."

His muscles were starting to protest, it had been a while since he'd dropped from a moving vehicle. He didn't miss it. If his body ached, Dakota must be in some serious pain. He indicated the bulky purse over his shoulder. "Got any aspirin in here?"

"Do you have a headache?"

"For you."

"We'll break them out and share when we get there, how's that? Boy, it's really dark out here, isn't it?"

His eyes had long since adjusted as he scanned their surroundings. Outside of town there was nothing to light their way but starlight, and that was blotted out by scudding cloud cover as the wind came up. "I'm fine."

"I remember. No drugs. Not even over-the-counter stuff."

The air smelled strongly of pine and dust as they walked, now in the middle of the dirt road, because either side was dense with thick shrubbery.

At the end of the road, they reached a large Quonset hut that served as the airport. The windsock stood out from its pole, flapping slightly in the wind, and the light above the steel door greeted them. He tried the handle, and thanked God it wasn't locked. He knew Dakota had given her last hurrah walking the mile to get here.

Rand eased open the door, noting that the light was on in the small office behind the counter, though not a soul was around. They walked through the silent hangar, where two Cessnas sat in the shadows, and entered the cramped, untidy office that smelled of jet fuel and dust. The wall clock showed it was just after 9 p.m. It felt a hell of a lot later.

As Dakota turned, he noticed the rip in the sleeve of her jacket for the first time, blood seeping a long wet stain on the fabric. He needed water, a first-aid kit—and to get her the hell back to Seattle.

"Someone left a note." She jerked her chin at the battered, paper-strewn desk, where a piece of foolscap with *MAGUIRE* scrawled across the top was propped against a bottle of wine and held down by a corkscrew.

Rand picked up the paper and sorted out the message among doodles depicting some sort of sprocket device. "The guy waited, but left after dark. He'll be back tomorrow morning. Let's see if there's running water and get you cleaned up."

"Excellent plan." She straightened her shoulders with a barely perceptible grimace of pain he would've missed if he hadn't been watching her so closely. "I don't know about you, but I need hot running water, a masseuse, and a chiropractor, not necessarily in that order."

"Let's hope we find at least one out of three." He smiled, because she honestly did need all three. Her hair was a wild tangle around her head and shoulders, the coppery strands filled with knots, leaves, and bits of twig. Her cheek had a raw scrape on it, and her face and clothing were filthy. The jackets she'd bought in Barcelona protected them from the worst of the road burn. Messy, dirty, exhausted, she looked like some mythical woodland creature sent to tempt a poor mortal.

Jesus. He must've hit his head to wax poetic at a time like this. "There's got to be some form of a bathroom around here."

They found a minute bathroom down a hallway from the office, equipped with a toilet and a sink. Dakota fumbled for the light switch, blinking into the sudden brightness. Clearly also used for storage, it was filled with stacks of boxes and odds and ends, including an enormous ashtray filled with a mound of cigarette butts drowned in coffee, or worse.

"I'll be quick."

He was caught by the light of humor in her pale green eyes as she wiggled her fingers for her tote. She was a mess, but the warm Dakota-scent of her skin, a scent no other woman had ever been able to duplicate with expensive perfumes and lotions, made his blood rush through his veins. "I want to look at that cut on the back of your arm. First let me get rid of this."

He picked up the ashtray with a rag he found in one of the boxes and carried it into the hallway. He came back and washed his hands, leaving the water running until it was hot.

"Take that off." He indicated the jacket.

She unzipped it and tossed it on top of the stack of boxes in the corner. "You're very bossy."

The skimpy tank top revealed where she was hurt. A few minor abrasions. The cut on her arm was the worst of it. There was a lot of blood. He crowded her against the sink, plopping her bag on a stack of boxes behind him. This was dangerously like old times, when they'd shared the bathroom before going to bed because to be apart for even those few minutes was too long.

She braced her hands beside her hips, which arched her back a little and showed the sweet plump curve of her breasts. When he raised his gaze to her face, her pretty green eyes glittered with amusement; she knew exactly what had his attention. She said with sassy good humor, "Apparently it's slipped your mind that I have two guns in that bag."

Rand grabbed a bunch of paper towels from the dispenser and tested the heat of the water on one finger. Satisfied, he wet the towels and squeezed them out. "*I* have the bag though, don't I? Turn around so I can clean that."

She presented her arm. The cut was long, but not as deep as he'd feared. He washed it gently to get out bits of gravel and debris, then went to work on various scrapes marring her fair skin.

"There's some hand sanitizer in *your* purse," she told him, her smile a little wilted. "Let's break out the aspirin while we're at it."

"Wash the parts you can reach while I look."

"Yes, sir." She washed her face with one hand, holding back her long hair with the other. Rand remembered Sunday mornings when she'd raced into the bathroom to wash her face and brush her teeth, then raced back into the bedroom to make love before he had to catch a plane back to LA.

He handed her more towels as she straightened, water dripping off her chin and eyelashes. "There's so much crap in here, I can't find anything. It's heavy enough to hold a bear trap." He handed it over. "Here, you look while I clean up."

Rand pulled his T-shirt over his head to assess the damage. Abrasions, a few holes, and dirt.

"Do you want me to—"

"Got it, thanks." God, no. He did not want her soft hands anywhere on his body. He washed as best he could, then dried off. It wasn't a shower, but it would have to do. They were both filthy. He looked up to find Dakota watching him in the fly-speckled mirror. She averted her gaze and finished going through her purse, placing his Glock and wallet on the edge of the sink. Her fingers shook.

"Need to pee?" he asked gently. She had passed exhausted and gone straight to being seconds from falling face-first on the floor, unconscious. He knew the signs. She nodded. Rand edged past her. "Get it done. I'll be right outside." He closed the door.

DAKOTA STARED BLANKLY AT herself in the mirror, then grimaced and shook her head. She looked almost worse than she felt. Her hair was a disaster, and her clothes were ripped. The scrape on the back of her arm stung like fire ants were attacking, and her muscles quivered with strain and exhaustion. "Oh, right. That's what happens when you get thrown out of a truck going the speed of light."

Rand banged on the door. "You all right in there?"

"I need ten minutes." Ten hours would be better.

"You have two."

She dragged her tank over her head, and shouted through the door, "What's your hurry, Maguire?" Then under her breath, "Ow. Ow. Ow." Every scrape and muscle she flexed made itself felt. "Seriously ow!"

"You're going to want to be horizontal in two minutes or less, trust me."

"Don't stand there listening to me, go find us something to eat."

"Minute forty."

She heard the scrape of his shoes on the cement floor as he wandered off. She wasn't crazy about her Wild Woman of Borneo look, but her brush had gone up in flames for the cause. Finding a scrunchie in the bottom of her tote, she finger-combed the debris out of her hair, tying it back so she could wash the ground-in dirt and assorted vegetation off at least her top half.

After using the facilities, she took out Rand's T-shirt and boxers from the day before, and her own clothing she hadn't had time to wash in Paris. Since she had no idea when or where she'd have another opportunity to do any more shopping, it was now or whenever as far as clean clothes went.

Using the sliver of rock-hard soap and hot water, she washed the handful of T-shirts and underwear, then hung everything on the towel bar to dry.

Resisting the idea that the floor was a good place to rest, she stripped off her ripped jeans and underwear, pulled on the black cotton drawstring pants, and dragged a clean but wrinkled tank top over her now swimming head. She leaned her hip on the sink to pull the tank down.

That depleted her last store of energy, and she began to shake in earnest. Shock, fear. "Ha!" Insanity.

"Dakota—"

She pulled the door open. Rand leaned against the jamb. He straightened, took one look at her face, and said roughly, "Damn it, woman!" And swung her up in his arms. "What the hell were you doing in there? Remodeling?"

"Beating your underwear on a rock."

"You're not making sense. Time for bed. Hit the light."

He turned so she could reach the switch. Dakota flipped it, plunging the area into twilight, then wrapped both arms around his neck, letting her head drop to his chest and the steady thump of his heartbeat. She closed her eyes. "Don't toy with me, Maguire."

The large hangar where the planes were parked was cool, but Rand's body felt blazing hot as he carried her to a far corner. "As wiped out as I am," she said against the steady pulse at the base of his throat, "I am *not* sleeping in some strange and skanky Frenchman's bed."

"It warms my heart to hear it," he said dryly. Rand's tenderness made her eyes prickle and her heart ache. He was only teasing, she knew, but it had been so long since he'd looked at her in any way other than with varying degrees of anger and mistrust. Too long.

He dropped to one knee, her body cradled easily in his arms. She tightened hers around his neck, not ready to break contact. "How very Prince Charming of you," she murmured, looking at him, grateful that the gloom hid her face.

His smile caught the distant light from the office, looking so sweet, so dear, that Dakota's throat closed. "Not a skanky Frenchman's bed," he assured her. "Just a pallet of packing blankets on the floor."

He lowered her onto a fairly soft surface, then pulled a dusty-smelling blanket over her. "This is about as soft, and fairly clean, as I could manage—damn it, you're shivering."

He lay down beside her, slipped under the blanket, and wrapped his arms around her. Pulling her carefully against his chest, he rubbed his hand up and down her back, her bottom, her shoulders. . . . "Reaction, and it's colder than hell in here." He rubbed a little more briskly, clearly forgetting the road rash. "Let's get you warmed up, then I'll see what I can find to eat around here."

"After-danger sex would probably warm me faster than a brisk back rub, Maguire." Despite the furnace of his body, she was freezing and couldn't stop shaking. However, the friction of his hands, the nudge of his knee between hers, was starting to warm her nicely.

"Oh, damn, sorry. Did that hurt?"

"No," she lied, because Rand touching her wasn't what had ever hurt her. Tilting her head, she kissed the underside of his prickly jaw. "Isn't that a thing? After-danger sex? If not, it should be written into the handbook."

She felt his smile against her forehead. "You were just thrown out of a moving vehicle—I don't think wild monkey sex is going to do you any good right now at all."

She didn't know about wild monkeys, but the sex part right now sounded good. She'd take what she could get when she could get it. "Would it do you any good?"

"Making love with you? Always." His warm hand slipped under her tank top to stroke up and down her back. "God, I'd almost forgotten how soft you are. We're lucky you got away with strained muscles, road rash, and every bone in your body broken. The latter could've been a real—goddamn it!"

She jerked at his intensity. "Oh, hell. Now what?"

"Just found another scar."

She relaxed. "We're both covered with them," she said reasonably, pulling his head down to kiss him.

"I hate that you were hurt," he murmured against her lips. "I hate that I wasn't—"

"Shh. No recriminations. Not tonight, okay?"

His knee was caught between her thighs now, and she shifted just enough so it could go higher, where the pressure would do her some good. Dakota slid her hand under his T-shirt, speared her fingers through the crisp, dark hair on his toasty-warm chest, and placed her palm over the steady beat of his heart. "You knew what you were doing. I wasn't worried." *Much.*

He laughed as he tangled one hand in her hair, sifting through the strands hypnotically. "Liar. Your 'no' was heard in California."

"It happened too quickly for me to be truly scared," she told him honestly. "And I trust you, Rand. I knew that you would make sure I was safe. Thank God for your expertise and experience so you knew what to do, and when and how to do it."

Dakota played with his nipple, which responded just as hers did when touched. "Although"—she rolled her head to kiss his chest, then his shoulder—"I will remind you that you owe me a boar's-bristle hairbrush. And sometime, preferably in the very near future, a deep soak in a bathtub filled with bubbles." *And you.*

Rand used to tease her about her love of bubble baths, until she'd introduced him to the pleasures of shoulder-deep hot water, slippery shower gel, and a shower wand.

"I enjoyed our baths." He rested his chin on top of her head as his hand changed direction to stroke a long glide down her spine. "The scented bubbles not so much." His hand slid inside the waistband of her drawstring pants to stroke her butt. Dakota wiggled closer and wanted to purr.

She ran her fingers through the springy hair on his chest; wanting the feel of it against her sensitized breasts. She caressed between his pecs as his knee rose a little higher. She was warming up nicely, and nuzzled the underside of his jaw, loving the scratchy, soft texture on her lips.

"Did you ever think how little time we actually spent together? Your job. My job . . ." He was stroking her with purpose. They both had on far too many clothes. "Out of about a hundred and four weekend days that year, we spent less than half of those together. I counted."

She brought her hand out from under his shirt and started the process of tugging it off. "That worked out to be forty-six days, including the four we took off to go to Napa." Being ambidextrous, she used one hand to tug the shirt up his chest from the front, and the arm she had beneath his head to snag it from the back. The man didn't stand a chance.

"So really," she told him very seriously between nibbles to his throat, "we knew each other for about six weeks." His ear was fair game, and she nibbled and laved it with her tongue until she felt the jut of his penis against her thigh. She painted a wet swirl, felt his responsive shudder, then moved down the tendons in his neck with licks and light nips guaranteed to drive him wild. "If you figure we spent three quarters of that time in bed, we really only spent about a week and a half getting to kno—"

With a shout of laughter, Rand rolled her onto her back, bracketing her shoulders with his arms so he could look down at her. He plucked a long strand of her hair off her nose, using it to paint delicate strokes across her lips. "Do you really want to talk about this now?"

"*This* is why we never talked before," she pointed out reasonably as she tugged his T-shirt up. He let go of her hair and helped her pull the fabric over his head, bunching it in one hand, and flinging it over his shoulder like a marauding Viking.

She arched her throat to give him better access as he kissed and nibbled his way to her breasts.

She melted at the first hot, wet sweep of his tongue circling the areola on her left breast.

"We had better things to do." The hot suction of his mouth made her back arch.

"Oh, verily," she teased breathlessly, spearing her fingers through his thick, silky hair to hold his head exactly where she wanted it. "We certainly did. But we didn't . . . get . . . to know . . ."

He slid down, lowering his head so he could nuzzle her belly, following his hands with his mouth as he slowly—painfully—moved, kissing his way up her torso again while he skimmed the tank over her head. Tossing her top aside, he looked down at her, eyes gleaming in the semidarkness. "My business was in LA, yours in Seattle. We did what we could, met when we could. . . ."

It had never been enough. Trips to and from airports, frantic kisses. Urgency. Heat. Passion.

"Hello sex," he murmured.

"Good-bye sex," she countered.

"Hello sex melding with good-bye sex. There went our whole weekend."

Neither of them had complained.

Dakota felt as though she were being given something infinitely precious in this moment. This slow build was something they'd rarely taken the time for. She knew it couldn't last, but she wanted to remember every brush of his hand, every stroke of his tongue.

"Talk," he murmured against the corner of her mouth, putting his palm to her cheek. "Later." His lips stroked tenderly over hers, once, twice. Soft as a butterfly's wings. Banking the power behind a touch so exquisitely gentle, so filled with intent, Dakota's entire body caught fire in response.

She lifted her head, drawing his head closer, fingers threaded in his hair. Rand's mouth crushed down on hers, his tongue spearing inside. Starving for this, she feasted on the taste of him. The brief encounter in the field earlier had just been a prelude, the hors d'oeuvre.

This was the main course.

✦ TWELVE ✦

Dakota smelled of unfamiliar soap and tasted of minty toothpaste. He barely tasted the lies. Rand didn't care. The press of her body and the ravenous heat of her mouth blotted out moral judgments or the need for full disclosure. He was drawn to her as he'd been to no other woman before or since.

Raw sex was what they both needed, not analyzing. Not thinking. Just feeling.

He moved from her mouth, kissed her throat again, but when he nibbled lightly, she froze and a whimper escaped her lips in a soft rush. He lifted his head. "Damn. Sorry. I forgot—" That she'd taken a beating an hour ago.

"I'm okay. I'm okay. Come back here." She guided his head back to her breast, and he felt her lips graze his temple as she did that sexy hum of arousal that shot his own lust-meter even higher.

She felt perfect in his arms. But then, she always had, damn her. He felt the soft, plump press of her breasts and pebbled nipples against his chest. Smelled her arousal and felt his own in every thudding heartbeat as she pressed full-length against him.

"Any special requests?" he asked against the underside of her breast. He nuzzled higher, closing his lips around the hard peak of her nipple, grazing it lightly with his teeth the way he knew she liked it. He wished there were more than the iffy light. He wanted to see her to compare his memories of her body with reality.

Her fair skin was incredibly soft and silky against his lips as he lazily trailed his mouth across each nipple, then breathed on her damp skin until she shuddered.

"No." Her sexy murmur was soft with amusement. "I'm enjoying your improv. Carry on."

"How's this?" He tugged the nipple into the heated cavern of his mouth, sucking delicately until her back arched off the blankets. "Good?"

In response she pulled his hair, and he returned to the other breast before moving down.

Tracing the circle of her navel with his lips and tongue, Rand slid one hand beneath the soft curve of her ass, lifting her slightly to his mouth.

He threaded his fingers through hers and held them over her head as he moved down her body. She'd always bathed before bed, but he realized he preferred her with the sexy smell of the day on her skin. Hell, who was he fooling? She could roll in a mud puddle and he'd want her. All the scents of her body turned him on. Shower or no shower, she always smelled of Dakota, and God only knew, that gave him an erection.

He trailed his lips across her belly. Her cool skin warmed to his touch, and he stroked his lips to the tender crease at the top of her legs. She slipped her fingers from his and trailed them up and down his arms as he moved her body where he knew she'd get the most sensation.

This was all for her.

Rand buried his face in the soft thatch of damp gingery curls at the juncture of her thighs, and inhaled the essence of her. The fragrance of her arousal almost made him come. He slid his hand up the inside of her thigh, and with his other, brought her hips higher, like an offering to his marauding mouth. The sharp sting of her nails in his skin hiked the ante.

He pushed her legs wider, opening the folds so he could suckle and tease her. Lapping the swollen bud until she shifted restlessly, Rand ran his hand down her leg, and she brought both up over his shoulders, opening herself for him.

Eagerly, crazed with lust, his dick so hard it was painful, Rand parted her dewy heat with his tongue and sucked on her clit. His name echoed in the vast open hangar, and her nails scored his shoulders as her hips arched off the pallet with a lightning-fast climax.

Dakota's hands tangled in his hair, a good hard grip that almost—but not quite—lifted his head from his target. He grunted in protest as he speared his tongue inside the slick heat.

She got a tight, stinging grip. "S-stop tormenting me, Rand! Make love to me. I need to feel you inside me—"

"Not yet." His voice, muffled as it was, was implacable. Too bad he couldn't taste her and make love to her at the same time.

She tried to shift her legs from his shoulders. "N—" Her order was cut off by a sob of pleasure jerking her body.

He slid two fingers inside her, and she arched again, rising higher in the cup of his hand under her butt. "Better?" He inhaled the sweet and salty of her, dragging as much of her scent into his lungs as he could. Nectar of Dakota. Yeah. Didn't get much better than this.

"I can't take any more!"

Rand smiled against her inner thigh. "Now?"

"Do it, you've made me crazy!"

In a smooth move, he surged up her body and plunged his throbbing dick inside the pulsing wet heat of her. Her feet crossed in the small of his back as she met each thrust with a countermove that flung him off a cliff. The shudders racked him for what felt like an eternity, and the space of a heartbeat. He collapsed on top of her, their sweating skin glued together as they panted and wheezed against each other's necks.

She lifted a hand to touch him, then dropped it limply to the side, too spent to move. "I suppose," she murmured weakly, her internal muscles still clenching around him, "it's a bit late to mention I have a family pack of condoms in my purse?"

Rand smiled against her sweaty throat. "The night's young. We both know sleep's highly overrated."

MONK'S EYES NARROWED TO dangerous slits as he enunciated clearly and succinctly, "Both dead." He didn't raise his voice, and it was not a question. His hands, relaxed and hanging over the arms of his chair, flexed. No fists. No overt show of anger. But inside he seethed.

Szik's eyes flickered from the medieval instruments laid out neatly on a chamois to the Cuban smoldering in the Baccarat ashtray on the small inlaid table beside his chair. The man couldn't get any pastier. He cast his gaze down again and licked his bloodless lips. "An unfortunate accident, Father. One that I deeply regret."

Deeply regret, you little turd? Deeply REGRET? All these years of meticulous planning, years of living an exemplary life, had just disintegrated in a puff of smoke, because the people he held accountable, the people he trusted in his own limited way, failed him. He should've known that if one wanted a job done well, one did it one's self. Unfortunately, he couldn't be in *two* fucking places at once. Monk shifted in his chair.

"Unfortunate *accident*? A high-speed car chase was an unfortunate *accident*? What other outcome could there possibly be when a man is chased by would-be assassins in the dead of night on an open road? If you had thought the scenario through, you would have ensured that Dr. North was secured safely somewhere else. *Before* he was killed."

"I failed you, Father."

Failed? Without Dr. North's input and expertise, it was impossible to go forward with his well-crafted, carefully thought-out marketing plan. No. Not impossible. Nothing was impossible. Her death made what he wanted to do more . . . challenging.

Monk was not in the mood to be challenged. He was not in the mood to have his plans thwarted or delayed. Yet here he was. Forced to endure all three.

"Was that irony, my son? Because the word *failed* is a gross understatement." Rapture labs would have to be established in key markets. That meant more time. More personnel. And more opportunities for people to cheat him. Szik was a necessary evil, and would have to be eliminated when the time was right. That was a task scheduled on his calendar, and one he had to do himself. Clearly, he could trust no one else.

This new development was unacceptable on every level. Sweat beaded his brow as he thought of the ramifications of not having the doctor's expertise and knowledge for this final, critical phase of the project. Years of grueling work were coming down to a two-week window. Monk had timed this like a precise Swiss watch. Every moving part had been carefully manipulated, and then put into play.

"I instructed that *only* Maguire be eliminated. I instructed that Dr. North be taken directly *to the lab*. Was that order too *complicated* for you, Szik?"

"No, Father. I would have gone—I would have gone myself, but you told me to—"

"It's my fault you failed? Is that what you're telling me, my son?"

"No, Father."

"You confirmed that both the man and Dr. North were inside the incinerated vehicle? That they are both indeed dead?" Monk still held a tiny spark of hope. She would be useful even if in traction. Burn victims were notoriously easy to control. Dead was final. Critically injured was something he could work with.

Szik's lashes fluttered, and his head bowed even lower. "Of course, Father."

"And Branah and Raimi?" Driving the vehicle sent to retrieve Dr. North. "What became of them?"

"I had them t-terminated, Father. It was made to look like a head-on collision."

He thought he was so damned clever. He wasn't paid to think. He was paid to make things happen.

Monk wanted to kill him. Quickly. He couldn't stand to look at Szik's face one more second. But sometimes expediency was not as satisfying as a slow, drawn-out conclusion. Why deprive himself of at least a modicum of pleasure? Slow was much more satisfactory. It would also show his other subordinates that when he gave an order, that order was to be obeyed. Instantly, and to the letter.

THEY LEFT AS SOON as the manager of the airport showed up the next morning. He bore a fat loaf of crusty bread, cheese, and strong coffee in a thermos. Fortified, they paid cash for the rental, and took off.

"For all he knows, we could be stealing this pretty plane," Dakota pointed out as they taxied down the runway. It was a perfect flying day, the sun shining, the air clear and still.

"He was reimbursed well," Rand said, scanning the fields as they passed to check for anything out of the ordinary. They lifted off without incident, and he allowed himself to relax for the duration. "I'll make sure he gets it back in one piece."

"Good." She settled more comfortably in her seat, looking fresh and pretty. She'd covered the abrasions on her cheek with expertly applied makeup and wore large sunglasses to shade her bright eyes.

She was dressed in fashionably wrinkled white cotton pants and an off-the-shoulder, long-sleeved black T-shirt that showed off her pale skin and two angry red scratches near her neck.

Her glorious hair, fiery and so touchable it took everything in Rand not to reach out and run his fingers through it as he'd done the night before, was corralled into a low ponytail. Despite the lack of a hairbrush, she'd managed to tie back the thick wavy length with a black-and-white scarf. She looked like she'd just stepped out of the pages of a fashion magazine. She had never looked like a chemist.

Dr. Dakota North was a resourceful woman.

"I'd hate to cheat him," she said, turning her head to give him a smile. "He brought us breakfast."

"He would've gotten an eyeful for his trouble if he'd shown up ten minutes earlier," Rand said dryly.

"True. This is nice, isn't it? Peaceful, drama free."

"Yeah. It's great." He wondered how long the détente and the peace would last.

An experienced pilot, Rand directed the rented Cessna toward Umbria's capital, Perugia, where the prison was located. He enjoyed flying, especially when he had terrific weather and a tailwind. The sky was a crystal-clear pale blue with ten-mile visibility and just a little haze in the distance as they flew over the mountains. He pointed out Mont Blanc and other landmarks on the route. They talked about food, and wine, and Zak and Acadia. Whom, Rand realized, Dakota knew quite well. Better than he did, given that he lived in LA and his friend in the Pacific Northwest.

"I don't know how you live with this sustained cloak-and-dagger stuff day in and day out," she said, peering down at what appeared to be a toy train cutting through brilliant green fields. "It's exhausting."

He smiled. "Hardly. This isn't how my jobs go normally. My team and I show up, we do our jobs without any drama or fanfare, and then we take a nice chunk of change home at the end of the day. In all the years since I started the security business, I've never once drawn my weapon. Never needed to."

"Good," she said emphatically.

"Just so you know, I'm determined to find whoever's behind this. For a dozen reasons, not the least of which is this might very well be the person who burgled your house, put incriminating shit on your iPad, and tried to run us down yesterday. The list is fucking growing by leaps and bounds."

"We're in this together." Dakota swiveled her head to face him, her eyes masked by large dark glasses.

"Yeah. We are." But the truth of the matter was that yesterday's high-speed chase had hit dangerously close to home. They could've been killed. *She* could've been killed.

He hoped like hell his father could provide some answers.

He rotated his shoulders to ease the tension, a product of anticipating seeing Paul again. His father wasn't an easy man—an understatement. He was a sanctimonious asshole, and a bully. Rand preferred keeping their face-to-face contact to a minimum.

Paul's assets had been frozen by his wife's Seattle lawyers until the charges against him were either dropped, or he was imprisoned.

It was Rand who paid the astronomical prices for the team of defense lawyers. That, and being civil, was the best he could manage.

Strapped in beside him, Dakota was holding the case that had contained the vials loosely on her lap, keeping track of where the second bad guy was. Currently, the GPS coordinates put the guy in northern Italy.

He didn't know what the guy was doing there, Rand thought, mildly annoyed, because he hadn't had contact with his men since the day before. But that could be for many reasons. He didn't want to believe they'd lost their quarry and weren't responding because they had fuck-all to tell him.

He regarded her thoughtfully. There was no sign of her being a white-knuckle flyer now. Stretched out as best she could manage in the confined space, Dakota looked as perfectly relaxed as a cat napping in the sunshine. As usual, she had her shoes kicked off. The shoes were sky-high black heels, which, like everything else they both wore, had been in her voluminous bag.

They had a tacit agreement to keep the personal from seeping into the already explosive situation, and when she wasn't making calculations on the handheld GPS, she spent the trip looking out the window or dozing.

Which was fine. Talking to Dakota was a minefield, and for the duration he'd like to bask in the warmth of the postcoital glow, and leave it at that.

Sex with her had been inevitable. The chemistry between them had never been an issue. That hadn't changed. At least she couldn't lie with her body; he knew that too well to be fooled by fake passion. Although he acknowledged to himself that a lot of men believed the same fucking thing. Still, he did know her body. Her mind was another matter altogether.

He checked the coordinates and landmarks. They were a hundred miles from the airport.

Umbria evoked the Middle Ages, with its mountains and hills, streams and valleys. The countryside was lush, the rolling green hills punctuated with the dusty gray of endless olive groves, emerald-green terraced vineyards, and orchards. The rustic landscape was dotted with historic hill towns of pinkish gray rock, set like semiprecious stones in nooks and crannies of vegetation.

He checked his airspeed for the descent. "We'll be landing in about ten minutes."

Dakota slipped her heels on. "How far is it to the prison?"

"Only about seven miles out of town."

She checked around her seat to make sure she had

everything stuffed back in her tote. "When were you here last?"

"I had to come early to set up security for the wedding, and made a quick trip here first." Paul hadn't been that pleased to see him. It wasn't like the old man had a social life—he was with the other inmates for an hour a day, with an hour outside, and had unlimited access to his legal team. One would think he'd be starved for any form of social interaction. Apparently not.

"How's your father doing?" Dakota shoved her sunglasses on top of her head, making the diamond studs in her ears sparkle in the sunlight streaming through the windows. "It must be hard for such an active man to be—"

"He's doing okay, all things considered." It was damned hard to dredge up the old resentment, considering the night they'd just spent, and in the bright light of day it was harder still to maintain his stance. It was what it was. No matter who was to blame, the bottom line was Paul was in prison, and it didn't look good for him being released anytime soon.

"Check the bad guy's location again before we land, would you? I'm surprised Ligg and Rebik haven't called in to let us know their status."

He'd called his assistant, Cole. Voice mail. He'd called Creed. Voice mail. He'd called his office in Los Angeles. His receptionist, Kristin, had answered. She was just as worried now as Rand—she'd thought he was with the rest of the team. It seemed that nobody knew where the fuck half his team was. They'd disappeared off the map and he was left out here swinging in the wind without help or backup.

Kristin asked if he wanted the men who'd just returned to head back to Europe, but after a moment, he said no. This wasn't a situation that required that many people. With two of his men on the trail of the bad guy, he figured that was sufficient. For now. Instead, he instructed her to have them check into the disappearance of the men they'd left behind.

This wasn't adding up, no matter how he looked at it.

It seemed a stretch—a *big* stretch—to think that the men were in cahoots with the bad guys. He'd known most of them from his stunt days. They were people, men and women, he trusted. But offer enough incentive, and a man could crumple as easily as a used tissue. He hoped to hell they *weren't* part of this. Right now Dakota's *don't trust anyone* philosophy seemed like a sound plan.

They'd lost one lead; he didn't want to lose the second. Rand had a bad feeling. Ligg was experienced and exceptionally fast on his feet. Rand trusted him to keep their quarry in sight without engaging. Once he'd questioned Paul, he planned to rendezvous with them and assess the situation himself—but he had to see his father first.

He couldn't believe how quickly and thoroughly everything had gone wrong. The wedding fiasco, the dead waiter, the mass murder in Barcelona, Ham's death . . . now an assassin on his ass. Hard to give chase when he was being chased himself. He hoped the lucrative deal he'd made with the guy from the flight school would prevent him from talking if anyone asked. Rand wasn't going to hold his breath. Rand knew the authorities must have his name by now, and there was a strong possibility, if it wasn't already done, that his photo would be next.

"Anything?" he asked, starting their descent while she was still rummaging in that bottomless bag of hers.

"Got it!" Dakota pulled the hard case and handheld GPS out of her bag again. "Hang on a sec." She quickly tapped in the longitude and latitude she was seeing in her head. Her ability was extraordinary, and uncannily accurate. Rand took back everything he'd thought when first Stark and then Dakota claimed to have this amazing tracking ability. Without her, he would've been screwed.

"He/she/it is now in a town called Berat, Albania."

"Damn it. I wish to hell I knew if Ligg and Rebik were close or looking for their asses with both hands, *miles* away."

"If they read their texts, they're right there with the bad guy."

When they hadn't responded to his voice mails, he'd texted both of them the GPS coordinates every hour for the last eight. There'd been zero fucking response. "Yeah. If."

"I can tell you exactly where they are."

"I *knew* you had a crystal ball in there."

"Something better and far more accurate." She shot him a sassy smile despite the edge to his levity, a smile that did a number on his heartbeat. She dove back into her bag.

As she searched for whatever, he powered back and leveled off, increasing the amount of pressure on the yoke, adjusting the aileron in the crosswind so the nose rose slightly. The wheels bit the tarmac with a screech, and he slowed and taxied across the runway's centerline to the private terminal.

"Hang on a sec—okay." She held the small aluminum case and the GPS again, then turned her head to look at him. He saw his own reflection, not a happy camper, in her sunglasses.

"Can you give me a minute, or do you want to wait until we're in the terminal?"

"Here." He applied the brakes and taxied in. "How are you doing this magic?" If she said she knew where his men were, she knew.

"I appropriated Ligg's sunglasses and Rebik's Swiss Army knife back in Paris."

"Devious."

The sunny smile disappeared as a cloud of hurt moved in. "Yeah. So I've been told."

THEY WENT TO RENT a car. "Let's get a scooter," Dakota suggested. "The wind in our hair, the sun on our backs?"

"Not much to protect us if someone tries running us off the road again."

She grimaced. "Good point."

Rand pointed to a sports car with the roof folded down. The kind of car he would've rented if they'd indeed come to Europe for their honeymoon. "How about that little blue job over there?"

Her face lit up. "Perfect."

It didn't take long to do the paperwork, and they were on their way. "You know, your father isn't going to want to see me," Dakota pointed out, holding her hair back and lifting her face to the sun. The wind teased bright banners of molten copper out in a stream behind her.

No fucking shit. Rand wouldn't have wanted to chit-chat with the woman responsible for putting him away in a foreign prison either.

Flanking the road were vineyards as far as the eye could see. "Were you serious when you said you'd testify on his behalf?"

She hesitated a beat too long, then said into the wind, "I'll try, but I won't perjure myself. Not for old time's sake. And not even for you."

"I figured. And this is a meeting better done alone. I know a decent hotel in Perugia—you can shower and rest up while I go see him." Rand wasn't looking forward to the visit.

He and his father had always had an adversarial relationship. His mother, whom Rand had adored, for all her faults, held the purse strings. Old oil money. His father hadn't liked toeing the line; instead of taking it out on his golden goose, he'd made Rand his whipping boy. His parents had been two dogs with one bone, each using their only child to motivate and manipulate the other. They'd professed to love each other, and yeah, his father had been devastated when his wife died. But for Rand, growing up in a war zone, their abiding love had been fucking impossible to understand.

Paul's imprisonment for the last two years was frustrating and depressing for his father, not to mention expensive and frustrating for Rand. Instead of assisting the legal team, Paul was constantly coming up with ways they could do their job better, which delayed proceedings while they tried to sort out his paper trail.

Rand tried to be understanding. Paul desperately missed his wife. He maintained his innocence to anyone who'd listen. Even if he was found not guilty of the premeditated murder charge, he'd certainly be imprisoned for involuntary manslaughter.

He'd been in Capanne prison for twenty-five months already, and he was understandably stir-crazy, as the Italian justice system moved slowly. Of course, he took no responsibility for his own delaying tactics and their effects.

Rand and Dakota checked into the small hotel. "Go ahead and go to the room," he said. "I'll probably be an hour or so. Then we can go and grab something to eat."

She shook her head. "I'm going with you."

"I don't think that's a good idea. He doesn't like anyone seeing him like that."

"Like what?" Dakota asked dryly, tucking her hand in his arm, steering him back outside. "In prison? Probably not. But we worked together for years, and he respected, if not me, then my work. There are questions I can ask him, or he may say something that you'd miss—I don't know, but if there's a chance he knows something, I want to be there. Four ears are better than two."

Rand agreed. He still wanted to give her an out. "He might not want to see you."

She shrugged, looking very French as she did so. "Let's deal with that if and when it happens."

He opened the passenger door. "Your chariot awaits."

"Barring people trying to shoot us or run us off the road, we can enjoy the short trip, right?"

He smiled back, unable to resist tucking a long strand of coppery hair behind her ear. "Right." He got in and started the car.

He had to gird himself for the upcoming confrontation—because a confrontation was always what their meetings were. He just wanted this one over with.

It was almost a relief to see the sign: *Casa Circondariale di Perugia.* Capanne prison. They had to show identification to the guard at the gate, a big fucking problem if they were followed, but there was no choice. They were allowed to pass through to the parking lot. More ID checks along the way. As they turned into the designated parking place, Dakota reached and laid her hand on his arm. "I know you've heard your father's point of view for the last two years, but I'm asking that you please keep an open mind right now. I swear to you, I didn't give Paul the drugs he administered to your mother. I swear on everything we shared. He lied to save his skin. I understand that need."

"Yeah. So do I. There's a lot of shit that doesn't add up. Let's go in and see what Paul has to say when you confront him face-to-face."

She bit her lip, her eyes shining as she said thickly, "Thank you."

"Don't thank me yet."

Dakota left her bag locked in the trunk, and they went through the process of being searched and checked in before being escorted to the visitors' room by two officers. Rand figured if he didn't ask if Paul would see Dakota, he wouldn't have the chance to say no.

His father was wearing regular clothes. Jeans and a sweatshirt over a blue dress shirt, and waited at a table, having been told he had visitors while they were filling in the required paperwork. Other than him, the large, sunlight-filled room was empty, but two guards were stationed outside. Paul had been a model prisoner and wasn't considered a risk. Clearly, the prison officials hadn't been sliced by his acerbic tongue.

They crossed the cement floor, their footsteps unmistakable on the hard surface. His father didn't look up.

Paul's style of dress and meticulous grooming hadn't changed despite his incarceration. A fit and healthy-looking sixty-seven, he had salt-and-pepper hair, buzz-cut close to his scalp to disguise the fact that it was almost nonexistent on top.

Rand knew his father was aware of their presence long before they arrived at the table in the far back corner. Paul liked to keep his back to the wall. The chairs scraped as Rand pulled two away from the table.

"Hello, Paul." Dakota curled her fingers around the back of a chair.

Paul lowered his glasses to glance up from the book he was reading. He ignored Dakota. "I saw you last week when you and Seth came. What's this visit in aid of?"

Rand tried to gauge the older man's reaction as he said, "Dakota flew in from Seattle because we had a situation at the wedding."

Paul removed his glasses, folding the earpieces before placing them squarely on top of his open book. He met Rand's eyes with no expression. Dakota had gone from Paul's most promising young chemist to the woman who'd framed him for murder, without any noticeable transition.

"My trial starts in days." His father folded his well-manicured, slightly arthritic hands on the table. "Is she here to *help* me this time, or is she going to fucking lie to keep herself pure and blameless?"

"She's standing right here, why don't you ask her yourself?" Rand suggested.

"Someone is demonstrating DL6-94's potential to prospective buyers." Dakota skipped the social niceties and got right to the point. "We believe someone intends to manufacture Rapture and flood the market with it."

"*Flood* the market?" Paul raised a brow. "Surely no one would *flood* the market. If, as you say, someone has their hands on a formula that the authorities believe was destroyed, one would think that they—whoever they may be—wouldn't be stupid enough to make the product that readily available. Not a good business model. That would drive down the price." He glanced at Rand. "How *was* the wedding?"

"Eventful, and not in a good way." He watched his father's face carefully to gauge his response. He sat down, because he didn't want to. He'd rather be outside in the fresh air. He wanted to be driving back to the small hotel and making love to Dakota. Hell, he wanted to be anywhere other than where he was. He'd taught himself in his mid-twenties that he wasn't the fuckup loser Paul insisted he was. But whenever he was near the son of a bitch, Rand felt diminished. Which in turn pissed him off. He was excellent at what he did, had been well respected in Hollywood, where his stunts had won him awards and the respect of his peers. Had a thriving, successful security business—

"Someone dosed the guests with Rapture," he said, cutting to the chase.

Paul's eyebrows rose, and it was like looking at himself in thirty years. Cold clenched his gut. Everything Rand despised in Paul was a character trait he himself carried. If and when he recognized a trigger, Rand did everything in his power to eradicate it.

"Impossible," the older man told him unequivocally, mouth twisting in derision as he put his glasses back on, adjusting the earpiece before saying, "The formula was destroyed years ago."

Rand gave Paul a cool look. "Apparently not."

His father's mouth tightened, and he waved a dismissive hand. He still wore the wedding band Rand's mother had put on his finger thirty-six years before. The light from the window on the opposite wall shone on the lenses of his glasses, obliterating the expression in his eyes. Rand didn't need to see it to know what it was.

"As usual, you don't know what you're talking about. You don't have the knowledge to differentiate between one drug and another, son. That would take an expert, and that isn't you." Rand had skipped the college education his mother wanted for him and left rainy Seattle and his father to go to Los Angeles at seventeen. He never regretted it.

"We're waiting for the toxicology reports to come back," Dakota informed him, not willing to play cat and mouse at his discretion. "We'll know then which team's formula is being used."

"You were the only person at Rydell who knew the ingredients of every one of those formulas. Rand has no further to look for his guilty party than the whore he's fucking." The insult was delivered without heat, his tone as level and even as if he'd just asked whether she'd like to sit down.

"Watch your goddamned mouth," Rand snarled at the same time Dakota leaned forward, her pale eyes glittering, although she didn't leap across the table.

"*Whoever* is responsible is stealing your thunder, Paul. *Someone* is riding your glory, profiting from your invention, causing chaos. You know the consequences of this drug getting loose on the streets. Millions of people are going to die if we don't stop it."

"*We?*" He cast out an all-encompassing hand, probably to indicate where he was. There was no *we*. It was her and Rand. Then he took off in an unexpected direction. "I didn't need six teams working on my formula. I had motive to produce the safest, most effective antidepressant on the market. It was redundant to have that many people working on the same thing."

She frowned. "You complained about the delays at the time. You said the more people working on it, the faster we'd get it to market. You pushed so hard."

"Too many cooks . . ." He sniffed, brushing an invisible speck of lint from his sleeve.

"Be that as it may, someone on one of the teams managed to get the formula out of the lab before everything was destroyed. We have to find that person, Paul, you know that. The consequences if we fail are astronomical. No matter how you feel about me personally, please help us figure out who could've done this. Please."

A small spark of interest flared in his eyes, then just as quickly disappeared. "You knew the individuals on each team far better than most. Who do you think?"

"I have no idea. Everyone worked in such small, tight groups, without sharing their progress—"

"You were quality control. You knew what was ordered by each team, how much was used, and their procedures. You tell me. What was the one ingredient we all used after the fifth trial failed?"

She frowned. "You mean the mastic? That was only a flavor enhancer." On *her* version of the formula. She gave him a curious frown. "Did your control group use it to do something more?" It was such an expensive and difficult ingredient to procure that several of the teams working on the formula just omitted it from their versions.

Paul didn't bother to answer. He didn't fidget or glance around, just watched her steadily from eyes unnervingly like Rand's. He changed gears again; it was disconcerting, and perhaps that was his intent. "Since it looks as though I'll be right here for the rest of my natural life, it begs the question: why should I give a flying fuck who does what on the outside?"

"You really are a piece of work, aren't you? Don't you bear any responsibility for *any* of this? Rapture was your baby from the start. Now you're disavowing your involvement? Awkward, when you're in prison for murder with your drug as the murder weapon."

His gaze locked on hers, piercing and ice cold. "Whether I do or not, next week the courts will decide if I'm responsible for premeditated murder, or if my Catherine's death was a terrible accident."

Catherine must've left millions when she died. That seemed like strong enough motivation to Dakota. Kill his wife, pin the murder on her, and walk away a rich, rich man. It seemed so obvious to her that she never had been able to figure out why it hadn't been obvious to his son.

✦ THIRTEEN ✦

So, you fucked up protecting these rich and famous friends of yours." Paul changed the subject on a dime. "Drop some names, so I can brag to my new friends."

His mild tone was edged with annoyance. Rand had heard it all his life, and he knew Dakota recognized it too. In the lab, Paul didn't do mad. He did intimidation. He was a master at making a tech, or a son, feel like an insignificant worm for even the slightest mistake or miscalculation.

Rand held his temper in check. Paul knew all his buttons and used them ruthlessly. He gave his father a succinct summary of what had transpired at the wedding, following it with the scene in Barcelona.

His father leaned forward over his arms, folded on the table. "Interesting."

"That's the best you can do?"

"Well, it's not as though I can go out and take blood samples and ask questions myself. Get your girlfriend to do it. But have her labs verified."

"You were singing her praises as brilliant and bold when you were at Rydell Pharma together."

"A lapse in judgment on my part. She was stealing from the company the whole time, selling Rydell formulas before the patents went through. They didn't fire her ass for nothing, did they? That's why she's diabolical. Pretty girls get away with a lot more than their less attractive sisters."

"Had any interesting visitors?" Dakota asked sweetly. "Heard anything from your friends in Seattle? What about the families of the other team members? How are they doing, do you know? Maybe one of them got their hands on the formula before the fire. The team was so small—"

Rand murmured a warning, "Dakota," under his breath. T minus five . . . four . . . three . . . two . . . one. Cue the explosion.

Paul swiped the book off the table with one impatient sweep of his arm. "What the fuck is this? Twenty Questions? I see my fucking lawyers, and I don't bend down for the soap. That's who I see in here day after day after day. Nobody gives a flying fuck that I'm stuck in here. Visitors? Fan mail from goddamned Seattle? Are you *kidding* me?"

The legs of Paul's chair screeched across the cement as he jumped to his feet. His face was flushed, his eyes glittering as if he had a fever. Flash temper. Rand stayed where he was.

His career was the only thing he could thank his father for. Paul's fingers mimicked Dakota's, curled over the chair back. "Who do you *think* has the fucking formula?" he exclaimed hotly. "She's sitting right next to you!" Removing the black-rimmed glasses, he cleaned the lenses on the bottom of his sweatshirt before looking at her, his expression inscrutable as he jabbed a finger in her direction. "*She* was quality control for the whole program. *She* knew every damn thing about that drug."

Dakota's eyes glittered with temper. "For God's sake, Paul—"

"I've told you this until I'm blue in the face. *She* saw the potential, and got rid of the competition. *All* the competition. Me. The rest of the team. The possibility that DL6-94 could've gone on to future approval by the FDA so it could help people like your mother. Dakota took all of those opportunities away.

"Once that drug was registered, she'd've missed her window of opportunity. She'll put Rapture on the streets and unleash a genie she'll never put back in the bottle. She's a sly, grasping, deceitful bitch. Watch your back."

"You're giving her a hell of a lot more credit than she deserves," Rand said dulcetly. "Didn't Rydell insist the formula be destroyed?" His father was delusional. Dangerously, chillingly delusional. Rand knew he had to get Dakota out of there before this situation escalated any further. A muscle twitched in his jaw as he got to his feet.

"Because she falsified—"

"*Bullshit.* Dakota's not the issue."

"Then who is?"

"Finding whoever's manufacturing this shit, and shutting them down."

"Good luck with that. Wherever you go, she's going to stick to you like glue. She's not *helping* you, you fucking moron!" He slammed his fist on the table so it rattled. "She's watching your every move to see what you *know.*

Fuck her, shuck her, and go back home. Dr. North's a dangerous woman. You should know, she fucked us *both* over."

The door slammed open, and one of the guards stood in the doorway. *"Che sta succedendo qui dentro? Non gridate. Fate silenzio!"*

DAKOTA FELT SICK TO her stomach. Paul wasn't giving an inch. He was going to keep insisting she was to blame no matter what. She cast a glance at Rand's set expression. She couldn't tell if he still believed Paul, or if he was seeing his father unravel as he tried to shore up his lies.

"Get me the lab work, give me something to do while I'm stuck in here," Paul urged Rand, ignoring the blustering guard, who retreated and closed the door behind him when they didn't acknowledge him. "*I'll* know if it's DL6-94 or something else."

"I've seen the prelim, the lab work," Dakota told him coldly. "And I'll confirm which version of DL6-94 is being used. Save us time, and do the right thing. *Do* you know who has the formula, Paul?"

"I'll let you know when I've taken a loo—"

Rand rose and shoved his chair back under the table. "It's more important right now that you work closely with your lawyers."

"They don't know what the fuck they're doing!" Paul's hair-trigger temper erupted and he flung the metal chair aside with a force that caused it to clatter into another table. "I've given them—*told* them—every detail!" Each word became more forceful, more furious as his temper boiled over in lava mode.

"They insist there's more. There *is* no more. Dr. North gave me medication for your mother. She assured me it was the Phase Three sample, assured me what she gave was well within safety levels in one-microgram doses." Rand stepped out of range as spittle flew. "I gave it to your sainted mother."

"That's absolute bullshit, and you know it!" Dakota said. No sudden moves, no show of her inner anger. "You could just as easily say you accidentally gave your wife the wrong dosage. That changed so often in trials that a mistake would be easy to explain away."

Paul righted his chair and brought it back to the table. He gave her a steady look as he sat down. "But you did give it to me, my dear. Mailed it to me from Seattle yourself. My lawyers have the proof."

Dakota's cheeks grew hot with anger. He was a puppeteer, yanking her string. Knowing exactly which way to pull for maximum effect. "Then someone set me up," she said, voice flat.

"Don't shout," he told her mildly, when she'd done no such thing. "We'll have the guards in here again telling us we have to break this lovely visit short." He picked up his chair, sat down, and lay an arm across the back of the chair beside his, looking relaxed and unaffected by anything she was saying. There was no sign that he'd lost his temper at all. It was chilling. "Convenient that you're here in Italy for the start of the trial. I'll let my lawyers know you'll be available to testify."

Her jaw ached from gritting her teeth. "I'll tell them the truth. Just like I did last time."

His small smile chilled her to her marrow. "You were fired for stealing and lying. I wonder whom the jury will believe when they see the surveillance video? A picture is worth a thousand words, you know. I wonder exactly what the penalty is for perjury in Italy?"

There was a dull roar in her ears. His tone barely changed, but the hair on her body felt as though she'd just gone through a surge of electricity. "What surveillance video?" Her lips felt numb as every fight-or-flight response urged her to run, not walk, away. Horror thrummed through her system, making her skin tight and itchy.

His small, cold smile disappeared. "We have a date-stamped tape of you going into the lab and appropriating the files only hours before the explosion."

The day she'd been fired. And those files had been found a year later on her iPad. Proof and more proof. All of it planted. "Impossible."

"Everything is possible, Doctor. A good thing for you to remember."

THEY DIDN'T SPEAK FOR the fifteen minutes it took Rand to drive back to the hotel. She preceded him into the room. He slammed the door behind them, making her flinch. "There was a damned good reason I didn't want you to go near him. You baited him," Rand accused, dark eyes flashing fire. His mouth was a tight, grim line. He didn't approach her, just stood on the other side of the large bed situated in the middle of the room.

She didn't need Rand's anger on top of her encounter with his father. Her mind was spinning, trying to assimilate all that Paul had told her. She tried to regulate her breathing, but her chest hurt too much to draw a proper breath. Fear was a cold, hard lump making her body shake. "*I* baited *him*? You must be kidding me! I have a right to face my accuser!"

"From a safe distance."

"There were guards everywhere."

"He can do a number on you without lifting a finger."

"I'm perfectly aware of that."

The enormity of her predicament overwhelmed her, and she couldn't handle Rand's anger right now. "I had to talk to him myself." Still shaken, her heart racing and her nerves stretched to the breaking point, she wanted time and space to process everything that just happened. Rand losing his temper was overkill, and likely to tip *her* temper over the edge.

"There was a reason why I didn't want you to go with me. I think that's pretty damn obvious. You being there achieved nothing."

That was so unjust, so unfair, so damned Rand, that she lost it. "Here's a thought. Did it ever cross your mind, even a *flicker*, that Catherine's death was no accident? That in fact your father killed her on *purpose*? That he brought her here to Italy, away from her friends, away from *you*, to do exactly what he did?"

He rounded the bed, his face filled with fury. She took a defensive step back, coming against the door. "Who the hell do you think you are?" The deadly edge to his words flayed her, as intended.

To hell with him. To hell with all of them. She glared at him, her cheeks hot with reciprocated anger. "I know what I'm *not*. A money-grabbing, dishonest *whore*. Isn't that what you called me when you told me to go to hell?" Those words yelled at her two years before when he'd called to break up with her still stung. Still wounded. The son of a bitch.

Her blood pressure throbbed behind her eyeballs. "I'll tell you who I *know* I am." Taking an aggressive step forward, she slapped a hand on his chest. "I'm Dakota North, I have a super-cool sixth sense that brought us this damned far. I'm a daughter to parents who think an A is for low achievers. I'm a freak. I'm a friend who's there when my friends need me, and I accept help from them when I need it. I'm a good if not *great* cook, and I'm claustrophobic. That's who I am."

He stuck his hands in his pockets, clearly in an effort to keep them off her neck, and snapped, "Thanks for the résumé."

"I'm not done." She gave him another shove. "I pay my taxes on time, I haven't had a lover since you told me to take a hike, and I sold my condo to pay my medical bills. I'll say this for the last damned time: *I did not give Paul drugs*—either approved or declined by the FDA. No. Drugs. Not even an aspirin. Whatever he did, he did it on his own. Which is why I'm not in prison and he is! Did I leave anything out?"

For a moment, she thought he wouldn't answer. His face was a hard, expressionless mask, but his hazel eyes glowed with . . . what, she had no idea. She was grateful that he'd missed the reference to the medical bills; no way she wanted to go there.

"The box containing the vial and wafers was post-marked Seattle," he said. "*Your* return address. With a fucking handwritten note telling him and my mom to enjoy their second honeymoon. I saw the note, on the custom notepaper your girlfriend Lucy gave you for your goddamn birthday."

"Her name's Lilly." Dakota had no idea who could've gotten their hands on one of the beautiful cards her best friend had made for her. "Where did you ever see anything I handwrote? Tell me that."

"Your fingerprint was on the vial."

"I worked for four years in that lab." She threw up her hands. "Of course my fingerprints were on the vial. My fingerprints were on *hundreds* of vials."

"And one just happened to travel all the way to Italy?"

Her hands dropped to her sides, and her stomach did a nauseating roll and lurch. She was sick of defending herself to him. Sick of trying to prove to the people she loved that she was worthy. Fuck them all. "Fuck you."

He narrowed his eyes, temper simmering in the glittering depth. "You don't ever say fuck."

"I'm saying it now. Fuck. Fuck. Fuck *you*."

He grabbed her upper arms. "Just look me straight in the eye and tell me the truth."

She didn't shake him off because her body felt too brittle to chance moving. Locking her knees, she stayed in his steely grip, meeting his hot gaze with one of her own. "I've looked you in the eye and told you the truth all along. It's not my fault or responsibility if you're too pigheaded and blind or too beaten down by your issues with your father to hear what I'm saying. I've tried to rationalize, to excuse your behavior. There are all sorts of abuses—but you're a big boy now, and your abuser is feeding you so much bullshit you need waders."

His fingers tightened like manacles on her arms. "Why would I believe you? The evidence was damning."

"*Faith*, Rand." Her throat tightened and her eyes started burning. "Talk about liars. You claimed to love me more than you'd ever loved anyone. You should've had faith that I wouldn't lie to you." But his pattern of mistrust started way before his father claimed she'd given him the wrong drug.

A muscle twitched in his jaw. "You didn't tell me about your sixth sense."

"God, Rand . . ." She didn't know where to begin with *that* one. She took a deep, painful breath into her restricted lungs. The knot in her chest reached critical mass and she felt tears welling. Damn damn damn. She blinked them back, staring at the ceiling, willing them to stop. This wasn't the time or place to unravel the entire spaghetti bowl of lies he believed to be truths. "Frankly, that's the least important part of all this."

His lips tightened. "A lie is a lie. It's a matter of moral fiber. If you're dishonest in the small things, then you'll be dishonest in the big things, and I won't tolerate being lied to."

"How damned sanctimonious of you. As if you've never withheld something or told a damned fib in your life." Dakota had never felt so fragile. Rand was the only person on earth she'd let come close enough to truly wound her. Being vulnerable right now infuriated her. She didn't want to be weak when she needed desperately to be strong and forceful. She'd done nothing wrong, damn it. "You won't tolerate being lied to? Really? With *your* parents? My God, they both fed you nothing *but* lies!"

"Now it's *both* my parents? Jesus, Dakota, really? You get caught in your web of lies time and time again, and your only defense is that *everyone* lies?"

"I didn't mention my tracking ability because *it wasn't relevant.*" *I couldn't bear for you to look at me like my parents do.* She'd been afraid; Dakota thought bitterly, he'd leave her. And he had anyway. But not because she had this stupid, freakish sixth sense. Because he'd believed every damned lie his parents had fed him. "Let me go. You hate me—it should be easy." His hands tensed for a second; then he released her and stepped back.

With effort, she controlled the trembling in her hands as she picked up her bag from the floor where she'd dropped it. "Tell you what. I'll give you the coordinates and location of your men, and the man carrying the vial. Then I'm done. You're on your own. I won't traipse all over the world to help someone who denigrates me and calls me a liar at every turn."

She felt adrift and afraid, and ridiculously, *infuriatingly,* she still wanted to hold on to him because he was big and solid and invincible. More fool her. She glared at him again instead. "I won't explain myself to you or anyone else, ever again. I am who I am. And if that isn't good enough, fuck you."

✦ FOURTEEN ✦

She looked magnificent with her red, orange, and gold hair a messy tumble around her face and shoulders. Her eyes looked larger and shimmered like rain-drenched spring leaves. She was furious, and she was deeply hurt. Seeing the pain she was trying hard to mask dismayed him. Her tears unmanned him, ratcheting his temper back under control.

Dakota was usually pragmatic, sensible, and even-tempered. It was one of the things he'd liked best about her. She was soothing in the storm of his life. But he'd never seen this vulnerable side of her. He'd never seen her cry. He felt a pang of remorse for coming down that hard on her. All his anger and frustration at the situation was spilling into every aspect of this aborted venture.

He reached out and brushed his fingertips across her hot, wet cheek, and said with aching tenderness, "Don't cry."

She jerked her head away, putting a hand over the rapid pulse at the base of her neck as her throat worked. Her eyes were hot, her mouth swollen and vulnerable. It took a moment for her to snarl, "I *never* c-cry."

She tilted her chin pugnaciously, her tear-filled eyes daring him to say one more damn thing. She didn't cry pretty. Her face grew progressively blotchy, and her nose was pink as tears streamed down her cheeks. She fought hard to control the sobs tearing through her chest. The sound made Rand's own chest ache, and something twisted knife-sharp inside him at her pain.

Her tears ripping him up, despite his determination not to be taken in by her. Dakota never backed down from anything. She confronted life head-on; hell, she'd go toe-to-toe with King Kong if she felt she was in the right. She stood there, braced—for what, he wasn't sure.

He'd cut off his own hands before he physically hurt her. But sometimes one didn't have to use physical violence to wound.

Furiously, she turned her bag upside down on the floor and crouched beside it to rummage through the mountain of contents. "W-wash your own damned un-underwear!" She tossed several clumps of black fabric in his general direction.

Sobbing so hard it was a wonder she could see anything at all, she continued digging through the pile, tossing out items as she went.

Rand sank to his knees beside her, putting his hands on her cheeks to lift her head so he could look into her eyes. She fought him like a wildcat, clawing at the backs of his hands, her nails scoring his skin. Sliding his hand around her nape, he gripped the back of her neck under the tangled mane to hold her still. "Don't." Just saying that one word ripped at his throat.

Pale eyes locked with dark. The rush of heat was hard, fast, and overwhelming. It always was when he touched her. He dragged her face up to his and kissed her. She tasted of salt and a deep sadness that killed him. Rand gentled the kiss, lowering her to the floor and coming down on top of her.

He murmured, "We'll figure this out. Together. I promise." He pulled her T-shirt over her head and tossed it aside. "Don't cry, sweetheart. Please don't cry." He tugged her bra over her breasts because he couldn't get to the clasp on her back.

Her nipples were a deep pink, hard and aroused, and she murmured low in her throat as he brought his mouth down to kiss her again.

Still kissing her, he pulled down the zipper of her jeans, shoved them down until he could wedge his knee in the fabric and maneuver one of her legs free. He ripped at the scrap of lace barely covering her, and wedged his hand between their straining bodies to free himself from his zipper as she clung to his shoulders.

He spread his hand under her to cup her ass, and with his other hand, guided himself into her wet heat. With a soft cry she wrapped her legs tightly around his hips and surged upward, meeting him halfway. He nudged her head back with his chin to expose her damp throat to his marauding mouth. Loving her, soothing her, arousing her.

He moved in counterpoint with her, feeling the way her body clung to his with each thrust and withdrawal. Feeling the shudder of her breath against his neck, and the wetness of her tears burning like acid against his skin.

She whispered, "Rand," in a voice that shook, and he thrust faster, harder, wanting to give her pleasure and stop her pain. Anything to stop the tears. Her fiery hair clung to him in long silken skeins, the strong filaments and the sweat on their bodies binding them. She arched against him with each thrust.

He lifted his head to look down at her. Her eyes were closed, her lips swollen; tears still leaked into her hair.

"God, I can't get enough of you." His voice was thick, his breathing labored as he pumped into her, feeling her body start to clench and tremble.

In response, she pressed her face against his chest and fell apart in his arms.

Only later, as he carried Dakota to the bed and covered her with the sheet, did he realize that other than that one involuntary use of his name, she hadn't said a word the entire time.

RAND SAT WITH DAKOTA in the offices of Paul's lawyers in Rome. His father claimed there was an incriminating tape proving Dakota had been instrumental in his mother's death. Rand wanted to see the damned thing with his own eyes.

He'd been here a couple of times, usually meeting with various lawyers on his father's case at the prison. The law office, on the Piazza Venezia, was ultramodern, all sleek black leather, chrome, and glossy surfaces. It looked cold, intimidating, and expensive. A stunning blonde with a centerfold's body sat behind a glass-and-chrome desk that was so minimalist Rand wondered how it stood upright. He figured the woman's large breasts, displayed in a low-cut black dress, stood with the help of augmentation surgery.

The lawyer had agreed to see him as soon as Rand could get to Rome. He should—Rand paid him a fortune to be accommodating. They'd made it there by late afternoon.

They were in the reception area of the high-priced law office, Dakota flipping a glossy Italian fashion magazine on her knee. Her legs were crossed, one foot bouncing as if she had her motor running. Her hair was tamed into a shiny coil at her nape, diamond earrings sparkling in her ears. She looked effortlessly chic in slim black pants and an off-the-shoulder black top, high heels, and a black-and-white scarf tied around her waist. Full makeup camouflaged any hint of tears, and she'd applied a delicate spray of familiar spicy perfume, just, Rand was sure, to drive him nuts. He wanted to take her right there on the law office's charcoal wool carpet. "You don't have to go in with me," he told her.

"Mr. Maguire?" An attractive brunette in a formfitting black dress similar to the receptionist's came toward him with a polite smile. "Signor Mancini is ready for you now. Please come this way."

Dakota tossed the magazine onto an almost invisible glass coffee table and rose with him. The woman led them down a wide, brightly lit hallway hung with modernist paintings that did nothing for him. Rand shot a glance at Dakota. She looked cool and unconcerned. Her lips twitched as she caught his eye. "Are you waiting for me to start sweating, Maguire?"

"I would be," he admitted sotto voce.

Her chin lifted as she gave him a calm look from smoky eyes that held no remnants of her earlier tears. "I don't have any reason to sweat."

Yeah, maybe not. Then why was he?

Their escort opened a twelve-foot-tall black glass door and stood back. "Mr. Maguire and Dr. North," she announced. Waiting for them to enter, she withdrew, closing the door quietly behind them.

The picture window on the far side of the room framed a spectacular orange sunset, the lights coming on in the square, and the immense white marble monument constructed for Victor Emmanuel II, the first king of Italy.

Octavio Mancini rose from behind the slab of black marble that was his desk and came forward, hand outstretched. "Rand, good to see you again." He was a distinguished man in his late fifties, with well-groomed dark hair graying at the temples and a small, trim mustache. He shook Rand's hand, then Dakota's, then led them to a small grouping of chairs beside the large window.

A tray was laid out on another barely-there low glass table. It held an artful arrangement of bottles, glasses, an ice bucket, and small china plates and napkins for the array of appetizers.

"I appreciate you coming forward on my client's behalf, Dr. North." Mancini motioned for them to be seated, and took the chair with his back to the sunset. "However, I don't think your testimony will be necessary. We have everything we need for a solid defense." His voice was polite, but he was clearly not a fan. But then, he was paid to believe in the innocence of his client, and as far as client and lawyer were concerned, Dakota should be the one behind bars.

"Paul claims you have an incriminating video of Dr. North," Rand said smoothly. "We'd like to view it."

Mancini glanced from one to the other, clearly puzzled as to why Rand was here with her. "We have two. Which would you like to see?"

Dakota, in the process of sitting down, straightened, her body stiff. *"Two?"*

The lawyer looked at Rand. "Is this something you wish to discuss in front of Dr. North, or should I have Rossella escort her out while we talk?"

"I don't think so." Dakota sat down, crossing her ankles as she leaned back in the chair, as if she had nothing to hide.

Rand's gut told him to listen to the subliminal message in her expression and body language. "I brought Dr. North with me so we could view the tape. *Both* tapes, if that's what you have."

"Very well." Using the phone on the table beside him, Mancini asked his assistant to bring the videos into his office. "She'll be just a moment. Sanbittèr?" He indicated the bottles of the aperitif soda on the nearby table. "Or a glass of Prosecco perhaps?"

Rand refused. Dakota accepted a glass of the white

wine, mostly, he suspected, because she needed some-thing to hold. He had the insane urge to shift over beside her so he could hold her hand in a show of solidarity and support. Not that she looked as if she needed it. She was composed and clear-eyed as she sipped the extra dry white wine, that he knew she hated, as they waited.

"What are these tapes?" she asked, the wineglass cra-dled between her hands.

"The surveillance tape shows you arriving at the lab and scanning the files the night of the explosion."

"Dr. Maguire asked me to scan some files for him a full two weeks *before* the explosion," she said calmly before taking a sip of wine.

"With due respect, Dr. North, I have watched these tapes many times, and both tapes have been verified by my experts."

Shit. This was not going to go well. He and Dakota both knew it. He didn't know how she could appear so composed.

The door opened and the brunette returned with two boxes. She went over to the large-screen TV on the far wall, then glanced at Mancini. "Which one would you like to see first?" she asked, her English flawless and almost unaccented.

The lawyer addressed Rand. "Your choice."

He wasn't ready to hear what the second incriminating footage showed. He had to remind himself that it wasn't Dakota on trial in Italy. The videos of her doing what-ever she'd done were to be used for his father's defense. If they were as damning as Mancini claimed they were, then she'd need a legal defense when she returned home. One damned thing at a time. "The lab."

The video was a compilation of security footage taken, according to the date stamp in the corner, the night of the explosion that had destroyed the lab, killing more than a dozen people.

At just after 8 p.m. on February 8, it showed Dakota driving into the lab parking lot in her white Range Rover. Showed her brisk progress through the drizzle as she crossed the lot, where twenty or so vehicles were parked. The lab was operational 24/7. The lobby cameras showed her walking in, sprinkles of rain on her shoulders and hair. The front desk was dark and empty, no security guard to check her.

"Where was the guard that night?" Rand asked.

"I have no idea. The night *this* was taken, everyone was in the rec room, celebrating Thom's birthday."

Rand glanced away from the image of Dakota walking down the clinically bright hallways to her lab and turned to look at her. "Thom?"

The pulse throbbing at the base of her throat was the only indication she was not as sanguine as she appeared. "Thom Haller was the guard on duty the night this was filmed."

"Jesus," Rand muttered impatiently. She had no fucking idea just how bad this was for her. "Who's on first? I just asked you—"

"Thom's birthday is on January sixteenth."

God. Even with irrefutable proof, she was trying to bullshit her way out of this. "You're mistaken. This was taken on February eighth. Look at the date stamp."

Her peridot eyes were unflinchingly steady as she said quietly, "I can read as well as you can, Rand. That date stamp was tampered with."

DAKOTA'S HEART POUNDED LOUDLY enough for her to hear as she observed herself walking through the empty halls. Her hands, wrapped around the cold glass, were clammy. The video hadn't been taken the night in question, but someone had gone to a great deal of trouble to make it look that way.

On the screen, she was wearing her black raincoat and boots. So it wasn't as if her clothing changed along the way and the manipulation could be easily spotted. She could just as easily have been wearing jeans or a cocktail dress under that coat. She always wore that raincoat because it was Seattle. It always rained that time of the year.

Her hairstyle changed slightly as she walked down the corridor, though. When she was working, she always wore it in some form of a braid to keep it out of her face. For a good minute, she had a French braid. As she unlocked the door to the main lab, it changed to a fishtail braid for an instant, and right back to a French braid. When the cameras picked her up again as she sat at the desk and booted the computer, it was in the fishtail again.

"Look at my hair, Rand. My braid changes."

"Looks the same to me," Rand said, totally focused as

he leaned forward, elbows on his knees, eyes fixed on the screen.

"This wasn't all taken on the same day, or even at the same *time* of day," she said impatiently. "Not only is my hair different, look at the neckline of my coat." She pointed. "Right there, you can see I was wearing a cream sweater!" A sliver of lighter fabric showed occasionally when she moved. But it was enough as far as she was concerned. "When I walked into the lobby earlier, I was wearing a gray blouse. You're the security expert. Surely you can see this has been manipulated?"

He put up a hand to silence her. "Hold that thought. Let's see the other one," he told the lawyer, his voice grim.

Mancini rose and popped out the disc, replacing it with the other one. He resumed his seat and swiveled to watch the scene, not saying a word, his face a mask. Rand didn't speak either as he saw her car pull up in front of his parents' Seattle home, all decorated for Christmas. She remembered thinking at the time how odd it was, going to all that trouble, when the couple wouldn't even be there for the holidays.

Seeing the image now, Dakota's heart sank as she saw her arrival had been recorded.

Of course Catherine and Paul had surveillance cameras at their big, expensive estate. It had never occurred to her to try to avoid them. She'd been to the house twice, the first time for Rand's and her engagement party.

She prayed like hell this wasn't the video from that night. She'd had a little too much champagne, and although she hadn't danced on the tables or run through the neighborhood naked, she had taken a little nap on Rand's childhood bed for an hour while the party had been in full swing downstairs. Rand had teased her awake, but she was embarrassed to have conked out on one of the most magical nights of her life. Worse, at her future in-law's home.

The second time had been when Rand's mother invited her to come over for a cocktail and a girls' chat prior to her and Rand's February wedding. She hadn't really looked forward to the social interaction one-on-one. She knew Catherine Maguire was clinically depressed, and according to Rand, her behavior was frequently erratic, and unpredictable, especially when she was under stress. The holidays, an extended vacation, and her son's imminent wedding, were all high-stress situations.

Now that Dakota thought about it, she realized that she'd had the same sense of uneasiness with Catherine that she'd had with Paul at the lab, the feeling that at any moment something could go seriously wrong.

Dakota had gone anyway. She hadn't seen Rand in weeks; he'd been on a two-week-long job in Vancouver, immediately followed by a security gig for another client in Brunei, and wouldn't be back for weeks. She'd missed him, and spending time with his mother was a way to keep him close. Besides, Catherine was about to become her mother-in-law; it would be a good bonding experience.

For reasons Dakota couldn't explain, as she watched herself walking up the driveway and crossing the lawn to the front porch, her heart started to hammer. God. Look at her. So happy, so in love, so filled with the joy of the season because she'd be sharing it with Rand.

Catherine came out onto the deep porch to greet her. Dakota remembered every second of the evening. It had been just before six, dark and icy cold. It hadn't rained all day, but as she approached the garland-swirled front porch, her breath preceded her, and her hands were jammed into the pockets of her coat.

The camera was at an odd angle, showing the back of Catherine's head, but Dakota was easily recognizable because the Christmas lights that twined around the pillars and along the gutters shone directly on her face.

She heard Catherine's cool, measured voice saying, "I know you're only marrying my son for the money. You aren't in any way good enough for him. Rand deserves someone on the same economic and social level as he is. How much money will it take to make you disappear into the sunset and find a nice rich old man to take care of you?"

"You're insane."

"That's a dangerous thing to say to my face, Dr. North. How much?"

"I love Rand. I don't give a damn about how much or little money he has."

"I'll give you two hundred and fifty thousand dollars to walk away."

Smiling, she said, "Not nearly enough."

Dakota frowned. What had Rand's mother *really* said before she'd answered that way? She couldn't remember. Yes, oh God. Yes she did. Implying that she and Rand couldn't possibly know each other well enough to marry with them living so far apart, Catherine Maguire had asked her how much time she and Rand had actually spent together in their courtship.

Not nearly enough.

"Now that we've established *what* you are, let's negotiate a price. You tell Rand that you've changed your mind when he returns. And do it with utmost sincerity," Catherine said coldly, her back to the camera. "I'll give you half a million dollars right now. Cash."

Catherine hadn't invited her inside, nor had this been the exchange out on the freezing-cold Christmas-wrapped damned porch. On the screen, Dakota saw herself shiver as she waited to be invited inside. She remembered that Rand's mother had been rambling about the wedding, the honeymoon. Paint chips and flowers. Dakota's mind had drifted down a similar and more concise path. She just wanted to go back to her condo, take a hot bubble bath, and curl up to wait for Rand to call.

Somehow the entire exchange had been transformed into something else altogether.

Rand's mother had handed her a thick envelope, which Dakota had smilingly accepted. In reality, it had contained an early wedding gift of tickets to Paris. Since that was exactly where she and Rand planned on going for their honeymoon, she'd graciously accepted and had given Catherine a grateful smile. Unfortunately, it had been absolutely freezing outside that evening, and on the video, Dakota's smile looked more like a rictus of contempt than a smile of thanks.

Dakota saw herself start to walk away, then turn back and say just loudly enough for the tape to pick it up, "I'll do whatever it takes to marry your son. Nothing can stop me."

The implication, Dakota knew, seeing Rand's expression as he watched her interaction with his mother, was that she'd do anything to marry him, up to and including taking half a million dollars and then telling his own mother that even Catherine wouldn't stand in her way.

Or worse, she realized with dawning horror, giving Paul Maguire a drug guaranteed to kill the very woman who stood in the way of Dakota's nefarious plans.

DAKOTA DIDN'T SAY A word after they left Octavio Mancini's office. Not even to ask where they were going as they drove through the bustling streets of the city. There were people everywhere, tourists and locals alike. Walking, riding bikes, and zipping through the traffic on scooters. Cars vied with pedestrians, and people crowded into the myriad of outdoor cafés, enjoying the balmy evening. The streets of Rome were alive and frenetic.

Rand expected her to blow up, to give him ninety-nine reasons why he shouldn't believe what he'd seen on those tapes. Instead, she'd settled back in her seat and not said a word in her own defense. The evidence was pretty fucking damning.

He drove to a small, out-of-the-way hotel he'd stayed at the last time he'd been to Rome. Dakota glanced around like a sleepwalker as he pulled up under the portico.

"What are we doing here?"

"We need a decent night's sleep before we catch up with Rebik and Ligg."

"I . . . sure." She popped her door and got out, standing beside the car as if lost, the warm breeze teasing strands of hair across her face.

And Jesus, after seeing those two incriminating tapes with his own eyes, he understood why. He smelled a setup. Even though it made no fucking sense at all.

Using cash, Rand made short work of checking them in. One room this time. He was afraid if he left her alone she'd fall apart or, worse, bolt. The elevator was minute, barely large enough to hold both of them, so he had to crowd her into the corner. Her respiration increased and she paled, but she remained mute.

"Breathe," he told her, concerned about her claustrophobia kicking in on top of everything else she'd gone through that day.

"I'm not sure I can," she admitted, voice flat. Her pale face was dewy with perspiration, her light eyes dull and lifeless.

The metal concertina-style elevator doors slid open on the third floor, and he put his hand on the small of her back as they proceeded down a narrow corridor. Her body stiffened, but she didn't shift out of his reach as he propelled her forward. Their room was at the end of the corridor. Rand unlocked the door and went in first to turn on the lights.

The bed took up most of the space.

"Where are you sleeping?" she asked dully, standing just inside the door.

"Right there." He pointed to the bed, then unhooked her heavy bag off her shoulder, tossing it onto the foot of the bed. "Go run a bath. I'll order room service."

She turned her head slowly, somber eyes flickering to his face. "I'm not h—"

"I'll order anyway." He took her by the shoulders and turned her toward the open bathroom door, flipping on the light for her. Reaching out, he gently tucked a flyaway strand of hair behind her ear.

For a moment, she simply looked at him, her pale eyes unguarded and stark with pain. Then she stepped back, out of reach.

"Take as long as you need," he said smoothly, not reacting to her withdrawal. "Food'll be here whenever you're ready."

She went into the bathroom and shut the door. Rand stood just outside, waiting for her to turn on the water. Finally the pipes rattled and he heard the gush of water on porcelain.

He cursed.

For years, he'd believed in her guilt. Now everything he thought he knew about her was taking a one-eighty turn.

Every step they took added yet another layer of complications. There was something he was missing, but what that was, he had no fucking idea. He rubbed a hand over the stubble on his jaw as he walked over to the window. They were both running on adrenaline. They needed rest and a decent meal. Then they'd have a no-holds-barred conversation and lay everything out on the table so he could make some kind of sense out of all this.

This time, he'd demand the truth.

Even if it was Dakota's version of the truth. It was obvious from her reaction that she doubted herself after seeing the tapes, and yet she'd been so certain before she saw them. What was real?

Pulling aside the drapes, he saw that their room was at the back of the hotel, facing a blank wall of the building behind it. Below was a narrow alley between the buildings, just wide enough to walk through. A fire escape right outside the window. Convenient. With a glance at the bathroom, where he still heard water running to fill the tub, he slid the window open and doubled over to step outside.

The flight of metal stairs had clearly been there for a very long time. Rand gave a fleeting thought to its maintenance as he went down. While he hadn't seen anyone following them since they'd left France, he wasn't taking any chances. It hadn't been Interpol or the local police shooting at them. Whoever those guys were, they'd meant business. Maybe they'd presumed he and Dakota had been killed in the crash. Maybe. But whoever wanted him— them—dead would eventually figure out that they hadn't been in the burning car. Then their pursuers would be back on the trail.

It surprised Rand that they hadn't been apprehended at the prison. By the cops, by Interpol, by the guys who'd tried to ram them off the road in France. In their place, that's what he would've done. Anyone who knew him must know that he'd show up to see his father eventually. It was just a matter of waiting, and he wondered why nobody had appeared yet. There'd been nothing on the news. Not anything he'd seen, anyway. Dakota had used her iPad to search the news online. Nothing.

He got to the bottom of the fire escape without incident. It had a tendency to shudder with every step he took, but it didn't pull away from the wall of the hotel with his weight.

He dropped into the alley and went left. At the end was a quiet street. Not many parked cars, but enough should they need to make a speedy getaway. He slipped back into the alley and walked through it to the other end. The street on this end was filled with people, lights, noise, and vehicles. A crowded outdoor trattoria buzzed with activity.

Left would get them quiet and the option of boosting a car undetected. Right would get them bustling streets and noise to get lost in.

Satisfied, Rand retraced his steps and scaled the stairs back to the room. The water was no longer running, and he didn't hear splashing. Concerned, he went to the door, tried the handle. The door was locked. There'd been a time when the door would've stood wide open in welcome; the bath had been one of his favorite places to make love to Dakota. "All right in there?"

"Terrific." She splashed. "Go away."

He went to look for a menu. She sounded more like herself. He put the image of her in the bathtub out of his mind. Wet skin, soft mouth. Pink nipples. Yeah, he didn't have *that* picture indelibly imprinted on his synapses.

After ordering a light meal, he requested they bring a computer to the room. Just to torture himself, he'd asked Mancini for copies of the two videos. He wanted to see them again. Frame by fucking frame.

The computer arrived a good thirty minutes before she came out of the bathroom wrapped in a white hotel towel that bared her long legs and hugged her like a lover. Her skin glowed from the too-hot water she was so fond of.

Seeing her damp and dewy, flushed and relaxed from her bath, made his blood race pleasantly through his veins. His gaze traveled over the curve of her slender shoulders, dotted with pale freckles, the clearly defined muscles in her slender arms, and the plump swell of her breasts confined by the towel.

She was his wet dream come to life. While there were only a few feet between them physically, Rand knew there was a chasm and two years' worth of pitfalls to trip them up.

Her hair was piled haphazardly on top of her head, long loose tendrils clinging to the water on her shoulders. "Where did that come from?" She jerked her head at the laptop on the desk in front of him as she secured the towel between her breasts.

She had gorgeous legs. Long, slender, and those too had well-defined muscles. His body burned. It took everything in him not to scoop her up, toss her on the bed, and say to hell with all of this.

"Hotel," he told her shortly, sounding pissed as his frustration mounted.

Rand had never felt such urgent, unrelenting lust for a woman. But there was no way to ignore what was going on. Where they were and why. The questions kept coming like fucking speeding bullets, with no letup.

Sex right now would allow them to forget, but after the sweat on their skin dried, they'd still be at an impasse. Rand realized there was no way around, over, or under this one. The only thing they could do was go through it. He sure as hell wasn't looking forward to the process.

She started rummaging around inside her bag on the foot of the bed. "See anything interesting?" she asked without inflection.

"Interesting viewing." Sound on and sound off.

"Are you going to just send me straight to the gallows, or will you hear me out?"

"I think I have a pretty good idea of what's been going on."

Her fingers curled into fists at her sides. She might've been dressed from head to toe in armor instead of a skimpy towel tucked over her breasts. Her eyes were level, her tone cool as she said, "Then that's that, isn't it?"

✦ FIFTEEN ✦

H
e was impossible to read, with his arm slung casually over the back of the boudoir chair he'd pulled up to the small writing desk. Dakota couldn't gauge his emotion at all. Why had he been so nice to her after he'd witnessed the videos? She knew she was innocent, but damn if she hadn't second-guessed herself after watching that crap.

His gaze was steady, his lips unsmiling. He got to his feet, leaving the video of her at his parents' house running.

"I'll grab a quick shower. Get dressed, put your shoes on."

"Why?" She cocked her head. "Am I going somewhere?"

"We don't know who's after us. I want to be ready to haul ass should anyone show up." He walked toward the bathroom. Four steps was all it took, bringing him a foot away from where she stood.

Dakota braced herself as he reached out. Before he touched her face, he dropped his hand. "We're going to untangle this damned Gordian knot. Together." His voice was soft, but grim as he added, "One way or another."

Her heart leaped. Did he not believe what the videos were telling him? "Rand—"

There was a knock at the door. He laid two fingers across her lips. "Save it. That's room service."

"Or cops or killers, or the paparazzi. Or all three."

He smiled slightly. "Or spaghetti and meatballs." He went to the door.

He let in the waiter with the cart, then tipped him and showed him out, turning off the computer as he passed the table. "This can wait until we've eaten."

Dakota stood in the middle of the small room as the bathroom door closed behind him. God—she didn't want to get her hopes up that for *once* someone believed what she'd been trying to tell anyone who'd listen for years.

Maybe he was just lulling her into a false sense of security while he called in the authorities. . . .

She dressed quickly in black drawstring pants, black T-shirt, and flat shoes. Then she walked to the window and held the drapes aside. There was a rickety iron fire escape right outside the window. It looked as if a strong wind would wrench it right off its rusty mooring to the ancient wall of the hotel.

Turning back into the room, she finger-combed her hair and started braiding it over her shoulder. She didn't relish making a run for it, but she would if necessary. Europe was a big place. Rand wouldn't find her, and she had the advantage. She knew where the second guy carrying the vials was. He didn't. Better yet, she thought she *might* have a clue—certainly something she was going to follow up on. With or without Rand's help.

The shower turned off and she pulled up a second chair to the desk, then took the covers off the meal he'd ordered. Thinly sliced steak on a bed of arugula, drizzled with oil and balsamic vinegar, and sprinkled with curls of cheese. Exactly what Dakota would've ordered for herself. She was surprised that he remembered what she liked to eat. She picked up the glass of icy-cold milk, he'd remembered as well, and sipped it while she waited.

When he emerged from the bathroom fully dressed, she saw he'd shaved. His hair was wet and scraped back, his version of combing. *Oh, God, Rand*—Dakota's heart hurt just looking at him. She pulled out a chair and sat down. She wasn't even remotely hungry, but she placed her napkin in her lap and picked up the silverware as he sat down opposite her. "This looks good. Thanks." Her reckless heart insisted on holding out hope that all was not lost between them. Despite the breakup and the passage of two years, Rand had not only remembered her likes and dislikes, he'd taken them into account now, even when he must really hate her.

He poured himself a glass of white wine. "Walk me through everything from your perspective."

"Starting when?"

"Let's start with meeting my mother before they left on their trip." He shoved the cork into the bottle. Too bad there was no shoving this situation back into the bottle as well.

"You saw what—"

The glass stopped midway to his mouth. "Dakota? I'm asking *you*. I'll start with saying that I watched that video several times. With and without sound. That was some creative editing."

Her fork clattered on the edge of her plate. The rush of relief she felt was staggering. "Oh, my God. I—"

"Save the editorial," he said grimly. "Just walk me through that night as best you can remember." He knocked back half the glass in one long swallow.

She told him about the initial phone call from his mother asking her to share a girls' night and talk about the wedding. The oddness of having the conversation outside on the porch in the cold. What Catherine had really said, and what she remembered saying.

Rand sliced into his steak, but didn't eat it. "What was in the envelope?"

"Their wedding present to us. Tickets to Paris and an itinerary."

"No money."

He didn't phrase it as a question, but she answered anyway. "No."

"If my mother had tried to bribe you as the video indicates, would you have told me?"

"Yes. Okay, maybe. I'm not sure. I thought our inter-action was vaguely odd at the time, but not odd enough to report to you. She told me she wanted to surprise you with the trip, and not to mention that they'd given us Paris as a wedding present. The fact that she'd invited me over, then not bothered to ask me inside, was strange, but I knew they were leaving the next day and probably had a million things to do. I didn't give it a lot of thought afterward. They left the next day for their trip, and I expected to see you for Christmas. I was going to feel you out about the trip. . . ."

"Instead, I was on my way to Brunei. By then my mother had already called to tell me her version of your conversation. I didn't know she had backup in case what she told me didn't stick. I kept waiting for you to tell me about it, and when you didn't . . ."

"Talk about the pot calling the kettle black," she said, trying her best to sound reasonable when she was feeling anything but. Losing her cool when he was sitting there prepared to listen would be counterproductive. But it would just be damn-well nice, if for *once* he believed her just because he loved her. "No matter what your mother told you, you should've come to me and asked for my side of the story."

"At the time, I was too angry to talk to you rationally, and by the time I'd cooled down, all hell had broken loose and my mother was dead."

"So when you flew directly back to Los Angeles from Brunei instead of coming to see me, you already knew it was over?"

"I was trying to justify to myself why it shouldn't be."

"Great." Dakota sat back farther in her seat. There was no space to get away from the pulsating raw emotion filling the room, swirling between them. "*That* didn't work in my favor, did it?"

"Actually, by the time I got to LA, I'd decided to take my chances and say to hell with all the damning evidence. I was going to finish up my business there, put everything else on hold, and come to Seattle. A week later, my mother was dead and my father was arrested."

"Then you had even *more* reason to break up with me,

right?" She remembered the conversation—if you could call it that—so clearly; she'd had two years to go over every word. He'd called from Italy and told her in no uncertain terms that they were done. *Whore. Money-grabbing bitch. Opportunist. Get the hell out of my life. Never want to hear your name. Over.* No room for her to get a word in edgewise. No defense.

Accused. Tried. Convicted.

It had almost killed her.

"Yeah. I did."

"Do you know that your father's lawyer called me a couple of days after your father was arrested?"

"To try to convince you to agree to testify on his behalf?"

"No. He asked me to e-mail a document to him that was on Paul's computer at the lab. He thought it would help his case."

"Who called? Mancini?"

"I don't think so. Maybe. It was a terrible line, and it was hard to understand that accent."

"Mancini doesn't have much of an accent."

"Then maybe it was someone from his office. I felt bad for Paul. And even though I wasn't willing to perjure myself for him, I thought that if I could send them what he was asking for, it would help him." *And help you understand how much I loved you, even though you refused to talk to me.* Every call she'd made to Rand had gone directly to voice mail.

Rand frowned. "Paul didn't mention a key piece of evidence that will clear him."

"Because I didn't find anything. That was the night the lab blew up."

"So you *did* go to the lab that night."

"On your father's behalf, yes. But Mr. Rydell saw me, called me into his office, and fired me on the spot."

"For what? You were one of their most respected chemists."

"Because I refused to testify on your father's behalf, because he said I had stolen files I had no business seeing——" The list went on. Dakota didn't want to relive that night; it was too devastating. "It doesn't matter now. He requested the company access cards back, and told me to clean the lab of my personal belongings. Which I was doing——"

"You were *in* the lab when it blew?"

"Fortunately I went to the supply room first, to put away the chemicals I'd been working with earlier. Writing the last few notes, trying to leave things in order even though I'd just been fired." She shook her head in bitter amusement at the memory. "If I'd just left after Rydell canned me, I would have been gone when everything went to hell. But there I was, when the lab exploded. The blast destroyed the wall between the lab and the supply room. . . ." *And damn near destroyed me too. I was knocked out*, she wanted to scream at him, *knocked out and left for dead.* It was only hours later that she'd been found under some debris by a firefighter in the cleanup. "No one was supposed to have been inside the lab itself. Seventeen people died that night. I was considered a suspect at first."

"No charges were made; Ham would have told me." He winced briefly, evidently thinking of the ex-cop and his death.

"I was in the hospital awhile."

He didn't move, but she sensed she had his full attention. "How long is awhile?"

"Three and a half months. The percussion broke so many bones I was Humpty Dumpty." Even now, when the weather changes, she knew it would happen before it made the evening news. Some things never healed right—like her relationship with Rand.

A stormy look darkened Rand's face. "Why wasn't I told about this?"

She gave him a wry look. "We were *over*. You'd made that crystal clear. You had your father to worry about, anyway. Things turned out fine. I'm fine."

"Now. No thanks to me. Jesus, I would've rushed to your bedside if I'd known."

"My friends knew what had happened." *My friends who hated your guts for the devastation you caused and for breaking my heart.* "How you broke up with me. They took it upon themselves to keep my condition quiet."

"Why didn't your parents call me? They had my number."

Dakota didn't move, but she felt the phantom pains radiating through her system. Her parents had been almost as debilitating to her psyche as the accident had been to her body. They'd finished off what Rand had started. She'd been a complete mess, both physically and mentally. "They'd told me all along that you'd leave. They . . . they did the best they could. They let me live with them as I recovered." The pain of physical therapy every day had been killer.

"You mentioned you sold your condo."

She shrugged. "Hospital bills add up."

"Dakota, I have more money than I can spend in a lifetime. You should've—"

Her small laugh was dry and brittle. "Asked for money from the man who had told me in no uncertain terms that I was a money-grabbing, opportunistic whore? Ask *that* man for help? I don't think so."

RAND WINCED. HE'D SPEWED a lot more. The surprise was that she'd remained on the line to listen to the vitriol. His mother had done a fine job filling his head with Dakota's transgressions. She'd sent a PI after his fiancée and given him the report right before he left on the Brunei trip. It had been devastating reading on the long flight from LAX.

It seemed that Dakota had a penchant for men with money, and was free in sharing her favors with those who had buckets. So while she was whispering *I love you* to him, who knew what she was saying to them? She'd been a busy girl, especially when he was on the road.

The PI report had been bad enough, but he'd been prepared to challenge her on what he'd read. Then his mother had told him about their exchange. He pushed at the steak on his plate. All she'd had to do if she needed money was ask. The PI report, with the chaser of his mother's anger at Dakota's willingness to walk away for money, had come as such a shock.

Dakota had never brought up money when they were together, and claimed to feel uncomfortable when he spoiled her with the occasional piece of jewelry. No, he couldn't care less about a woman liking the security of cash; it was that long list of men that had sent him over the edge.

Jealousy had eaten at him like acid. Each memory of them making love was now tainted by the thought—the image—of her doing that same act with someone else. He didn't give a shit about the money. Rand would've given Dakota the inheritance from his maternal grandfather; it was the basis of his mother's fortune and the bone of contention between his parents for as long as he could remember. In his family, money was, above all else, a bargaining chip.

He'd been struggling with all that when his mother had died, and his father accused of Dakota's murder. He'd had a full fucking plate. "I didn't give a damn that you wanted to marry a wealthy man," he told her. She gave him a steady look over the table. Neither had eaten more than a couple bites of the meal. She pushed her plate a few inches away in a final gesture.

"I wouldn't have cared if you were dirt poor. Your loss that you didn't believe that."

His fingers tightened on the stem of his glass. "What about the other men?" *Did you tell them the things you whispered to me late at night? Did you stroke your foot up their calves and nuzzle their chests and tell them how much you loved them?*

That got her attention, and she frowned. "Other men? What other men? I had two lovers before I met you. Three lovers isn't considered a lot by any stretch of the imagination."

It was Rand's turn to frown. "My mother showed me the report from the PI who followed you for months." A four-inch-thick red folder, secured with a rubber band, with a stark white label affixed to the front that read baldly *DR. DAKOTA NORTH*. He'd known before he snapped the band off that opening the file was going to change the entire course of his life. "There were nine men. The meetings photographed and documented. Dates, times, places."

Dakota leaned back in the chair with a shake of her head. "Wow. She was dedicated, that's for sure. Add *that* to the doctored video, and I guess you have your answer."

No, goddamn it. He not only had no answers, he had a shitload more questions. "Let me make sure I have this in a nutshell." He dropped his hand to the table, realized it was clenched into a fist, and flattened his fingers on the surface. "My mother hired a PI who gave her a thick file on your raunchy activities over several months. There's a video—doctored, you claim—of a conversation that never happened on my parents' front porch. . . . And you're saying it's all lies, that someone has gone to all this trouble just to set you up. Do you see how this all looks incredibly coincidental and farfetched?"

"Oh, yes. I certainly do. I think that was exactly the goal." Her eyes glittered. "Now I have a question for you. *Was* your mother trying to set me up? Was she trying to get you away from me, or was this someone else's manipulation? Because I have some pretty out-there opinions about all this."

He hadn't listened before; he would listen now— though he felt his shoulders rise defensively. She still had the power to hurt him. "And those are?"

"Given that I know absolutely that none of these things are true or even remotely as they seem, I think we're both being manipulated."

He leaned forward, folding his arms on the table. "A conspiracy theory? Seriously? You think we were *all* set up by my mother? You, me, Paul?"

"I don't see how this could all be your mother's doing, although God only knows, this is Machiavellian enough to lay at her feet. But she's not doing it from the grave. Yet everything about this seems to me as though a puppeteer is pulling strings to suit a bigger purpose. Doesn't it look that way to you?

"Think about it, Rand; go all the way back." She leaned across the table, staring intently into his eyes. "Your mother believes, or is *fed*, a pack of lies about me, which she promptly feeds to you; then she's killed, and your father convinces you that I'm to blame. So neither of us has the other's support, neither of us knows the whole story. Then the lab is destroyed. Then the wedding that *you're* doing security for is sabotaged, using a product connected with your father, whose formula was supposedly destroyed years before. *Then* hired killers somehow manage to find us over and over, and to top it all off, Ham is dead and half your security people are missing in action. Have I left anything out? Probably. But let's start there, shall we?"

"No. Yes. Possibly." He was shaken; when she laid out the sequence of events that way, it was inescapably disturbing. "But I don't know who could be doing it, much less why. Obviously not my mother. Yes, I admit that the doctored video and PI's notes could certainly have been her motherly way of making sure I didn't marry you. But since she died two years ago, we know that at the very least, the rest of this is someone else's work." Rand mulled over the notion, concentrating on the events surrounding his breakup with Dakota. Even if his mother hadn't suffered severe and debilitating depression, she'd been a vindictive and manipulative human being all his life. She used her wealth as a club to make people do what she wanted them to do. Rand. His father . . . The list was long. He wouldn't—couldn't—negate Dakota's theory. His mother had been capable of all that. And more.

It wasn't his mother's actions that killed him now, though. It was his own. By blindly believing the reports she'd shown him, he'd allowed her venom to poison what he had with Dakota. He'd never even considered that there might be a flip side to the coin, making it that much easier to believe the lies he'd been fed.

In a way, he had almost welcomed his father's version of events; it had justified his suspicion, his rejection of the woman he'd sworn to love forever. He'd been blind, yes, but he wasn't entirely blameless, and the realization hit him hard.

He drained his glass, then reached for the bottle to

refill it. "If it's an enemy of Paul's who's running the board," he said flatly, "he's won that part of the game. Unless there's a last-minute piece of evidence they've missed, Paul will be in jail for the rest of his life."

"Not necessarily, if Mancini's law firm is worth what you're paying them. They have those discs," Dakota pointed out. "They're damning, and he'll use them to sway the jury into believing that *I'm* the one who is guilty. Your father could walk."

Rand met her intense eyes. She looked exhausted; the smudges of shadows under her eyes had nothing to do with the crappy lighting in the room. Her pallor had everything to do with him. If her conspiracy theory proved true, his entire family was responsible for ruining her life. Him included. "Mancini won't be using the so-called evidence. I called him and told him they were fakes. I also told him that I had some serious questions about the 'experts' he hired to look at them, and that I expected him to get me some answers."

Her expression barely changed, but he saw a small flicker of hope in her still features. "When?"

"When you were taking your bath."

"You saw them just a few times. What made you change your mind?"

She'd been in the bathroom longer than she realized. He'd watched them each a dozen times. In slo-mo and without sound. He'd been in the movie business. He knew about dubbing and splicing and creative editing. "I know *you.*"

The harsh light glittered on the rim of tears welling in her eyes. She blinked them back, and Rand saw her throat move as she tried to swallow her emotions. "Don't—" She had to swallow to get the words out. "Don't say that unless you mean it. I'm at the very end of an incredibly short rope here."

For Dakota, who'd gone through so much, no thanks to him, to admit vulnerability, made Rand's chest ache with compassion. He reached out and covered her icy fingers with his. "I have no idea how or why these things have been put into place, but I believe you. I'm so sorry I didn't believe you before."

She couldn't prevent the raw sob that ripped her throat, but she put up her free hand to check him when he rose from his seat. Rand sank back down, turning her hand and lacing his fingers with hers.

He poured her half a glass of wine and pushed it in front of her as she struggled for composure. "You won't like it, but drink a little anyway."

She pulled in a deep, shuddering breath, lifted the glass, and drained the fine wine like medicine. "*That* is truly disgusting." She put the glass down and grimaced, making Rand smile.

"You should probably try to get some sleep. We've been going nonstop for days—we should take advantage of this short respite."

"Unless the good guys or the bad guys knock on the door," Dakota pointed out dryly, reading his mind. There was the glimmer of them together that he'd missed for the past two years. The way they could fin-ish each other's thoughts, knew the other person. It had been so painful when he'd thought that he didn't know her after all. And now . . .

"We can talk about this—figure it out—tomorrow when we're both fresh."

"Oh no. You don't know how long I've had to mull this over. Examine and reexamine every detail. Who knows what tomorrow will bring? I'd rather hash it out now. Do you mind?"

No. For the first time in a *long* while, he was breathing easier. He too wanted everything out in the open. "What's your theory?"

"At first I thought someone was setting *me* up for a fall. Now I'm not so sure. Let's just go with your mother being overprotective and wanting someone better for you. Malicious mischief, nothing more. But then she's killed. Paul believes with utmost sincerity that I was the one who sent him the drug and the wafers so he could administer the DL6-94.

"We know—*I* know—that wasn't the case. What if someone wanted Paul in jail? Who could have benefited from your mother's death, from getting Paul out of the way and leaving you isolated?"

"Nobody." Rand pushed her plate back in front of her. "Eat while you talk. Yeah, I inherited a chunk of change from my mother, but let's agree that I'm not behind all this, okay?" He saw a hint of a smile on her face, and drew another breath before continuing.

"If I die, everything goes to a foundation my mother set up for research into depression. Nobody would personally benefit from *my* death. So the who and why?" He shrugged. "No idea. I agree that someone is manipulating the players, but, and I hate to say this, I *do* believe you're the target. Forget my mother's shit, which I don't think was related to the rest of it.

"Someone is responsible for splicing and dicing the video from the lab. I think that footage was taken over the span of several weeks. Then, to solidify the case for your presumed guilt, you were sent to the lab the night of the explosion. I'll check with Mancini, but I'll bet that wasn't anyone from his office who called you."

"After seeing the video, I'm damn sure it wasn't. Someone wanted to implicate me in corporate espionage long before your father was put in jail. That footage was taken in October and November. A good four months before your mother died in Italy. The security firm never kept surveillance tapes for more than a couple months, but someone made sure they had what they needed for the blame-Dakota reel."

She took a bite of the arugula and chewed, then stabbed the air with her empty fork. "Someone wanted to implicate me in the explosion at the lab."

Rand, who had followed suit and taken a bite of his steak, suddenly had a hard time swallowing his food. "Or kill you."

"They almost succeeded." She shrugged, not giving anything away with her expression and leaving Rand to imagine how hideous and terrifying the experience must have been. "Bummer for the bad guys, yay for me. Next step, if the explosion didn't take me out of the picture: have me arrested for corporate espionage? And if that doesn't work, use those videos to prove that I wanted your mother dead, and therefore I'd be an accessory to murder, if not an outright murderer?" Her fingers tightened in his.

Rand took a sip of wine to ease his tight throat, then said, "Some pieces fit, others don't. It all sounds both plausible and, quite frankly, like one of Seth Creed's movies."

She smiled. "Blockbusters, all of them."

"Okay. Let's try something else. What if you *aren't* the target? What if this person used you to get to *me*, knowing you were my Achilles' heel?"

She smiled slightly, a spark of hope igniting behind the pale green eyes. "Was I?"

"In ways you can't imagine." But that was a conversation for another time. "Let's try this for an alternate theory. First, breaking us up. It almost killed me when I saw the proof of your infidelity." He put up a hand to stop her from speaking. "Then my mother dies from a drug you and Paul were responsible for manufacturing. Paul is arrested. There's a damn good chance he'll rot in prison. And while I have no love for him, he is my father. I don't want that for him."

"If we go with this train of thought, that you're the target of all this—we were intentionally broken up," Dakota agreed. "The wedding you were hired to protect was targeted in a very personal and specific way. They could've used Rohypnol, if all they wanted was a scandal-worthy party. But it was *this* drug. *Our* drug, the one your father and I worked on." She exhaled, then sipped the glass of milk. "Someone seems to have worked very hard to manipulate you, your father, and me. None of what we know adds up to any real solution. Yet nothing about any of this feels coincidental. Does it to you?"

He looked grim. "No. It sure as hell wasn't a coincidence that Rapture was used there."

Dakota tapped her fingernails against the edge of the ceramic plate. "Where are the good guys? Not that we'd be any happier to see them than to see the bad guys—but where are they? Even though we used mostly cash, we still used a credit card for the car in Perugia, and had to leave passports for ID at several hotels we stayed at. If the police and/or Interpol knew who we were in Barcelona, they should've been able to follow you to the *moon* with that kind of information. They should be right here at the hotel with us, ordering dessert."

"Therefore we weren't made at the bank. Not by the good guys, anyway. Another issue of concern: why my men haven't made contact in forty-eight hours. It couldn't just be bad cell reception, not for that long. And . . . yes, that is freaking weird. Ham was two feet behind me in the catacombs when he was shot. I wasn't touched. Yet we were almost shot and killed en route to see Paul."

"True. But no one seems to have followed us here, right?"

"This feels like," Rand said grimly, getting to his feet, "you and I are being *herded.*"

Her eyes went wide. "But why? What could they possibly hope to gain?"

"That's what we're going to find out."

"IT'S TIME TO GET rid of those who no longer benefit us, and put the final clue in place, Szik."

"Rebik and Ligg?"

"This time, I want you to travel to do the job. Go to Albania and dispatch them personally. I don't want anyone to see you. Do you understand?"

"Yes, Father. Should I dispose of Rand at the same time?"

"Not now. She'll only go forward if he's with her. There's no point separating them now." Monk threw him a bone. "You can have him when we have her."

Szik's face lit up, his eyes glittering with excitement. "You trust me that much, Father?"

Monk forced his lips to curve into a benevolent smile as he gazed with flat eyes at his most faithful servant. "You are the only one I trust, my son."

Szik fell to his knees and sobbed his gratitude as Monk brought the lighter to the end of his cigar.

RAND WAS RIGHT. WITH the threat of a hit team chasing them, and the GPS location of the carrier of the missing vial leading them, it did feel suspiciously as if someone was manipulating their every move. Certainly people other than Zak Stark knew about her tracking ability. She'd been mentioned in the local papers several times, if nothing else. There was no resisting the easy strength of Rand's grip as he bracketed her face with both hands. "You're frowning."

She gave a half-laugh, putting her fingers around his wrists to remove his hands from her face. Looking at him made her heart hurt. She wanted to believe that he believed in her, but experience told her that what she was feeling was wishful thinking.

Nobody made such a fast turnaround. Not with all the damning evidence against her. Not a man as steadfast as Rand had always been about things being black or white. "This situation warrants at least a frown," she pointed out, not pulling him away but instead running her fingers lightly around the strong bones of his wrists. She loved touching him. That never changed. She loved his physical strength, and God only knew, right then, his physical strength was incredibly seductive.

He bent his head, blocking the light. "I'm sorry. I'm so goddamned sorry." And then he kissed her so gently, so tenderly, tears prickled behind Dakota's lids. Her heart swelled and her chest felt tight as she opened her mouth and welcomed him inside.

She slid off the chair and allowed herself to lean on him as he stroked her hair, which was still wound in a braid down her back. That would last about two seconds—his fingers expertly combed through the still damp strands until her hair was draped in a damp cape over her shoulders.

She felt ridiculously safe right now. Stupid, all things considered. Dakota fitted herself against him, felt the hard ridge of his erection, yet she sensed no urgency from him as, still kissing her, he backed her against the bed.

He lowered her to the mattress, coming down beside her, and she broke the kiss. "I—"

He murmured, "Shh," and placed a finger gently on her parted lips. His eyes, a dangerous forest green, turned even darker as he cupped her breast. He made no move to get her naked in thirty seconds flat. Instead, he caressed her through her T-shirt and bra, until she moved restlessly under the slow caresses that weren't nearly enough.

He petted her, teased her nipples, and kissed her so that they had to pull apart and gasp for air. She loved the musky scent of his skin that even the hotel soap couldn't mask. Loved the feel of his cool, damp hair as he slid his lips down the arched curve of her throat. She loved the hot, sweet pull of his mouth as he closed his lips around her nipple through two thin layers of fabric.

He stroked a line from her collarbone with a gentle finger, nudging her farther up the mattress, coming to rest between her upraised knees.

Eyes closed, she stroked his nape as he kissed a path up her throat and took her mouth again. Slow, sweet drugging kisses that made her blood surge urgently through her veins. She felt the glide of his hand under her T-shirt, then the brush of his fingers inside her bra.

Rand wasn't just making love to her, but worshiping her with a tenderness that both broke her heart and made her want to fly. It had been so long, so very long since he'd believed in her, and it came through in every touch. They made love slowly, as if they had all the time in the world and no one but each other. An illusion, but one Dakota clung to as he kissed his way down her body. She was willing to put aside both the past and the future. Because the truth was that all anyone ever really had was the present. And the present was perfect.

✦ SIXTEEN ✦

Are you sure Rebik and Ligg are dead?" Rand repeated the next morning as they ate breakfast. The outdoor area of the trattoria was doing a brisk business. Nobody was listening to one more couple crammed into the narrow space, with tables placed cheek by jowl to accommodate as many people as possible. A line was forming near the door to the restaurant.

Dakota swallowed a mouthful of eggs. "Positive. I don't see their numbers anymore." She'd known in the early hours of the morning when she'd gotten up to pee, and checked. But she hadn't had the heart to wake Rand to tell him. It served no purpose to rouse him from the first decent night's sleep he'd had in days to tell him something he couldn't fix. She'd crawled back into bed, tucking herself into the warm spoon of his body, and gone back to sleep herself.

They'd both woken feeling refreshed. No crazed killers or determined officials knocked down their door in the middle of the night. Nonetheless, she'd had to tell him his men were dead before they left the room to go eat.

Now they sat outside an out-of-the-way, family-style trattoria having breakfast, and Rand placed his coffee cup on the table with a *thump* of disappointment. "Not that I don't believe what you're telling me," he assured her with a squeeze to her fingers, threaded in his. "I just need confirmation that you aren't having a . . . glitch. Damn it to hell. We've gotten this close, and now the trail is cold?"

"No, it isn't cold. We know your guys found the person carrying the vial, because they were in the same place as his coordinates when they died."

"Fuck it! Who the hell's killing my men?" He kept his voice low, but it took an effort. Rand ran a hand around the back of his neck, frustration in every line of his body.

"I don't know who, but I know exactly where it happened. I marked it on the map while you were in the shower. But I have another idea. Something Paul said yesterday."

"Since we both know Paul is only out to protect Paul, implicating you in my mother's death . . ." Rand shoved his fingers through his hair in frustration. "Can we believe whatever it was he said?"

"I don't know, but I have a feeling this might be worthwhile. When we were talking about DL6-94, he mentioned mastic. Mastic is an ingredient that some of our control studies used. I was more concerned with getting a stable product than I was with taste. But Paul implied that the mastic wasn't for taste. That it was an important ingredient in Rapture."

She picked up her cappuccino and cradled the shallow cup in her palm. "*Pistacia lentiscus* is found all over Mediterranean Europe, but the subspecies on our approved supplies list came from only one place, in Greece. Specifically, the peninsula of Mount Athos. And how did I remember this small, insignificant detail, you ask?" She took a sip of creamy coffee and looked at him over the rim. He obligingly raised his eyebrows in inquiry, a slight smile on his lips. "Because when I was researching it and where the plant grew, I learned that this is the area that has all the monasteries, and that no women are allowed to go there. The details stuck in my head."

Rand smiled. "And of course you wanted to go immediately and pick the leaves yourself."

She smiled back, taking inordinate pleasure in their simple camaraderie. Looking for emotional pitfalls was exhausting business, and she was more than willing to take advantage of the current détente. The sun shone, a couple nearby was laughing, and a small bird near her feet looked up, hopeful for a breakfast crumb. The last time she'd felt this happy, this content, was when Rand had taken time from his busy new company to take her to Carmel for the weekend, a few weeks before everything in her life had blown to hell. Literally.

No. I'm not going there. Not now. She was going to enjoy every damned second of this morning for as long as it lasted. "Something like that. We used the tree's resin, not the leaves. It oozes out of the bark. When the resin dries, it's mixed with the other ingredients. Actually, it's been used in medicines for centuries, not to mention chewing gum, foods, and cosmetics. It's in lots of products."

"Then what makes the mastic used by Rydell different or special? It seems as though your clue is giving us a needle in a very large haystack."

"The mastic that's used in this application can only be found in two places in the world. *Two* places." Her heart started beating faster with anticipation as she realized she could be onto something. This could be the real clue to finding the person responsible. "The Greek island of Chios has one subspecies, but that proved unstable for our purposes. The one we used exclusively is harvested in very small amounts in the Mount Athos region. I think we should go there and see what we find."

"I hear you." He considered her suggestion for a moment. "But I'd prefer to go to Albania, and the last place my men were alive, to search for clues. Someone killed them, and that someone might be the same person we're following."

Dakota put a free hand on his rock-hard forearm. "While I appreciate that you want to check on your men, my instincts say we should head directly to Mount Athos. We're running out of time and we can't do both."

Rand gave her a half-smile as he lifted his butt to pull his wallet from his back pocket to pay for their meal. "Do you have a manly disguise in that bag of yours? A nice mustache and goatee perhaps?" He laid a handful of euros beside his empty plate.

Dakota stroked her thumb on his warm skin on the back of his hand, which was lightly clasping hers. She loved his big hands. Loved the look of them, loved the feel of them touching her skin, loved the strength and the gentleness when he made love to her. "It never occurred to me," she teased back. "But I bet I can improvise. Would you make love to me if I were a man?"

"I'd make love to you *pretending* to be a man," he said dryly, bringing their joined hands to his lips and kissing her fingers. "In the dark," he said with mock firmness. "With my eyes closed. After confirmation that everything that should be there *was* there." The waiter came and took the check and money off the table. Rand indicated there was no change and rose, still holding her hand.

On the street, he paused. "Albania first. To make arrangements to ship the bodies home, if nothing else."

"The coordinates for the guy carrying the vial are still there," she admitted, hitching her bag higher up her shoulder. "Please tell me we won't be driving—my butt hurts from all this sitting."

"No, we'll fly."

RAND IDENTIFIED THE SWEET, sick smell of death the instant he stepped into the hangar. Beside him, Dakota slapped a hand over her nose and mouth as she got a whiff and gagged. "Wait here," he told her grimly. The large doors had all been shut—but not locked—when they arrived. With no windows or cross ventilation, the heat was oppressive, even though it was barely noon.

"No."

His fingers tightened around the grip of his Glock; beside him, Dakota had her tiny S&W special in her hand. He didn't like her being there. But then, he hadn't wanted her anywhere near him at the start of the trip. Life was fucking funny that way.

The hangar, large enough to house a commercial 747, held only one small, bright yellow Air Tractor. "Shit," he muttered under his breath as he approached the aircraft cautiously. If he was ID'ing it correctly, it could have a payload of up to a thousand pounds of . . . airborne Rapture?

Dakota closed the gap between them. "What?" she said, barely above a whisper.

"That's an ag-plane." Rand recognized it from a stunt he'd done in a movie several years ago. "A crop duster," he clarified. Question was, had the load been dropped, or was it still sitting in the tanks?

"Stop!" Dakota grabbed his arm.

Rand paused, noting the bodies of his men beneath the fuselage and the lifeless white of their eyes.

"They'll still be dead in two minutes! I'm sorry, Rand, just give me a minute." She pulled him back, sticking her weapon into her bag as she rustled around for something else. "Let me find . . ." She pulled out something—not the gun he'd instructed she keep out and ready at all times, but something in a sealed package. A second package quickly followed the first.

"Just put this on." She ripped one of bags open with her teeth. "If that's a crop duster, chances are it's got Rapture in it, on it, near it. Your men certainly took a big hit." She shook open a mask and handed it to him, before tearing into the second one.

He put the elastic over his head. While it was only made to prevent smoke inhalation in a residential setting, it was better than nothing. Her resourcefulness impressed the hell out of him.

Rand helped her adjust her mask over her face and the wig she was wearing, then gestured for her to retrieve her gun from the bowels of her bag.

Together they approached the plane and the two dead men beneath it. Dakota crouched beside Ron Ligg and pointed to his open, staring eyes—fully white. He'd received a massive dose of Rapture. Same for Derek Rebik.

Had the payload already been dropped, or was it a disaster about to happen?

Rand climbed up into the small cockpit and turned on the engine. It roared to life. He looked at the gauge. The hopper capacity was eight hundred pounds, and the level showed . . . eight hundred pounds. Relief flooded through him, and his fingers gripped the controls for a moment before he shut the engine off. His ears throbbed in the aftermath.

God. If this shit had been sprayed . . . anywhere, anytime. The death toll could've been in the thousands, possibly hundreds of thousands.

Emerging from the cockpit, he stepped onto the wing, then jumped down and walked around to look at the tank under the fuselage. Aware that Dakota watched anxiously from a safe distance away, Rand quickly removed the regulator and pressure valve, rendering the spray boom inoperable. He shut the cover, pocketed what he'd just removed. "Okay," he said, double-checking that the cover was secure. "We're outta here."

He heard a slight scuffle and muffled shout, and spun, ripping off his mask, tossing it aside, and raising his gun in what felt like slo-mo. "Shit." A trap.

Six armed men dressed in airport coveralls formed a semicircle, boxing them in. One man had Dakota. Her mask had been ripped away, and she looked more pissed than terrified.

A military-looking guy with a buzz cut gripped her from behind, his arm wrapped tightly under her breasts, his engine-greasy hand covering her mouth. The semiautomatic in his other hand was pressed to her temple. He did not look friendly.

The short and wiry guy beside them, booted feet spread, had his weapon trained on Rand. Rand focused on the muzzle at Dakota's head, ignoring the five who had him in their crosshairs. He could make a shot or two, maybe three, but for Dakota, there was no wiggle room.

"Drop your weapon," the man holding her said in strongly accented English, bending her into his chest so she was off balance. Cheeks flushed a pissed-off pink, eyes wide over his fingers, she tried to maintain her balance and pull away at the same time. She used both hands to pry his fingers away from her face, bending them back until he let go. Of her face.

She dug her nails into the forearm clamped across her body. The guy didn't so much as flinch. Didn't stop her trying to break free. "Shoot the son of a bitch!"

Rand's heart did a tap dance, and his finger squeezed the trigger. "Who do you work for?" he demanded, ignoring her request and the other men closing in as he concentrated on the guy he figured was in charge.

Buzz Cut looked taken aback: "Drop your weapon or the girl dies."

Rand allowed his gaze to flicker to Dakota. They'd snatched the wig off and tossed it on the floor. Her hair tumbled in a crazy, bright cloud around her shoulders— something that a son of a bitch like the man holding her could use to keep her tight in front of him. Rand had to force his eyes away from her to concentrate on her captor.

"Razor's Edge," she told him meaningfully.

In which he'd doubled for Jackman, and saved the girl by shooting the bad guy who was holding her in the head, missing her by inches. Those had been blanks. And he hadn't given a fuck about the actress. Eyes on the man behind Dakota, Rand shook his head. Not just no. But no way in hell.

The guy wasn't familiar, but his type was. Military. Buzz-cut black hair, pug nose, strong jaw. No fat. Just slabs of rock-hard muscle. Trained. They were a good thirty feet apart, but Rand could see his dead black eyes over Dakota's bright head.

"Go for it," he said coldly. "The girl means nothing to me. And feel free to shoot me. Policia e Shtetit are on their way. We called them to come get the bodies." He jerked a thumb over his shoulder. "They'll be here before you turn around. I hear Peqin is particularly nice in the winter months."

The high-security prison was known for its inhuman treatment of prisoners and complete disregard for human rights. Albanians had a profound mistrust of the justice system, and just the word Peqin stopped the men in their tracks.

For a few seconds. Then one of the men flanking Buzz and Dakota fired a hail of bullets from his semiauto. The barrage missed Rand by several feet, but he felt the breeze go by his ear. Buzz snapped out a command in what sounded like Greek and jerked his chin; his men closed in on Rand—no weapons.

So they wanted them alive; something to consider later. If there was a later.

Rand spread his feet, adjusting his weight over his knees as the five men rushed him. He'd trained for these kinds of kick-butt action scenes, rehearsed the hits to make a scene look as authentic as possible in front of the camera. Over and over. Cut after cut. He had muscle memory on his side. But since he didn't have the directive not to shoot anyone, he fucking fired into the mob.

One down, four to go. He slammed the Glock on the closest guy's nose with a gratifying crunch. The man howled and dropped, blood gushing from his nose and mouth.

The next guy, silver hair, baby face, rushed him from behind, but Rand had already spun, leg extended. His foot slammed up into the guy's jaw. *Crack.* Blood sprayed from baby-face's mouth and nose. He was unconscious before he hit the cement.

Defense. Offense. Kick ass. Blood pumping. Mind moving three steps ahead as he circled.

Momentum building, Rand went headfirst into the next guy, ramming him in his hard belly and wrapping his arms around him like a wrestler going for the tag. Someone kicked him as he was getting up; pain radiated down his side. He stumbled from a punishing blow to the back of the head. Ignoring the black snow in his vision, Rand grabbed the man's hand, bent back his fingers like twigs, taking him to his knees. Then Rand brought up his knee into his esophagus.

He staggered to his feet and swung back to see Buzz half-carrying Dakota from the building. Fuck it! Everything had been a diversion. It was *Dakota* they wanted.

Razor's Edge. Without hesitation or finesse, he fired. His bullet hit Buzz in the temple, and inches over Dakota's head. She let out a bloodcurdling shriek of surprise as he crumpled behind her, almost taking her down with him.

The last man standing was better at taking orders than at improvising; the loss of his leader slowed him down. He fumbled for a better grip on his weapon and grabbed at Dakota's arm as she tried to get out of the way. She swung her purse and slammed it into his head, making the shot he was about to fire go wild. She ducked as it ricocheted off the metal ceiling, sounding like a bullet in a tin cup.

White-faced, the asshole swung the weapon in Rand's direction, shouting at the others to get up, to help him, in a combination of Greek, Italian, and broken English. His call for help needed no translation; he was out of his depth and he knew it.

Dakota lunged at him, slamming her body against his arm, and again the shot missed the intended target. His semi went, spewing ammo as it cartwheeled in the air to slam into the corrugated metal wall behind them. It was a fucking miracle that they weren't all dead where they stood.

The idiot and Dakota crashed to the cement floor in a tangle of arms and legs.

Two of the attackers had made it back to their feet, streaming blood, and they converged on Rand, hell-bent on vengeance. He kicked out, making one guy jump out of the way. The other thug put on a surprising burst of speed and grabbed him in a bear hug from behind. The man tightened his hold, squeezing the air from Rand's lungs as he swung him in an arc like a rag doll. The Glock slipped from his bloodless fingers.

He used the guy's momentum to lift his legs, giving him his full body weight so the guy staggered backward just as his partner came at Rand with his fists.

Rand took a punch to the jaw. His head snapped back, and he tasted the metallic tang of his own blood. Even as his eyes watered from the blow, he shot out a foot.

Thwak.

His foot slammed down on the man's thigh. He felt the vibration travel all the way up his own leg as he heard the crack of bone. The man howled and dropped.

Rand struggled in the implacable grip of the last man standing, panting and trying to break loose as the steel bands of the guy's arms squeezed until black spots danced in front of his eyes. He slammed his head back, heard cartilage crunch, and jumped out of the way as the man fell full-length, face-first, into the cement.

Lungs heaving, he swiveled his head to find Dakota across the hangar. The place was littered with bodies. He swiped his hand under his bleeding nose. It hurt like hell, but he laughed anyway at the picture she made.

She was straddling the man's chest, her little pea-shooter pressed to the guy's left eye. Her hair streamed in a glowing waterfall down her back. She turned her head, her eyes glittering in the muted light. Her position was overkill, because the man was quite dead.

Rand went over and grabbed her arm to haul her to her feet. "You okay?"

"No, I'm not okay. This really pisses me off. Who the *hell* are these people, Rand? And what do they want?"

Holding her arm in a gentle but unyielding grip, he did a visual inspection of her from top to toe. She didn't seem hurt, thank God. He tucked a long strand of bright hair behind her ear, the backs of his fingers lingering on her warm cheek. "We could stick around and ask them when they wake up."

She growled low in her throat, making him smile, despite his throbbing nose and aching ribs.

"If you'd done *that* in the first place"—she indicated Buzz—"you would've saved time. How badly are you hurt?" She ran her hands over his face, murmured "Sorry," when she touched a tender spot, then ran her hands over his shoulders and chest.

"I did stunts like this for years, and got paid a shitload of money to do it." Except that a faux blow, no matter how realistic-looking, didn't hurt.

He retrieved both masks from the floor, and picked up the wig as well, handing them to her as they went outside. "This was incredibly foresighted of you."

"Thanks." She shoved everything into her bag. "I'm sorry about your men, Rand."

"Me too. I'll make sure their families are taken care of." He breathed deep. "My men must've disabled the plane. When I turned the engine on, a few of the dashboard lights stayed dark. But someone will be back to offload the Rapture and transfer it to another plane."

"We can—"

"I jammed the tanks. Plane won't fly, and they won't be able to empty the tank to transfer the liquid. Not for a while, anyway. I'll call the authorities after we leave, warn them to bring in a hazmat team and clear the area. I thought you said this stuff was too unstable to transport in a plane."

"A crop duster would work for an airborne application because it flies so low the stability of the product wouldn't be affected by altitude." She closed her bag and faced him. "You're certain it wasn't dispensed?"

He shook his head. "Not yet. Tanks are still full." They had the plane locked and loaded, ready to disperse Rapture, and his men had been killed . . . so why the hell was the plane still just sitting in the hangar?

"Thank God. Now what?"

Rand rubbed his hands together. "Call in some favors and get the hell out of here before we're asked questions we can't answer. I'll claim their bodies later, once this is all over. We have to get to Greece."

They were damned fortunate. Neither had been badly hurt or worse, and Rapture hadn't been misted over an unsuspecting city. Rand called it a good day.

THEY FLEW THE CESSNA they'd rented in Fontainebleau to Thessaloniki in northern Greece. Once again, they went under the radar with no flight plan. Their flights alone broke so many laws that if he was caught, the book and the whole damned library it was in were going to be thrown at him.

Not on his list of things he gave a shit about right then.

He and Dakota boosted a car at the airport and drove the hundred and fifteen kilometers to Nea Roda. Rand switched vehicles halfway, and then again twenty-five kilometers outside of the small tourist town.

There'd been no indication that anyone was following them, yet he'd felt eyes on his back, off and on, the entire trip.

"If nothing else, when we're caught, we're going to get nailed for grand theft auto," Dakota said, sitting back and kicking off her shoes. She was wearing the short black wig, blowing around her cheeks from the open window. She didn't seem concerned by the possibility that they'd be thrown in jail sooner than later.

"You can always tell them you were a hostage," Rand told her lightly, turning into a half-full public parking lot. "Grab your stuff. We'll walk from here."

"I wouldn't let you take the rap alone. These guys were after me too."

There were only a few hotels on the narrow peninsula with its spectacular beaches and touristy shops. Rand didn't want to check into a small, intimate hotel, not this close to the endgame. The biggest hotel, however, was closed for renovation. "Excellent," he said, seeing the sign and the scaffolding. The defunct hotel would be perfect for one night.

"The hotel not being open is a *good* thing?"

"It is for us. We don't have to present our passports or ID to check in."

Dakota lowered her sunglasses and gave the building a dubious look. "It looks as though it might fall down around our ears."

"No construction workers. It's perfect."

They blended with a group of tourists, picking up camping supplies, then casually strolled around the back of the hotel.

"Empty," Rand noted as he walked right in through an unlocked side door. It was screened from the street by a hedge that seriously needed trimming and watering.

"Well, that was anticlimactic," Dakota said as they made their way up the wide, uncarpeted staircase to the second floor.

"You'd prefer we were being chased?"

"The way my heart's pounding, we might as well have been. Do you think the bathrooms work?"

He pushed open a door at random. "Let's see." The room was empty, the carpet ripped out. It was stuffy from the day's heat, but it had been swept clean. Dakota reached through the curtains and opened the window, which looked out over the weedy swimming pool behind the hotel, letting in the warm late-afternoon breeze. It smelled like the ocean.

For the first time in what seemed like forever, Rand felt that he had a moment to catch his breath. He went into the bathroom, flushed the toilet, and tried the taps.

Dakota tossed her heavy bag into a corner and was standing back from the window looking out. "We have a toilet and cold running water," he told her, coming up behind her to wrap his arms around her waist.

She crossed her arms over his and laid her hands on his forearms as she leaned into his chest. "All the comforts of home."

"About three hours of daylight left. Want to grab a shower while you can still see where everything is?"

"I know where everything is, but you can always come in and remind me."

He smiled against her hair. "Let's check the location of the bad guy first."

Dakota shook the metal vial case in her hand. "Just did. Strangely," her eyes shone with excitement, "moving this way. Who would've thunk it?"

He let go of her and stepped back. As much as he wanted the moment to stay frozen in time, and to take her up on her offer of sharing the shower, they were here with a purpose. He wanted to leave at first light, preferring not to be trying to read a map by the beam of the small flashlight.

They'd bought a map of the area earlier. Rand spread it out on the floor, folding it so that it was a square showing the peninsula of Athos. The area was thirty miles long and about seven miles wide. He shook his head as he realized that he was automatically converting kilometers to miles; old habits died hard. "Show me."

Holding her trusty GPS, she sank onto the floor on her knees, leaning over to look. "On the western side and up a bit." She placed a fingertip on the monastery of Xenofon, then slid her finger a little farther north. "Right about here."

Up a bit looked like five or six miles. And while the peninsula was dotted with monasteries, all of them marked on the map, there was nothing in the spot Dakota was indicating. He didn't ask her if she was positive. If she said the guy was there, he was there.

He was through doubting Dakota North.

"I see roads on the map; are we driving?" she asked.

"Nope. Those roads are more like glorified goat paths. The going would be *very* slow and we'd stick out like the proverbial sore thumb; we might as well call ahead and tell them we're coming." He flipped the map over, pointing to a small inset listing travel services. "We could catch a tourist boat, followed by either a long walk or, according to this, an unreliable thirty-minute bus trip. Followed by another hike."

It seemed that every option guaranteed they'd be spotted. He briefly considered an airdrop—but the sound of the plane would alert those on the ground, and it would also involve more people. Right now, Rand trusted no one. Other than Dakota. Well, almost no one. He pulled out his phone.

"Are you calling a cab?" Dakota sat back and grinned.

"Calling your boss again." He reached out and brushed his hand over her bright red hair as the phone was picked up on the other end. "Who do we know with contacts in Greece? Mount Athos area, to be precise," he asked Zak Stark without preamble.

"Be more specific," his friend said, not asking for details about the why and how of Rand's situation. "I'll make a call."

Rand was very specific, then disconnected. "He'll call back," he told Dakota.

"Zak knows people."

"He does indeed."

Rand pulled out the travel guide and settled beside her on the floor, leaning against the wall. She lay down, placing her feet in his lap. With an arm flung over her eyes, she ordered, "Read to me."

Rand ran a finger up and down the arch of her bare foot. "According to the protocol of the monastic state, only men are allowed to visit Agion Oros, Mount Athos to you, and even then, it's a lengthy, time-consuming process to be approved for entry."

"We're going to sneak over there?"

"*I'm* going to sneak over there with Zak's help. *You* are going to stay right here and direct me in."

She lifted her arm off her face and gave him an incredulous look. "Are we playing this same song again? Remember the loss of cell phone connection in Paris?

What if that happens again? If we lose contact, then you have no clue where to go. They could be anywhere in, what? More than two hundred square miles? That's ridiculous. I'm going with you."

"If we're caught, it's going to be ugly. *Very* ugly. International-incident ugly." Like dead ugly.

She put her arm back over her eyes. "Then we better make sure that we aren't caught. Furthermore, if we don't catch this bastard and stop him, it's going to be very ugly for thousands of people."

He couldn't argue with her reasoning, so he settled in to wait for Zak, gently rubbing her feet and enjoying the brief lull in the action.

Zak called back ten minutes later. "I have the name of a fisherman in Trypiti who'll give you some useful gear and firepower. He'll take an extra boat, escort you to Dafni. You're on your own for the last leg; looks like a little under seven miles from the port to Mount Athos. My friends need more info, but you'll have backup if you want it. Can you give me something to give them?"

Rand wasn't going to say no to backup. His own men were dead or AWOL. He gave Zak a quick rundown of the events to date. When he was done, he snapped his phone shut, gave Dakota's feet one last squeeze, and announced, "Change of plans."

THICK, SCUDDING CLOUDS OBLITERATED the sky as the wind came up, making the watery vista as dark as a witch's heart. The darkness was oppressive, but it lasted only a few minutes before that batch of clouds blew aside and the stars and moon appeared to light their way again for a few minutes.

God, Dakota looked at the gleam of white highlighting the choppy waves, *we're in the middle of* nowhere. And nowhere was noisy. The slap of the waves on the hull, the splash of oars, the sound of the wind, the *thump-thump-thump* of her own heartbeat resonating in her ears.

The little boat, which seemed ridiculously small for the three of them at the start of their journey, now seemed insanely tiny on the vastness of the open water. The fisherman turned off the engine twenty minutes before, and he and Rand were rowing hard against the swells. Wishing there'd been a third set of oars so she didn't feel useless, Dakota huddled in the middle, hanging on to her seat with both hands for dear life.

They'd agreed on no talking the closer they got to the steep and rocky coast. Sound carried over the water, their escort had told them when they'd left three hours ago. She didn't have the energy to spare, anyway.

Dakota gripped the wood seat on either side of her hips. Not that she could feel it; she'd lost sensation in her hands and feet. Whatever was covered by the black slicker she'd pulled on was wet, and whatever wasn't covered by the slicker was wetter. The two men didn't have time to worry about being drenched as they fought the choppy water to keep the boat afloat and in the direction they wanted to go.

The fisherman sat in back, Rand facing her in the front of the boat. The oars dipped and gleamed in the intermittent moonlight. Silver streamers poured off the oars with each upward stroke. Splash, dip, lift. Rhythmic. Dakota concentrated on Rand's heavy oilskin jacket.

She now knew firsthand that one could have claustrophobia in the middle of the ocean. Okay, strictly speaking, it wasn't the ocean, just a sea. Thank God she wasn't seasick as well. She wasn't sure *how* she wasn't seasick, because the angry waves slapping against the wooden hull made the boat go not only up and down but side to side. At times, she was sure it levitated.

If it weren't for the oppressive sensation caused by her claustrophobia, her fear of drowning at any moment, and the realization that once they set foot on land she could be killed, this would be the adventure of a lifetime. Icy water splashed over her shoulders.

Against the darkness, the GPS numbers glowed brightly in her mind's eye. Their quarry was well ahead of them. Barely moving. Had he arrived at his final destination? Their final destination? They were going to find the lab when they reached land, she was sure of it. Sure, and terrified of what, or whom, they'd find.

As if he knew what she was thinking, Rand leaned forward and gripped her fingers. Wait a minute—why wasn't he *rowing*? As much as she wanted his hands on her, right now she'd prefer they were firmly gripping the oars. What on earth was he doing?

He let go of her hand to wrap his arm around her shoulders. Warmth. Comfort. The bump and scrape as the small boat struck the rocky beach. Rand anticipated their arrival, she had no idea how, since there'd been no indication beforehand.

He spoke a few low words to the man who'd rowed them across the water; then she helped him untie the second boat from the first with mostly numb fingers, and the two of them climbed ashore. In moments, the fisherman was back on the water without a backward wave.

The wind off the water was cold, and she shivered as she helped Rand slide the even smaller boat up the rocks to the tree line ten feet away. The rocks were slippery underfoot and Dakota moved carefully; this wasn't the time to twist an ankle, or worse.

"Okay. You can use the flashlight—keep the beam low, and cover it partially with your fingers. Yeah. Like that." She held it so he could see to tie the boat to the twisted trunk of an old olive tree.

Rand shrugged off the backpack he wore and tossed it aside as he started unzipping his slicker. "Sorry, but we need to leave our jackets here for the return trip. We won't need them when we get up top."

She wasn't too sure about that. It might be summer, but until the sun came up, the wind had a bite. She was already chilled, but she stripped off the slicker. The wind sliced right through her wet clothing, shrinking her skin a size, as she handed him the jacket. "I'm glad to hear that you believe we'll *have* a return trip."

He stuffed both into the boat, securing them under the bench, then picked up the pack. "Let's get some branches, make sure the boat's well covered, and get this show on the road."

They broke off a few leafy limbs from the surrounding shrubs to hide the boat, then stood back and waited for the moon to reappear, to see if they needed to add more. After a few minutes, when the moon coyly remained in hiding, they decided there was no more time to waste, and it would have to do.

The breeze smelled of the ocean—salt and iodine, with a faint tang of licorice. The mastic used in Rapture. So it *did* grow here. Her heart did a little skip and a jump, a combo of terror and exhilaration.

Rand took her hand just as she was about to shove it into her armpit for warmth. His fingers closed around hers, warm and strong. "There's an abandoned monastery just over this rise," he said, pitching his voice low but carrying over the susurrus of the waves lapping at the smooth stones of the beach. "We can change into our dry clothes there."

The incline from the sliver of rocky beach was steep, an almost vertical fifty or sixty feet. Six stories. Dakota gave it an assessing glance when the moon reappeared. Holy hell, it looked dangerous, especially in the dark.

"Maybe there's a way around . . . ?" she suggested hopefully. She'd never gone up anything more arduous than a flight of stairs in heels.

Rand squeezed her fingers. "Trust me. This is nothing compared to the north face of the Eiger," he teased. "Come on."

He gave her hand a little tug, and they walked to the base. The cliff wasn't *exactly* vertical; there was a slight incline, and the face was covered with rocks and small shrubs and grasses. "Plenty of handholds, you'll do fine."

"I'm glad you have that much confidence in my ability," Dakota told him dryly. "You do remember I've never climbed anything in my life, right?" She paused as she considered the unpredictable moonlight. "I suppose I could hold the flashlight in my teeth—"

"No. We're exposed out here. I'll help you. All you have to do is trust me," Rand assured her, stuffing the backpack under the front of his T-shirt. She winced. It must be icy cold and wet against his skin, but he didn't even flinch.

"We're going up side by side. Grab the back of my jeans with one hand, use the other to grab what you can. Just hold on. I promise I won't let you fall."

"I don't think that's such a good idea." Dakota looked up the face of the cliff. "My extra weight will pull you over."

"No, you won't. I'm used to carrying a hundred-pound pack. Hell, one time Gideon Stark and I carried Zak halfway down Mount Reiner when he broke his leg."

Dubiously, Dakota curled her fingers into the waistband of his jeans. The wet, cold fabric of his shirt fell over her forearm, but his skin was warm against her cold hand.

He glanced over at her. "Ready?"

"You bet. This was on my bucket list."

His teeth flashed white. "That's my girl. Hang on tight. Here we go."

He was an experienced climber, with absolutely no fear. This must be very tame for him, she thought, as he talked her through every step and every handhold, waiting to make sure she was okay before going on. It was painstaking going. "If I weren't here, you'd be leaping from rock to branch, stone to twig, right?"

"If you weren't here, this wouldn't be nearly as much fun."

Dakota smiled as she wedged her sneakered toe into the hard dirt and shifted her free hand a little higher. "Liar." She knew he and the Starks had been climbing buddies for years. Zak had told her about some of the wild adventures they'd gone on. Including Rand's heroism when he'd carried him down that mountain. This wasn't even in the same league.

Holding tightly to his jeans, she placed her feet where he indicated and trusted him to get her to the top safely. He reminded her to pause every time she grabbed a branch for leverage and, when she dug a toe in for purchase, to make sure it would hold her weight. She appreciated his caution. Six stories wasn't high for him, but it might as well have been Mount Everest for her, and she was grateful for all the help he could give her. And for the darkness that prevented her from looking down.

Suddenly there was a *thump-thump-thump*. For a moment, Dakota thought it was her own heartbeat. As she strained to listen, she realized it was the repetitive beat of wood striking wood. Over and over and over again, echoing out of the darkness across the water. It did sound like a rapid heartbeat, and seemingly from all directions. Feeling like Spiderman clinging to the cliff-face she cocked her head. "What *is* that?"

✦ SEVENTEEN ✦

It's eleven."

The sound seemed to be resonating inside her head. Disconcerting. "That's a *clock*?" Dakota whispered, clinging to a prickly shrub. The gong was as good an excuse as any to pause to catch her breath.

"A *semantron*, a long wooden cymbal. One of the monks hits it with a mallet every night at eleven o'clock. Used to call an hour of private prayer. Keep moving."

She pulled herself up, using her legs and Rand's momentum. "How do you know that?"

"Read it back at the hotel. How're you doing?"

"Much easier than I thought." It was only half a fib. When she got home, she'd have to use that gym membership she'd had for a year and used only three times.

Since Rand was doing most of the heavy lifting, they made it to the top of the bluff without incident. As she climbed the last few feet, Dakota wasn't surprised to find herself sweating despite the cold, her arms and legs shaking with muscle strain. She was the least athletic person she knew, and she was proud of herself for not shrieking like a girl and begging to be left behind with the boat.

Rand clambered over the edge, then hoisted her beside him. She took a hasty step away from the drop-off before glancing around to get her bearings. Brushing the dirt off her hands onto the seat of her uncomfortable wet pants, she caught glimpses of the telltale glint of the ocean far below, hearing the soft susurrus of the waves spilling over the rocks.

It was a very, very long way down.

They were in a copse of trees, hard to identify, as they were just denser black against the darkness. Whatever the species, the thick foliage sheltered them from the wind, but the damp fabric of her clothes felt clammy and cold. "We should change."

"Our helpful fisherman escort said there's a ruin just through the trees north of here. Let's go where we'll be more protected." He took her hand, opening her fingers. "Your gun, ma'am." He placed the small .38 in her palm.

Five bullets were all it held, but it made her feel marginally better. "I hope I don't have to shoot more than five people," she whispered, only half-joking as she adjusted her fingers on the grip. When he'd taken it from her in Albania, she'd hoped that was the last time she'd ever have to see it.

"Or attempt to shoot one person more than five times."

"Or shoot anyone at all," she murmured fervently. She could barely see him in the dark, but heard him shifting around, presumably arming himself as well.

"Want this now?" He nudged her arm with her tote, which he'd stuffed into the backpack for the boat trip.

She took it, slinging the strap over her shoulder. When this was all over, she was going to find the smallest purse possible, and carry nothing but a key and a lipstick in it.

Taking her free hand, Rand said, "This way," very softly, leading her across the ankle-high grasses into the trees.

"We have a flashlight," she reminded him as she walked into a low shrub and had to do a little dance to get around it.

"Tree cover."

It was a nifty trick that he could speak so softly and yet she could hear him perfectly well. Walking with him on a windswept bluff in the pitch dark, knowing what they were up against, made her shiver with trepidation. She tightened her fingers in his, and he used his arm to draw her hard against his side.

Their hips brushed, their thighs moved as one. Dakota could smell the heat of his body and the tangy scent of the soap he'd used in the shower earlier. She wanted to stop. To hit pause, and just stand there with him to enjoy this moment of peace and quiet. Unfortunately, she knew they were in the eye of the storm.

Zak had promised backup. Where and how, she had no idea. Either way, she was damn glad she and Rand didn't have to do this—whatever this was—alone.

The air was warmer as they moved between the trees and smelled strongly of pine, underscored by the smoky, resiny, aromatic scent of the evergreen shrub that produced the mastic for Rapture.

She touched the side of her purse with her gun hand—wasn't *that* a weird observation?—and felt the familiar, smooth oblong of the vial case through the fine-grained leather, saw the numbers gliding through her mind. Moving the heel of her hand, she picked up the second GPS string of numbers from Rand's sock. Without a map, she didn't have much information, but knowing Rand was beside her gave her a starting point. The other set of numbers was fairly close as the crow flew. Except she knew that on the peninsula, cut off from the mainland by Mount Athos, hills, rivers, and deep valleys, nothing was as straightforward.

Geographically, they were closing the gap.

She hoped Paul's unintentional clue would be the key to finding the lab. Her shoulder hit a tree trunk with a dull *thud*, but she didn't cry out in surprise. A city girl, Dakota found the night silence spooky, and she was glad to hear her heartbeat and the soft crunch of their feet on the dirt and scrub grass.

"Okay?" Rand asked quietly, his fingers tightening around hers.

She nodded, realized he couldn't see her, and whispered, "Peachy." She had no idea how he knew where they were going, since it was completely dark. He must have eyes like a bat. Or was that ears? Radar? Instinct? Or all of the above. Maybe he was just damn good at this undercover security stuff. For a second, she allowed herself to wonder what their lives might've been like if he'd remained a stunt coordinator, and if he'd trusted her. What kind of life would they have had?

She'd never know.

After about ten minutes he let go of her hand and turned on the powerful flashlight, keeping the beam low and partially covered by his palm. She tucked her fingers under his arm and closed the small gap between them.

The narrow beam, filled with small flying insects, led the way through the rocky ground scattered with clumps of grass, a large tree trunk, and the occasional looming shrub. "How are our numbers?"

"Holding steady."

"The ruins," he announced, letting the narrow beam illuminate the walls.

Ruins was right. The structure had four broken-down stone walls and no roof. Rand led her "inside" and scanned the walls with the light. No bigger than ten by twelve, it had once been an outbuilding of some kind for a long-vanished monastery. Now it was nothing more than a pile of rocks.

He set the light on a protruding rock, pointing it at the ground, and dropped the backpack beside it. "Strip."

She plopped her tote down at her feet. "You say that to a woman holding a gun?"

He slid his hand under her hair and pulled her forward. "I can because I have a bigger gun."

She tilted her face, and her lips were right there as he closed the gap and kissed her.

Too short, but definitely sweet. He looked into her eyes as he lifted his head. "Change quickly. Let's get this over with."

Dakota pulled dry jeans and long-sleeved T-shirts out

of the backpack, held one of each closer to the meager light to check the size, and handed him his clothes. She tossed hers over a nearby rock and quickly stripped to bare, goose-bumpy skin. It felt liberating being outside on a black night, completely naked. Too bad they couldn't linger. She toed off her shoes instead of reaching for Rand.

Rand leaned over and rubbed down her chilled skin with something dry, running the soft fabric all the way from her shoulders over her breasts and down her belly. "I hope that isn't your nice, dry shirt," she scolded, leaning into him, then backing up because he still wore his cold, wet clothes.

"You have goose bumps."

She smiled. "You can't *see* my goose bum—"

"About time you got here," a man said without inflection. "While this is touching, we expected you two hours ago." He stepped into the small stone ruin to join them.

CONFUSION STAYED RAND'S GUN hand, but he guided Dakota behind him as he stared toward the voice of the man who shouldn't be anywhere near this place.

The faint beam of the down-turned flashlight glinted momentarily on Creed's gun. "Seth? What the hell are *you* doing here?" The director was so out of context that Rand wasn't sure whether the man was his old friend Seth Creed or his doppelgänger. It would've been helpful if the damned moon would make an appearance. All that was visible were several black shapes beyond the broken wall behind Creed. The narrow beam of the flashlight did little more than make the director's features marginally easier to identify.

Dakota crowded against his back, her cold fingers brushing the small of his back.

"Let Dr. North dress, fellas," Creed said helpfully. He stepped aside so that several men could come up alongside Rand. "A little crowded, but we're all friends here."

No, Rand suspected they weren't friends at all. "Make it fast," he murmured to Dakota, who was shimmying into her jeans, still vulnerable behind him. The darkness concealed her now, but that wasn't going to last.

Rand was aware of the man beside him a nanosecond before he felt the hard, unmistakable jab of a muzzle hard to his jugular. He didn't dare move, or Dakota would lose him as a human shield. A second guy grabbed him by the arm and started patting him down. Found the Glock, stuck in the front of his jeans, then patted down his legs and got the knife in his ankle sheath.

The shadowy men stepped back. "He's clean."

"I'm not putting on a striptease here," Dakota said curtly, coming up flush behind Rand. He felt her tuck the .38 into his waistband. She pulled his shirt over it, and shifted away. "Turn your backs!" He heard the rustle of fabric and the brush of her arms and knees against him as she finished pulling on her dry clothing in the shelter of his body. "I don't know what's going on, but whatever it is can wait until I put my shoes on."

"You're a very difficult girl to pin down, Dr. North."

"That's because I'm not a girl," she said with asperity, stomping her feet into her sneakers. Rand recognized that tone in her voice, knowing it didn't bode well for whoever was on the receiving in. "What's this all about? What does a film director have to do with Rapture?"

"I made a movie by that name a couple years back, remember that, Maguire?" Yeah, Rand remembered. Creed had told him the stunts in it were going to make his career as a stunt coordinator. He'd felt indebted to the director for the opportunity then. But he sure as hell didn't now. "Bring them along," Creed said to his men, his shadow drifting toward the opening between the crumbled walls. He added to Dakota, "It was the last job your very talented boyfriend did before he quit the biz."

"News flash, neither of us works for you, so stop giving us orders." Dakota slipped her hand into Rand's as they stepped onto the grass beyond the close confines of the walls. The other shadows crowded around them.

Creed chuckled. Amiable, good-old-boy laughter that hinted at beers shared and fun times.

Jesus. This didn't compute. "What are you doing here, Creed?" Rand's footsteps slowed. Dakota's quiet, "Don't!" motivated him to keep walking more than the hard jab to the ribs with the barrel of a gun. Damn it to hell.

"This way. I have a car. A luxury here but, I find, a necessity if one doesn't want to traipse all over hell and go by foot like the monks do. It's six miles to the lab, and I don't want to tire you out. It's going to be a big night for you."

The way Creed talked in circles and in an unrelentingly cheerful tone made the hair on the back of Rand's neck lift in warning. His flight-or-fight responses were on red alert. He tried to assess his surroundings as they walked. It was pitch dark, he had no fucking idea of the lay of the land, and these guys were heavily armed. All he had were his wits and Dakota's pea shooter. "What the fuck's going on?"

"Dr. North is necessary for further work on Rapture," Creed said as if this were a normal conversation over lunch at the Ivy.

Rand's gut clenched as he realized Dakota had been right all along. They'd wanted her, and he was the vehicle to get her there.

"I stopped working on DL6-94 two years ago," Dakota told him, her voice flat. "I don't have my notes, and I sure as hell don't remember any of the formulas. Frankly, even if I did, I'm not going to be part of turning this drug loose on the world. Just save time and take us back to the boat."

"You *have* all the notes, Dr. North. If you can't access them from that reportedly clever mind of yours, you can retrieve them from your iPad."

Her reaction was instantaneous, and she stopped dead in her tracks. "You son of a bitch! *You* were the one who set me up? *Why*, for God's sake? I don't even *know* you!"

Rand felt as though he'd fallen into some sort of hallucinogenic rabbit hole as beside him Dakota's entire body bristled with fury. "*You* robbed Dakota's house?

Set her up to be convicted of a felony for stealing trade secrets?"

"Not *personally*. I have people for that. And I can assure you, Dr. North, you might've been *accused* of economic espionage, but never *imprisoned*. That was merely a means to an end. Here we are," Creed said cheerfully, opening the back door. No light came on. "I'll sit with you and keep you company. Stavros, get in the other side beside Dr. North."

"Means to what end?" Rand demanded as Dakota slid into the car, before he got in beside her. He squeezed her fingers as Creed crowded in on his left. The other guy got in on the other side of Dakota, squashing them tight as fucking sardines in the back of the vehicle.

Creed didn't respond.

What purpose could he possibly have for setting her up in such a Machiavellian way? The end result was obvious. He needed her here to work on the old formula. "How did you know about this particular drug? Did Paul mention his frustration over the years as the teams worked out the kinks to get the drug to market?"

Creed hadn't been interested in an antidepressant. Fucking hell. Paul must've told him of the formula's aphrodisiacal properties. Avarice was behind the director's bizarre behavior. He must've discovered that the drug was unstable, and with Paul in prison, he needed a chemist intimately familiar with the formula to fix it.

He'd gone to extraordinary lengths to get Dakota to Greece by the most convoluted methods possible.

"All it needs is Dr. North's experience and a little fine-tuning."

With a sinking heart, Rand heard the smile in the older man's voice. *He* was a dead man walking, and Dakota, once she'd stabilized Creeds multibillion-dollar product, would be expendable.

Except the formula couldn't be stabilized. He squeezed her slightly clammy hand in warning, but he knew he didn't need to caution her not to blurt out that little factoid. First Seth would force her to prove that was the case. Then he'd kill her. It was just a matter of timing.

Four men got into the front seat, and the car rolled across the rocky ground, lights off. There was nothing around them but inky black. No sign of the ocean or the moon. Just a sense of motion and the crunch and snap of the tires going over rocks and shrubbery.

"This is all very double-o-seven," Rand said dryly, hoping like hell his eyes adjusted soon. "Where are we going?" Not that he'd had any choice, but getting into the car was probably a fatal mistake. Not knowing their destination made formulating a plan of escape tricky. His mind was going a mile a minute as he tried to think three steps ahead. Unfortunately, he couldn't see three *inches* ahead.

Not even the dash lights shone, making the darkness complete. The man driving must be wearing night-vision glasses, because otherwise he was driving blind. Fucking dangerous, close to a six-story drop-off.

"I'll show you Dr. North's state-of-the-art lab before we make arrangements for your departure, Rand. You'll be impressed, Dr. North."

"I've seen state-of-the-art labs before." Her voice remained steady, but Rand knew her well. She might've seemingly taken the quick gun battle at the hangar in Albania in stride, but right now the cumulative experiences of the last few days were catching up with her. She was understandably, justifiably scared. "I'd prefer to leave now."

"After all the trouble I went to getting you here? That's not very sporting of you, Doctor."

Without the distraction of visual input, Rand immediately picked up the nuances of what Creed was saying. "What do you mean, 'trouble'? What did you do to get Dakota here?"

Creed chuckled. "How far back do you want me to go? Let's see . . . We could start with the actor I hired out of Central Casting to play the private detective for your mother. He was an *excellent* investment. I thought the actress portraying Dr. North was particularly talented. You saw the stills. An amazing likeness, don't you think? The wig she wore had to be custom-made, of course. Dr. North's hair is so distinctive. I knew you'd look no further than the hair for your proof, buddy."

Not the manipulation of a possessive mother. A deliberate act with far-reaching consequences. "Did my mother know he was fake?"

"No. Which made nutty, fucking fruitcake, bat-shit crazy mommy's performance so much more sincere. Manipulative bitch fell into the script as if well rehearsed."

"You cut and dubbed the video of Dakota and my mother talking at the house?" Shit. Of course he had. Rand wanted to punch him. "Did you kill her, you son of a bitch?" he demanded, a nerve in his jaw twitching.

Dakota murmured, "Rand," and he realized he'd been squeezing her hand hard enough to hurt her. He eased his grip, apologizing by stroking his thumb over the backs of her knuckles.

Christ. They'd *all* been set up by this egotistical son of a bitch. His mother, Paul, Dakota, and himself. Mere pieces in an elaborate chess game for Creed's amusement.

"Me?" The director's voice tinged with satisfaction and a trace of amusement. "Good Lord, no. However, I did make sure Dr. North was fired. Damned inconvenient that she still happened to be in the lab the night I blew it; she was supposed to leave right away, not linger. Very diligent of you, Dr. North, but ultimately *extremely* inconvenient. The explosion almost killed you."

"It was extremely inconvenient for me too, you sick fuck!" Dakota snapped. "Not to mention the small inconvenience of murdering all those innocent people."

Creed chuckled. "Had to get rid of any remaining evidence pertaining to Rapture and anyone who might be able to reconstruct the successful tests." Creed shifted slightly in his seat. "You were the one who showed me how to detonate the C-4, remember? It went off better than I expected—you'd be proud of what a good pyrotechnic student I was."

"Jesus, Creed. That explosion killed a dozen people—"

"Dr. North wasn't supposed to still be in the building when it blew, over diligence on her part, and a small miscalculation on mine. I must admit, I had some tense moments when she had to spend so long in the hospital."

"Sorry my recovery was so inconvenient."

"The planning was meticulous until you were foolish enough to stay in the lab after you were fired. Your protracted hospital stay put us back several months."

"Well, seeing as how you put me there, that's hardly my fault, now is it?"

Rand felt Creed's body tense beside him. He didn't like someone questioning his fucking loony-tunes plans any more than he liked actors questioning his directions on set.

"If your intention wasn't for Dakota to be arrested for stealing the formula, what was the point of going to all the trouble to make it appear that she'd done so?" Rand asked as the car slowed into a sharp turn. Were they almost at their destination?

"A precaution. Burning bridges for her. Really, who'd hire a chemist who'd steal company secrets? No one."

"So you made sure she was out of work after you put her in the hospital."

"And homeless," Creed added with a smile in his voice.

"A prince of a guy," Dakota said tightly.

"Then it was a matter of getting her to come to us."

"Kidnapping would've been more expedient," she pointed out grimly.

"You're far too stubborn to have cooperated with us if we'd resorted to kidnapping and coercion. We wanted you to have no where to turn, to be completely out of options."

Rand shifted, wishing he could see Seth's face. Dakota's .38 was a reassuring hard knot in the small of his back. But he couldn't reach it easily, and in the close confines of the car it would probably do more damage than good. Creed had always been a well-prepared, meticulously organized director. Rand already knew the men in the car with them were armed to the teeth. All weapons trained, point blank, at him.

"Who's 'us'?" he asked.

"You, my friend, unfortunately were—and are—expendable. Just a means to an end. Amanda and Jason's wedding cost me a fortune. But I consider it a lucrative investment. A twofer, as it were. It not only demonstrated the wonders of Rapture to our buyer but also coerced Dr. North to come to Europe, even if it meant interacting with the man who broke her heart. The obvious use of Rapture ensured that she'd come racing to your side to help you."

"You were responsible for dosing the wedding guests?" Rand said bitterly. "Talk about Machiavellian and convoluted. All that as an inducement to get Dakota to come here? My God, you are seriously fucked up, you know that? That shit is nothing more than poison."

"Oh, I know," the director said almost proudly. "When we were showing it to our buyers in Spain, they wanted to see what the effect was when Rapture was airborne. We fed it through the air-conditioning system. It was very gratifying. We let the salesman keep whatever he took from the safe. An employee perk," he said, chuckling.

"You were right," Rand told Dakota, then addressed Creed. "Who was that demo for?"

"Eastern bloc mob. Those petty criminals have the green, and plenty of it. A very lucrative deal. They put in their first order yesterday."

"And in Paris?"

"Another salesman. One of our best street-drug men. He scored big with that buyer, a dealer who holds a monopoly on almost half of Europe. We gave him France. No need to be greedy. We're all going to make a great deal of money with this venture. That idiot salesman had to party afterward, happily talking about things he had no business sharing. Partaking of the product is not allowed. His death was inconvenient when we were in such a critical phase of operations."

"Tragic," Rand muttered.

"We tried to take Dr. North at the hotel in Paris," Creed said conversationally. "But when our men arrived, she'd gone into the catacombs in search of *you*, my friend. Ahh, true love. Even her severe claustrophobia didn't deter her as we'd hoped."

Thank God. Even though Rand knew he would've ripped Europe apart to find her, it could've taken two lifetimes to locate her out here in the middle of the Aegean Sea when he'd had no fucking clues. "Why was it necessary to kill Mark Stratham?"

"Ah. Ham. My man didn't realize that you'd switched and taken the lead in the tunnels until the deed was done. Ham was one of us. Another unfortunate death whose blame I lay squarely on your shoulders, Rand. He'd been most useful, helping us keep track of you."

Shit. "How many of my people work for you?"

"Out of your entire west-coast office? Twenty to thirty percent? The one's you brought to the wedding? Five."

"Cole Phelps?"

Creed waved a hand. "Your assistant proved to be far too diligent and inquisitive."

"You killed him." The anger Rand felt was hard to contain, but he had to do so if he and Dakota had a snowball's hope in hell of getting out of this clusterfuck alive. He didn't recognize his own voice as he demanded, "How many others?"

"They were either with me or against me. It was survival of the fittest. I'm proud of the way you've made Maguire Security the best in the business, Rand, I genuinely am. I always liked you. Smart. Resourceful. Honest. You're a likable guy. Everyone has been extremely enthusiastic about the work you do. I'm sorry that you won't be around to hear the accolades at your eulogy. I'm sure everyone's warm and fuzzy comments will bring a tear to the eye. But the end justified the means. To get Dr. North, we needed you to be in place. Black knight to white queen. The circle of life."

"Let me kill him first!" With flailing fists, Dakota lunged over Rand's lap to get at Creed. Rand used his shoulder to block her, and she subsided, vibrating with fury.

"Chess and Disney cartoons, Creed?" The sound of the tires changed several minutes before. An even roughness. Cobbles? Chiseled stone? Still not a glimmer of light. "Maybe you should've picked up the fucking phone and filled me in on your plans. Then perhaps I would've been more goddamned cooperative."

"You did give us the runarou—we're here," he finished abruptly.

HERE, DAKOTA SAW AS she and Rand were shoved into the ancient stone building, looked like an orthodox church, with muted stained-glass windows, rough-cut stone floors, and breathtaking paintings and mosaic works of art propped against the rough walls by a careless hand.

While barely illuminated by the spare glow of tall white taper candles, the paintings still looked as though they'd been finished yesterday. It was a room of about thirty feet by fifteen. No furniture, just the double rows of flickering candles leading straight to the door she saw in the back.

Seth Creed walked on her left, his leather dress shoes clicking on the hard, gritty floor. There was a faint smell to him that she'd tried to place in the car. Almost like the smell when her hair got caught in the hairdryer . . . Other men walked two behind, the rest on either side. More heavily armed men waited outside the door. Great. This just got better and better. They were outnumbered and outgunned. Basically, Dakota thought, tamping down hysteria, they were screwed.

Their captors all wore black pants, military-style boots, and long-sleeved black T-shirts. They were hung like Christmas trees with weapons—guns slung over their shoulders, knives in boots, handguns in harnesses, goggles around their necks. Night-vision, she presumed. Rand having her tiny, girly .38 gave her no sense of security at all, faced with all this impressive weapon power. She darted a glance at his face as he walked in step with her.

He appeared only mildly interested in what his friend was telling him. She, on the other hand, was riveted, because the closer they got to that damn door, the harder her heart pounded, the sweatier her palms became, and the more terrified she was.

"How did you get my fingerprints on the vials and letter you sent to Paul?" It was just one of a dozen questions she wanted answered. At this point, she didn't actually care, but talking was better than listening to their footsteps leading them to God only knew what.

"That was a stroke of genius," Creed said, pleased as hell with himself. "You actually held the vial and wrote the letter yourself."

"I most certainly did n—"

"That lovely little nap you took at your engagement party?"

"I— *Flunitrazepam!*" She slapped her arm over Rand's chest as he lunged. "Don't. It makes no difference now."

"He drugged you!"

She nodded. "Rohypnol." Known as the date rape drug, and she would've done just about anything under the influence, and not remembered a damn thing when she woke up. No wonder the lawyer experts could prove she'd written that letter. She had. If she hadn't been so hot and sweaty and pissed off, her blood would have been freezing at this new information.

"I'd like to kill you slow and with my own fucking bare hands, you sack of shit," Rand told him. "But I want you dead too badly to draw it out."

"Death has no fear for me."

"Let's see how you feel when my hands are around your goddamned throat, and I'm squeezing the life out of you." Rand's fury was palpable.

Dakota placed her hand on his arm, acutely aware of the inequity between the number of men in the room and the strength of their firepower. All Rand had was a six-inch gun with five bullets. "Let's see what's waiting for us before you turn feral, okay?"

"I'm not going to *turn* feral," he snapped. "I *am* feral."

The sound of the men's boot heels echoed off the bare stone walls. It was cool inside—the stone must keep the heat of the day out—and she shivered, more from nerves than the temperature. The air smelled . . . sweet. Medicinal, not rose-scented, thank God. It would be the height of stupidity to attempt to dose them with Rapture. Unless Creed was a voyeur, in which case she'd just added another level of freak-out to what they already had.

She shot a curious glance at Creed walking on the other side of her. He looked like someone's favorite uncle. Almost as tall as Rand, he had receding, fine, medium-brown hair and wore Coke-bottle-thick, black-framed glasses. He was dressed in khaki chinos and a pressed, long-sleeved blue dress shirt, buttoned to the last button under his prominent Adam's apple. A less scary guy was hard to imagine. But here he was.

"What do you hope to gain by mass-producing Rapture, Creed?" Rand asked. "After the first billion, the money won't mean a damn thing."

The director's steps faltered, and he glanced at Rand over Dakota's head. He looked genuinely puzzled. "It was never about the money." Then he proceeded toward the arched door in a ten-foot-thick wall.

"Then what?" Rand demanded. "Power? Notoriety?"

One of the knot of men waiting for them opened the beautifully carved wood door, and they passed through into a much brighter space. Dakota didn't have time to take in anything, as Creed suddenly dropped to one knee beside her, head bowed. She glanced at him in surprise. Odder and odder. "What the h—"

"I do everything for Monk," he said reverently. "Hello, Father."

Next to her, Rand went stock-still, then bit out incredulously, "Yeah. Hello, father."

✦ EIGHTEEN ✦

The room was lit by the steady flames of a dozen oil lanterns placed on several of the sterile-looking white work spaces lining the walls. Rand had been inside the labs of Rydell Pharmaceuticals a couple of times to pick Dakota up. This was a quarter of the size, maybe a tenth, but a perfect reproduction of one of the team's testing units. He saw her eyes widen as she too looked around.

Other than walls that had probably been constructed a thousand years before, the space looked no different from the labs she'd shown him. Creed was right. State-of-the-art. Top-of-the-line. Scary as all motherfucking hell.

Computers, ventilated hoods, glassware, electron microscopes, analytical machines—Rand heard the throb of a generator close by. Or perhaps it was his own erratic heartbeat. "How did you escape a maximum-security prison?" he asked his father, who wore a monk's rough-spun robe, complete with an ancient-looking silver cross on a heavy silver chain around his neck.

Paul looked at him over the flame of his lighter as he touched it to the tip of his cigar. "Walked right out the door. As I've so often done in the last twenty-five months and three days." He smiled. "Money oils a lot of wheels and greases many palms. My life in Capanne was *quite* pleasant. I had servants"—he reached out a hand and drew Creed to his side—"like faithful Szik here, and—"

"His name," Rand snapped, "is Seth Creed."

Paul shrugged. "His adopted name. But my Szik is from Budapest, not so, my son?"

Creed bowed his head. "Yes, Father."

Rand rubbed his hand over his jaw, sick to his stomach. He got no sexual vibe from the pair. He suspected that the bond they shared was nothing so normal, that what these two shared was complicated and depraved. Whatever the sick relationship ran on, it appeared they were more king and a serf, puppeteer and his puppet, than sexual partners. "So Creed's worked for you all this time?"

"And he hired you at my request."

"Fine. Great. Whatever," Dakota said, moving slightly in front of Rand. "What's your point? Because I'll repeat what I told your puppet there—I'm not going to help you in any way whatsoever. Not now, not ever." She folded her arms over her chest and spread her feet. "White queen to black whatever."

The corner of Paul's eye ticked for an instant, or perhaps it was Rand's imagination. "Do you think something like this operation happened overnight?" Paul asked as if she hadn't spoken. "I knew I needed Dakota to work by my side if I wanted to produce a stable version of Rapture for transportation. Only small batches, of course. Everything will be made right here on Agion Oros."

"Dressing like a monk doesn't make you a monk. What's going to happen when the real monks who live here discover you?"

"I *am* a 'real' monk." Paul made air quotes. "I've been coming here for twenty years. Everyone *knows* who I am. We keep to ourselves and pray." He smiled coldly. "Or rather, *they* pray, and I work in my lab. To each his own."

And then, in a non sequitur: "Do you really think for a moment that the two of you met by *accident*?" Paul's smile didn't reach his eyes. But then, it never did.

"What are you planning to do? Keep me under lock and key forever?" She huffed out a fuck-you breath. "In case you haven't noticed, women haven't set foot in this place in several zillion years. Someone's bound to notice when you have to go on a run for tampons and chocolate."

Again he spoke over her as if she hadn't said anything. "I knew that if Rand saw Rapture in action, he'd recognize some of the symptoms, know it was from Rydell, and call you for help."

Rand gave him a cold look, but he'd changed his depth perception, so while it looked as though he was focused on Paul, he was actually seeing everything behind him. "I didn't," he responded evenly as he estimated the distance to various items around the lab that could, and would, be used as weapons the second he considered it time to make his move.

The electron microscope was only a dozen feet away, looking suitably lethal as a weapon. He'd start with that.

Creed stood, head bowed, beside Paul. The four black-garbed men they'd come in with were stationed in the corner, heads bowed in respect to the son-of-a-bitch psycho to whom he had genetic ties.

The windows had been boarded from the outside, and there were three, no, four doors. How the fuck was he going to get them out of here? Zak Stark was supposed to be sending in some counterterrorist group as back-up, but Rand had no idea when, or even if, they'd show. There was also the unwelcome possibility that they'd already been taken out by Creed's muscle.

"I didn't know that it was the same drug Dakota was working on. We didn't do a lot of talking," he told Paul, easing Dakota a little behind him as she crowded close. God, was she trying to protect *him*? "And even if I had, Dakota was the last person I would've asked for help, since I believed she was responsible for putting you in jail."

Not to mention all the bullshit his mother had fed him, and the proof, impossible to dispute, that he'd seen with his own eyes. What in his life had been real? Rand wondered bitterly. His entire life had apparently been manipulated and twisted to suit Paul's every fucking whim. He'd thrown away the one truth—Dakota—for his unworthy parents. He *deserved* to be shot for his fucking stupidity. He was in the right place for that to happen.

"Yet another way you failed me," Paul told him shortly. "I knew she was the love of your life, son. I worked with what I had. I need her to stabilize the formula for mass production, and you were worthless at keeping her in line."

"Well, you didn't get that right either. She was the last person I would've called, even if it had occurred to me do to so. I didn't want her anywhere near this clusterfuck. I asked a friend for hel—" His voice choked off as he saw a gleam, a spark of satisfaction flash in his father's eyes.

Jesus. He stiffened. He'd been keeping Stark apprised of everything that was going on. Was Zak Stark a part of this too? Because if he was, there was no goddamned cavalry charging to the rescue, now or ever. Was the small boat still where they'd left it at the base of the bluff? Hell, could they even get back there in the pitch dark? And that was if they weren't shot or otherwise rendered fucking dead.

"Yes, Stark," Paul said with a self-satisfied smile. "I knew our girl had gone to work for him last year. Nothing escapes my notice. I banked on him sending her to you. Either way, I won."

"Are you deaf or just stupid? Let me repeat this more slowly," Dakota said, taking an aggressive step forward, and only Rand's fingers on her wrist kept her from going right up to Paul. Fury made her voice hard as she bit out, "I. Will. Not. Help. You. Or work with you. Or advise you. Or anything else with you. Go. Fuck. Yourself."

Paul continued to ignore her, but the tic under his right eye got more pronounced. "Since your mother believed *everyone* was out to get her money, she bought into the betrayal story hook, line, and sinker. I knew she'd go running off to show you that carefully constructed dossier, but the PI screwed up and gave it to her too soon." Paul folded his hands inside his sleeves. "It took a lot of work to get Dr. North here where I need her."

Rand considered the weight of a calibrator on a nearby worktable as his second weapon. "What do you mean, a 'lot of work'?"

"You were supposed to go to Paris for your honeymoon after your romantic Valentine's Day wedding. You would have encountered a tragic accident, Dakota would have gone somewhere to recover from her deep sorrow. Instead, she'd have been here with me. With her help, I could've gotten Rapture on the market two years ago."

"Did you kill Catherine intentionally?" Rand asked flatly.

"She was my final test. Rapture built up extremely quickly in her system. I thought she'd last at least another few weeks. Her premature death was very inconvenient."

"Inconvenient, you sick fuck?" Rand lunged for him, hands outstretched to grab him by the throat. Creed jumped forward and stuck Rand's own weapon in his face. Son of a bitch was expressionless unless he had his glowing eyes on Paul.

"The lab's impressive," Dakota inserted, drawing Rand back and giving him a moment to assimilate all the information. He kept his fingers more lightly banding her wrist. "How long has this, this abomination—and God, yes, I mean the bunch of you as well as the lab—been in an area that's counted among the most holy places in the world? Why haven't the monks shut you down and tossed you into the Aegean?"

"We built the lab three years ago. They have no idea it's here, and they don't ask questions. They think we're here year-round. We come into a small cove under cover of darkness by boat. Our closest neighbor is more than ten miles away. No one comes out to this old monastery. Dangerously unstable, the local residents believe. They think I'm a saint for living in such onerous conditions without complaint. A perfect location, with an abundant natural resource right at our fingertips."

Dangerously unstable sounded damned good to Rand. He could work with that—he'd been doing it his entire life.

"SZIK, TAKE DAKOTA TO her quarters," Paul told Creed when Dakota yawned—not from exhaustion, which she felt in spades, but from fear. She was too wired to be tired and knew her body just needed the extra oxygen. But whatever delayed the inevitable was fine with her. She yawned again for good measure.

"As impatient as I am to get started, clearly she's tired and needs to rest before starting work," he concluded.

"Wherever Dakota goes, I go." Rand wrapped his arm firmly around her waist, pulling her tight against his side. Very helpful, since Dakota's knees were decidedly shaky. She felt as though she'd been dropped into a bad play and someone had forgotten to give her the damned script.

"And we're not staying," she added for those who hadn't got the memo.

Paul withdrew his black-framed glasses from his pocket, unfolded them, and, in no damn hurry, put them on his nose. His chest rose and fell with a soft sigh as his magnified eyes gave her a steady look. "I'm afraid I must insist."

"I'm not afraid to decline," she countered. She had no idea how they were going to get the hell out of there. None. Before Rand was able to get off five shots from her little gun, the men would shoot him on the spot. He was redundant now. They all knew it.

"Stalemate, Paul," Rand told him. "I know her well. Once Dakota makes up her mind, you might as well give up."

Maintaining eye contact with her, Paul told Creed, "Shoot him."

She stepped in front of Rand, her body blocking his. "Go ahead. If you shoot him, you'll shoot me." Rand's big hands closed in a punishing grip around her waist. She stood her ground, on her tiptoes to cover as much of him as possible. "We'll die together and you still won't get your damned drug stabilized. Save the blood and gore, and let us go."

Paul gave a small signal, and the four men rushed forward to block her and Rand's movements. Boxed in, they had no options. Dakota stayed where she was, despite Rand's painful grip on her hips as he tried to move her out of the way.

"What kind of father are you that you'd kill your own son?" she demanded, digging her shoes into the ancient stone floor for purchase.

"The kind who never wanted a dependent, but caved because the bitch wanted a kid, and she held the purse strings. The more she loved him, the less I could tolerate either of them. Szik, come here," Paul said without a hint of inflection, yet the hair on Dakota's body rose and her blood ran cold.

Seth Creed, powerful, award-winning Hollywood director, dropped to one knee beside Rand's father. He started unbuttoning his shirt.

Rand's fingers gripped her waist so hard Dakota could feel his heartbeat in his fingertips. She could hardly breathe as she stared, transfixed.

"Jesus," Rand whispered as Creed's shirt dropped to the uneven stone floor. From below his collarbone all the way into the waistband of his khaki slacks, his pale, hairless torso was covered with scars. Neat, systematic. Straight lines and small circles. Some old, some fresh.

Paul had played a cruel, macabre game of tic-tac-toe all over him.

Bile rose in the back of Dakota's throat as Paul removed a lighter from the pocket of his robe and brought it to the tip of the cigar she'd forgotten he was holding. Rand's hands slid from her waist, his arms circling her body, holding her hard against him. She strained to get free, to help Creed. To beat the living crap out of Paul. To puke. "My God! Don't—"

He lit and puffed. Lit and puffed. Checked the tip, then nodded to Creed.

Head bowed, the director extended his left arm, palm up, bracing it on his bent knee.

Rand's arms were a steel corset around her ribs, cutting off her circulation and restricting her breathing. Nevertheless, she wasn't capable of taking in air anyway, her vision reduced to a pinpoint on the tableau of the two men just feet away.

Head cocked slightly, Paul looked down, clearly searching the mess of angry red and white scars before firmly applying the red-hot tip of the cigar to the inside bend of Creed's elbow.

The director neither flinched nor made a sound as his flesh sizzled. The sweet, sickly smell of burning flesh made Dakota gag. Black snow obliterated her vision, and she sagged in Rand's grip. One second she was limp and nauseated; the next she was shoved hard, propelled toward Paul and Creed without warning. She crashed into them, landing hard in a tangle of arms and legs.

One of them was heavy on top of her, and she lay on a man's leg or arm. She couldn't see anything, but all hell was breaking loose—shots fired, men yelling, the pounding of running footsteps, chaos. She didn't know whether to cover her head, run and hide, or find her .38 and use those five damned bullets.

She struggled to break free, shoving at Creed's bare shoulder, seeing the deep slices and cigar burns on his skin up close and horrifyingly personal. "Get off, get off!" She shoved at his chest, trying to roll him off her midriff. He was a deadweight, and heavy as hell. Nearby she saw Paul's broken glasses and his outflung arm. He wasn't moving.

She flinched as shots were fired; a man screamed. More shots. More shouts. Glass breaking. Metal hitting metal.

She used every ounce of strength she had, and finally Creed flopped over like a dead fish. Panting, Dakota came up on her elbow beside him. She tried to make sense of what she was looking at. There was a large, gory hole where his head should be. She tasted bile and tried to scramble away backward like a crab. "Oh, my God, oh, my God!"

Something incredibly loud exploded out of sight, and she flinched as she staggered to her feet. She slipped, righted herself, and saw that she was crouched in a glossy pool of bright red blood, which was spreading on the stone floor.

HIS SICK FUCK OF a sperm donor wanted Dakota alive. Rand was expendable. Rand almost missed the subtle order to take him down as Paul and Creed performed their bit of theater.

He'd seen a movement out of the corner of his eye and shoved Dakota the hell out of the way as one of Paul's men tried to separate them. It was a split-second decision to get her away from him before he was attacked or shot at point-blank range. A through and through would seriously injure her, if not worse. He wasn't taking any risks with her life.

He'd thrown her a lot harder than he intended in his haste. With a shriek of surprise, she went barreling into

Paul and Creed like a bowling ball into two pins. They all crashed to the floor.

As the first guy reached for him, Rand grabbed the muzzle of his Uzi with one hand and shoved his palm directly up and into the man's nose, wrenching the weapon out of his hands and breaking his nose at the same time. With the element of surprise on his side, he swung the butt of the submachine gun and used it to deliver a swift uppercut to the jaw. His opponent went down without a murmur.

The next guy, big and rock-solid, grabbed Rand around the waist and tried to squeeze the life out of him. As he felt a rib crack, then another, Rand headbutted him. The guy just squeezed harder. There went another rib.

Number three came up beside them, hit him on the side of the head with something fucking hard, and made him see stars. Rand fumbled the automatic into position in his numb fingers and popped him. At this close range, it was a very effective deterrent. Blood splattered on his face and chest. Three dropped to the floor. Out of the game.

The man holding him in such a tight embrace stumbled over the body, and he was free. Rand stomped him. Not very effective in running shoes, but the man stayed down, looking dazed. Rand bent and grabbed his weapon.

He heard the shot, felt something icy cold then fiery hot on his upper arm, and knew he'd been hit. Didn't hurt.

There were a hell of a lot more men in the room now, as the ones outside poured in to see what the commotion was about. Several converged on him at once, firing wildly. They were piss-poor marksmen, but even bad marksmen eventually hit what they were aiming at. The next man was firing as he ran. Number six came in from the left; number seven and eight discovered pretty damn fast how inaccurate the shots were when they were in motion.

Shit exploded as they converged across the lab, firing wildly. Fragments of smashed glass flew, instruments clattered to the floor, and a stained-glass window shattered, rainbows of glass splintering once more on impact with the hard stone floor.

Flashing a glance at Dakota, who was tangled up with Paul and Creed, Rand opened fire with his newly acquired Uzi. Six hundred rounds a minute. Range two hundred feet. He could take them all out in seconds. If the fuckers weren't shooting back. He spun, squeezing off a barrage of bullets, attempting to drop as many as possible before they shot him.

Number eight fell, eyes staring sightlessly at the domed ceiling. Six crumpled and lay still.

His weapon was out of ammo. Rand tossed it aside and brought up the second. But before he could squeeze off a shot, there was a round of weapons fire from the sidelines.

He brought the automatic up as more black-garbed men appeared out of nowhere. He was only ten feet from where Dakota had just struggled out from under the weight of Creed and Paul.

He ran, yelling her name. Skidding to her side, he grabbed her arm and hauled her closer. Her clothes and hands stained with shiny red blood. "Are you hurt?" he demanded, even as he pulled her behind him, his attention fixed on the new arrivals.

She was breathing hard. "Blood's not mine."

"Good, that's good," he said, relieved, but now concentrating on the new threat. This batch looked a damn sight more professional than the others; this was serious firepower in the hands of men who knew what the hell they were about. Six of them, dressed from head to toe in unrelieved matte black.

He squeezed off a shot. *Click.* Fuck.

They were out in the open. Out of options. He reached back for Dakota's .38. Point and shoot.

One of the men yelled, "Maguire?" even as he fired off two shots that struck the last two of Paul's men as they fumbled to their feet. They both dropped.

"Hot damn," Rand said, wrapping his injured arm around Dakota. "The cavalry's arrived."

The men moved around the lab with ruthless efficiency while Rand went to check on Paul and Creed. It was immediately clear that Creed had shot Paul point-blank and then turned the gun on himself, thereby putting a period to all Rand and Dakota's unanswered questions. "Maybe we're better off not knowing all the answers."

She leaned into his side. He stoically didn't wince as his cracked ribs screamed for mercy. "We would've been better off not having any questions in the first place," she said dryly, shoving her hair over her shoulder. Rand reached over and picked bits of glass and plastic out of the tumbled curls.

A short, wiry man in his early forties approached them, and Rand automatically tensed. "Dr. North? What's the protocol for incineration of Rapture?"

Her face was pale and bloodstained as she told him, "It burns at eight hundred and fifty degrees, with no emissions of substances that pollute the air, water, or soil. If you can cremate the lab at that temp, you'll be doing humankind a big favor."

The man's lips twitched. "Yes, ma'am. We'll take care of it. There's a chopper outside waiting to take you to safety. As soon as you're clear, we'll make us a big old bonfire."

AND A FANTASTIC BONFIRE it was, Dakota thought, sinking back into Rand's arms as the pilot circled the massive blaze. "Those poor, unsuspecting monks," she whispered into the headset, as flames leaped hundreds of feet in the air and thick black smoke made the pilot warn they were going to make fast tracks out of there.

Dakota was fine with that. She closed her gritty eyes, listening to Rand and the men who'd accompanied them discuss various methods of igniting explosives until their voices faded to black.

✦ NINETEEN ✦

They were on a private plane. A private plane with a bedroom and a bathroom in back. The last three hours passed in a kaleidoscope of events that Dakota knew would take a long time to unravel, let alone process. Right now she was too spent, too numb to even try.

"Take a shower. Sleep," Rand told her, his expression closed. Beyond the door between the aft cabin and the front cabin, half a dozen black-garbed men talked in low voices. She'd barely noticed them as she and Rand had been escorted to seats in the back to buckle up while the plane took off from a tiny airstrip somewhere in Greece. Before that, there'd been a helicopter ride.

Once the plane reached cruising altitude, a guy came over to offer them food and drink. They both declined. They were both liberally covered with blood. None of the men seemed to mind that it got on the buttery soft, camel-colored leather seats. Another man showed her the bedroom with two narrow single beds in the aft cabin. Rand thanked him curtly, and went inside with her, his eyes scanning her face. "Are you sure you weren't hurt?"

"Positive. None of this is mine. You, on the other hand . . ."

"I'm fine." He put a hand on the door handle. "I'll be right outside if you need me."

I need you in ways you can't even imagine, she thought dully. "I don't."

She stared at the solid surface for a moment after he shut it behind him, then gave herself a mental shake. She stepped into the tiny, beautifully appointed bathroom, and closed and locked the door.

She took a too-quick shower to get the blood and dirt off her. She would've liked to stay in the tiled stall for the entire twelve-hour trip back to Seattle; she wasn't sure if she'd ever be clean. But Rand pounded on the bathroom door what seemed like a second later. "You all right in there?"

She twisted off the water. "Peachy," she yelled, grabbing the towel off the rack and blotting her hair. She had no clean clothes, so she wrapped the towel under her arms before opening the door. He was standing at the foot of the bed closest to the tiny bathroom. He too had showered, but he'd been given clothes by their testosterone-charged hosts who'd swooped in and blown everything to hell on Mount Athos.

He was barefoot, wearing dark pants and a body-hugging black T-shirt that showed off his abs, his biceps, and the long jagged scratch down his left arm, which looked as though it needed stitches. More scars.

She looked from the angry cut on his forearm to the inscrutable expression on his face. "Pretty fancy plane, with two bathrooms." And two, comfortable-looking, flat surfaces just feet away.

"I'll start off with an apology."

She raised an eyebrow. "Only one?"

His lips twitched. "These apologies come wrapped in batches of twenty."

She went to the head of the narrow single bed and sat down, then swung her feet up, crossed her ankles, and leaned back against a padded black-leather headboard. "Go ahead." She tucked the loose end of the black towel over her knees, which were still wet. "Start anywhere you like. They don't have to be in order of importance."

"There is absolutely no excuse for my lack of faith in you. None. But in my own defense, I had a couple of shit experiences in my early twenties. One, when a girl-friend made a pass at my father, and my mother paid her to break it off with me. That wasn't trumped up—I was standing right outside the door when she took the money."

"Told to be there right *then*, no doubt, by one of your loving parents, as a sacrificial lamb."

"Yeah, in retrospect. Probably." His deep, rich voice sounded raw, his control not as firm as it usually was. A muscle clenched in his unshaven jaw. She could feel the tension in him, but he didn't reach for her, merely shoved his hands into his pockets.

In contrast to his calm demeanor, the crackling intensity pulsing off him transmitted itself loud and clear. The small cabin wasn't big enough for him, or what he was saying and feeling right then. Dakota knew he wanted to pace away the feeling churning inside him, but he was so controlled that no one else would've seen it. "We all betrayed you in our own fucked-up ways."

"True."

"The entire Maguire family owes you an apology," he said thickly. "But since I'm it, I'll speak for all of us."

"Don't apologize for Paul. . . ."

"No." His nostrils flared, and he flushed along the blades of his cheeks as his eyes turned to slate. "I'll apologize for myself. I was a dick."

"True," she said again.

"I should've trusted in you, and at least *asked* you about the PI's findings. Let you tell me your version."

"Let me tell you the *truth*, you big jerk."

"Yeah. The truth would've gone a long way toward preventing all of what I put you through."

"It all boiled down to trust. You didn't have it."

"I've learned from my enormous screw-ups, believe me."

"Frankly, I think you had cold feet *before* we got married," Dakota said. "You wanted to believe all the lies you were fed, so it was easy to convince yourself that a report from a PI, with pictures, was the real deal."

"Believe me, I didn't have cold feet. I loved you more than life itself, and your perceived betrayal derailed me. In a major way."

"It killed me that you believed your father over me," she countered. "Worse, that you wouldn't even listen to my side of the story." She met his eyes and saw the pain he didn't mask, and despite her own pain, felt his. Damn it, she didn't *want* to be reasonable, or let him off the hook. But if she wanted to dream of a future with him, they had to deal with the nightmare of the past.

"I had no idea that your mother had hired a PI to spy on me. Nor could either of us have possibly known that Seth Creed would hire actors to play all the parts that convinced her that I was exactly what she'd been telling you I was." She waited for him to sit on one of the beds, but he remained where he was, hands stuffed into his front pockets.

"At the time, I had to force myself to get over it. Had to remind myself that your relationship with Paul was precarious at best before your mother's death. Worse after. Then compounded by the loss of your mother."

It was his turn to raise a brow. He did it much better than she did. He'd had practice. "Are you *defending* my dickwad actions?"

"I'm helping you move along," Dakota said reasonably. "How many batches of twenty apologies do you have? If this is only number one, we need to speed things up. It's only a twelve-hour flight." His eyes narrowed, and she said mildly, "That was a *joke*, Maguire."

He took one hand out of his pocket and squeezed his forehead as if his head was about to explode, then shoved his fist back.

Dakota got up on her knees to close the gap between them, since he seemed incapable of doing it himself. Somehow along the way, she crawled right over the towel she'd been wearing. Rand's eyes flared as she walked on the mattress toward him on her knees, naked. "Eventually I got it. You and your father had such an adversarial relationship, and you'd just started mending fences. You wanted to believe he wasn't the man you'd grown up with, wanted to believe him incapable of murdering your mother. You believed he was innocent, because you wanted to believe in him again."

"Yeah. That. In a nutshell."

Dakota didn't care about apologies, or explanations, or about rehashing their entire European extravaganza. There'd be plenty of time to do all that. Later.

There was only one thing she had to know now. She tucked her fingertips into the waistband of his pants and gave him a little tug. "Hold off on those apologies. I have two questions for you."

"Shoot."

"A poor choice of words, all things considered," she said with a small smile. "Do you love me?"

"Do I love you?" he repeated incredulously, his face tight. His eyes flared with something savage as he took in her naked body and clinging wet hair, but he remained planted in place, hands fisted in his pockets. "I never *stopped* loving you."

"Excellent to know." She flipped open the button at the top of his fly with two fingers. He was commando, which was handy.

"What's the second question?" he asked hoarsely, burying all ten fingers in her hair and pulling her face up to meet his descending mouth.

Dakota smiled against his lips. "Is that door locked?"

Fantasy.
Temptation.
Adventure.

Visit PocketAfterDark.com, an all-new website just for Urban Fantasy and Romance Readers!

- Exclusive access to the hottest urban fantasy and romance titles!

- Read and share reviews on the latest books!

- Live chats with your favorite romance authors!

- Vote in online polls!

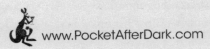

www.PocketAfterDark.com

26119